"SEARCH THE PLACE!"

Napoleon's lieutenant ordered his men.

I froze. My Melisse, my small daughter. In that great cedar chest. They would surely find her.

I rushed to the garret while they were searching the second floor and sat tensely on the edge of my cot until I heard their heavy boots coming up the steps.

They burst into the small room and stared at me. "Oho!" said one, "the crazy niece has come up to greet us. My God, she's as beautiful a piece as ever drew breath beneath the dirt."

Another one came directly to the chest where Melisse was hidden.

"Please, *mon capitaine,*" I said timidly, my stare vacant, "Tis only my linens stored—for the time when I am wed."

"Ha, Francois, she hopes to be wed, the little *insense* niece."

"I'll not wed her," Francois said coarsely, "but, by God, I'll bed her!" and suddenly he was upon me. One big hand caught in the neck of my dress, grasping all my garments and with a single, swift movement, ripped dress, petticoat and chemise straight down the middle.

I lay there naked, screaming and screaming . . .

Liliane

by
Annabel Erwin

A Warner Communications Company

WARNER BOOKS EDITION

ISBN 0-446-79941-6

Cover illustration by Jim Avati

Warner Books, Inc., 75 Rockefeller Plaza, New York, N.Y. 10019

A Warner Communications Company

Printed in the United States of America

Not associated with Warner Press, Inc. of Anderson, Indiana

10 9 8 7 6 5 4

For the real Lillian,

with love

Liliane

PART ONE

CHAPTER 1

The May night was black as the heart of a Paris chimney as I fled that dangerous city with my small daughter held close to me. Clasping the reins tightly, I rode astride the big gelding as no lady would. But who was to see me? No one, I prayed fervently. The countryside spread out darkly on either side of a thin dirt road between Paris and Marseilles. In Marseilles I hoped to find the friends Jacques had named for me as he gasped out his life on the floor of the little *pension* room we had shared.

I must slow the gelding, I thought with sudden panic. He could not gallop all the miles to Marseilles at once. His big body was hot against my bare legs where I had pulled up my thin summer dress and petticoat.

Early in the night, Mélisse and I had run from the *pension*, taking nothing with us but the clothes we wore, and mounted Jacques's horse. There was no guessing how far he had ridden the gelding before he reached us, but the big animal had not seemed too tired as we galloped swiftly through cobbled streets and down twisting lanes until we reached open country. Now I drew back on the reins, looking behind me. Surely I would hear the pounding of hooves if I were pursued. There was nothing to break the late spring stillness but the sound of crickets in the hedgerows and ditches beside the road, and the soft plop of the gelding's hooves in the dirt.

When my husband had stumbled into our bedroom a few hours before, I could hear his rasping breath, and I knew he was mortally wounded before I could strike the flint and light a candle. When I did so, my fears were confirmed. His white summer uniform was bloodsoaked across his chest and he sank down on the floor before my horrified eyes.

"Liliane—take Mélisse and run. I am discovered—Napoleon's lackeys will be here at any moment. My horse—just outside——"

I said frantically, "But you need a doctor, Jacques. I should ride to get one!"

He shook his head and coughed thickly. Blood trickled from the corner of his mouth. "I've three bullets in my chest. Go to Pierre Dumaine, the *aubergiste* in Marseilles—*L'Auberge de l'Abbaye.* He and Aimée are old friends of mine and hate all Napoleon stands for. They will give you shelter—hide you." His lids fluttered and in the candlelight the old familiar nightmare of flight enveloped me.

I stooped to him and caught up his hand. There was blood warm upon it where it had trickled down his sleeve. For a moment there was a reassuring pressure, then it relaxed suddenly. His eyes were still open, but there was no life in their glassy depths. Jacques was dead and the moment I had feared for months had come upon me. There was no one in Paris I could trust, because of my husband's plots against Bonaparte. Jacques and a small band of soldier patriots had tried to stop the juggernaut that was Napoleon's vaulting ambition, but one by one they had been murdered, quietly and without any resultant furor. Now my husband, one of the last of the group, was gone.

I snatched up a dress and donned it swiftly. Then I went to her cot and roused my Mélisse. She was almost four, a quiet, subdued child, marked by the secret existence we had been forced to lead these last years since my husband had turned against his idol, Napoleon.

Now, as the big gelding cantered along the road, I felt Mélisse melt against me in slumber. While we covered the miles at a slower pace, I let my mind slide back over the years—nearly nine years ago, when my sister, Yvette, and I had fled to Paris with Tante Genèvre, my mother's maid. We had left behind us our mother and father, le Comte and la Comtesse de Belvoir, in our deserted but beautiful chateau. Our parents had known they would soon be taken prisoner to stand before Robespierre and the Committee of Public Safety, and they knew the guillotine would be their fate. Though Robespierre was long dead now, I shivered remembering the day I had glimpsed him, a pale little man, pale of skin and pale of eye, as he walked among a group of his Jacobins on their way to watch the guillotine perform its function, while France ran red with the blood of her aristocracy. He was not robust, a small, cruel man, a fanatical man.

Tante Genèvre had taken us to Paris, where we had melted into that fear-ridden city. There, she set up a millinery shop with the money my father had given her. She had struggled to teach us the trade those months of 1793. Then had come the fateful day when she sent us to deliver bonnets to one of her customers on the rue St. Antoine. It was near the Bastille and as we moved down the crowded street, we wondered at the milling mass about us.

Yvette whispered to me, " 'Tis the tumbrils coming! Hear them creak?" She was sixteen and I was fourteen, and we stood on tiptoe to see over the heads of the gawking crowd that lined the cobbled street. I could hear the groaning of unoiled wooden wheels as they slipped jarringly over the rough road. Then suddenly we could see them coming. There were three carts, one following the other. To our horror, the first contained our mother and father and two others. I smothered a cry as I saw how ragged and dirty they were from their long imprisonment. Mother's beautiful brown-gold hair was in wild disarray and her face drawn, but her loveliness seemed undimmed to me. Our father, his black head bent to hers as he kept his arm firmly about her, was clutching the sides of the wobbling cart, which was drawn by a gaunt horse. The horse was urged on by a dirty, bearded peasant. The peasant spat at the watching people lining the street and laughed, pleased to escort the hated nobility on their way to Robespierre's justice.

That was the day we saw Robespierre. He was coming from a tall brick building, surrounded by the black-clothed Jacobins and the Committee of Safety, and his pale eyes were fixed on my mother and father, who stood proudly erect, their resolute faces set against breaking.

All around us rose the whisper, " 'Tis Robespierre—'tis Maximilien Robespierre himself, going to see justice meted out to *les aristocrates.*"

Yvette and I clutched hands and followed after the tumbrils to the huge iron gates that led to the square where Madame Guillotine performed her service. The crowd pushed in after Robespierre and the Jacobins, to watch the macabre events. We could see the top of the guillotine from where we stood.

Yvette was weeping, but I was dry-eyed in my horror, and I pulled at her hand, saying, "Come, Yve—we shall not stand here and watch our mother and father die. Come, let us go to the house of Madame Gautier and deliver her bonnets."

Then as we pushed down the crowded street, my tears too deep to flow, I clenched her hand tightly. "Do not cry so, sister. They will suspect us of being sympathizers with the nobility. Maman and Papa do not want that. Remember when he said, 'My daughters, hide with Genèvre. Let no one know who you are. For you are quite old enough for Madame Guillotine. Take care, for Maman and I want you to live—all of life is before you.' Have you forgotten?" I asked fiercely.

"No, Lilibel," she said, calling me by the diminutive she had given me at my birth. She smothered her sobs as we hurried down the street. "But how can you be so calm —so cold?"

"I despise the Jacobins and Robespierre," I said, "and all the murdering scoundrels who traffic with them. My hatred dries my tears! They are decimating our France!"

I had taken both boxes in my hand in order to give Yve the chance to dry her eyes swiftly. Now as we neared Madame Gautier's house, Yvette turned to me. "Give me back my bonnet, Lilibel, the one I made for her. I want to present it myself." Yve, as I had called her since babyhood, was always very possessive of her things. We had shared nothing material in our childhood; she insisted on her toys belonging only to her and mine to me. Though we were of a size now, we did not trade clothing as so many sisters did, which I thought rather sad because it would have doubled our meager wardrobe. But I shrugged it off. Yve was Yve, and I loved her devotedly.

After that, we delivered the bonnets and returned to Tante Genèvre's shop where we had sleeping quarters and a small kitchen at the rear.

Now, years later as I swung along the country road, I looked up at the starless sky and thought of my sister Yve, safely married to her American tobacco planter in some faraway place in the New World called Virginia. She had been there nearly eight long years.

I determined to write her as soon as I reached Marseilles. We exchanged letters at least twice a year. They were written in English, as I had set about to learn the language of my sister's adopted land. It took so long for a letter to make its way across the wild reaches of the Atlantic and my address was always uncertain. But when she had written, Yve always expressed love and concern for me, and now at last, I would ask her for refuge. I could not stay in France with Napoleon's hounds on my trail. Surely Yve would send me money to come to her. At the thought, my throat drew tight with longing to see her. Yve and I looked somewhat alike, but she had great eyes as blue as a delft bowl, while mine—alas, I did not know what to call my strange amber eyes. They were large and thickly fringed with lashes like Yve's, but their color changed with what I wore from gold to pale green, with brown flecks in them. I had often wished them to be like Yve's. Now my small Mélisse had Yve's eyes, and for that I was thankful.

The last letter I had from my sister had been rather unsatisfactory, but that was because she was a young mother with a young son who took up much of her time, I was sure. She had not seemed especially happy to have a son; I thought she had probably hoped for a daughter first. But she said her Andrew was so proud of little Andy that she was content.

The night dragged on and we passed through several sleeping towns, large and small. At last, the unsettling false dawn came and went as the gelding plodded tiredly onward. Dawn itself found us near a stone farmhouse, and Mélisse was speaking plaintively of her hunger. I saw a woman come out of the house and throw a pan of water into the grass. Smoke was curling lazily from a chimney.

A little behind the house was a byre and outside it two fat cows, their udders tight with milk, stood looking hopefully at the woman who turned and went back inside. I guided the horse down the lane toward the house, too tired to think what excuse I would give the woman for seeking food.

I dismounted, carrying Mélisse in my aching arms. My hair tumbled down my back and I tried to adjust a skirt that was wrinkled and uneven from being stretched over the saddle.

The woman's eyes widened when she opened the door at my knock. "Please, madame," I said, improvising rapidly, "my little daughter and I are on our way to my mother in Marseilles. We have come from Paris and we are very hungry."

"All the way from Paris—in the night?" she asked sharply. Then, looking down the lane to the road, "Is someone after you? You have broken the law?"

"Oh, no, madame," I said hastily, my tired heart giving a great bound. "I am just widowed. My husband was very old and died of apoplexy——"

"Why then have you no money? Why did you not stop at Lyons to eat?"

"My husband had not been able to work," I said, aware that Mélisse was rigid with fear. "He left us nothing—that is why I go to my mother in Marseilles."

"Well," she said grudgingly, "come in." She led me into a broad kitchen with a great fireplace, which emitted the smell of frying meat. She had batter in a bowl and was preparing to put it in a skillet over the fire.

In a moment, two great boys came in with their father from the stables at the rear. It was her husband, Monsieur Hebert, and the boys were Etienne and Michel. I had introduced myself as Madame Aubert and my daughter, Mélisse.

Now as we all sat down to eat, her husband asked me for the news from Paris, revealing that they were ardent admirers of the great Napoleon.

I told them that Napoleon had established a new order of knighthood, the Legion of Honor, and that all prefects of departments and all mayors of cities were appointed by him, so that not a vestige of provincial or municipal freedom remained. I tried to sound as though I thought this a fine thing. It galled me to pretend, but they were all jubilant. The two young boys remarked that as soon as they were of age, they planned to join Napoleon's armies. I swallowed the bracing French coffee and ate the hotcakes and meat thankfully, even though I knew this family would turn Mélisse and me over to the police without hesitation if they had a remote idea of our identity.

The woman had been watching Mélisse like a hawk, which made me even more uneasy. When we finished eating she said, "You two may rest awhile if you like. Etienne will feed your horse—he looks tired." My apprehensiveness grew.

I said carefully, "I think we had best go on, though you have been more than kind."

"It is for the child I am kind, madame," the woman said sharply. "She looks as if she could use the rest."

The man and his sons got to their feet and, without further comment, clumped out of the house to attend to their chores.

"I thank you, Madame Hebert," I said, smiling brightly, "but Mélisse will sleep while we ride."

" 'Tis near three hundred miles to Marseilles."

"*Oui*. That is why we must travel on." I tried desperately not to sound as frightened as I felt.

Madame Hebert shrugged eloquently. "Very well. Let me pack up some meat and bread and dried fruit for you, then."

My tension eased and I said gratefully, "That is most kind of you." I was amazed at her generosity as she pulled a great leg of mutton from a carcass that was still roasting on a spit at the fire. She took two loaves of bread from a black brick oven at the side of the great fireplace. She was equally generous in pouring dried apples and peaches into the sack she handed me.

"You are indeed kind," I murmured, clutching Mélisse with one hand and the bag of food with the other. "This should last us all the way to Marseilles."

"That is what I intended," she said roughly, "and it is because of the beautiful child. See that she sleeps as you ride."

I nodded vigorously, made my *adieux*, and mounted

the tired gelding, hooking the bag of food to the saddle as I put Mélisse upon him and clambering up myself.

It was not until the farmhouse was far behind us that I dared to stop. We found ourselves in open country and there was a haymow in a field beside the road. I saw no sign of habitation about, so I guided my weary mount to the hay and allowed him to feed, while Mélisse and I crept into the hay at the side and slept like the dead until the following morning.

All the way into Marseilles it was thus. Three days and three more nights we spent traveling, sleeping in thickets of trees and haymows and stretching Madame Hebert's supplies to last us until we finally reached the teeming city of Marseilles, late the fourth day. A stranger there, I did not know where to turn, but I asked a passing man where I would find the tavern known as The Abbey and Pierre Dumaine. He gave my ragged appearance a disapproving glance. His glance at my child was even more reproachful. It was plain to see he thought me a poor mother who would take a child to a tavern at that hour.

"They are kin of mine. I am a widow now, come from Paris."

His eyes softened, and he gave me explicit directions on how to find L'Auberge de l'Abbaye and its *aubergiste*. Marseilles was cleaner than Paris, I supposed because of its proximity to the sea. I followed the winding streets into the heart of town, passing shops containing all sorts of foreign goods. I perched uncomfortably at the side of Jacques's saddle, trying to adjust Mélisse, who had been remarkably uncomplaining for one so young. She seemed to sense the desperation of our flight from Paris, and clung to the saddle in an effort to help me.

At last, not too far from the harbor, where I saw a forest of ships' tall masts rising above the warehouses along the docks, we came to L'Auberge l'Abbaye. I could have wept with joy at the sight of the sign hanging over a broad heavy door. There was a big window of many square panes beside it and I could see the many tables and chairs inside.

Dismounting, I took Mélisse into my arms, and we stepped through the door. It took a moment for my eyes to adjust to the candlelit interior. Then I saw several bearded sailors sitting at three tables, decanters of wine at hand. They all eyed me curiously. I ducked my head, holding Mélisse close, and hastened to the counter at the rear. In a whisper, I asked the mustached man there for Pierre Dumaine.

"I am he," he said in a guarded voice. His weathered face put him beyond forty. "What do you want, madame?"

"Can we talk in private?" I asked, low-voiced. "I am Jacques Sevier's widow."

His eyes widened and he beckoned me silently to follow. We went through a door at the rear, where I saw living quarters. There was a narrow stair nearby that wound up to a second story. A woman sat mending clothing in a chair by a window.

"Aimée, this is Jacques Sevier's widow," he said quietly.

"Widow! *Mon Dieu*——" she whispered. "Jacques—dead?"

I said rapidly, "Near five days ago in Paris—he barely reached our *pension*—shot through the chest. He died in my arms and I had to flee for my life, for the Bonaparte's soldiers were seeking him even then—and all connected with him, of course."

Her eyes filled with tears and I looked at her, wondering at my own dry eyes. It had been so long since Jacques and I had shared real love for each other. Since the birth of Mélisse, he had lost himself with a fanatic's zeal in plots to assassinate Napoleon, though he was a lieutenant in Le Bataillon Cinq, and had been for nearly four years. In July of 1798, Jacques had been given a battlefield commission for gallantry in action, when Napoleon and his armies took Cairo in faraway Egypt. Jacques had been wounded in the arm, but not badly. He worshiped Napoleon at the time. Then finally he had seen the long shadow of tyranny cast by his commander. After that, he had been home even more rarely, and I had insulated myself against the moment of his loss. I would grieve later, but not now. Not when my child and I were so weary from the nearly four-hundred-mile journey from Paris.

Pierre Dumaine took charge. "That horse outside—is it yours?"

I shook my head. " 'Twas Jacques's."

"Then we must get rid of it and his saddle at once. I

shall go now and sell them at the marketplace. Aimée," he continued rapidly, "we will let Madame Sevier and Mélisse stay in the garret. The soldiers will be seeking her before the week is out, I have no doubt. Go in, my dear, and close the inn. Tell the sailors our niece from the country has come to stay with us—that my brother has died."

Aimée, a woman near her husband's age, looked frightened and left the room. She was gone for some time and I could hear the sailors grumbling loudly as she bade them leave. She returned and led us up the steep dark stairs that twisted around the second story and up to the garret. It was very clean, though sparsely furnished with two cots and a washstand holding the usual pitcher and bowl. No rug was on the bare floor and the single peaked casement window was closed, making the small garret room stuffy and hot. Aimée went directly to this and flung it open, letting the warm evening air blow in across us. The air was filled with the odors of a harbor city, the fragrance of spices, mixed with the strong odor of fish. Buns were baking somewhere near, too, for there was the faint scent of bread mingled with the mixture.

"I'm hungry, Maman," my daughter whimpered. We had finished Madame Hebert's sack of food early that morning.

Aimée Dumaine stooped and caught Mélisse up in her arms. "What a beautiful *jeune fille!*"

Mélisse turned terrified eyes to me. "She is so afraid of strangers, Aimée," I said apologetically, reaching for her. " 'Tis the life we have lived since Jacques involved himself in secret opposition to the Corsican."

Aimée handed her to me. "I understand, madame—Liliane. I know the little one has lived with fear," she said sadly. "We have lived with it for years, all of us."

"Since the Terror," I replied bitterly, stroking Mélisse's silken head, remembering. The guillotine, that instrument of *mercy* designed by Dr. Guillotin to save victims from the agonizing wait for the ax, was burned into my brain as I had first seen it. The tall, gaunt scaffold, holding the blade at the top like a huge, slanted and severed head itself, waiting to fall upon the innocent neck of each victim in turn. I could see the basket of bloody heads, filled to the brim beside it.

I closed my mind and said, "We are very hungry. We have ridden day and night to reach you. Jacques, of course, gave me your name."

"Jacques was like a son to us. His father's farm was next to ours and he grew up fishing from the river near our house. We had no children and we loved him dearly."

"He never mentioned you until he lay dying—but that is not surprising. My husband became very closemouthed about every part of his life, when he pitted himself against the Bonaparte."

"Napoleon Bonaparte—the Corsican, parading himself as a Frenchman." Aimée spat contemptuously, then said with a shrug, "I shall fix you something to eat. But first, you see that large chest at the end of the attic?

Mélisse and I stared at the great coffinlike container, made of cedar. " 'Tis a linen chest," Aimée continued, crossing and flinging back its lid. It was packed to the top with neatly folded linens, but Aimée reached in and lifted carefully and lo! A long shallow shelf of linens came out, revealing a large empty space. Large enough to conceal two men.

Aimée said sharply, "Mélisse, this will be your hiding place. If soldiers should come stamping into our tavern, speaking loudly and angrily, you must wait beside it—and I will come to hide you. You must promise not to say a word until Maman or I come and lift the lid. Do you promise?"

Mélisse was trembling, her great blue eyes wide, but she promised.

"You are a good girl, *ma petite*," Aimée said, briskly replacing the long tray of linens and closing the lid softly. "Now you two wash up and I will fix you something to eat."

Later that evening, as twilight was dying redly in the west window of the garret, I put the sleepy Mélisse in one cot and flung myself wearily on the other without removing my soiled dress. I would act as a kitchenmaid, and I was to be a touch simple-minded if accosted by anyone at all. Jacques, it appeared, had written regularly to the

Dumaines, but he had always been somewhat embarrassed to speak to me about his background because I was the daughter of a nobleman, brought up in one of the great houses of France. It was an odd situation; I had married him mostly because I was alone and frightened after Tante Genèvre died, but also because he was not of the aristocracy. At the time, I had thought that would insure a certain stability and stolidity. But he had proved as breakneck and headstrong as any of the young noblemen with whom I had grown up. And he had died as they died—violently.

Now I tried to unleash my grief for him, but still tears would not come. He had been young and very full of life. But it had been so long since we had shared our nights, so long since he held me in his arms and whispered of love. Somehow, it was as if he had been gone a long time already. Now I was with these friends of his, who knew all about me, while I knew nothing of them except that they shared Jacques's violent hatred of Napoleon. And they were going to try to give me a safe haven until my sister could respond to the cry for help I had written less than an hour ago.

Pierre had taken the missive, sealed it with his own sealing wax, and walked down to the harbor with it. He knew several ships' captains who plied the Mediterranean and Atlantic between Marseilles and Virginia's port cities of Hampton and Norfolk. He would give one of them my letter and explicit instructions on where Yve's home in America was—up from Hampton, past Norfolk and Williamsburg, and twenty miles beyond to a farflung tobacco plantation called Cloudmont, on a river named James. Yve had written that the family was an illustrious one, having settled in America over a hundred years ago. Her husband was Andrew Madison, and I visualized his house as a somewhat rough building, like a frontier outpost, which was what America represented to me. There would be few comforts, despite my older sister's hyperbole in trying to make it sound civilized to me. She had briefly mentioned his mother and sister, a brother who was a sea captain and a brother who had died in a hunting accident. I could not sort them out in my mind; there were children too, but she was vague about them. She indicated that Andrew loved his family well, and I knew that went against the grain with Yve. She was as possessive in her love as with her belongings. It was part of her charm, for she made one feel so warm and wanted when she chose to love.

I struggled up tiredly and began to divest myself of my dress and the thin petticoat beneath it. Snuffing the candle, I stood in my chemise before the window, looking out on the street and rooftops beyond. Candles and lanterns flickered in some of the shops and in the windows above, where their owners dwelled. The sky had lost its last faint blue tinge and stars were beginning to prick the vastness. The air washed over me and I could detect many new flavors in it as the May night wind cooled my body. There was the fragrance of coffee and molasses and something like new hemp rope, and suddenly, at last, I cried hard for Jacques.

The days slipped by and I worked behind the bar and in the kitchen. I pretended to be simple-minded and foolish, a hard role to play, for it was so miserably monotonous. The work I did was the most grueling I had ever done and I was so weary when I fell on the cot in the garret that my sleep was deep. Still, toward dawn, I would wake in a sweat, for nightmares were frequent. Always I was running away from nameless terrors, too horrible to be clear. I woke from them tired before the hard days began. I had never done such menial work and in order to keep my sanity I tried to think of Yve and her home and the freedom that would be mine in America. Mélisse kept to the garret, where no one could see her, playing with the meager toys we were able to make or find for her.

Even though I wore shabby dresses, my face smeared with ashes, my thick brown-gold hair bound in a nondescript gray scarf, and a large apron covering my breasts, I was constantly accosted by the rough sailors who frequented the place. Some of them were brazen enough to grab at me as I served them wine, and I was always in a state of anxiety. Every day, when I heard the sound of horses on the cobbled road before the tavern, I feared it was Napoleon's soldiers come for me.

Once, as I came from behind the bar, a towering young French sailor caught me about the waist and pulled me to him, saying, "Foolish or no, you need a good lay with a man like me! Come, girl, let's find a room——"

Pierre came from behind the bar. "Unhand my niece, m'sieu. She is simple. Surely you would not take advantage of a girl who is *folle!*" He took my arm, but the sailor jerked me away and into a powerful embrace. He was drunk and he said thickly, "Foolish or no, I'll wager she'd be a wanton bedmate."

Pierre struggled with him, but the sailor was so large, he sent him staggering with one blow as I struggled desperately in his embrace. The other sailors looked up with interest now. I turned my eyes to them with entreaty and cried out my distress.

Pierre turned on them furiously. "Will none of you help a poor *idiote?*"

Then at last two of them got up and seized the sailor who held me. "Come on, Demeaux, let the wench go. She's crazy. You can find plenty others down the street who'll be much more cooperative."

The young sailor released me, cursing his shipmates roundly. I turned and fled to the back rooms, and Aimée said I did not have to go out again for the remainder of the evening. I sat in the dark of her sitting room, counting the days since Pierre had mailed my letter to Yve. It took three months to get to America and three more for a reply, unless the winds were very advantageous; I could not hope for a letter before October. Depression settled over me like a heavy oppressive cloud.

The following morning I could not stem the tears when I talked to Aimée. "I fear my letter has gone astray. I should write Yve again!"

"Non, non." Aimée said harshly. "It is too great a risk. All our friends in Marseilles, and the sailors, believe you to be a feeble-minded orphan, Audette Dumaine. The slightest mistake, the least clue to your identity, and we could all be hauled off to the guillotine!"

Each day that passed was a torment to me, for each day we served the rough sailors who came to the tavern and I played the idiot, dirt-smeared and ragged. Yet a spark of hope flared at the sight of an occasional ship's captain at the bar. Still no letter came.

Napoleon's soldiers came instead. It had taken them

more than three months to track me down, but the Corsican's followers were tenacious and brutally effective. I was behind the bar polishing glasses when we heard the stamping of their horses and their imperious pounding at the door. A group of newly arrived American sailors sat at two tables.

Wild panic flooded me, but Aimée was swifter than a striking snake. She had me on my knees before the great fireplace on the west wall of the tavern with a bucket of sudsy water, a scrubbing brush in my hands. I sloshed water on the hearth and began to scrub. She was on her way to hide Mélisse before the first man came into the room.

Pierre was now polishing the glasses. He said heartily, "Welcome, *mes amis*. Come in, come in! Always happy to serve the soldiers of our great leader, the Consul Napoleon."

There were four of them, a lieutenant and three of his men. "And he will soon be your emperor, peasant," was the lieutenant's arrogant and unfriendly reply.

" 'Tis what we all hope for," Pierre said smoothly, "for we are ardent supporters of our leader."

"You lie, dog!" the lieutenant spat. "The stableman, Donne, swore it was you—you are Dumaine, of course? who sold him Sevier's horse and saddle last May."

The American sailors were watching them alertly now and with a touch of hostility.

"But that horse and saddle I sold last May were given me by a Monsieur Ducayet, for a greatly overdue bill."

"Who is that scrubbing the hearth?" the lieutenant demanded.

" 'Tis our niece—an orphan from Lyons," Pierre said. "She is touched." He pointed to his head. *"Idiote."*

The lieutenant looked taken aback. He stared at me for a moment or two. Twisting my head upward, I ran a hand freshly smeared with ashes over my face and looked at him with mouth agape.

"Dirty wench—but those eyes. . . . Pity."

In the meantime the other soldiers had gone through the tavern like a whirlwind, cursing as they upset chairs, broke glasses at the bar, and tipped over kegs of spirits searching the corners. The American sailors were beginning to mutter angrily among themselves.

The lieutenant said sharply, "Search the rest of the place, Gaston—François—Maratte. Don't leave a corner, a cupboard, a box without investigating!"

I froze. My Mélisse in that great cedar chest! They would surely find her!

Meantime, the American sailors were rising from their chairs and grumbling, asking what the furor was about. Pierre tried placating them with fresh wine. The lieutenant began to explain to one great sailor with a barrel chest and long muscled legs. The other three soldiers went stamping up the stairs, and I took advantage of the lieutenant's preoccupation to follow them swiftly, unobtrusively. I must protect Mélisse at all cost!

I went straight to the garret and sat tensely on the edge of my cot until I heard their heavy boots coming up the steps from the second floor.

They burst into the small room and stared at me. "Oho!" said one, "the addled niece has come up to greet us. By God, she's as beautiful a piece as ever drew breath beneath that dirt!"

Another one came directly to the chest where Mélisse was hidden beneath the tray of linens.

"Please, *mon capitaine*," I said timidly, my stare vacant, " 'tis only my linens stored away—for the time when I am wed."

"Ha, François, she hopes to be wed, the little *simple* niece."

"I'll not wed her," François said hoarsely, "but by God, I'l bed her!" And suddenly he was upon me. One big hand caught in the neck of my dress and with a single swift movement, ripped dress, petticoat, and chemise straight down the middle, the two halves falling loosely away from my nude body.

One of the soldiers laughed. "Dieu, what a body to be wasted on a feeble-minded wench!"

I began struggling wildly as François flung me on my cot. I lay there naked, with the halves of my garments about me, and a great searing scream welled up in my throat and burst out. I screamed and screamed as François's heavy body came down on mine, holding me immovable, pinned beneath him.

"Alors, François!" said the one called Gaston. "She's like to wake the dead—shut her up before you have your way with her!"

Still the screams were welling out of me and then his sinewy hand was clamped over my mouth. I bit it hard, and with a roar of pain, he struck me such a blow I was almost senseless for a moment. But in that moment I heard a loud stamping on the stairs and suddenly the American sailors, followed by Pierre and the lieutenant, were in the room.

"Get off that girl, you bastard!" shouted the sailor with the great chest, and before the man above me could move, he was hauled roughly to his feet and struck such a blow that he fell to the floor. "What kind o' men are yer, to rape a poor addled girl?" he bellowed.

I reached down and caught up the thin blanket to cover my nakedness and sat quivering while the men milled about the room.

"You're an officer," said the American sailor furiously to the lieutenant. "No officer in America would allow his men to rape while searching a home or a business!"

The lieutenant looked taken aback. Surrounded as they were now by nearly a dozen burly sailors, he blustered in English, "These people are accused of harboring traitors to Napoleon!"

"So you think raping an addled girl'll help you find them, eh?" The sailor towered six inches above the lieutenant.

"Gaston, François—Maratte? Have you found anything?" the lieutenant asked brusquely.

François gave him a surly glance. "*Non*. These people harbor no one."

Though it was only minutes after that before they were gone, it seemed an eternity. They left threatening to talk to neighbors and keep an eye on the *auberge*.

Aimée gave me one of her dresses, which hung on my slender form like the rags I had discarded. Then I let my little one out of her prison in the chest. She was trembling and silent and we clung together seeking comfort from each other. She was so pale and slender from the lack of sunshine it wrung my heart. Oh, God, if ever I reached America, she would play in the sunlight and eat of all the good foods that were grown by country people!

Our life never settled down after that, if ever settled it had been. We lived in terror that the soldiers would return, and as October drew near I despaired of ever hearing from my sister. I lost weight, and my hands had long ago grown calloused from the rough work I did.

Just when I had given up all hope, a tall, burly American captain came into the inn. He was very discreet. He had two brandies, Pierre told me later, before he asked quietly for Madame Sevier.

He produced a letter which he gave to me and then, oh, wonder of wonders! He took from his pocket a leather bag that contained more gold than I had seen since long before my father and mother were beheaded. I offered to pay him with some of the contents of the bag, but he said he had been well paid for his service already. Then I took both letter and bag gratefully and scurried to the garret, where I hugged Mélisse in wild abandon and lit the candle, for twilight was falling fast. Winter was coming rapidly to Marseilles.

"My darling Lilibel," I read. "I am sending you three hundred dollars in gold. I do not know what that is in francs, but it will be enough to get you to me, where you will be safe forever from that evil man Napoleon. I cannot tell you how happy I am that you and Mélisse are coming to live with me. God knows, I need you, little sister. I need your strength, your marvelous way of putting things in the right perspective. I will not tell you of the *ménage* we have here. I will let you see for yourself, but I need you as much—nay, more than you need me. *Vite, vite,* my darling, hurry to me in America as I hurry to pen this and send it right back to you and precious Mélisse. You say she looks like me. How happy for me! Your loving and devoted Yve."

I read it three times. It was short, but it said so much that I wanted to hear. I was welcome. I was wanted. My daughter was wanted. I did not even wonder that Yve failed to mention her own adored son and her beloved husband. She had been hastening to finish and send the letter back by the messenger who had brought it.

I kissed Mélisse and whispered, "My love, we are going to Tante Yve in America, in a strange place called Virginia. And you are going to be so beloved, you will forget all your fears—all our terrors here in France."

On the third of October, 1802, we boarded the *Maidee Love*, an American schooner carrying a cargo of Sèvres china and French silks to Hampton, Virginia. I took with me the scanty wardrobe that Mélisse and I had acquired over the past six months, lip slave, rouge, rice powder, kohl, and a small vial of perfume, purchased at the last minute as a sop to my vanity. I wanted to look my best when I met Yve's family.

Unwilling to wait for a schooner fitted for passengers, I bought passage on a freighter, and our quarters were crew's quarters. They were stuffy and cramped, without a porthole. It was like being in a large box with two beds built into opposite walls. My heart fell at the prospect of making the three-month voyage in such prisonlike surroundings.

As the days strung out, even Mélisse's and my walks around the deck, a necessity for our health, were an ordeal because of the rough jokes from the sailors. If the six months at the *auberge* had been harrowing, the three-month voyage on the *Maidee Love* promised to be hell, for the seas grew rougher in November, eliminating even our walks. Our damp sour little room was so miserable, we spent much time in the galley, for there was a fire there, and usually hot coffee.

When we were almost to Hampton in Virginia the worst of the storms struck. I had not been really frightened until evening came on, though the captain had bade us stay in the galley because of the angry seas.

I could hear the wind howling in the rigging, for the men had long ago reefed the sails. It was impossible to talk over the wild noise of the storm. The cook, a fat, cheerful man named Kirk, from a place called Massachusetts, stayed behind his little bar that divided the galley into two sections, the kitchen and the dining area. The ship rolled so violently on its sides that it was impossible to stand, so Mélisse sat upon my lap in one of the chairs that was fixed to the floor.

Real fear took me when the captain entered, a bleeding gash over his left eye, and a great combing wave rushed in before he could slam the door against it, swirling across the floor to wet my little half-slippers and the hem of my gray wool skirt.

The captain bellowed, "Kirk, we've lost Edmonds and Ramsey and I haven't seen Johnson in over two hours. Is there anything you can give the crew?"

"Biscuits, sir. An' cold coffee. I just put out the fire. I'm feared to keep one goin' the way she's fightin' the seas."

"I feared it might be so. Cold coffee'll be better than nothing, though. I'm going to send them in, two at a time —those that are left."

He turned and spoke to me, "Madame, you and your little girl—I think 'twould be better if I lashed you into the chair." He eyed me where I sat clinging to Mélisse with one hand and holding on to one of the upright columns in the room with the other.

"But captain, if there is danger the ship might sink——"

"The lifeboats ride heavy seas better than a ship, madame, for they are lighter."

"You mean there's a possibility we shall have to take to the lifeboats?" I asked, swallowing down the thick fear in my throat.

He took rope from a wall cupboard nearby and bound first me, then Mélisse in my lap, to the chair.

"There is always that possibility, madame," he said. "That's why we carry them." The door opened and as he left, the seas washed in once more, but this time I lifted my wet, chilled feet above the floor, still holding tightly to Mélisse.

By now it was black as pitch beyond the window. The lanterns above us swung with crazy ease backward, forward, and to the side. I was shivering uncontrollably, though my gray wool was a heavy material.

Cold wind swirled wetly in with the waves as the sailors came in, blue with cold, to drink the coffee Kirk handed out to them. I thought the whole world must be made of ice, before the last of them left.

The ship rolled sickeningly and I clutched my pale, silent Mélisse. Her little hand was cold through the damp wool of my sleeve, and her small, white face frightened me further. She had endured so much. Surely we would survive this last terror. Surely a merciful God would not let us come so near my sister's home as this and then condemn us to death in the black depths of the Atlantic!

All through that eternal night, the ship tossed and wallowed in the mountainous swells created by the storm. Exhaustion finally claimed both my child and me, and toward dawn we slept.

I could not believe it when I wakened with a start to realize the ship was not rolling so wildly. I looked toward the galley and saw Kirk starting a fire in his iron oven. When he saw I was awake, he brought me a cup of hot coffee, which I took gratefully.

"Ma'am," he said quietly, " 'tis Christmas morn."

Two days more after that dreadful Christmas Mélisse and I endured aboard the *Maidee Love*, and it was with incredulity that the two of us debarked at last at Hampton, about noon on the twenty-eighth. The captain escorted us to a nearby inn, where we ate hurriedly in order to catch the coach for Williamsburg. As Mélisse and I mounted the coach step, the captain said briefly, "Madame, you've a long way to go yet. I advise you to stay the night at Christiana Campbell's hostelry in Williamsburg. Ye've had a hard voyage."

I scarcely heard him, so full of fever was I to reach Yve. My heart was suddenly bursting with excitement and hope. It communicated itself to Mélisse and she held my hand with warm, tight little fingers as the coach clattered off down the road toward Norfolk.

"Maman, we will be safe at last, *non?*"

"Yes, yes, my darling!" I replied, hugging her fiercely.

Finding safety at last was not to be so easy, but for that brief little moment I was sublimely happy, and I knew I would not pause in Williamsburg. I was far too anxious to see Yve, to feel welcome, to be somewhere I could call *home.*

CHAPTER 2

The hired coach lurched heavily in the deep ruts of a winding road and I put out a hand to see that my sleeping daughter was not disturbed beneath the blanket covering her. Drumming rain had given way now to the sharp crack of sleet against the rumbling vehicle. It was black as pitch in the coach and very cold, for the storm we had encountered at sea had followed us inland.

Miserable myself, I felt sharp compassion for the driver, Mr. Hawkins, who was perched on the box and receiving the full fury of the stinging particles of ice. Surely we would soon be arriving at Cloudmont! The first leg of the journey on land had been a long, tedious ride in a larger coach with the three other passengers from Hampton. It was dark when we reached Norfolk and it was later still before we left Williamsburg, where the other passengers had debarked. I had hired the man Hawkins and his coach at a stable between Prince George Street and Duke of Gloucester Street, and he had driven us out of Williamsburg, past that small city's flickering lights and through the long night.

Yve had written that Cloudmont was not too far from Williamsburg, but with the foul weather slowing us, the miles had crawled past all too slowly. I drew my threadbare fur-lined cloak more closely about me and leaned back against the cold leather upholstery of the rocking coach. I let my mind slide back over the three-month voyage from Marseilles, back to Paris and Jacques and further —to the days and nights of horror and the memory of

Maman and Papa in the tumbrils on their way to the guillotine. I thought of that too often, I scolded myself, and squeezed my lids against the vivid vision.

That was all past. I was safe here in Virginia and soon to be with Yve, who had married so well. My little Mélisse and I were far from the suspicion and intrigue of France under the wily Napoleon. I tried to relax, but without success; it was too cold, too damp.

The coach swayed and I felt it each time the driver turned sharply. The sleet seemed heavier, beating a thousand tiny drums on the frame of the vehicle. I shivered, dreading the moment when I would have to descend from the coach into the weather. God willing, the house would be near the drive and Mélisse and I would soon be within the warmth of Yve de Belvoir Madison's arms. My eyes stung with tears at the happy thought. Hugging Mélisse, I was thankful that she had slept nearly all the way from Williamsburg.

The coach lurched to a stop. A moment later the driver opened the door and peered into the blackness that enveloped me. "Madame, we are at Cloudmont—at the back. The front faces the James River and I have brought you up to the visitors' entrance. Give me yer hand and I'll help ye down."

"My little one is asleep. I must waken her. One moment, please." I spoke in a low voice.

"Don't wake 'er, madame," Mr. Hawkins said, brushing wind-driven ice particles from his brows and beard. "I'll carry 'er inter the house fer ye. Here I'll wrap 'er in the blanket and she'll not feel a touch o'weather."

I was aware of a pale golden light upon us before I realized that it came from a pair of oil lamps burning at either side of the door. Looking up at the looming bulk of a great three-storied house, with vast wings extending out from the main body, I was amazed by the size of the structure. Even in the dim light I could see that it was Georgian red brick, and it appeared large as a castle to me, not at all like the rough log house I had envisioned.

I drew my cloak about me and swiftly followed the driver to the door, where he shifted the bundled Mélisse in his arms and lifted a heavy brass knocker. There was no porch over the massive granite steps, no protection against the hissing sleet that was driven against us by gusting wind. I was conscious of the trees towering overhead as their branches made snapping noises in the gale. The sound of the brass knocker was faint amidst the noises of the storm.

As we waited the wind swept under my light wool skirt, swirling icily about my ankles. I wore the sky-blue wool Aimée and I had made. My gray dress had suffered from the sea that swept the galley and I hoped to renovate it as soon as I was settled. My little half-slippers, the only shoes I possessed, were poor comfort to my numbed feet. The small bonnet tied fast about my unfashionably long hair was no protection at all. My hands had been chilled so long in their thin kid gloves that they felt numb and frozen as I clutched my large reticule. Yve knew I could be here by late December. It was the twenty-seventh—no, the twenty-eighth. It would soon be New Year's. Surely I had been expected to arrive at any time!

I swallowed down sudden uneasiness, realizing the lateness of the hour. I should have abided by the captain's suggestion and spent the night in Williamsburg. That would have timed my arrival at Cloudmont at the dinner hour the following day, instead of the small hours of the night. Ah, I was too anxious! Eight years it had been since I had seen my quick-tempered, vivacious Yve.

During our long wait, I glanced up at the driver. He gave the gleaming knocker two more raps, this time with a fierce urgency that rang out hard.

"You won't have to return to Williamsburg in this weather, Mr. Hawkins, will you?" I spoke with concern, lifting my voice above the howling wind.

"Bless ye, no, madame," he replied, holding Mélisse easily in the crook of his arm. "Mr. Madison has a place fer hired teams and fer their drivers, too. He's famous fer his kindness and hospitality."

My spirits lifted. It made my sister's husband suddenly more human. In Yve's few short letters, her love for Andrew Madison had been a strong thread. Yet there was something else in those brief, infrequent letters that had disturbed me—a feeling of concealment, of gay determination to overlook some of those who peopled Cloudmont, some for whom she had little liking. But if a hired coachman had kind words for Andrew Madison, he must possess at least some of the noble traits that caused Yve to love him so desperately. Yet time was drawing out and the ice storm buffeted us as we stood on the granite stoop before the door.

"Knock again, Mr. Hawkins. They surely lit these lamps expecting our arrival," I said, forcibly restraining a violent shiver. Another moment and my teeth would be chattering.

"Lanterns always burn at the doors, front and back, of Cloudmont, madame," replied the coachman, and he reached to knock again.

But the door opened under his poised hand, and a tall, cadaverous man stood holding a crystal-chimneyed candle in one bony hand. His nightshirt hung down beneath a heavy topcoat.

"Aye, 'tis Henry Pepper himself," the coachman said heartily, pushing me inside as Pepper dropped back. "And were ye not expectin' Madame Liliane Sevier, man?"

A lugubrious smile lit the man's long, frightening countenance. "Ah, Madame Sevier—to be sure." Then mournfully, " 'Tis a sorry welcome for you."

Shadows leapt about us in the gloom of the biggest foyer I had ever seen. A sense of indefinable foreboding closed in on me. I watched Henry Pepper swing the heavy oak door shut on the stormy night as we moved further into the great room. The silence about us was abrupt and complete. I had a shadowy impression of exquisitely carved paneling, sideboards, paintings, and even chairs in the foyer, which was as large as a ballroom.

"Oh, but it's not sorry," I began breathlessly. "No matter how bad the night——"

"Who is it, Pepper?" A deep male voice shouted from the gloom at the top of a long, square-turned staircase.

" 'Tis young Mistress Madison's sister, Madame Liliane Sevier, from France at last, sir," Pepper replied.

"My God——" The voice broke off. Then strongly, "I'll come down immediately."

We three, Hawkins still holding the sleeping Mélisse, stood waiting. My eyes strained into the black upper regions of the house. I was still shivering, my anxiety increasing steadily.

After a long silence, Pepper said awkwardly, " 'Tis like the master's gone for a dressing gown, madame."

"I should have stayed at the hostelry in Williamsburg—come at a more propitious time," I murmured through a tightened throat. "But I am so eager to see my sister——"

Why wasn't Yve flashing down those long polished stairs? By now I had expected to be clasped in my sister's warm embrace. I yearned for that comfort with an intensity that brought tears near the surface.

"Nay," Pepper said kindly, his long face morose. " 'Tis only right you should come as fast as you could, madame." His sad, portentous air added unaccountably to the dread suffusing me.

The figure now emerging at the foot of the dimly seen staircase compounded my feeling of dread. He came forward with a swift stride, a dark robe belted about a narrow waist.

"My dear sister-in-law—Liliane," he said in a deep, resonant voice. "Welcome to Cloudmont, and please accept my apologies for meeting you in this manner."

I looked up into a dark, saturnine face that appeared slightly drawn. There was no smile on the firm, clean-cut lips, and the black eyes were unreadable. There was something in his manner that turned dread into near panic.

"I—I had so hoped to see Yve—at once, monsieur." In moments of agitation, my accent became more marked. "Can you not inform her that I am arrived?"

Andrew took a quick step forward and put an arm about my shoulders. "My dear, your sister—my wife, has been very ill."

In the strained silence that followed his words, a standing clock in the vast foyer chimed the hour of two. Hawkins said quietly, "Here, Henry, hold the little one, and I'll get madame's baggage for 'er."

Henry Pepper put the candle in its glittering chimney down upon a nearby side table and took my child carefully into his long, thin arms. There was a cold gust of air as Hawkins opened the door and vanished into the storm.

I drew a long, quivering breath. "Then, Monsieur Madison, surely I can be taken to her at once. She will want——" I broke off, fighting back tears.

"She is sleeping," the man said brusquely, "and God

knows she needs to sleep." Then abruptly, "Pepper, go rouse Mrs. Beady and have her fix something hot for madame. She appears near frozen. Here, I'll take the child." He lifted the sleeping Mélisse from Pepper's arms, adding, "We shall be in the library. Tell her to prepare a large pot of hot chocolate and a sandwich of that turkey we had for dinner tonight. Bring the candle, madame—Liliane—and follow me. It is cold here in the great hall."

I wanted to protest that I would not wait, that he must take me to Yve at once, but I found myself obeying the firm voice and trailing after my brother-in-law as Pepper disappeared into the shadows behind us.

There was a dim red glow in a large fireplace and a gentle, pervasive warmth filled the room. The mantel was exquisitely carved, and I realized at once that a master craftsman must have done all the wood in the house. Furniture loomed large and comforting in golden light from the candle Pepper had handed me. I placed the candle upon a small table of polished wood beside a long, deep couch and looked about me. The walls of this room were covered with shelves of books. There must be thousands of them, I thought as I glanced at shelves that stopped only at the ornately carved molding that ran around the decorated ceiling. There was a desk too, of immense proportions, crouching like a beast in its lair near a floor-to-ceiling window.

Andrew Madison laid my child carefully on the big couch, tucking the blanket about her gently and pulling aside the portion that covered her face. "Ah," he said softly, "she's lovely. Lovely as my Yve."

"Yes. I wrote my sister how much her niece resembles her," I replied, refusing to let my voice tremble.

He looked up from beneath black brows and murmured huskily, "You resemble your sister as well, Liliane—except that Yve's eyes are so blue."

"Mélesse's are blue like my sister's. Mine are"—I sought for a word to describe my strange, honey-golden eyes with the brown flecks in them—"hazel, I think."

"I regretted that I did not get to meet you in Paris before Yve and I left after our wedding, but as you recall, the circumstances were—hectic. You are aware I was there on business when I met Yve and fell so deeply in love with her." He motioned me to take a large Hepplewhite chair near the fire and seated himself in its mate across from me.

I put my reticule on the floor beside the chair and began pulling the gloves from my numb fingers. "Tante Genèvre was too ill for me to leave her and attend your wedding. I had to stay with her, for she was—dying. She had saved Yve's and my life, you know, when the Jacobins were howling for all our heads. We were fourteen and sixteen, quite old enough for the guillotine."

He nodded. "So Yve told me. Was your sea voyage a pleasant one?"

I thought fleetingly of the long, arduous journey beset by violent winter storms at sea and the dreadful Christmas just past. I realized he was trying to divert me from my sister's illness and it increased my uneasiness.

I began, "Monsieur, I must——"

"Please call me Andrew. After all, we are related. And may I call you what Yve always calls you—Lilibel?"

"Of course," I replied automatically. Another man was entering the room. From the corner of my eye, he looked even taller than the man seated across from me. I turned. He stood watching me, an oil lamp in his big hand. His eyes gleamed black in a heavily tanned face. Little lines fanned out at the corners of his eyes, as if he had narrowed them often on far horizons—and perhaps laughter was his companion much of the time. His dark face was somber now, and his resemblance to the man before me was undeniable.

"I heard the knocker. This must be Yve's little sister, Lilibel." His voice was a shade deeper, even more commanding than Andrew Madison's, as if he were used to issuing orders that were obeyed at once.

"Come in, George," Andrew said to his brother. "I hope the noise has not roused the rest of the house." There was a faint touch of an unnamable emotion in his low voice as he went on, "I have told Lilibel how ill her sister is—that she must not be disturbed."

George's black eyes went to his brother's swiftly before they fastened on me with sharper intensity.

"Oh, monsieur—Andrew," I put in swiftly, "if only I might look at her! I would be quiet as a mouse. I——" I faltered. "It has been so very long and she is all I have left except my Mélisse."

Andrew spoke with quick tenderness, "You have a great many left in the world now that you have joined us, Lilibel. We are a large and closely knit family. You will find yourself surrounded by relatives."

"Indeed you will," George echoed as he placed the bright lamp on a nearby table and seated himself in a tall ladder-back chair near me. "There are two other young widows and our mother in the house, and your Mélisse has three young cousins." He smiled and his teeth gleamed white in the sun-browned face.

Despite fatigue and fear, I was aware of an excitement stirred by these tall, vital men. An instinct deep within me quivered in response, which surprised me faintly, for it had been long since I had thought of men and their attractions.

"My younger brother has been captain of the *Tern*, transporting Madison cotton and tobacco to our foreign markets, for more than six years," Andrew said, a little smile creasing his sober countenance. "He returned—rather reluctantly I fear—last month to join me in the production of our commodities."

George's laugh rumbled in his broad chest. "Our father was a firm believer in primogeniture. Our older brother, Thomas, adhered to it too, but when he was so untimely taken from us eight years ago, Andrew became master of Cloudmont and he, like our President Jefferson, does not believe in it. So the prodigal has at last returned home to his inheritance, as Andrew suggests—reluctantly."

I was confused by his terms and his discourse, and my desire to see my sister, even though she lay desperately ill, smothered all other thought. "Please, gentlemen, I beg you—just let me look at my sister."

Henry Pepper appeared in the room, carrying a tray with a silver pot and two china cups and saucers beside the sandwich upon it. He was followed by Hawkins.

"Ah, Master George has joined you, sir," Pepper said, as he placed the tray on the round table beside the oil lamp. "I shall get another cup for him."

Hawkins began, "Mr. Madison, sir, 'tis a foul night and I was wonderin' if——"

"Of course, man. Go into the kitchen and have Mrs.

Beady fix you something hot. Charles is in Norfolk on business, but Noah will see you bedded down in the coachman's house. You know where to find him. And there will be a place in the stables for your team, as well as feed."

"Aye, sir. Thankee."

"Mrs. Beady will give you breakfast in the morning and I will settle your fee at that time." Andrew was pouring the steaming chocolate into two cups.

"Madame Sevier has already paid me, sir, so after breakfast I'll be on me way back to Williamsburg." Bowing, he left.

George Madison rose and went to the fireplace, where he lifted a huge log effortlessly from a wrought-iron basket and laid it upon glowing embers. He took a polished brass poker from a stand nearby and shifted the glowing coals. A bright blaze sprang up, sending out reassuring warmth.

My frustration was mounting. My chilled fingers closed upon the delicate saucer held in Andrew's big, steady hand and I took a sip of sweet, hot liquid. It warmed me as the leaping fire did, and feeling began to flow back with a tingling sensation.

"Eat the sandwich, my dear," Andrew urged. "You are so pale. We don't want you coming down with an illness, too." His smile was compassionate as he took up his cup of chocolate.

As Pepper returned with a cup and saucer for George Madison, he murmured, "Sirs, I have put Madame Sevier's portmanteau and valise in the room Mistress Madison had us prepare for her."

"Good, Pepper. You may retire now. We will see madame safely to her chamber." Andrew poured a third cup of chocolate and handed it to his brother, who now lounged against the mantel. Apparently, he was a restless man.

George's black eyes twinkled. "A tot of brandy would have been more to my liking—and more in line for our half-frozen sister-in-law, I'm thinking."

"A little innocent chocolate will do neither of us harm, George," his brother replied with a faint smile.

I said slowly, "Since it is apparent you will not permit

me to look in at my sister, Andrew, perhaps you will tell me from what illness she suffers."

" 'Tis a fever that has settled in her lungs. We should not disturb her in any way."

His voice was strained. With the warmth of the drink and the fire stealing through me, I felt a touch lightheaded. "Then surely she has a nurse with her—if she is so terribly ill."

"I secured the best I could find. She has been ill but three days," replied Andrew, finishing his chocolate and placing his cup and saucer on the silver tray.

Presentiment crawled through me. These two men who were watching me so narrowly knew more than they were telling. I placed my half-finished sandwich on one of the delicate china plates and sipped the last of the chocolate. In some dim recess of consciousness I noted that the china was exquisite, as fine as any we had long ago in our great château outside Paris. I had thought I was coming to some pioneer settlement on the edge of a wilderness, yet all about me in this house were signs of gracious, even opulent living. I had put Yve's description of the house down to her desire to reassure me only.

I sighed, leaning my head back against the cushioned chair. The blessed warmth that had stolen through me was a soporific. Despite worry about Yve and the unwelcome alarms at finding myself in strange surroundings once more, I was growing heavy-eyed.

George came forward and leaned over me suddenly, his dark, hard features near my own. A sharp emotion surged up, accelerating my heartbeat. He said, "Come. You need sleep more than anything else, little Lilibel." I allowed him to pull me to my feet. His big hands were warm and slightly rough as they enveloped mine. Tired as I was, I was shocked wide awake by the vital and electric response that coursed through me at his touch.

He took up the oil lamp and led the way. In a few moments, we had climbed the stairs, traversed a wide hall, and arrived in a large room on the second floor. I sensed that it was in the east wing off the central section of the enormous house. Andrew carried Mélisse tenderly in his arms up the long flight of stairs and laid her on the big bed.

A fire was burning brightly behind a firescreen, laid no doubt by the grim but thoughtful Henry Pepper. There was a small crib not far from the big bed that stood in the center of the room. A rush of gratitude made my eyes sting. Dear Yve! She had thought of that, I was sure. No doubt this was her small son's crib, now outgrown, as the boy was six.

"Would you like breakfast served you here in the morning, so you may sleep over your long, tiring journey?" Andrew asked courteously, taking my hand in a welcoming gesture. To my annoyance, a flood of feeling similar to that I had known at George's touch engulfed me. Dimly, my tired mind registered danger in my response to these two powerful men.

"No," I replied. "I should like to breakfast with the family. And I hope to see Yve as soon as possible, you know."

"Good!" George said with his quick smile as his brother joined him at the door. "You're going to find yourself surrounded with family, Lilibel. God knows, *I* have—and how I've longed for my mistress, the sea!" He closed the door on his laughter.

I leaned against it for a moment. Fatigue lay heavily on me, dimming apprehensions for Yve, dulling my astonishing reaction to these two men. Mélisse did not rouse from deep slumber as I carefully disrobed her. I put a warm flannel gown from the canvas valise on the child and placed her small body in the crib, drawing the covers gently about her.

When at last I took the little flight of three wooden steps up into the high feather bed, I sank down into its warming depths with a prayer of thankfulness that I had completed the long, harrowing pilgrimage and was safely under my sister's roof. Tomorrow—tomorrow, surely they would let me see Yve, no matter how ill she was.

Despite near exhaustion, I wakened early and lay in the soft folds of the bed, observing my surroundings. In dim light that filtered through the drawn folds of blue brocade on the north and south windows, I could see that the room was huge. The fire, burning cheerfully in a marble-manteled fireplace, had been laid afresh while I still slept.

There was a couch and several chairs about it and a great armoire in one corner of the room, with mirrors gleaming on its doors. A fine imported rug covered the polished floor, its flower motif blending with the blue of drapes and bedcoverings. There were matching blue curtains about the testered bed, held back with velvet ties. I had not drawn the bed curtains, wanting to be aware if Mélisse stirred. Blue was a favorite with Yve, and it was reflected in every accouterment in this exquisite bedchamber.

Renewed anxiety descended on me as I thought of my sister. Surely Yve would be improved this morning. She was so vital, so vivacious. Possessive she had always been, jealous of her own, but so charming withal—nothing could happen to Yve!

In the crib, Mélisse suddenly flung an arm from the covers. I looked at the sleep-flushed little face, my heart contracting with love. This child was all I had to show for the feverish days of my hasty and short-lived marriage.

I rose from the bed and moved silently to replace the coverlet over the arm of my rosy child. It was still very early. I stepped to the great windows on the north and drew aside the drapes to look down at the rear of the house. I was astounded by the complexity of outbuildings and gardens that met my eyes. All the buildings were of the handmade red brick that formed the main house, and beyond them stretched a vast bowling green. There were formal gardens on either side of the bowling green, intricate and beautiful, one being laid out with the *fleur de lis* motif in English boxwood hedges. Dark green boxwood was everywhere, low hedges bordering walkways and flowerbeds, which were bare now, and high hedges dividing some of the outbuildings from others. Tall trees, many of them bare of leaves, bordered both gardens and paths.

One large building with two stories looked as if it housed carriages, with living quarters directly above. Beyond it a church steeple thrust into the cold blue sky. The whole was meticulously kept and beautiful to see under the bright cold sunlight that had come with the clearing of last night's storm. Looking down the curving road, I could see where the coach last night had turned and lurched, bringing us down the visitors' approach.

Much farther away, beyond tall, black-green pines on a

rolling hill, I glimpsed several large barns, which I was to learn stored cotton and housed the drying tobacco leaves as they were cured.

Near the buildings I took to be the carriage house and stables, a slender young black was feeding a pack of lean hunting dogs. They leaped about him as he threw food to them. As I watched, a man emerged, and I recognized Mr. Hawkins as he strode swiftly down a side path toward the stables. In a few moments, he would have his team harnessed and hitched to his racketing coach and be off in the cold morning sunlight for Williamsburg.

Swift with curiosity, I went to the windows on the south and drew the drapes, revealing vast, rolling terraces of lawn and shrub of garden and hedge that stopped a quarter-mile away at the bank of the James River. It was a broad and shining river, lovelier than any I had ever seen. Not even the Seine was more beautiful.

The sudden realization that my feet were very cold turned me at last away from the windows. Silently I gave thanks to the maid who must have replenished my fire earlier, for it was burning steadily and warmly and the room was quite comfortable, except for the floors. That was good, for my meager wardrobe boasted neither dressing gown nor robe.

I moved to pour water into the china bowl on the washstand and bathed myself quickly in the cold water. There was a bar of lavender-scented soap, a touch of Yve that comforted me. Its faint fragrance clung as I dressed in my best frock. The dress was made of pale rose corded silk, rich and heavy. The bodice fit snugly across my high breasts up to a demure black velvet bow at a round collar. The skirt was a long narrow drape with but one thin petticoat. It had been Aimée Dumaine's best dress, cut down to fit me.

Seating myself at the broad dressing table, I took out my pot of rouge, brushing my pale, delicate features with the faintest of color. It would cheer Yve to see her sister looking well despite the ordeals I had suffered. With that thought uppermost, I dusted my straight nose with rice powder and rubbed my lips with the rose-colored salve I had brought from Marseilles. I even touched my lids very faintly with kohl. It was regrettable that my long hair was not as fashionable as my remodeled dress, but I had not found opportunity or money to have it cut and styled before my hasty departure. Nor did I possess one of the extremely short curled wigs that were so in vogue. Touching my wrists with the spicy perfume I had indulged in with some of Yve's generous gift, I turned away from the mirror.

I noticed a second door at the opposite side of the room and went to explore it. I found it opened into a passageway, lighted by two windows, one on the south and one on the north. There were two doors across the hall that I knew must be additional bedrooms.

As I turned back, I heard a soft rap on the door beside the fireplace. At my soft call, it opened, and a tall, slender black girl came into the room. Her head was bound with a bright yellow cloth and in her ears were two small gold studs. She was exceptionally beautiful in a strange, exotic way. Her smile revealed perfect white teeth, but there was a haunted, appealing look in her luminous eyes which immediately aroused my sympathy.

"I am Judith, madame, maid to Miss Laura, and she sent me to ask if I might help you this morning—perform your toilette or dress your hair—but I see I am too late." Her voice was soft, almost educated.

"That's kind of you, Judith, and of Miss Laura, to think of me."

As Judith came forward to look down at Mélisse, enchantment spread across her even brown features. "Madame, your little girl is beautiful," she whispered. "The most beautiful I ever saw."

Flushing with pleasure, I murmured, "Thank you, Judith."

The big dark eyes came to my face and the young woman added, "No wonder—your beauty is the same."

"You are very kind," I replied, "and I can return the compliment." I added, "I shall have to wake Mélisse soon. The breakfast hour must surely be upon us."

"Would you like me to dress her?"

Before I could answer, there was another, more decisive rap upon the door. My skirt rustling richly, I went to open it. But it opened before me and in the aperture stood a majestically tall and handsome woman. Her snowy hair, like a cloud wreathing Olympus, was piled high. Heavily fringed black eyes were so like those of the two men who had greeted me last night, I knew the relationship at once.

Judith said gravely, "Good morning, Mistress Madison. I were sent by Miss Laura to maid for madame, but she don't need me." And she took her quiet departure as Mistress Madison gave me a quick smile that revealed beautiful teeth, remarkable in one who must surely be in her fifties.

"Liliane, my dear!" Her voice was low, well modulated. As she took me in her arms the faint scent of lavender enveloped me, and I thought fleetingly that possibly it had not been Yve after all who had carefully placed the soap in the dish for my morning toilette.

Releasing me, she said, "I am Andrew's and George's mother and you will soon meet my daughter, Mary Madison Jackson. Call me Cornelia, dear. I'm so *glad* you're here at last!"

"Thank you." Then, swiftly, "Is my sister better? May I not see her now?"

A look of acute distress crossed the strong, handsome features and was smoothed away with apparent effort. "Come, my dear." She led me to the brocaded couch before the fire. "I must tell you about our dear Yve."

A strange numbness washed through me. Disaster had followed me since that dreadful day when Yve and I had stood in the Paris street and watched the tumbrils creaking and scraping past. I repressed a scream now, as I had on that day ten long years ago.

Cornelia Madison took my hands in a warm clasp. "My darling child, Andrew and George thought you far too weary last night to be struck another blow, but you must be told now. We buried our beloved Yve yesterday morning. She died of a congestion in her lungs three days ago."

The older woman would have taken me again into her arms, but I drew back, bracing myself against the sickening shock of knowing my sister was lost to me forever.

My voice was muffled. "And all the time I was in the coaches yesterday—hurrying to reach her—she was already gone." I thought, *I knew last night. I sensed it all along and refused to face it.*

"She was ill such a short time. Only three days. And she did not suffer long, Liliane. She loved you very much."

"I loved her," I replied in a dead voice. "Now there is no one left—except my Mélisse. No one."

Her words were swift and sympathetic, "You must look on us as your family, dear. Yve wanted it so. *We* want it so. She told us of your dreadful experience during the time of the Terror in France, of your trusted servant, Genèvre, taking you at your parents' request to hide you in Paris. She even told us of the unfortunate circumstance that permitted the two of you to see the Comte and Comtesse on their way to the—guillotine." This time she succeeded in putting her arms about me, and drew me near. "You have stood so much. Your husband's murder, and your narrow escape to Marseilles. Now that you are with us, you must forget all that."

I pulled back and looked at the woman with tear-filled eyes. My face was perfectly composed but scalding tears would not be denied, and they rolled down my cheeks. I said thickly, "But Yve is gone. My sister is *dead.* Now I shall never see her again. There is nothing you can say, madame, that will ease my agony or comfort my soul."

For a long moment, Cornelia Madison looked into my grief-stricken face, which I held firm against crumpling. Then in a slow, measured voice she said, "It has been said either death is a state of nothingness and utter unconsciousness, or there is a change and migration of the soul from this world to another. Now if death be of such a nature, I say that to die is to gain, for eternity is then only a single night."

I fixed my eyes on the woman's face in surprise and brushed at my tears with my hands. Cornelia continued, "After all, who is really to say whether you, who must go on living, will be happier than she, who has left this life for another?" There was genuine understanding in the dark eyes that looked into mine, as she added slowly, "Give us a chance to make you happy, Lilibel. Sorrows are lessened when they are shared, and we shall share yours—— Ahh! What a lovely little girl!"

I turned to see Mélisse, who had flung back the covers and sat looking at us from the crib, her tangle of black curls falling about her shoulders, her gentian eyes puzzled.

"*Maman, q'est que c'est*——"

"*Parlez anglais, ma chérie.* We are at Tante Yve's house now, and this lady is your Uncle Andrew's mother."

Cornelia, who had followed me, stood at the crib, her face lit by the warmest and most endearing of smiles. "Call me Aunt Cornelia, Mélisse, for I am indeed your great-aunt. You must hurry and get dressed, for Mrs. Beady has prepared a beautiful Virginia breakfast for you and your mama—and your young cousins, whom you will soon meet. Aren't you hungry?"

"*Oui*—but yes, Tante—Aunt Cornelia."

Before I could forestall her, Cornelia had lifted Mélisse from the crib and was carrying her to the couch. The child put her arms trustingly about the woman's neck. This surprised me, for our secretive, fearful existence in France had made her panicky with strangers. I went to the portmanteau to get a dress and undergarments for my daughter.

"Oh, but you *are* a lady!" Cornelia was saying admiringly. "And all of us had been expecting a baby."

"I'm four. I was four years last July," Mélisse was saying gravely in her lilting child's voice. I marveled anew at the older woman's charm for my child. By the time the two of us had finished Mélisse's quick toilette, my little daughter was completely won by Cornelia Madison.

I was not so taken. There was something about this regal woman who was capable of such winning ways, such warmth, and such educated philosophy that made me reserve judgment. As we readied ourselves to leave the bedchamber, I stopped short. To my dismay, tears clouded my eyes, and such a wave of homesickness for my sister swept through me that I was powerless against it. Cornelia gave me a knowing glance.

"Come, dear," she said gently. "I know how you feel, but believe me, being with others who love you is the best source of comfort."

"But she's dead," I whispered. "I can't believe it. I can't comprehend it. How can you possibly know——"

Cornelia spoke with sudden bitterness. "I know. I lost my firstborn and beloved son, Thomas, in a hunting accident eight years ago, and there hasn't been a day since that I haven't wept for him. Not a moment that I don't miss him still, even with my other three children about me." To my surprise the black eyes were brilliant with unshed tears as she added, "I would to God it had been I who died that day. I would gladly give my life for any of my children." The strong mouth trembled before iron control triumphed. She said with sudden determined gaiety, "Ah, Mélisse, your little cousin Andy is only a little older than you, and you two shall have great fun. My daughter Mary's children are older. Amanda is fifteen, while Timothy is a big boy of ten."

She continued telling us about the family as we made our way down the long hall and took the stairs. Laura Landon Madison, who was childless and Thomas's young widow, lived with the family at Cloudmont as well, she informed us. Mary's husband, who had been much older, had died of a sickness of the heart five years before. The two sons, Andrew and George, completed the immediate circle, and according to Cornelia, all were most anxious to make me and my daughter welcome additions to the large family.

We reached the great hall and I paused, swept once again by the enormity of my sorrow, but I drew a long breath and followed Cornelia, who gave me another of her heart-warming smiles.

"Don't have misgivings, my dear," she said kindly, guiding us to the rear of the great hall. "Your life must go on, and you will find our large family an antidote to sorrow. You will see."

Nursing my grief, I wished strongly and briefly that I might be alone with it, but I squared my shoulders and followed Cornelia and Mélisse into a great room that seemed filled with people. With difficulty, I returned their ready smiles.

CHAPTER 3

"We've been waiting for you!" cried a young woman with fashionably short curling hair that looked like honey-colored silk. Her eyes were the clear blue of a summer sky and her morning dress, snugly fitted about her full breasts and falling straight in the new waistless look, was of pale blue and accentuated the beauty of her eyes. Her swift smile put an enchanting dimple in her left cheek.

"That is my daughter-in-law, Laura, my dear Thomas's widow," Cornelia said briskly, and began introducing the others in the dining room one by one.

I was conscious of a great sideboard against the wall opposite a row of tall, cream-draped windows that looked out on the rear. The sideboard was laden with platters of steaming food. Three maidservants hovered near a tall, handsome older woman in a maid's apron, who stood quietly near a door that led to another large room. I was to learn later that Cloudmont was the only plantation mansion to have recently added a great pantry connecting the house to the kitchen. The older woman's features were classic and her black hair, showing only a little gray, was draped softly about her face, which still bore traces of an extraordinary beauty. I registered her cold, interested scrutiny and her air of authority. Henry Pepper, a frown of concentration on his morose face, gestured to the maids and they darted back into the pantry to fetch more food.

On the great linen-covered table there was the mellow gleam of silverware, sparkling crystal, and china, thin as a wafer. A child's table, set for two, stood near the windows. A richly gleaming sterling chandelier holding at least fifty unlit candles hung above the big table.

Cornelia turned to me. "You know my two sons, Andrew and George, and here is Mary, my daughter, sadly also a widow. These young scallawags are my grandchildren, Timothy, Amanda, and Andy." The three youngsters studied Mélisse and me, smiling politely. Fifteen-year-old Amanda had a look of wisdom beyond her years in her knowing blue eyes, as thickly lashed as her grandmother's black ones. Her gleaming brown hair, tied with a blue velvet bow, fell below her waist. I detected a barely concealed hostility in those young eyes.

During the introductions, I noticed that Andrew wore a wide band of black silk on his right arm, which was startling against the light brown brown wool suit, but none of the women wore mourning. I realized with an ache that I had no black dress I might wear to mourn my sister.

I forced a smile for the tall, dark young matron who was Cornelia's daughter. Mary was attractive in the same fashion as her two handsome brothers, yet in her the family look was inexplicably flawed. She was full bosomed to the point of voluptuousness and her mouth was too ripe, almost loose in its sensuality. Her large eyes were beautiful, heavily lashed and delicately shadowed under fine brows, and when they rested on Mélisse they glowed with love ready for the accepting. Yet when they swung to meet mine, their coldness was unmistakable. The overripe mouth moved in a smile that was not echoed in those eyes, and I knew a prickle of dislike.

The young ones had drawn near Mélisse, smiles less tentative and more encouraging. I murmured, "They are lovely children." Timothy, the ten-year-old, was swaggering a bit. His black hair had obviously been slicked down by his mother.

Andy, Yve's six-year-old son, stood slightly back from the others, and he was handsomest of all. His hair was not black like Yve's and Andrew's, but a soft, light brown, and his eyes were a lighter blue than Yve's. I wanted to seize and hold him to me as the last part of my sister, but I knew that would never do, for the child's expression was one of wariness. Mélisse was transfixed by her first cousin, lips parted, small face alight with pleasure at finding him so near her own age.

I stooped swiftly to Andy, my rose silk skirt in a graceful pool about me on the floor. Smiling at the other children as well, I said, "Andy, I am your Aunt Lilibel. Did your mother tell you that your little cousin Mélisse and I were coming to see you?" From the corner of my eye I watched Mary's and Laura's close observation as I talked to my nephew. Could there possibly be jealousy in it? I discounted the sudden intuition. I was too shaken by my sister's recent death to sort out my confused impressions.

The boy nodded, his smile polite as he stepped back and skillfully evaded my embrace. "Yes, Mama told me."

I rose to my feet and acknowledged the amenities regarding my journey by the cold-eyed Mary and the fair Laura. George and Andrew asked gravely after my health and I replied that I was well under the circumstances. Nothing was said of the fact that the brothers had not apprised me of my sister's death. It appeared to be tacitly understood by all that their mother had undertaken that sad chore and disposed of it.

Then, with Cornelia leading the way, we all took places and served ourselves from the rich spread of food on the sideboard. The maids served Andy and Mélisse at their miniature table by the windows, which revealed the long vista of gardens and bowling green, bordered by the myriad outbuildings. Timothy, with his older sister, was permitted to sit at table with his elders, which no doubt accounted for his swagger. The tall, handsome woman in a maid's apron poured coffee and remained nearby to serve as requested.

I looked at the luxurious appointments in the room and commented on their beauty. I was amused to recall that I had been prepared for a rude dwelling and a rough life.

At my compliments, those at the table launched into a spirited history of the house. Andrew informed me that the first Madison, the original Thomas, came to America in 1700, determined to have the best and not be beholden for it. He not only raised fine tobacco, he warehoused it himself in Hampton and shipped it on his own ship to foreign markets.

George, eyes twinkling in his sun-browned face, added,

"Jefferson once remarked that Virginia planters were a species of property annexed to certain mercantile houses in London—but he wasn't speaking of Madisons."

Laura said with a touch of sarcasm, "My family was not so shrewd as the Madisons, who achieved their wealth and luxury by their own initiative and cleverness in both producing *and* shipping." She turned deliberately wide eyes to me. "Why, Lilibel, the first Thomas Madison had such scruples and high moral standards that he had no slaves at all on this great plantation."

"Really?" I replied noncomittally. I had little patience with this family chatter when Yve lay buried only twenty-four hours ago.

There ensued a sharp exchange between Andrew and Laura regarding slavery. It appeared that Laura had brought the first slaves to Cloudmont as part of her dowry, and while her husband had been willing to keep them, Andrew was not. He was now in the process of educating them preparatory to sending them as free men and women to the North, where they might take up their lives in happier circumstances. As the exchange continued, I learned that Laura's old home, Landon, on the York River, had been permitted to run down, while Andrew had kept Mary's home, Jackson's Landing on the Chickahominy in good repair and producing.

Mary sent Laura a black look, but said to me, "Andrew is far ahead of his time in knowledge of soils and their ingredients, Lilibel. He's made a study of it." She turned to Laura and, in a tone laced with pure venom, said, "As for Landon house itself, even *you* refuse to live in that draughty old ruin, Laura."

A delicate flush mantled Laura's face and she bit her soft lip. Her eyes on Andrew were bitter.

He said a touch wearily, "Laura, you know how tobacco exhausts the soil. Even cotton leaves it depleted. And you know well enough we are in the process of plowing fertilizers and nutrients into Landon soil right now."

"You cannot convince the ignorant of your wisdom, Andrew darling," Mary said, with tenderness. "*We* know you are doing the best for all of us."

"That will be enough of such wrangling, my dears,"

Cornelia said firmly from the end of the snowy-linened table. "After all, Lilibel has suffered a great loss and I think we should converse on things that would comfort her, for we share her grief." She bent a kindly glance on me.

Laura said with quick contrition, "Your sister's presence shall be with us always." But I sensed there was no depth in the amenity.

"She was a beautiful woman," Mary said in a cold, measured voice, "and we miss her. We thought it better not to remind you of her loss, or we would have spoken of it immediately." I knew a faint, inexplicable repulsion as Mary tightened her overfull mouth.

Cornelia, whose dark eyes were undeniably sympathetic, added, "You must not think us unfeeling because we do not wear mourning. We will not attend any of the parties this season out of respect for Yve. Though of course we must have our traditional Open House, for the custom has not been broken in over fifty years. Not even during the war against England."

I was thinking of Yve's few but disparaging comments on these two young widows and Cornelia. Yve had little time for anyone who took Andrew's attention from herself, no matter how briefly. Upon reflection, it seemed to me that Yve's love for Andrew had been the paramount theme in those infrequent letters. She had averaged only two letters a year—letters lost when I fled Paris seven months before.

Covertly I studied the handsome people around the table as they engaged in lively conversation, and the thought that had been lying at the base of my mind since Cornelia Madison had told me of Yve's untimely death rose up, and I faced it. I really had no claim on these people. They were making me welcome and it was obvious they wanted me to make my home with them, yet I felt alien. But where could I go? The money Yve had sent me was exhausted. The last of it had gone to pay Mr. Hawkins for the long, rough coach ride to Cloudmont. As if in answer to my thoughts, Cornelia spoke.

"You know, Lilibel, we in Virginia adore large families. The bigger, the better, and heaven knows we've room for an army here at Cloudmont. Thirty-four rooms." She paused and smiled. "In fact, at the start of the Revolution, we almost housed an army—the British." Her face grew suddenly hard and secretive as she added, "My husband and his men—dissuaded them." Then with a determined smile, "I yearn for more grandchildren, but my Mary's a picky one and though she's had suitors, she hasn't chosen to remarry. As for that rascally George, who knows when he will settle down with a wife?"

George laughed aloud, "I married the sea years ago, Mother, and she's a changeable, jealous mate."

Cornelia gave him a reproachful glance, "But you've given up the sea."

"For a while. We shall see after a year how I like being a landlubber."

Cornelia turned back to me. "I am so glad you came, Lilibel, for now I have two more to love." Her eyes on me were so warm, so welcoming that my own filled with tears of gratitude.

"I feel I have no claim on you, madame. I really should make my own way in the world. Tante Genèvre taught me millinery——"

All the women broke in at once, Cornelia's voice rising above the rest. "Liliane," she said sternly, "you have the greatest of claims. That of blood. Your daughter is first cousin to our own adored little Andy. Let us hear no more talk of this—making your own way. Cloudmont is your home and there is love aplenty to go around."

Andrew's eyes drew me. He was looking at me steadily, his black gaze compelling. He and his brother had the same heavy-browed scowl, which reminded me of an eagle I had once seen in captivity at the château years ago. And as the eagle's had done, his fierce stare made me catch my breath.

He said quietly, "This is indeed your home—and Mélisse's." It was said with such finality that I could only murmur an assent as we all rose from the table. The servants stood by respectfully as the family filed out.

Even so, my uneasiness was not laid. It clung through the morning as I became better acquainted with the children and the adult residents of Cloudmont. Cornelia showed me through the vast house and the two wings off the main structure. She asked if I liked my room, which was near hers. My room was on the east end and I realized then that the broad windows on the north looked out over the rear yards, and while it was enormous, it was not so large as those I had seen in the main and central section. The servants' rooms were on the third floor, as were the nursery, schoolroom, and children's rooms.

Cornelia took me through them all, saying, "They're all comfortable enough, most with fireplaces of their own as you can see, but so many stairs are wearying. You can come here and watch the children take their lessons with Seton, when you like."

It was easy to discern from Cornelia Madison's conversation as the day wore on that although the broad acres and ample house at Cloudmont set the stage for independent, dignified, and gracious living, their lives were not carefree. The management of Cloudmont was a heavy and multifarious responsibility. Plans had to be made and executed for maintaining the many buildings about the house, for allocating fields to the several crops—and here Andrew's studies of soil played a great part in his plan, for refertilizing the acres and rotating the crops. He had to oversee the planting, harvesting, and providing of food for many men and animals. Further, he had to secure a money income by the sale of tobacco, cotton, and other commodities. There were unwilling laborers to be pushed to their tasks and problems as numerous and varied as the complexities of human nature to be settled among his tenants and the slaves. Even with his brother, George, now shouldering a portion of the responsibility, it sounded a killing job to me. Cornelia did point out that he had the help of a fine overseer, Jacob Worth, who was of invaluable assistance, and of Charles Alexander, a source of even more help, who was now in Norfolk attending to Madison business at the warehouse there.

Later, Cornelia and I had tea in the morning room, where we could look down the long, landscaped distance to the sparkling James River. As she filled our cups she confided, "I'm afraid Andrew is a little autocratic and opinionated, but those can be good characteristics when properly channeled. George is equally commanding, having captained the *Tern* for so many years. He's been back but a month now and so far he and his brother have gotten along very well together, coordinating the work between them. And Charles, whom you will meet when he returns from Norfolk, is really indispensable. Thomas, of course, was absolute in his mastery over Cloudmont, for he believed, as his father did, that the eldest son should inherit entirely."

"That's what George meant when he made his remark about primo—primogeniture?" I asked, sipping my tea. Laura and Mary were engaged elsewhere in the house and the children were playing in the nursery. Cornelia and I were cozy together by a glowing fire.

"Yes. My husband thoroughly endorsed the practice. At his death, a little over twelve years ago, everything went to Thomas. But you see," she said pensively, "Andrew has been greatly influenced by Thomas Jefferson's principles, and he does not believe in primogeniture at all." She poured herself a fresh cup of tea and stirred in sugar and cream thoughtfully as she continued, "All three of our sons were educated at William and Mary University. We would have sent them abroad for their education, but they would have none of it. They are very patriotic. Thank God, they were too young to fight at the time of the Revolution. Their father died of an old wound suffered in the fighting early in that war." She sighed. "Well, the boys traveled the world over when they graduated, but I fear their education is not as extensive as it might have been had they agreed to go to England."

Finishing my tea, I remarked, "I really should go up and finish arranging my clothes." I thought of my sparse wardrobe. It would certainly take a short enough time to hang my meager garments in the armoire and fold my lingerie into the tall chest of drawers.

"Of course, my dear! I have talked so—I do hope it hasn't tired you?"

"Of course not. I should love to continue after I put my things in order. Some must be laundered——"

"I shall send Clementine and Abigail up to help you. Have you trunks to arrive later?"

I smiled, "No, Cornelia. I brought everything in the world that Mélisse and I possess in my portmanteau, valise, and reticule."

"My dear!" Cornelia was shocked. "We must go into Williamsburg soon to outfit you and Mélisse."

"I feel too beholden already," I protested.

"Now, none of that," Cornelia was brisk. "You are my daughter now, and I shall take great pleasure in buying you some of the new pretty fashions that have just come in from your own France. I've friends in Richmond who get the latest fashion magazines from France and England and there are two seamstresses, two sisters there, who can copy anything." She looked at me approvingly. "I'm so glad you haven't succumbed to this craze of cutting off all the hair. I can always tell when a woman wears a wig, no matter how cleverly wrought it may be—and I think they are quite hideous."

I sighed. "I must admit, Cornelia, that much of my unfashionableness is due to lack of funds." I had wanted very much to cut my hair the new way, but I had little chance to do so. And I was entranced by the new wigs, but they cost a great deal.

"Hmmn. Well, some good things spring from impoverishment, my dear. I think these new Empire dresses we are all forced into, with the waistline directly under the bosom, are most unbecoming. Mark my words, we will return to the full skirt eventually and women's waists will be in evidence once again."

I gave her a faintly mischievous glance. "In Paris, now, these simple frocks are very sheer—so sheer that the ladies' limbs are almost visible, and much of the bosom is exposed as well."

Cornelia smiled. "Yes, I've heard of Madame Récamier—and there was the wife of a French diplomat in Philadelphia at a social gathering. A friend of mine who attended wrote to me jesting that she had privately dubbed the lady Eve and her dress, the figleaf."

I laughed aloud for the first time since I had learned of my sister's sudden death. "*Vraiment,* Cornelia, I have no figleaves, but I must go put away what I do have." I went on, with genuine relief and gratitude, "You cannot know how happy I am that my small daughter is so taken with her cousin and all of you."

Cornelia said seriously, "Love is rarely unwelcome—and we all love your Mélisse. I'm sure Seton Cambridge will find her quite irresistible. You will meet him when he returns from Richmond, where he has gone for the holidays. He is our tutor as well as pastor. When he has finished with our youngsters, he conducts classes in the church every afternoon for the tenants' children and the slaves as well."

"I look forward to meeting him," I replied as we left the room together. I took the stairs upward from the great hall, marveling anew at the carved banister and finials and the exquisitely wrought paneling in the great hall. Below me, I heard Cornelia calling for the maids as she went from the hall into the dining room. Above me I heard the voices of Mary and Laura raised in anger. Laura was saying, "You do the boy a great injustice, taking his side every time he quarrels about his lessons, or correction! He must be disciplined or he will grow up a weak, useless creature."

"You have no sympathy with that poor, motherless child, Laura," Mary blazed. "Your heart must be made of stone!"

"That's a lie—I love him better than you do, or I wouldn't demand that he be disciplined."

"Andy does not need discipline. He needs love now, more than ever——" Mary broke off as she saw me coming toward them and her face smoothed, the jealousy and animosity wiped away as if by magic. Laura, not too well disciplined herself, was slower to disguise her rage and frustration.

As we met, I said awkwardly, "Cornelia and I have just had tea. I think you both might enjoy a cup. It is still in the morning room. The pastry is delicious."

"I shall have some," Mary said blandly, refusing to look at Laura, who flung herself on down the stairs without further speech.

I continued toward my room, somewhat shaken by the passions I felt in the two young women. Evidently my sister's child was the source of great dissension between his two aunts. It was a curious circumstance, as if they were rivals for the child's affection. I sensed that the hostility between them ran deep.

At the turn in the hall, I was startled to see the tall, handsome woman in maid's apron who had overseen our breakfast step out of the shadows. Her face was closed but her dark eyes were brilliant and I had the feeling she had witnessed the altercation between the two young women and was pleased by it. Still, her face was composed as she gave me a beautiful smile and said, "I am Louise Alexander, madame, head housekeeper. I hope you are feeling better—after learning of the sadness that has been ours at Cloudmont."

"I am very well, thank you."

"Forgive me, but you do not seem at all like your sister." Hers was the first of many discomfiting comments I was to receive regarding Yve.

"No, Yve was more vivacious than I." I smiled. "A much wittier person."

"Yes," replied Louise, "but you also seem gentler, more thoughtful—less unkind."

"My sister was never unkind," I said coldly, looking into the face of this once beautiful woman, who seemed to be a servant, yet did not walk or speak like one.

"But she was, madame. And not entirely without cause." With that, she gave me another cold smile and began her descent of the stairs with a stately step.

I stood looking after her, puzzled and more than a little resentful. True, I had not seen my sister in many years. It was possible that she had changed, but if so, something must have precipitated that change. I could not imagine the old Yve being deliberately unkind. And what did Louise Alexander mean—*not without cause?* I was still pondering the strange conversation when I entered my bedroom.

A few minutes later, the two servants joined me in the large, warm bedroom. I had seen them serving at breakfast but I had not yet met them personally. Clementine Carpenter was a plump, fresh-faced Londoner, recently indentured to the Madisons, and Abigail MacTavish was a Scotswoman with a somewhat dour expression that concealed a warm heart. Her head was a mass of beautifully coiffed red hair. She promptly informed me that she could dress the most recalcitrant hair in most beautiful fashions, her eyes fastened on my unshorn tresses with undisguised pleasure. She also told me proudly that she had been with the Madisons for fifteen years, and received excellent pay for her services.

Though they did not remark on it, I knew they were both scandalized by the poverty of my wardrobe. I saw them exchange glances as they brushed and shook out the two modest dresses and hung them in the great empty armoire at the end of the room. They spoke to me with sympathy of my loss and remarked on how beautiful Yve had been. It seemed to me that they were careful in their praise of her beauty, as if that were all they dared remark upon.

Clementine, plucking forth undergarments that I had delicately embroidered from the portmanteau, cried, "Ah, ye make 'em like your sister did, madame. So dainty and lovely!"

"You mean my sister, in all this luxury, made her own undergarments?"

"Aye, she said as how the American seamstresses did work too coarse to her taste," replied Clementine, placing the embroidered silk things in a long drawer of a tall mahogany chest. "She had on a nightdress she made herself on the very night she died."

"Did she have a doctor—a nurse to care for her during her illness?" I asked abruptly.

"The master'd sent for them from Richmond. They got here after Mistress Yve died. But her illness was such a short one, ye know." Clementine glanced uneasily at Abigail, whose lips had thinned.

Abigail said firmly, "They had old Mincy Delafield to tend her. She's better than any doctor. She delivered Mistress Yve of young Andy."

"I heard nothing about this—Mincy." I was still smarting under Louise Alexander's remark that Yve had been unkind. "I was told only that Yve was desperately ill of lung congestion. Tell me about it, Clementine."

The maid's cheeks pinkened as she pushed the heavy drawer closed on neat, small piles of lingerie. "Ma'am, I—'twould be more properlike if ye were told by Mistress Madison."

"Mistress Madison is dead," I responded. "You tell me."

"She means the old Mistress, madame," Abigail interceded for the flustered Clementine.

"I was told that my sister had the finest nurse that could be found to care for her."

"She did, madame, but it was too late," Abigail spoke with finality. "Mincy Delafield is a braw doctor and nurse and nigh onto a witch with her miraculous ways."

I asked quietly, "Which of you found my sister dead?"

Clementine made a strangled sound. "Madame, the master was with her when she died—he and Mincy. I—none of us *found* her after she died."

I said slowly, "Did she *say* nothing to any of you after she grew ill?"

"Oh, yes'm," Clementine said artlessly, relieved that the conversation had taken a turn in which she felt able to answer freely. Abigail's reproachful glance was ignored. "She just had a bad cold to start with and was not too sick the first two days. But it grew worser in the night. She must've been out of her head then, fer when I took breakfast to her the next mornin', she was in a pool o' sweat an' I couldn't wake 'er. I closed the window an' covered her up again an' run to Mr. Andrew's room to tell him."

"She was unconscious?" I asked incredulously.

Abigail broke in. "She had a ragin' fever, madame. The cold had gone into her lungs."

"But Clementine said she was in a pool of sweat. I've never heard of sweat with a fever. You sweat only when the fever is broken. And the window was open on her, you say?"

Abigail said angrily, "Tina, you've upset Madame Sevier with yer idle tongue. Mistress Madison would be furious with ye!" Clementine's eyes widened with fear, but Abigail turned to me soothingly. "Madame, 'tis like that young Mistress Yve opened that window to cool off when her fever first come up an' then it broke afterwards. 'Tis what Mincy says. If ye talk to the master, I'm sure he'll tell ye all about it."

I looked at the two disturbed servants. They were observing me with a touch of wariness. I sighed wearily. "You are probably quite right, Abigail. I loved my sister dearly. Like most bereaved people, I suppose I want someone to blame for the brutality of fate."

"Aye." Abigail nodded wisely. "I felt the same when me mother and father passed on. Y'know, madame, ye're a fair and bonnie lassie." Tidying my brush and comb and jars of cosmetics, she added, " 'Tis pretties than yer sister, ye are."

"Thank you, but I can't believe that. Yve was beautiful."

"Aye, that she was, but ye've a warmth about ye, me dear, that lights ye like a candle in a dark room," Abigail replied, taking the empty portmanteau and putting it on a high shelf in the armoire. She turned to leave.

"Come along, Tina. Madame Sevier, please forgive Tina. She's not been here but three months—Tina, ye shouldn't be sniffin' madame's bottle o'scent!"

"Ah, but 'tis lovely, Abby. Madame, do let Abby smell?"

I laughed at the childlike delight on the maid's young face. "Of course. It's *parfum.* I bought it before I left Marseilles." With a piece of the gold my *kind* and *generous* sister had sent me, I thought fiercely.

Abigail put her sharp nose to the stopper and rolled her eyes upward, her fiery pompadour bobbing. " 'Tis sweeter'n Mistress Madison's sweet Williams in the summertime," she said. "Come now, Tina. We must help Beady with supper. An' 'tis likely madame will want to rest. I know that long sea voyage, and well do I remember me seasickness." The two made me a brief curtsey and went out, closing the door behind them.

When they had gone, I sat down on the brocaded couch before the comfortable blaze in the fireplace and reflected on my curious anger at learning a few of the intimate circumstances of Yve's death. Except for the black silk band worn by Andrew Madison on his sleeve, there seemed to be no mourning in this house. I had the feeling that life was proceeding just as it had before death had struck down my sister. I knew mourning would not bring Yve back to me, but it did seem that respect demanded further recognition of her passing.

Yet I was at a loss to know just what it was I expected of these people. They had spoken of Yve's beauty, they had voiced grief and offered me a certain consolation; but had there been a lack of real love in their voices? After Louise Alexander's implied indictment, I suspected them all of not really mourning. But surely it could not be *relief* that restrained their sympathy!

No, I was forced to recognize that no amount of mourning would be enough for me, and with that knowledge, an inner anguish eased somewhat. There were the children to think of, all playing together now in the big, bright nursery on the third floor of the east wing. They were full of life, unaware of the inevitability and the sorrow that was death. It was best for all of us that there be no going about clad in black, with subdued voices and drooping spirits. I felt that Yve would not have wanted that for her little son, Andy.

The two days before the new year of 1803 went by swiftly. I was constantly astonished by the metamorphosis of my child. Mélisse was entranced by her older cousins and they by her. Even the mature and somewhat hostile Amanda was warm and loving toward Mélisse. As for Mélisse herself, after just two days in their company she had become a bubbly, joyous little girl, full of ready laughter at the boys. Surprisingly, she was highly voluble—half in English and half in French when excited. Her use of two languages caused the other children to view her with respect as well as genuine affection. In fact, the whole household fell in love with her. All the maidservants, the cook, the sad-faced Henry Pepper, and even the reserved Louise, showed warm affection for my child.

In those first days, I made the acquaintance of all those in the household. The downstairs maid, Bibsey Turner, who with Louise took care of the first floor, was newly indentured for four years, having come from London on the same ship with Clementine. She was a pug-nosed, pert little creature with short black hair and blacker eyes, and she made no bones about the fact that she had come to the New World with the intention of serving her term of indenture and catching an American husband.

Louise Alexander impressed me more than the others, despite her comment about my sister—or perhaps even because of it. I sensed a biting honesty in her. She had been serving the Madisons for twenty-seven years, and she went about her duties with all the aplomb of the lady of the house. She was a touch intimidating, I thought, and better educated than the other servants. I sensed but was at a loss to understand the strange, restrained animosity between her and Cornelia Madison.

On my second day, I was introduced to a thin, spectacled young man with scant brown hair and a large Adam's apple. He was courteous and friendly, was Seton Cambridge, and had the air of one always extremely busy. Each Sunday, he preached a sermon in the Cloudmont church, as well as handling his duties as tutor and teacher for the whole plantation. His classes for the slaves were one more evidence of the Madison men's well-known intention to educate the slaves who had come with Laura's inheritance, teach them a trade, and free them. In the interim, they worked Madison fields and handled Madison stock, as did the Madison tenant farmers.

In the two days preceding New Year's Eve, I did not leave the house, but in the talk that swirled about me, I learned something of the operation of a large tobacco and cotton plantation. I saw little of Andrew and George, for despite Andrew's recent loss and the holiday season, he and George were immersed in riding their acres, conferring with the overseer, the servants, and farmers, and working long hours in the large plantation office at the end of the west wing, where all the papers and accounts were kept.

I felt myself sliding into the ebb and flow of life on this vast tidewater estate. The custom of the New Year's Eve Open House for all their friends and neighbors would not bend to mourning, and I watched the plans and preparations for the event go forward.

On the morning of the eve of the new year, as breakfast was finished, Laura suggested that she, Mary, and I go horseback riding along the James River.

"It's turned into such a beautiful day—it's a little warmer, too." Laura gestured out the window at the brilliant sky and sunlight. "Besides, everybody here will be getting ready for the guests tonight. We'll only be in the way."

"You two go," Mary said. "Mother will need my help here, Laura."

Laura's laugh held a touch of malice. "You don't fool

me, Mary. You don't like to drape all those skirts over a saddle and bump along in the cold wind."

"True, I don't care for it too much," Mary replied, with an edge to her voice. "But I did promise to help Louise supervise the decorations in the great hall and drawing room."

Laura made an impudent face. "Lilibel was brought up on a large estate in France, so I'll wager she loves to ride. Wouldn't you like to go with me, Lilibel?"

"Indeed I would," was the ready reply. I longed to get out of the house for a time. "But I have no riding habit."

"You're too small for any of mine or Mary's," she said, eyeing me judiciously. Then with inspiration, "There are all of Yve's. I'm sure she'd want you to have them—and her other beautiful clothes, as well. Were you two not of a size?"

"We always used to be," I said, my throat tightening. All Yve's beautiful clothes. It would break my heart to wear them. Yve would not have liked sharing them, either; but that was certainly no reflection on her. It had simply been her nature.

"Then it's settled. Come, I'll take you to Yve's room and you may make your choice." Laura seemed as authoritative in her bright, airy way as Cornelia and Mary. I wondered uneasily if there were not more than occasional clashes between the strong-willed women who inhabited Cloudmont.

I followed Laura up a long stairway lined with oil portraits and down the hall, decorated with occasional pedestals bearing marble busts and interspersed with vases of holly, pyracantha, and pine. There were still more portraits hung between the doors leading to rooms, and I knew I must be looking at several generations of Madisons. I stood a moment before the open door to Yve's room. I had seen it fleetingly when Cornelia showed me the house, but now I looked at it with sharp clarity. As in the room I had occupied the last three nights, blue dominated the decor, the brilliant blue of Yve de Belvoir Madison's eyes. The room was on the south side of the house, looking out on the terraced lawns that ran to the James River. It was spotlessly clean and smelled faintly of lavender, evoking a vivid memory of my bright, beautiful, and animated sister.

Laura led me to the broad, mirrored doors of an enormous fruitwood armoire and flung them wide. "There," she said, gesturing to the racks of clothing. Opening several drawers in a tall chest, she added, "Take your pick. I'm sure Yve would rejoice to think her sister was receiving them instead of the servants—or charity." There was an amused skepticism in her words. And it irritated me, but I thought of Yve's fierce possessiveness and knew that it had no doubt been a source of some trouble.

"The dressing room is beyond Andrew's," Laura continued, pointing, "and his room opens into it. Meet you in a trice, my dear, after I change."

When Laura had carelessly closed the door to the room, I stood in sudden silence, rooted to the spot before the open armoire. *Andrew's room.* He and Yve had not shared a bedroom. Cornelia had not made that plain when she took me over the house.

I wheeled around, looking at the smooth bed, pristine under a blue taffeta spread. My sister had died there, the cold winter wind blowing on her in a pool of sweat. Yve had always been susceptible to colds. Yet there was something in me that raged silently against such a slight illness causing her death.

I fumbled through the clothing in the armoire and pulled forth a blue velvet riding habit—it must have been a favorite, for it showed hard wear.

Uneasily I began to don my sister's riding habit.

CHAPTER 4

Laura looked me over as we met in the bedroom door. "Hmmm. That blue velvet was Yve's favorite riding habit. You just might give Andrew a bit of a jolt were he to see you in it." She sounded as if she might enjoy that, and I was struck anew by the feeling that there was a deep, unbridgeable hostility between Andrew and his brother's beautiful widow.

"I thought of that," I said quietly, adjusting the blue hat on my dark hair and following Laura down the stairs, "and that may well be why I should not avail myself of my sister's wardrobe."

Laura shrugged. "I'm sure it won't matter if you borrow this once." Her dimple showed in a sudden smile. "Come, we'll go out through the pantry and kitchen to the stables. 'Tis nearer."

The kitchen, enormous and warm, was the scene of fragrant activities in preparation for the night's festivities. Louise Alexander, Abigail, and Clementine were trimming pie crusts, stirring mincement, and peeling crisp apples. Bibsey Turner was mixing a batter on one of three long tables situated conveniently about the room. Samantha Beady, the cook, was a fleshy woman, and her round face was now pink from tending the great brick and iron ovens built into the walls of the kitchen. In the vast open fireplace a fire was smoldering under several pots, and a great haunch of beef roasted on a spit before the flames. The mouthwatering aromas of fruits and meats hung in the warm, spiced air as Mrs. Beady glanced up to see the two of us enter.

"Lor' luv me, mistress, but ye do look almost the spit o' yer sister in them clothes o' hers." The protuberant blue eyes crinkled at the corners in a quick smile. "An' terrible pretty, I might add."

"Thank you, Mrs. Beady. It's been so long since I've been on a horse." Seven long months since that wild ride to Marseilles, I recalled with a shudder. Brushing the dreadful memory aside, I returned her smile.

I drew the cold, fresh air deep into my lungs as we stepped outside. The sun was bright and warm despite a touch of ice in the air, and I looked at the winter-bare rose and camellia gardens and brown, empty flowerbeds with an appreciative eye, knowing that spring would bring acres of beauty to life. The dark green English boxwood emanated its strangely pungent fragrance as we made our way past the gardens to the stable.

Along either side of the bowling green stood the brick buildings that I had glimpsed from my window the first morning. Laura pointed absently. "That big one with all the tall windows is the orangerie, where Andrew keeps all sorts of citrus trees in great pots, as well as tropical plants of great beauty, which are set out in the gardens during the summer. We have oranges, lemons, and limes as a treat occasionally, though not many of them."

She pointed to a tall brick building farther down the wide graveled walk. "That's the smokehouse. We have our meats, hams, beef quarters, bacon, turkeys, and game birds in there. There's a constant smoky fire kept going in the center and the meat hangs from the beams. The smoking preserves it indefinitely, and it is delicious. Over yonder is the storehouse, where all the tools and implements are kept for distribution to the servants and gardeners. And beyond that is the overseer's quarters—Jacob Worth's—it's that nice-looking brick with white trim. Yonder are the gardeners' quarters and the icehouse." She looked at me and laughed suddenly. "Did you know we have ice for our tea and our drinks all summer? In another month, the servants will go down to the James River during a hard freeze and cut out great blocks of ice to be stored in the icehouse for next summer. Down there is the wash house and laundry yard. And way on down there the slave quarters. Tom had them built especially when I came to him as a bride from Landon House with my people."

I was hard put to take it all in, so vast and complex an establishment was Cloudmont. I murmured, "Belvoir Château was not nearly so large. I do not see how Andrew manages all this himself."

"He doesn't do it by himself," Laura said shortly. "He has plenty of help, as you will see in time."

We drew up before the great carriage house next to the stable and Laura called, "Noah! Where are you?"

I looked into two open doors of a fine black carriage as Laura called again and a grinning black face appeared from around the vehicle. The boy held a soft polishing cloth in one hand and a long-handled brush in the other. There were other doors that were closed and I assumed more carriages were inside, as well as space for visitors' vehicles.

"Yes'm, Miss Laura." Noah was very young and there was mischief in the grin. Behind him I could discern a towering figure, a giant black man.

Laura said quickly, "What are you up to—and who is that with you?"

"I'm just gettin' the last of the mud off Master Andrew's carriage, ma'am—an' it's only Railo with me."

"Railo—" Laura's lilting tones changed to exasperation. "I suppose you're here to see Judith again. Does Mr. Livingston know?"

The black stepped out, his powerful shoulders bulging against a linsey shirt, great thighs pushing against the coarse homespun breeches. "Yes, Mistress Laura. He knows I'm away to see Judith. I been tryin' to get this worthless Noah to run see can she come out." There was great dignity about him, an air of competence that stirred respect.

"Railo, it would be far better for you to forget Judith. You know Mr. Livingston will not sell you—and I just can't let Judith go!" Then in a softer voice, "Noah can go get her as soon as he saddles up for Madame Sevier and me."

"You ladies goin' ridin'?" Noah's grin broadened.

"Saddle up Missy for me and—" she paused, eyeing me appraisingly. "How good a rider are you, Lilibel?"

I smiled. "I can stay on." There was no need to tell Laura Madison that I had grown up with a horse under me.

"Then saddle up Dandylion for Madame Sevier, Noah. Madame is Mistress Yve's sister."

"Yes'm. I figgered that when I seen her," he said, sobering. "Powerful sorry fer your loss, ma'am."

"Thank you, Noah." I was not sure if my eyes stung from the cold air or from the sympathy in the boy's young, compassionate face as he turned and walked to the stables.

"Railo," Laura began, when Noah had disappeared, "I do wish you wouldn't worry Judith—especially when you know nothing can come of your relationship."

"I love Judith, ma'am." The ebony face was set and there was no humor in the glittering black eyes as they rested on Laura's fair face.

"Does she love you?"

"She ain't said yet, ma'am. But my heart tells me she do."

"I declare, I don't know what I'll do if she sets her mind to marry off Cloudmont."

"I ain't askin' her to come to Livingston's, ma'am." His voice was like flint.

"Well, it's too far for you to commute every night," she retorted.

"Every night, yes'm—but once in a while, ma'am?"

"We'll see," Laura's face had softened despite her annoyance. "Go on up to the house, Railo, and tell Mrs. Beady I said to send for Judith. I'll wager Mr. Livingston hasn't given you too much time for courting."

A faint smile flickered on the black face. "No'm, he sure ain't." He turned his broad back and trotted up the graveled path to the big house.

Laura, observing him, said thoughtfully, "I'm not sure Jabez Livingston *has* given him time off for courting Judith. Railo is the most intelligent black at Livingston's plantation and he's been his foreman for four years—but he's a bit too smart and independent for his own good."

"For Livingston's good, you mean, *n'est ce pas?*" I asked dryly.

She gave me a sharp glance. "I meant for Railo's good. Jabez Livingston is a hard man. Ah, Noah, here you are."

The slender black boy came out of the stables leading two beautiful mares, their breaths cloudy in the crisp morning air. "I don't know whatever I shall do without you, Noah, when the Madisons let all my people go," Laura said mournfully, as he held her foot while she mounted.

"Reckon I might stay, Miss Laura, did you pay me good wages like ol' Mister Pepper gets," Noah replied with another grin as he helped me mount.

"You little opportunist," Laura laughed, touching the mare with her heels. "I just might do that."

As we started off, I said, "You didn't tell me what those little whitewashed buildings are down there—"

"Yes, I did—those are the slave quarters. Each one has its own garden at the rear." As we passed, several black women and some small children in the little yards looked up and waved to us.

"Tom had no qualms about owning slaves, like his brothers have. See that"—Laura pointed to a much larger brick building with a spire far beyond the white-washed wooden cabins that housed the slaves—"That's the church where Seton Cambridge preaches on Sundays and holds classes for the slaves and the tenant's children. The family cemetery is next to it."

"I suppose Yve is buried there," I said thoughtfully.

"Yes. Would you like to see it? Andrew's ordered the stone from Richmond. Her grave is still unmarked."

"I'll wait until the stone arrives," I said, thinking, *she isn't there. Only the shell that housed her spirit lies beneath the dark soil of Virginia.*

Laura took a circling path south toward the river as we angled toward the front and away from Cloudmont, the gravel giving way suddenly to the leaf-covered floor of the forest.

Laura spoke with sudden heat. "I hope you don't think—— Well, in spite of what you may think of me, I would gladly pay Noah. He's marvelous with the horses and he is equally good as a house servant, helping out when we entertain. And I *have* approached that tight-fisted, hateful Jabez Livingston about selling Railo to me—all because I've seen that *look* in Judith's eyes when we speak of him. But Jabez wouldn't sell him for a million sterling. I'm not an oppressive slave beater, you know."

I looked at her in surprise. "I don't sit in judgment on you, Laura. We have something in France much crueler than slavery."

"You mean Napoleon?"

"Napoleon and Madame Guillotine, who murders the innocent along with the guilty."

"Ah, I forgot your parents for a moment, Lilibel."

"I can never forget."

Laura was silent for a moment, then quietly, "But we shall make it so pleasant here for you that your sad memories will ease. Come. Can you gallop? We are nearing the James."

I nodded and the two horses broke into a swift, hard gallop through the bare maples and lindens along the worn, sloping path. In a few moments, we broke into an open stretch, and before us spread the shimmering water of the broad James River. I caught my breath with pleasure. It was beautiful, sparkling as the sunlight twinkled on its smooth, gentle flow toward the distant sea. Laura slowed her horse and the two of us walked our mounts along the bank, looking at the shining water in silent delight.

"This is tidewater country, Lilibel. Up above the fall line begins the piedmont."

"The foot of the mountains?"

"Yes, piedmont—the word is French, isn't it? It's the high country, where the tides no longer affect the flow of the rivers." We sat silently admiring the river for a moment, then Laura said, "You know, when the first Thomas Madison settled here in 1700, he was given a grant of a hundred thousand acres by George the First. He had all his help imported—the best Newgate prison had to offer, George says—as indentured servants. But after they served their term of indenture, he leased them each twenty acres of land for life. Of course they had to give him ten percent of their crops, and help him with his harvesting and planting. But it still works that way, and that's why there are no slaves at Cloud——" She broke off as a furious pounding of hooves came to our ears. We exchanged startled glances.

Suddenly a man on horseback burst from the woods. When he saw us, he pulled back on his horse so savagely that the animal rose upright and pawed the air. This did not dislodge the rider, who remained in the saddle with muscular grace. Our two mares moved nervously, disturbed by the precipitate appearance of the gray stallion and its rider. I had a flashing first impression of a classically handsome face, marred only by drawn black brows and a look of anger.

As the horse settled down and I could observe its rider more closely, I saw that his tumbling black hair was in disarray, his jaw was strong to the point of obstinacy, and he wore with arrogance a look of good blood. There was a leashed violence in his movements, as if he bore a volatile spirit and vitality too great to restrain.

"Charles Alexander!" Laura exploded. "You've scared Missy and Dandylion near to bolting!"

A sudden warm laugh broke from him. "Then I should have had the pleasure of rescuing two beautiful ladies—and receiving the gratitude of at least one." His black eyes went over me like lightning. "You must be the sister we've been looking to arrive."

"Yes, I am Yve's sister," I replied. There was a recklessness in Charles Alexander that reminded me faintly of Jacques.

"When did you return from Norfolk?" Laura asked sullenly. "I thought you were going to stay a week at least."

"And miss the Open House? No indeed! I arrived about half an hour ago. I finished the business George sent me on much sooner than we thought. I've been remembering all those remarks you made about my low birth and background when I proposed marriage to you, and I've had time to become fairly angry. So, I came to talk to you, Noah told me where to find you."

"Noah should have minded his tongue!"

Charles Alexander turned from her suddenly and bowed to me, saying compassionately, "Your sister was a fine lady. Her loss is a great one." He looked into my eyes soberly and I felt my heart warming toward this handsome, imperious young man.

Laura said coldly, "Lilibel, Charles is the son of Louise Alexander, our chief housekeeper." She urged her horse forward. She had spoken her dismissal of the man.

I was astonished, for there was an authority about him that belied his humble birth. I did not let my horse follow Laura's. I stayed to say, "I'm very pleased to know you, Mr. Alexander."

"Call me Charles, madame. Everyone does." He spoke as if he had been well educated and my puzzlement grew.

"Come along, Lilibel," Laura called impatiently. "We must return in time for lunch, despite all the hubbub that's going on today."

I loosed my horse and Charles eased alongside of me, saying, "Mistress Laura is an impatient lady—as you will come to know. Albeit a charming one, when she chooses."

Laura gave him a disdainful look over her shoulder and stepped up the gait of her horse. "Do you mean to ride with us?" Her rudeness was unmistakable.

"Indeed I do. Even without a courteous invitation." He let Laura go on ahead and fell in beside me once more. "Madame Sevier, I am the jack of all trades at Cloudmont, doing what Andrew and George request. Sometimes I keep books at the warehouse in Norfolk—that's where I've been this week. Sometimes I help oversee our harvests, and I have made several voyages on the *Tern*. Indeed, George and Andrew think now that I would be a good captain to transport their cotton and tobacco and wheat, this year. But I hate to be away from Cloudmont so long. You see, I love the plantation life."

"You must be a brilliant man to be accomplished in all those things," I said admiringly. Laura's back was ramrod straight before us.

"Oh, I am, to be sure," he replied in mocking tones. "I graduated from William and Mary University, as did Thomas, Andrew, and George. My *humble birth* notwithstanding. Thomas Madison senior thought I had promise." A rollicking laugh broke from him, making his handsome face even more winning. "Laura doesn't think so, however."

Laura turned. "I think you're horribly cocky and conceited, Charles. You know well enough how I feel about you."

"I know how you *felt* about me—until you suddenly changed."

Tension between the two drew out. I was uncomfortably aware of the emotions swirling between them and of the strong attraction. I knew that in the caste system that existed in every country, Charles, as the son of a common domestic servant, could scarcely hope to wed a planter's daughter—nay, a planter's wealthy widow.

Charles turned his smile on me. "I came out here to have words with Laura, before I even reported in to George on my trip. But finding she has so charming a companion seems to have dissipated all my anger."

"You were angry with her?" I glanced again at that straight, uncompromising back ahead of us.

"I was. I am. Laura has led me on and now she vows she cares nothing for me."

"A simple little flirtation," Laura flared, half turning to look back. "That was all it ever was, Charles, and you know it. Now you're being a dreadful bore. I really don't want to see you again."

He shrugged eloquently. "That will be hard to do—since my duties and the family welcome bring me often to the big house and always around the estate."

"I wish you'd go off on the *Tern* again," she said angrily. "Andrew and George need a new captain for her. You should be mindful of how good they are to you and——"

"I have been offered that position, but I prefer to stay and help manage Cloudmont."

"You would," Laura said, under her breath. Then loudly, "I do wish you would leave Liliane and me to finish our ride in peace."

His face darkened before he smiled again at me. "I've received my *congé*, madame. I shall leave you two to your ride. Good day to you." He wheeled the big stallion and was gone in an instant.

Laura dropped back beside me. "Don't be taken in by him, Lilibel," she said exasperatedly. "He's a handsome devil and takes shameless advantage of it. He's left a string of broken hearts in Richmond."

"I can believe it. He has great charm."

"The Madison charm," Laura replied derisively.

"But—I thought you said he was Louise Alexander's son?"

"So he is—but his father was the senior Thomas Madison. He's a woods colt, born on the wrong side of the blanket. 'Tis common knowledge."

I was taken aback by the casual delivery of this fact. "Then he is half brother to Andrew and George—and Mary."

"And my husband Tom, who had little use for him. The old gentleman provided well for Charles. Sent him to the university, saw to it that Louise had a permanent position in the house, and that Charles will always have a place at Cloudmont. He lives in very handsome quarters above the carriage house—a place of his own choosing, I might add."

"This must be very hard on Cornelia," I murmured.

"On the contrary, she is very fond of Charles. It's his mother she can't accept. But she endures her, and with grace, I think."

I began, "Charles seems such an intelligent and ambitious man. Surely his good qualities make up for——"

"Being a bastard? I think not. He's very adroit, but he carries a chip on his shoulder and I'm sure in his heart he resents the fact that none of Cloudmont can ever be his, nor the Madison name. He's very handsome," she added pensively, "and being a widow can be very—lonely."

I gave her a searching look. "You are so beautiful, Laura, I should think you would have been remarried long ago."

Oddly, she flushed, and there was a touch of guiltiness in her voice as she said, "It's true I've had opportunities, Lilibel. But, as Cornelia says of Mary, I'm picky, too. I'll not marry a paunchy old planter with a dozen half-grown children. Nor a wild young buck who will give me trouble." Her voice hardened. "And certainly not a man who cannot claim his own father, nor an inheritance."

We rode on in silence, while I drank in the sweet, clean air and reveled in the sunlight. I digested what I had learned of my new home and the people who inhabited it, and felt my own sorrows dim under their impact. The river beside us made a hushed, soothing sound and I felt my spirit, so torn by Yve's unexpected death, take a first tentative step toward healing.

"Did you see Yve before she died?" I asked quietly.

"Yes. I helped Cornelia nurse her, at first. Yve was a very nervous person. Did you know that, Lilibel?"

"No. She was as gay and normal as any eighteen-year-old the last time I saw her. Tell me about the last day," I said, keeping my voice casual, "or before that, Laura."

"Well—I remember she was happy enough as a young bride. I was not that involved with family matters until Tom died. At one point, I moved back to Landon House and tried to live alone with only the servants about. In fact, I was practically a hermit for several months. I had the fool idea that I should be independent, run the plantation myself. What an idiot I was!" Her voice was bitter, and I felt these words were dredged up from some still deep and hurtful place within her. "An idiot in so many ways. I stood it almost a year when finally, at Cornelia's insistence, I came back to Cloudmont—that was shortly after little Andy was born. It was an especially hard time for Yve." She spoke haltingly, her voice troubled and her eyes on me were beseeching. "Your sister was a —a difficult little person. She was very unwilling to share——"

"You mean she was possessive," I cut in shortly. "I know that. But it has its good points—she made you feel so beloved, when she cared."

"Well," Laura said uneasily, "that may be true, but frankly, Lilibel, she did not seem to care for any of us but Andrew. And she was a very tense person."

"In what way, Laura?"

"She had difficulty sleeping. She used to complain about it. And she was restless, too, wandering about the house and gardens at all hours. Finally a doctor from Richmond prescribed laudanum, which seemed to help some. But she seemed peculiarly susceptible to colds."

"I know. As a child she suffered greatly in the winters at the château. Who is Mincy Delafield, Laura?"

The blue eyes flew to me. "Where did you hear of Aunt Mincy?" she asked in surprise.

"Clementine and Abigail told me she attended Yve at the birth of Andy—and she was with her when she died. Who is she?"

"She's a midwife, and a magician with medicines as well. She's delivered over a thousand babies, black and white, including most of us at Cloudmont, and she's a better physician than any of those butchers in Richmond. She loves the children, and 'tis a rare treat for them when they are allowed to spend a night with her in her cozy cabin."

"Could I meet her? Where does she live?"

"She lives in her own little cabin on a bit of land my grandfather bought for her when he freed her. 'Tis between Landon plantation and Livingston's."

"She's—she was a slave?"

"Yes. She came from South Africa on a slaver in 1750. I don't think even she knows how old she is. She's very kind and gentle and she saved my mother's life when she was a baby and had whooping cough. That's why my grandfather freed her and gave her a cabin and land of her own."

"Will you take me to see her, Laura?"

"Now?"

"No—I know we must return in time for lunch. But perhaps one day after the new year."

"Why?" Laura asked bluntly.

"I wish to ask her about my sister's final moments," I replied sadly.

Laura's glance at me was sympathetic. " 'Tis a great pity you had to lose her."

"Yve was charming," I said painfully. "She was always the first of us to make friends with strangers." The odd tightness in my breast that I had known when I first set foot in Cloudmont was upon me. I could not argue with the powerful intuition that there was something hidden from me about Yve's death.

"You sit a horse beautifully, Lilibel," Laura said with determined cheerfulness.

"Thank you," I replied absently. "Yve and I were taught to ride by the time we could walk."

"What was it like—being the daughters of nobility and living on a beautiful estate in France?" Laura was trying to divert me, and I permitted it.

"Not so very different from life here at Cloudmont—which surprises me. I had thought life over here would be much rougher."

"It has its dangers. In August, two and a half years ago, an insurrection of slaves broke out near Richmond and they marched on the town. A thousand of them organized the rebellion under the command of two strong, intelligent leaders. They perfected their plans in secrecy. They were to attack the city by night, kill all who resisted, divide the women and the spoils, seize all arms and munitions of war, and free all the blacks throughout the state."

"*Mon Dieu!* What happened?"

"But for Providence, it would have succeeded. They assembled six miles above the city, armed with axes and scythe blades, and the massacre and burning of Richmond was planned. The police were feeble in Richmond, the town small and scattered, the militia and citizens totally unprepared, and the attack would have been disastrous. But a violent storm came on, with heavy rains that swelled the streams and impeded their progress. And thank God, a young slave attached to his master swam the river and gave warning. The storm slowed the insurrectionists, giving the militia and the countryside time to gather. The slaves, finding their purpose discovered and resistance massed against them, scattered and fled. Most of them got quite away, but they caught a couple of the ringleaders and hanged them."

I shuddered. "How can you be so calm, Laura? I should think all of you would be terrified all the time. You know they must *hate* being owned."

She shrugged. "They make the finest servants, and some of them are quite loyal. All of *my* people are, and that's why I hate for the Madisons to free them." She added, "When you've lived with the system, as we do all the time, you will grow more calm about it. The blacks are very primitive—one more reason for keeping them."

I did not reply, for I felt that Laura was wrong. At my silence, she said defensively, "I know you probably disapprove. God knows, there are enough Virginians who do, too. For many years now in every one of our governing bodies, there's been some fool legislator trying to put an end to the 'evil practice,' and I quote. In 1778, Thomas Jefferson finally got a bill passed outlawing the importation of slaves to Virginia. But it's meant nothing. Smugglers still do a brisk business and the slaves already here have children, so it's still very much a going business in Virginia. After all, the big plantations all depend on slave labor, and they support our country. We can't all be as liberal and selective as Andrew and George Madison." She cocked her head to one side and asked, "Who served you on that great château in France?"

"We had a great many servants, French, like ourselves, but woefully ignorant. Some of them betrayed us to the revolutionaries, but Tante Genèvre, Maman's personal maid, fled with Yve and me to Paris and hid us before they took my mother and father before the Commune. *Les citoyens!*" I spat suddenly, for the words tasted sour in my mouth.

"Where did she hide you in Paris?"

"Did Yve never tell you? Tante set up a milliner's shop with the money my father gave her and passed us off as her orphaned nieces. 'Twas when Yve was delivering a hat to the home of Citizenness Valois she met Andrew Madison. He had come to Paris to buy silks and chinaware. Yve was running down the hall with her hatbox and bumped into him as she rounded a corner. It was very romantic."

"I can imagine," Laura said dryly.

"I understand that in America there were many who identified with the lowly French peasantry who threw off the shackles of their king."

"Yes," Laura said. "At first. But I also remember the outrage that followed when we in America learned of the wholesale killings."

I sighed. "It all seems very long ago."

"That is well," Laura said kindly. "Time is an unguent to such wounds." Then putting her heels to her mare, she added, "We must hurry now. Beady will be serving the noon meal soon."

I trotted beside her and spoke with sudden stiffness.

"This evening will seem strange to me. In France, after a death in the family, there are no celebrations."

"My dear," Laura said gently, slowing her pace, "we all mourn Yve, but they have been sharing a welcome to the New Year at Cloudmont with their neighbors for many long years. Yve would be the first to say the tradition should not be broken. There will be no dancing this year, though—and as you know, we are not attending any of the other open houses out of respect to your Yve."

When I made no response, Laura edged her mare near, put her hand on my shoulder and looked into my tear-filled eyes. I blinked rapidly and Laura moved away, but the two of us rode back to the big house in companionable silence.

The noon meal brought a contretemps of its own that added another facet to Thomas Madison's illegitimate son, Charles. His relationship with Laura was intriguing, and over dessert, I learned more about him.

Andrew said casually, "Charles, I want you to be ready to sail with the *Tern* as captain in March. As you know, the last of the tobacco in the warehouse goes to England then."

Charles looked at him squarely. "Not this time, Andrew. You know my preference for Cloudmont and its affairs."

Andrew's jaw tightened and he said heavily, "Cloudmont and its affairs are bound up in the *Tern*. You have done well as captain and you are needed in that position."

A white line formed around Charles's well-cut mouth and a little vein in his temple throbbed. "Andrew, Will Morgan is better qualified than I to captain the *Tern*, and you know it. I prefer to see to the crops themselves—the spring planting—the warehousing of those crops."

Andrew's black brows drew together and I sensed a general tightening of nerves about the table. Andrew's voice was harsh. "You will do as I——"

George cut in smoothly. "Since you are bound that one of us shall sail with the *Tern*, Andrew, I will do so if you do not settle on Will Morgan."

Charles's face had paled and Cornelia looked distressed. Even Mary's pouting lips had tightened, but her large dark eyes on Andrew were worshipful. Laura looked studiously at her plate.

Andrew turned on George. "I need you here, and you know it well."

Charles's face set and his voice was flat and cold. "But obviously you do not need me, and I do not fancy the life of a seaman. I shall take the first opportunity to find employment elsewhere."

Louise stood in the pantry doorway, very straight and very still. Laura's great blue eyes blazed with unconcealed fury. I thought, *Andrew is a man who enjoys bending others to his will.* Cornelia had spoken the truth when she told me he was autocratic.

George's easy laugh broke the tension. "Andrew, Charles is one of us. He will do as he chooses. If you cannot feel easy with Will as captain, I shall go myself. I welcome the prospect."

A harassed look crept over Andrew's handsome features. "You know I want you here with me, George, and you gave your word you would try a planter's life for two years."

"Then make your peace with Charles's desire to lead a planter's life, brother." George's twinkling grin took the sting from his words and Andrew's brows smoothed.

Charles, whose reckless smile had returned with George's intervention, said, "I share with you, Andrew, the desire to do what makes me happiest."

"Very well," Andrew replied. "Will Morgan will captain the *Tern* on this voyage at least."

With his lightened tone, there was a general relaxation and the conversation turned to other things, but I had learned that Charles Alexander had a will as inflexible as any of the legitimate Madisons.

Later that day I happened on a second puzzling revelation about these people with whom I had come to live. I had put Mélisse down for a nap, washed and arranged my hair especially for the evening's festivities, and then restlessly sought Cornelia, with a view to making myself useful.

I went directly to the morning room, where Cornelia kept the household accounts and paid the servants their stipend twice a month. I was about to enter when I was halted by the sound of her urgent voice.

"Andrew, you know I do not want the servants in the cellars. Only Henry Pepper *knows*, so you and George and Henry can fetch the wines and liquors for this evening."

"Mother, they would never find the passage. 'Tis sealed over so it looks like part of the wall. They'd be most unlikely to press about, seeking the opening."

"But they might. Servants are very curious—you should know that, my son. They knew more about your relations with Yve than you did yourself, I'll wager." Her voice was tired. "We have been over this before, Andrew."

"I know, Mother. And why you will not allow George and me to remove those——"

"That's enough." There was a shudder in her voice. "We will not discuss it. It shall never be used again. You know how I feel about the whole episode and the terrible circumstance that brought it on so long ago."

Evidently the huge cellars that underlay the main section of Cloudmont were forbidden territory. And they *were* huge. Laura had told me they contained a Madeira and cheese store, a bin cellar, a small beer cellar and strong beer cellar, a cider cellar, and various storage cellars for wine. I had paid scant attention to the dark, narrow door, a sort of indentation near the rear door to the great hall, that led to them. Now my curiosity was stirred, but I cleared my throat and made noises of entry.

The two of them presented closed and contained faces to me as I entered. I said, " 'Tis so cheerful in here with all your pots of growing things, Cornelia. May we not have a little tea together?"

Immediately their faces cleared and she said quite cheerfully, "Of course, my dear Lilibel. I shall ring for Bibsey to bring it at once."

The day's third revelation was the most unsettling. In fact, it came that evening as I was dressing for the New Year's gathering. Mélisse looked at me with troubled cornflower eyes. Sitting in the middle of the great testered bed with the heavy velvet curtains drawn at the corners, she peered round at me and said, "Maman, Andy says that Tante Yve is dead—she was his maman."

Smoothing on the same rose silk dress Aimée Dumaine and I had cut down for me, I went to the bed and stooped to kiss my child. I had refused to wear any of Yve's fine clothes, despite Laura's urging, and Cornelia and Mary seemed relieved. Cornelia had vowed she was going to take all of Yve's clothing into Richmond and give them to the minister's wife there.

Taking Mélisse into my arms, I murmured, "*Chérie*, Maman told you all that—that Tante Yve was very ill and died——"

"*Oui*, but Andy says she hated him."

My fingers tightened on my daughter's arms as I held her away, staring with horrified eyes into the delicate little face.

"And Maman, Andy says he hated her even more than she hated him and he's glad she's gone." Mélisse's round blue eyes looked wondering into my paling face.

"Mélisse, did he say *why?*"

"Only that she did not love him."

"*Bon Dieu!* That is a lie! Someone has poisoned the child against his mother!" I felt panic swarm through me as I sought a reason for the incredible thing Mélisse had told me. "I will talk to his *grandmère*."

"No, no, Maman! You must not! Andy told me it was a secret that he hated her, and no one knows except Amanda. He made me cross my heart and hope to die not to tell."

Suddenly it came to me that it was possible these monstrous lies were a defense against grief for the boy. Grief worked strangely on one. I recalled sharply how I wanted to lash out at everyone, even Yve, when our parents had been guillotined. It was easier to believe it was inverted grief than to suspect these kindly women of poisoning a child against his mother. Yet somehow, the little boy's statements reinforced the nebulous feeling I had that Yve's death contained a mystery.

"You must never tell, Maman," Mélisse said urgently in French. "For then Andy would hate me and I could not bear that."

"*Parlez angalis, ma petite*," I said automatically, tying the ribbons at the throat of Mélisse's nightdress. "I promise to keep his secret. Now you must go to sleep like a good girl."

Mélisse had refused to sleep in the crib after the first night, protesting that she was no longer a baby. But she did not want a room alone on the third floor with the other children. I had ruefully agreed, for the time being, that we sleep together in the broad bed, and Cornelia had stored the crib in the attics.

"*Maman, s'il vous plait*—will you please leave the candle lighted? It is so very dark in here without it."

I looked at the candle, standing tall and straight in the carved crystal chimney, tears of wax graceful along its sides, its brightness a defense against shadows that reared up about the bed.

"Yes, my darling. But you must promise not to touch it when I am gone." I would come back in an hour and extinguish it, when she was safely sleeping.

Mélisse agreed, snuggling down cozily in the covers. I stirred up the fire in the large fireplace, laying another small log upon it before I replaced the screen. Quietly, I left the room, at Mélisse's sleepy request leaving the door ajar.

I paused at the landing. A hum of voices and the music of happy laughter came to my ears from the great hall below and the drawing room. My heart twisted in sudden pain. Yve should be here beside me, laughing like that, merrily introducing me to the strangers now in the house. A few more steps downward, and I could see the crowd of people below, nodding, talking, animated, joyous with the joyful season.

As I stood observing them morosely, a carriage rattled up outside and Henry Pepper, his long countenance set in unaccustomed lines of cheer, went to open the door at the visitors' entrance. Still, I stood in the shadows of the stairs and watched as he ushered in a party of four—two men and two women. They were young, as young as I myself, and handsomely dressed in the latest fashions. The men wore the slim, close-fitting pantaloons introduced in America by my own countrymen and the women had their hair cropped in a profusion of short curls, visible as they took their hooded cloaks from about their heads and handed them to Henry. Their fine silk dresses made mine look quite seedy and out of style, which it was.

I lifted my head high and took the rest of the stairs as the four drifted after Henry Pepper toward the drawing room, through the milling crowd in the great hall below. I stepped down into what seemed an ocean of people, their clothing bright and rich, their faces warm with drink and good spirits.

As Cornelia had promised, there was no dancing, out of deference to the Madison family loss, but gaiety pervaded the room. The guests moved back and forth between the great hall, the drawing room, and the huge dining room, where I knew the buffet covered every available space from sideboard to the table itself. I had seen the savory dishes that graced the board. Indeed, I could not recall even in the happier days at Belvoir anything to equal the lavish spread for the guests at Cloudmont. Along with roast goose, smoked turkey, and glazed hams, there were beautifully browned game birds, dove, quail, and pheasant, with every side dish imaginable and sweetmeats to make one's mouth water.

Cornelia and Andrew spied me standing in the doorway to the drawing room and came forward swiftly. They bore me away between them for a lengthy round of introductions. So many names and faces! I was sure I would never be able to remember them all. Some were from adjoining plantations, but a great number had come by carriage all the way from Richmond and Williamsburg. Cornelia took mischievous delight in pointing out to me with a whisper which of the beautifully dressed women wore wigs.

I made a special note of those introduced as near neighbors and dear friends. Among them were the Clayton Reeds of Tulip Grove plantation. With Clayton and his wife, Grace, was the oldest of their four children, young Clay, a tall, well-built young man with a drowsy, endearing smile and twinkling brown eyes.

Cornelia said lightly, "Clay is unhappy because Mary will not let Amanda come down. She feels that Amanda is still too young for a strictly adult gathering such as this."

"But she is fifteen," I said involuntarily, and was rewarded by a flash of smile from Clay.

"I share your astonishment, Madame Sevier," he said

with a slight bow. "I have thought Amanda quite grown up for two years now."

Andrew said, smiling, "Well, Clay, we all know that you are indeed grown up, since this is your first year in William and Mary."

"And my mother has allowed me to attend functions such as this for two years, sir," Clay said coldly.

Grace, blonde as her husband was dark, and quite regal, said coolly, "That was because I felt you were quite old enough to refrain from remarks such as that."

Young Clay flushed and his father laughed good-naturedly, slapping his back. "Your mother knows how to keep her young ones in line. Now fetch her a glass of punch."

"Yes, sir," replied Clay, and hastened to do as he was bid. Cornelia moved on to another couple, who were much older, nearer Cornelia's age.

"This is Evan Montague and Helen, his wife, Lilibel. They live at Lindens, just down from the Reeds' Tulip Grove."

The Montagues' hair was iron gray, but their faces were curiously unlined and youthful. They told me they had two daughters, both older than I, who had married merchants and lived in Richmond. The daughters had driven to Lindens to spend the holidays with their parents, and they were presented to me; Marie Stafford and Amy Graves with their tall, pleasant husbands, Lamont and Anthony. Both daughters greeted me warmly. Before we could move on, the two older Montagues told us enthusiastically about their four grandchildren, two from each daughter, three boys and a girl.

When at last we were able to detach ourselves, we found the Chenaults, Vance and Sara, waiting to be presented. They had left five small children at their Rosehill, which was the first plantation west of Cloudmont on the road to Richmond. Vance was very tall and thin; his wife, Sara, was short, blonde, and plump. She laughed a great deal. I liked them both, as I had the others I met.

Cornelia and Andrew left me then, to go and greet others coming in, and as I stood chatting with the Chenaults, Mary approached. Her voluptuous body was well defined by an exquisite rose satin dress and her black hair curled about her face in the latest style. Altogether she presented the luscious beauty of a full-blown rose. Still, the gross sensuality of that full, loose mouth, smiling now, stirred the uneasiness I had first felt on meeting her.

She caught my arm. "Come, Lilibel—Vance, Sara, do forgive us, but Mother has sent me to fetch Lilibel. We've not eaten since tea."

As we made our way to the dining salon, Mary asked, "Did Mélisse get to sleep before you had to leave her?" Mary's enveloping family love had taken my daughter into its folds, for which I should be grateful. Yet my feelings about Mary had not coalesced. There was something in the young woman that turned my affection into a strange leaden thing, sluggish and slow to move in her direction.

"Almost," I said briefly. "I must go extinguish the candle I left for her soon."

"Send Clementine," she said briskly. "Everyone eats all evening—right into the new year. Some sit and some stand. We don't try to serve at table, there are so many."

"Indeed there are," I murmured as I accompanied her into the dining salon, where we both filled plates with the tempting foods so plentifully displayed there.

I followed her back into the drawing room and we seated ourselves on a small sofa, balancing plates on our knees, as we conversed about the people attending the party. I had the feeling that Mary had accepted me, mainly because of Mélisse but partly because she found no irritant in me. So far, I had presented to her a façade as bland as a pudding.

All of the maids, including the regal Louise Alexander, wore starched white aprons over neat gray frocks, and went about among the guests with platters of food for individual helpings. Henry Pepper, when not tending the door for new arrivals, supervised Noah who had been recruited for house service on this occasion. Noah was resplendent in a red coat with brass buttons and a pair of tight black breeches. His young face was solemn and concentrated as he went about with a tray of glasses of whiskey for the men and wine for the ladies.

New guests kept arriving and Mary and I ate between conversations and new introductions constantly being made. I stopped trying to keep track of names, merely smiling at everyone who glanced my way. When we had finished eating and Bibsey Turner retrieved our empty plates, Mary urged me to mingle with the guests.

"They are so impressed that we have another member of the French aristocracy in our home. Most of them know of your flight to escape Napoleon's soldiers. You're something of a heroine, Lilibel." And she left me.

I remained on the sofa. I did not feel like a heroine. I felt alien among these ruddy, jovial Americans of British descent. I looked about the sea of bright clothing and brighter faces. Laughter was louder now, unrestrained, and conversation rapid and animated. Life had closed over the place where Yve had been; it was as if my sister had never existed here.

Cornelia brought up a man and woman to meet me, John and Lucy Stuart from Richmond, who were staying a week with the Reeds at Tulip Grove. They were young and spirited.

"These are our dear friends in Richmond," Cornelia said. "We visit often back and forth. John is in the mercantile business. They have three small children they left in Richmond while they came for the last of the holidays with the Reeds."

Lucy was fair and lively and I took an immediate liking to her. Her quiet husband was of medium height and also fair, with dark blond hair.

"Oh, I am so anxious for you to come and spend a week in Richmond!" Laura exclaimed. "I've already asked Laura and she is coming this month. But I would like you all to come!"

I said slowly, "I would like to come, but I am not yet adjusted to my new home, Lucy."

"Oh, I know. Cornelia says it will be a month before you all can come. Still, Laura is such a sunshiny person, I shall be most happy to have her. She and I seem to have so many things in common."

"Lucy loves houseguests," Cornelia put in, smiling. "But the fact is, Lilibel, we own a large town house in Richmond, where we can stay quite comfortably and do, in the spring and sometimes during the worst of the winter."

" 'Tis more fun when you are all at my house. Laura would be quite lonely racketing around in that great house of yours on Broad Street."

"That's true, Lucy—but when we all come to Richmond, we shall stay in the town house, and we shall visit often with you."

Lucy made a little *moue*. "I shall accept that, then, Cornelia. I do so look forward to the days when you ladies come to shop and socialize in Richmond."

We were joined by others then and the conversation veered to other things. Laura was the center of a group of admiring males. The dashing Charles Alexander, apparently accepted by all, was among them, as well as the less attractive but intense teacher-minister, Seton Cambridge. The Reverend Cambridge was flushed with drink and the intoxication of Laura's ready laughter. It was easy to discern that his emotion for her was near worship.

"You're a solemn little owl," said a deep, drawling voice beside me. I looked up into the quizzical black eyes of George Madison. He eased himself down beside me on the couch, adding, "I suppose you feel a touch of strain among so many obviously ungrieving strangers." His tone was light and I could not tell if he really possessed an insight to my emotions, or was merely making conversation.

"Yes," I replied abruptly. "It seems very strange and —irreverent."

He stretched long legs out before him and leaned back against the damask sofa. He shrugged his shoulders. "This is a custom of long standing. Our grandfather died December twenty-eighth in 1780, but the Open House was held as usual." His eyes on me were sharply observant as he added, "I don't think you resemble Yve at all. The others are merely searching for a resemblance when they say you favor her."

"I thought there was a strong family resemblance," I said stiffly.

He shook his black head, a white smile in the suntanned face. "You're much more vulnerable than Yve, and more beautiful. Your sister was a—well, obstinate is the only word for it. A possessive and self-willed woman. It was very hard for her to get along in a house full of equally obstinate women in Cloudmont. Now you are a gentle, compassionate creature, and intelligent. It shows in the set of your mouth, in the expression in those remarkable golden eyes of yours."

My mouth firmed. "Appearances are deceiving. I am not so vulnerable as I may appear, monsieur."

"Do call me George, dear sister." He was laughing.

"I am not your sister. And I think you mistook courage and strength for obstinacy in my sister, George."

He laughed again, easily. "She was not the woman to take kindly to my brother's—peculiarities."

"What are you trying to say?" Anger and suspicion were rising swiftly.

"Only that their marriage was a stormy one. Andrew is a hot-blooded man, or should I say hotheaded? Traits we Madisons can't seem to lose."

"Then you are a hotheaded, hot-blooded man?"

"But too shrewd, madame, to bind myself to a woman who would try to change me." He was laughing outright once more. "Which is why I am a bachelor."

"Are you, in a roundabout way, trying to tell me that my sister's marriage was not a happy one? That Andrew was unfaithful to her?"

"It was probably as happy as such a state can be. It is my considered opinion that marriage is a miserable state—to my mother's great distress."

"With your attitude," I remarked coldly, "remaining single should be very easy. No woman in her right mind would have you."

His laughter this time was hearty. "I wish it were so. The traps set for a single man of means are most delightfully disguised, and it takes a wary gentleman to sidestep them."

"You should have no trouble at all, George. You are a very wary man indeed. But I can assure you that you are safe in my presence. I do not intend to marry again, ever."

His black eyes gleamed. "Never?"

"Never," I replied resolutely.

"Was it such a disagreeable experience then?"

I flushed. "It wasn't disagreeable at all. I was very happy." This was not entirely true, but this tall, lean man had succeeded in pricking me. "And you have added to my doubts regarding my sister's death—which confirms some conclusions of my own." I was aghast at these words that escaped in anger. I had to restrain myself to keep from putting a hand to my wayward lips.

"And they are?" His eyes were alert, yet veiled now.

I swallowed and improvised rapidly. "I thought perhaps my sister might not have fought her ailment, might not have cared to go on living. If what you say of her marriage is true——"

"I don't think that's what you meant at all," he cut in with frightening insight. "I think you meant to imply that my brother aided your sister in her departure from this world to the next."

My heart was pounding, but I managed a Gallic shrug. "If she felt he no longer loved her, so he might. She could have willed herself to die. That was the possibility I had in mind." I was terrified now. If any of those in Cloudmont knew I had any suspicions about Yve's death, might their welcome be suddenly cooler? I gave my adversary an innocent and slightly sad smile. He was studying me and I felt menace in those dark, deceptively twinkling eyes. I made an elaborate sigh. "I am a fool, of course."

"I think not," George drawled, his eyes lazily exploring mine, then dropping to my mouth. "I think you are probably one of the most beautiful and most intelligent women I have ever met." Then, as if divining my fears, "I do not think I shall mention your—ah—misgivings to anyone. It would surely further distress my already grieving brother."

"You are right." I restrained a rush of gratitude. "I am probably far from the truth. My sister was not a girl to give up her life easily. Least of all—how did you put it? For peculiarities in an adored husband." In this, I knew I spoke the truth.

George agreed readily. "Yve was a fighter. But even Aunt Mincy couldn't fight and win against deep pneumonia."

"I'm sure that's true," I agreed, but I was thinking, *especially pneumonia aided by an open window on a winter's night, and a pool of sweat.* I forced a distracting smile and said, "It has come to me that all four of the women in Cloudmont now are widows, with one grieving widower. Do you not think that passing sad, George? How long has it been so?"

He downed the last of his drink and set the glass on a nearby table. "It came about so gradually, I've not thought about it. Our father died twelve years ago and Thomas was killed eight years ago. For a while Laura tried to live at Landon's, but it was too lonely. She returned to us about six years ago. Mary's husband was much older than she—and I don't think she was ever very happy away from Cloudmont. He died of a failure of the heart—— Ah, here come the Livingstons, bent on meeting you, apparently."

I looked up to see bearing down upon us a stout couple in their late thirties. The woman was rather overdressed and wore a fixed smile; her husband was ruddy-faced with a great beak of a nose and thin, cruel lips. He reminded me somehow of Robespierre. I felt a curious revulsion even before they spoke.

The feeling was compounded when Noah, hastening to bring a fresh glass to George, collided with the woman as she stepped into his path. She recoiled as his tray slipped and glasses splintered on the floor. "Careful, you fool!" she lashed out. Then she struck out at George, "George Madison, you and Andrew are idiots about your slaves! A good beating would serve this one right for his clumsiness." Her furious glance seared the astonished Noah.

He said fearfully, "I 'pologize, ma'am. It were an accident."

"Don't give us such a lie, boy," Mr. Livingston said menacingly. "You *meant* to knock Mistress Livingston aside. I know you people, especially ones like you who have been promised freedom."

"Now, Jabez," George drawled, a muscle in his jaw quivering with repressed anger, "Noah's a good man and I can't have you make a simple accident into a crusade. Noah, please serve me another drink when this is cleared away. Now Mistress Anna, come let me introduce our sister-in-law from France."

Noah, his eyes narrow now with anger, bent to the task of putting the bits of shattered crystal on the tray trembling in his hand. He mopped up the liquid, which just missed the Oriental rug, with a heavy napkin, and was swiftly gone. But something rank and unwholesome permeated the atmosphere, and I tried to put on an expression of serenity as Jabez and Anna Livingston nodded to me.

They were neighbors, living beyond the Lindens, furtherest west of Cloudmont, and were most anxious, they said, to make me welcome. They added their condolences on the death of my sister.

I made the proper and courteous rejoinders to their interested questions, but the queasy feeling that some new terror had been loosed in the house would not let go its hold.

When I intercepted one of the glances that Noah sent the voluble Livingstons as he silently placed a fresh whiskey at George's hand, I caught my breath. Noah's eyes held what had glittered in the eyes of people lining the streets when my mother and father had jolted along in the wooden cart that hauled them to the guillotine. It presaged the spilling of blood. It was universal in the eyes of those too long oppressed.

I realized with a sinking heart that possibly death lurked not only inside this great mansion, but outside it as well.

CHAPTER 5

On New Year's Day, I mentioned my fears casually to Mary. She had just presented me with a length of fine cambric and one of muslin, and was burrowing deeper into a chest at the foot of her bed for some matching ribbons and pins. "Is it often that the slaves rebel against their slavery, Mary?"

"If you're like Yve at all, you can sew better than any sempstress Mother has," Mary was saying. "What did you say?"

I repeated my question less casually. Without looking up Mary replied brusquely, "Periodically they do, sometimes with disastrous results. It's something we try not to think about—and anyway, they all know that *we* are going to free our slaves as soon as they have mastered a trade." Then, looking up, "Here is a packet of needles, and I will help you with the fittings when you're ready." Her sudden laugh was a touch malicious. "After all, a little longer and that rose silk will take root on you."

"You are too kind," I said coolly. "I really don't deserve so much. After all, our relationship is—tenuous."

Mary's glance from under dark winged brows was faintly reproachful. "But it is firmly rooted in blood, through Mélisse."

"But I am no relation at all." I pursued the subject to see what this woman's reaction would be.

"But you are Mélisse's mother, and she is first cousin to our own darling Andy." Mary wore a determined expression. She added a bit coldly, "And as her mother, you are most welcome. You must stop feeling that you are among strangers—and come to look on us as your own people, which we are."

"I shall do that, Mary," I replied with sudden contrition. After all, if I was going to stay at Cloudmont, and I knew I must, it should be done graciously, for these people had certainly been gracious to me.

"I know you will be lovely in those, when they are made up." She nodded at the materials over my arm as she closed the chest lid decisively. "We always give each other gifts on New Year's Day. I've two pipes and some of Cloudmont's finest tobacco, properly shredded and stored with apples for six months, for Andrew and George. And a wool scarf I've knitted for Mother." The change in her expression when she spoke of her family was startling. Her eyes glowed and her face changed from handsome to beautiful. She added carelessly. "These are my gifts to you, Lilibel."

"What a lovely tradition," I said with regret. "And I've nothing to give anyone."

"You have given us the best gift of all—Mélisse," Mary said firmly, adding hastily, "And yourself, of course." Then slowly, "You really are not at all like your sister, you know."

"I *am* like her," I replied swiftly, nettled. "We grew up together and——"

"I meant no disrespect to the dead." Mary shrugged. "You have her high spirits, but you are gentler, more tender. Children—you seem to love them very much."

"You mean my sister did not?" I checked my rising temper.

"They made her very nervous." Mary looked directly at me and her eyes were cold once more. "Nay, I must tell you the truth. She had no use for children."

"I can scarcely believe that. She wrote me she was so proud when they put Andy in her arms—she wrote that only three months after he was born. And Yve was always fun to be with." What she had actually written was that *Andrew* was so proud. I had assumed *she* was, I reminded myself with sharp honesty.

Mary's look at me held a faint trace of sympathy. "Well, to be charitable about it, Aunt Mincy said it was a terribly difficult birth and Yve was in bed near a month afterward, weeping most of the time—and would not nurse Andy. Indeed, Mincy said she could not. I suppose those things would take a toll on a woman's disposition." Her voice hardened as she finished. "But she was—really cruel to Andrew."

I tried to stem my anger at this woman's cold self-possession, so oddly at variance with her voluptuous body and passionate mouth. "In what way was she cruel to Andrew, Mary?" I kept my voice low.

Mary eyed me speculatively and her dark gaze changed subtly. "My dear," she said gently, spreading her hands in an appealing gesture, "let us not talk of these things. They are past, and all things are forgiven in death." She changed the subject. "Would you like to cut the patterns now? I can bring an extra pair of scissors and help. I know I'm not so clever with a needle as you and Yve, but I can try."

I swallowed my anger and met her halfway. "Thank you. I really need a new dress to please your mother. I fear if I show up once more in that rose silk, she will weep with vexation."

As we started from the room, Amanda burst in upon us, followed by a flushed and panting Bibsey Turner.

"Mother—Clay Reed has come to call on me and Bibsey won't let me go in to greet him until I tell you!"

"Mistress Mary, you *told* me not——"

"Amanda," Mary said severely, "I have told all the servants that you are to receive no gentlemen callers until you are seventeen. You know that very well."

"But Mama! Laura was *married* before she was seventeen. So was Grandmother—and so were you!"

"We were all married much too young. Such marriages are the source of great heartbreak. I will not have it happen to you. The matter is closed."

"Oh, Mother!" Amanda cried, and burst into tears. Bibsey turned to flee, but Amanda jerked around and cried, "Don't you dare tell him I can't see him!" Bibsey teetered uncertainly in the doorway.

I interceded swiftly. "Mary, why do you not go and sit with the young ones, while they visit? My mother did that when I was fourteen, and for the very mature young Yve when she was but thirteen."

Amanda's tear-filled eyes swung to meet my compassionate ones. Astonishment and suspicion fought with disbelief in her face, as her mother said doubtfully, "So young as that?"

I smiled. "It takes a great deal of the urgency out of the determination to meet, Mary, when they are allowed to do so under the parental eye."

Mary's eyes changed, and I felt a sudden reluctant pity, for there was pathos in them as she said slowly, " 'Twas my father who sat with me when Joanthan Jackson proposed. I was barely fifteen."

"That was very young," I agreed. "And your answer was yes?" I smiled again, hoping to strike a lighter note, for there was suddenly sadness in the air.

"My father said Yes," Mary answered sourly. "My Amanda was born well before I was sixteen. And I had to take over a large household at Jackson's Landing on the Chickahominy River, long before I was old enough to accept such responsibility. I would spare my child that experience."

I felt I should not have intruded my opinion, but being hoist upon it, I said defensively, "This lad is but seventeen, Mary, with three more years of college ahead of him. Surely matrimony is far from his thoughts."

Mary was beginning to hesitate, and I pressed my advantage. "His feeling for Amanda is probably one of friendship and admiration. Sitting with them, you could surely nip any serious intentions in the bud."

"You are quite right, Lilibel," Mary said, surrendering abruptly. "Come, Amanda. I will sit with you while you visit with young Clay."

Amanda sent me a swift questioning glance as Mary handed her scissors and box of sewing equipment to Bibsey, saying, "Take these to Madame Sevier's room, Bibsey. And Lilibel, I shall join you afterward for our sewing." Mother and daughter left the room together, Amanda obviously restraining her flying feet. I could not tell if I had made a friend in Amanda or not.

Following Bibsey down the hall, I met Cornelia and Abigail. Glancing at the materials I carried, Cornelia asked, "Where are you going with all that, my dear?"

"Mary has kindly given it to me to make myself two new dresses," I replied. "Would you and Abby like to come see the patterns and the materials?"

Cornelia hesitated and replied slowly, "Abby and I are going to do—something I have put off too long."

"You're going to pack up Yve's—things?" I guessed their project from Cornelia's hesitation.

Cornelia's dark eyes on me were faintly apologetic. "I should have done it immediately, but it's such a—painful chore, and I have had to do it for my husband and my son—it was easier to put it off." She cleared her throat. "You needn't worry about it, dear. I shall save all her personal things, and you can go through them later when your grief is not so fresh."

"I should like to help," I said, quietly but firmly. "Let me put these things in my room and I will join you in a moment."

After I had put the materials on the wide bed in my room, I returned to the hall, where I met Andrew standing with his mother outside Yve's door. His black eyes wore a haunted look as he said to me, low, "Mother told me—are you sure you want to help with this unhappy necessity?"

"Yes, Andrew," I replied. "I feel it is my duty to assist your mother." But in some secret compartment of my brain, I was thinking guiltily there might be some clue as to why my sister had been as unhappy and nervous as people claimed.

Cornelia said, "She agrees with me, Andrew, that we should give Yve's clothing away. She doesn't wish to wear it herself."

Andrew's eyes were inscrutable as he said, "I'm grateful for that, Lilibel. I am reminded enough of my loss without seeing her personal clothing each day." He turned and went down the hall to the stairs.

Going through Yve's clothes was more difficult than I had anticipated. Her undergarments touched me particularly and I was silent as they passed from hand to hand, to the large box Abigail had brought for the purpose. The long stays, which went from breast to midthigh and laced up the back, were carefully embroidered with minute pink roses, a skill taught to both of us by the talented and beloved Tante Genèvre. Her chemises were exquisitely decorated and of the sheerest muslin and silk.

Abigail, folding them respectfully, murmured, "Seems a pity, Mistress, that these must be given away."

Cornelia made a small, distressed sound. " 'Tis something that must be done. 'Twould break Lilibel's heart to wear them—and they will serve some worthy lady well. The minister's wife will see to that." She went to the dressing table, where she lifted a polished sterling box to her lap. When she opened it, a red plush interior could be seen, a sparkling in the crimson depths. "Lilibel, come look at her jewels. We buried her in her wedding rings, but these were the ones Andrew bought for her on his trips abroad. They will be for Andy's bride one day, when she is mistress of Cloudmont."

I stood looking down. There were sapphires and rubies, diamonds and pearls. The green of emeralds glowed from a pendent necklace and earrings. Cornelia explained, "Of course, the family pieces—the Madison diamonds and pearls—are in the safe in the library, but Yve wore them often and they were lovely on her. They were hers to wear, as they had been mine, then Laura's until she was widowed."

"Ah, Laura wore them, too?"

"As Thomas's wife and mistress of Cloudmont."

I was silent, letting a small diamond bracelet swing from my fingers as I thought about this. Laura had been mistress of Cloudmont before Yve. And Cornelia had been mistress for many years before that and was now titular mistress once again—unless Andrew should marry a second time. And if Andrew had been as unhappy as George and Mary suggested, that could be a time far away. It appeared a very safe wager that Cornelia Madison should be wearing the Madison diamonds and pearls for any number of years. I glanced at her swiftly as her snowy head was bent over the jewels. Being mistress of Cloudmont, even with a thorn like Louise Alexander ever present, could be addictive.

At last the box was filled, and two more that Abigail had been sent to bring. Yve's large armoire and the tall chests were empty now. I was astonished at the number and variety of fashionable outfits my sister had acquired through the eight years of her marriage.

My feet were exactly the same size as Yve's, and I allowed Abigail to persuade me to keep several pairs of the dainty half-slippers and small boots my sister possessed. Andrew would not notice them.

When I took these and placed them in the armoire in my own room, I stood looking at them thoughtfully. They were beautiful, in their many colors and with their tiny heels and narrow ribbons and laces that fastened them to the foot. The boots were of the finest leather, supple and soft. I had tried them on and they clung to my narrow, high arches as though made to my foot. I closed the mirrored door, wondering why, of all clothing, shoes should be the most evocative of their departed owner, and the saddest.

I was swallowing at the lump in my throat and blinking away tears when a great racket sounded beyond my bedroom door. It came from the far hall that led to the east wing stairs. There were shouts of "Grab him! Hold on—Grandmother will get us for letting him run in the house. Quick! There, Mélisse, you let him get away again!" I heard the pelting of light feet and more screams of laughter.

I flung open the door and stepped out, to collide solidly with Andy. The two of us sprawled on the floor together. The boy recovered quickly and jumped up, looking down at me with frightened blue eyes. With my skirt to my knees and flat on my back, I stared back at him and burst into unrestrained laughter. A small black-and-white spaniel leapt at my hair and began pulling at it with puppy jaws.

When Andy saw my laughter, his handsome face registered first surprise, then relief, and at last wild hilarity. Timothy and Mélisse joined in the general fun as I clutched at my tumbling hair, pulled from its pins by the eager puppy, which would not let go of a long, tangling curl.

"Oh, you rascal—do let me go!" I panted, between gusts of laughter. "Help, help! Children—do get him!"

Andy was pulling the puppy from my hair as George came bounding up the narrow staircase.

I hastily pulled my skirt down about my ankles and attempted to rise. Since this was New Year's Day, all the men were at home. Even Charles Alexander was somewhere in the house, I knew, to eat the festive dinner with us later. To my annoyance, my foot slipped and I tumbled down once more, which sent Timothy, Andy, and Mélisse into gales of fresh merriment. The puppy, excited by the laughter, ran round and round our small group.

George, smiling broadly, stooped to catch both my hands. Pulling me to my feet, he said, "What a pretty picture," his eyes bright with amusement.

"Certainly a funny one," I replied breathlessly, reaching for my tumbling hair, which hung to my waist now and was completely unmanageable. I laughed again and looked at the beautiful child. "What's your puppy's name, Andy?"

"Domino," the boy said, still laughing. "He was a Christmas gift from Uncle George and Grandmother says I must keep him outdoors—but I shall change her mind," he said confidently. "See, he wears a little black mask across his nose—that's why I named him Domino."

"He looks like a little bandit, but he's a beautiful puppy," I said, stooping to stroke the silky black head. My hair fell about my face again and the puppy plunged to bite at it.

"Here!" George said firmly, lifting the spaniel and my brown-gold hair with it. "I'll admit that's a great temptation to play with, but you must learn to be a gentleman, Domino. And gentlemen, alas, cannot always do what they want in polite society." His black eyes met mine with a mischievous twinkle and inexplicably I blushed. I looked away swiftly.

His words triggered a belated apology from Andy. The young face sobered swiftly and a trace of fear returned. "Madame—Aunt—I hope you are not hurt. I'm sorry I tripped you."

"You didn't trip me any more than I tripped you," I said with a smile. "We did it together, I believe."

My nephew's smile returned slowly as his uncle put the puppy back into his arms. Timothy cried, "Come on, Andy—Mélisse—we can go play with him up in the schoolroom. Grandmother won't know!" The three of them pelted up the narrow staircase leading to the third floor.

I looked after them thoughtfully as their slender little figures went past the south window on the stairs and disappeared. George was watching me alertly when I faced him.

I asked abruptly, "Why do you think my nephew fears me?"

"He always gives his friendship slowly, Lilibel," George replied.

"You and Mary and Laura would have me believe it is my sister who has taught him to fear. Only Cornelia and Andrew have refrained from indicting her," I said bluntly.

"Give them time," he replied with a cynical smile, as his big hand closed over my arm. It seemed to burn through the thin silk of my sleeve and suddenly the narrow passageway seemed intimate and slightly dangerous. My heart began to pound.

"What were you doing up here anyway?" I asked breathlessly, making a feeble effort to release my arm. As before, his touch filled me with a kind of wild uncertainty in which desire and common sense fought. Instead of letting me go, his big hand tightened over my arm, and he followed me back into my room. Indeed, he steered me there.

"I was told by my mother to pursue those scallawag children and see that they put the dog back into his kennel by the stables." There was hidden laughter in his voice as I proceeded under his firm hand to the door into the broad hall that led back to the central section of the house. "But you have distracted me, my dear. I shall tell her that I couldn't find them." In the hall, he added abruptly, "And *you* are afraid of *me*. Why?"

My recent experiences with men, Napoleon's soldiers and the sailors on the *Maidee Love*, had made me suspicious of all men's motives, but I did not tell him that. Instead, I jerked my arm vigorously, without succeeding in pulling from his hold on me.

"Let go of me," I panted, for I found myself fighting an absurd desire to throw myself in his arms. George Madison was a singularly dangerous man where my feelings were concerned.

He loosed my arm with a suddenness that made me reel slightly, and his voice was cold. "You are a fool, madame." His stride lengthened as he drew away from me. Over his shoulder—"New Year's dinner will soon be served, and I meant to escort you to the drawing room for a glass of wine beforehand."

All at once I was burning with mortification and an overwhelming desire to right things. "Oh, George, I apologize if I offended you. But you must admit that you are—abrupt."

He did not wait for me, but continued his way to the stairs. Though I ran a few steps, I drew up short, quelling the urge to take his arm. "I'm—I *was* afraid of you, but I misjudged you. I'm sorry." He continued down the stairs ahead of me. "What of the children?" I said.

"I shall send Bibsey to the schoolroom to fetch them." He did not look back at me and I followed him silently down the stairs and into the great hall, and through it to the drawing room, where we came upon the tableau of Amanda entertaining Clay Reed under the dampening watchfulness of Mary Jackson.

Amanda's and Clay's strained greeting gave me the excuse I sought, and I caught George Madison's sleeve. "George, I believe I would like a small glass of wine, after all. And I so adore the morning room. Could we not have it there?"

Laughter was twinkling once more in George's black eyes, but it was for the blushing Amanda, agonizing under her mother's frown while she sought for nonchalance with her eager young beau.

"Of course," he replied, carefully refraining from touching my arm as we took the two broad steps down from the drawing room into the long, bright morning room. George stepped to the pantry door and in a moment, Henry Pepper entered with a bottle of Chablis and poured two glasses of the clear golden liquid for us.

George watched me without expression and said nothing. I had offended him with my vaporings, I thought, infuriated by my reactions to this man. And he had reduced me to apologies, something I had not engaged in since my childhood days with my imperious sister. Thus we sat in tense silence, for I vowed I would make no further overtures, and thus Andrew found us.

"I have been sampling something stronger than wine," he greeted us, striding in from the pantry, his handsome face wearing a broad smile for me. He approached, glass in hand. "This is something we have your countrymen to thank for—a rare inspiration on their part—brandy." He took one of my hands and brought it to his lips, which were warm upon it for a fraction longer than my countrymen would have indulged in, I thought, had they been so recently bereaved.

"Sir, you are as engaging as any of my countrymen," I replied, more admiringly than necessary. But under the goad of George's cool, contemplative eyes, I smiled with all the charm I could muster and motioned Andrew to a seat beside me on the small couch. I then spent one of the most uncomfortable half-hours I could remember, for George was cool and noncommital, without his usual mocking laughter. And I, on the other hand, allowed a towering rage at him to fill me. While Andrew sat quietly immersed in his own thoughts.

Mary permitted Amanda to ask young Clay Reed to have New Year's Day dinner with us and he was delighted to accept. So, when we joined the family at table, I was able to take my thoughts from the boorish George Madison and put them on more pleasant subjects.

At the table, the two young people forgot the strain they were under when they had sat with Mary's eagle eye upon them, and seemed to relax enough to enjoy each other thoroughly. Cornelia, to everyone's amusement, drew Domino, the spaniel, like a magnet. Having easily escaped the children and the half-hearted attempts of the servants, the dog was now lying across Cornelia's feet, and remained there during the entire meal.

"Domino knows who has the softest heart in the house," George said to his mother.

"He simply *must* be put out after dinner," she said. "Heaven knows, you'd think the little creature would lie in front of the warm fire."

Though Andy called him repeatedly from the small table where he and Mélisse sat beside the north window, Domino refused to budge from his nest on Cornelia's slippers. George and Andrew, despite their mother's demurs, talked during the meal of crops and cargoes, of soil problems and solutions. It appeared to me that they consulted with Charles Alexander as much as they did with each other, while he sat at table with all the aplomb of one of the family.

After the meal, young Clay took his reluctant departure. A glowing Amanda waved from the granite stoop at the visitors' entrance as his horse clopped down the road. The rest spent the balance of the day in their own personal pursuits. And I, insisting that Mélisse take an afternoon nap, fell soundly asleep beside her.

Two days later, Sunday, after an early breakfast, we all trooped down to the small church. I noted with surprise that the English tenant farmers and their families were coming through the woods and up the various lanes, while Amanda's slaves were already seated when we entered. The little church was soon filled to capacity.

Seton Cambridge, clad in the kind of long black robe I associated with chief justices in France, took his place at the pulpit, and there delivered the longest, most sleep-inducing sermon I had ever heard. It was my introduction to the Protestant service, and I tried desperately to stay awake. I had great difficulty in smothering my yawns. Seton might be an excellent teacher, but he was a very dull preacher, for I noted that my neighbors were likewise hiding yawns. It was only when he began a long prayer that I was able to focus on his words. He prayed for many of the things I prayed for, and I was able to echo his words in my heart.

It turned bitterly cold the second Sunday in January. After we had all returned from church that morning, Laura left us to go and pack her portmanteaus and valises for her visit to John and Lucy Stuart in Richmond. Immediately after the noon meal, taking her beloved Judith with her, she went out where Noah and Henry Pepper were waiting with the carriage.

The horses stamped their feet and blew cloudy air from their nostrils as we all bade her good-by. It seemed to me that it hurt her most to leave Andy. Mary watched jealously as she embraced the boy, and I could swear tears sparkled in Laura's eyes.

"What would you like your Aunt Laura to bring you, darling?" she asked as we stood about the carriage in the graveled courtyard.

"A surprise," he said, tucking his small hands into her muff.

"I *shall* surprise you, Andy, with something that will be great fun!" She caught him to her and kissed him warmly.

"Laura, the child will freeze to death out here—we shall all freeze!" Mary said sharply and she came forward, catching Andy's arm, pulling his hands from the muff.

"Noah, you and Henry drive carefully," Cornelia admonished the two who sat muffled to their ears on the box.

"Yes'm," Noah grinned. Going into Richmond was a great treat for him, even though they would have to return in the morning.

In a few moments, the carriage clattered down the road, spewing gravel from beneath iron-rimmed wheels. We did not stay to see it disappear, for the cutting wind drove us inside.

"*Brrr*," Mary said as we stepped back into the rear of the great hall. "A few more days of this, Mother, and we shall be ready to cut ice from the river and refill the ice-house."

"Indeed we shall. There should be enough to fill it to overflowing before the week is out if the temperature holds."

Domino, exhilarated by the cold, ran wildly among us, to the children's delight.

"I knew when George gave you that animal he would wind up underfoot all the time," Cornelia said resignedly, as Andy hugged the puppy to him.

"Spaniels make good house pets," Mary said indulgently, watching the puppy lick Andy's face. "I read once that the king of France had several, which slept at the foot of his bed. Is that so, Lilibel?"

"So 'tis said," I replied, thinking sadly of Louis and Marie Antoinette, who had died as cruelly as Maman and Papa.

The temperature held and Ephraim and Joshua Landon,

the two chief slaves among Laura's people, went down to the river with several other men from the quarters where they chopped the ice into huge squares and loaded the service wagons with it. They hauled it back to the ice-house, a dark, cellarlike place covered with thick layers of logs, sawdust, and earth, where it would remain unthawed until the long, hot summer days.

George and Andrew spent much of their time in the plantation office, a huge room with windows facing north, south, and west. Charles Alexander was with them often. He was nearly always at table with us for meals and Cornelia seemed to bear him a deep and genuine affection, which surprised me, considering the chilly constraint between his mother and her. George, Andrew, and their half-brother made frequent trips to both Richmond and Norfolk, which were west and east of us respectively. They had business in Williamsburg and Hampton as well. When they were at home and not involved with the plantation accounts, they spent much time with the tenant farmers on the huge estate, laying plans for the spring plantings. Their warehouses were checked when one of them went into Norfolk.

One dark, cold January evening as I sat alone, sewing by the oil lamp in the library, I heard a clatter at the rear followed by a banging door and the buzz of male voices. I could distinguish Henry's. The other man was either George or Andrew.

It proved to be George. He came into the library, the cold fresh smell of the night still clinging to him as he flung off his greatcoat, and greeted me. Pepper, following, took up the greatcoat and said, "I'll bring your brandy immediately, sir."

I put down my sewing and watched as George went to the fire, flung a large log upon it, and maneuvered it in line with the brass poker. A shower of sparks flew up. It was hard for me not to watch George, for every movement of his big, graceful body invited my eyes.

"How is it you are up so late—and alone?" he asked.

"I was restless. And I might as well put my sleeplessness to advantage." I spoke coolly, and took up my sewing. "And what brings you home alone—so soon?"

"Dull business. I am to start the men loading the last

casks of tobacco on wagons tomorrow. Andrew wants them in the warehouse in Norfolk by the end of next week for shipment to England in March."

Henry Pepper entered with the brandy on a silver tray. "Is there anything else, Captain?" he asked.

"No. I'll keep you up no longer, Pepper. That will be all." His dismissal was firm and Pepper departed silently.

George sipped his brandy slowly and I could feel his eyes on me. I glanced up once swiftly, caught their gleam, and a vulnerability crept over me before I could tear my gaze away.

"How fortunate I am," he drawled, without moving, "to find you unsurrounded by my ever-present family."

My heartbeat stepped up, but I said reprovingly, "You sound as though your family troubled you."

"So they do—on occasion."

"They are wonderful people," I said firmly, "and they have been most kind to me."

"I should like to be most kind to you." There was a hint of laughter in the husky voice.

"You have been," I replied blandly. I should have put my sewing aside and gone upstairs immediately, for there was danger in that warm room, and I was none too sure of my resistance to the determinedly single George. Yet there was in me a perversity that made me lift my thick lashes slowly and smile at him.

He returned the smile, twisting the brandy-glass stem in his big hand as our glances held. My face was hot and I knew I was inviting trouble, but I felt reckless suddenly, and uncaring, for under George Madison's lazy eyes I was young and desirable again, and it was a pleasant sensation.

He finished the brandy and set the glass aside, getting to his feet with a singularly catlike movement. He came to stand before me silently and the turbulence within me increased. I refused to look up at him towering over me. I continued sewing, aware of the polished Hessian boots just before me.

With unexpected gentleness he reached down and plucked the sewing from my hands and tossed it into a nearby chair. Taking my hands in his, he pulled me to my feet. I stiffened as he took me into his arms.

His very deliberateness was a deterrent to struggle. I had been wondering how it would feel to be pressed close to that long hard body, to have those strong hands caress me. Now he lifted my face to his and I was powerless to resist the surge of desire that flooded me when his firm, warm mouth closed over mine.

Caught in a gust of passion, I returned his kiss wildly and my arms twined about his shoulders as I strained against him. I could feel the electric shock that went through him at my response and suddenly he reached over and extinguished the oil lamp.

He swept me into his arms and strode sure-footedly through the room and into the great hall. As he took his mouth from mine, reason returned dimly through the mist of my emotions, and I realized what I was risking—my whole future—and with a man who had no intention of marrying me.

"Where are you taking me?" I asked thickly as he began to go up the stairs.

"To my room, darling—where we will not be disturbed." His voice went over me like a caress, but I stiffened in his arms.

"Put me down, George. I have been a fool. I have no intention of yielding to you."

For an answer he held me more closely and his little laugh was triumphant. "But you will."

Abruptly he halted and a flickering light spilled over us. I turned from his shoulder and saw Mary, clad in her long white nightgown, holding a wavering candle.

"Oh—'tis you, George." She sounded disappointed. "I heard voices earlier and I thought 'twas Andrew returned. What is the matter with Liliane?" There was disapproval in the question.

I took the opportunity to push myself free and regain my feet. "I turned my ankle on the first step," I replied breathlessly, "but 'tis all right now." I took the last three steps and said over my shoulder, "Thank you, George, and good night to you both."

As I hurried down the dark hall, I heard Mary asking her brother about Andrew and why he had not returned with him. I did not hear George's reply as I reached my bedroom and hastily entered, closing the door firmly behind me.

How close I had come to succumbing to that man's charm, and without a word of love spoken between us.

I did not stir up the fire, but undressed in the cold and crept into bed beside my child, shivering more from the narrow escape from my own nature than the cold January night. It must never happen again.

The following morning I refused to meet George's eyes at the table, and for the next two days I saw little of him as he supervised the loading of wooden barrels of tobacco leaves from the tobacco barn to the several wagons for transportation to Norfolk. I was further relieved when he left the third morning for Richmond, and my days settled down once more in the pleasant routine at Cloudmont. I missed Laura and I missed our horseback rides. Mary did not like to ride and so I concentrated on my sewing. Near the end of January, I viewed my handiwork on two new gowns with pride in my accomplishment. The muslin, a pale orchid trimmed with cream lace, had long, tight sleeves and a short scooped neck with a ruching of the lace about it. The cambric, a delicate beige, had short sleeves, but there had been enough of the material for me to make a self-lined pelisse, which was both warm and fetching when donned with the simple frock. I had worn them both before the end of January.

During those cold, bright days, I came to know Timothy and Andy better. Andy gave me his wary, tentative smiles more and more often. His remarkable confidence to my daughter regarding his mother was never mentioned, by me or by Mélisse, who had apparently forgotten all about it. The young Amanda remained aloof and suspicious, keeping her distance with me. Neither her mother nor grandmother made any comment on her attitude, though I felt it must be plain to see.

Timothy, on the other hand, accepted me with a boyish enthusiasm that warmed my heart. He was bright and eager and asked me to teach him French. This desire on his part lasted through a week of early morning lessons and faded as his schoolwork under Seton Cambridge increased. Mélisse liked the gentle young teacher and he had put her to learning the alphabet during his morning lessons with the other children. By the end of January she was able to recognize all twenty-six letters, though she was still unable to reproduce them all.

The day before Laura returned to Cloudmont, two facts were revealed to me—the depth and source of Amanda's suspicions of me, and Railo's desperate risks in coming to see Judith.

Both came about because of my yearning to get out for a brisk canter on Dandylion. Mary had been disapproving that morning when I told her of my intention to go riding, and she urged me to go no further than down the long lane to the tobacco fields and return. She was fearful I might lose my way, and in this I concurred.

Coming from my room clad in Yve's old blue velvet riding habit, which never failed to provoke a vow from Cornelia that we would soon go to Richmond for new clothes, I came upon Amanda. As she stepped up the central stair landing on her way to the third floor, she stopped dead still at the sight of me.

"Ah, *chérie,"* I said warmly, "I am going for a ride on Dandylion. Would you not like to go with me?"

She expelled her breath as I drew near and said softly, "For a moment—in the dim light, you looked like——"

"Like Yve?" I cut in. "They always said there was a strong resemblance, and in this light I must have given you a start. But she was much prettier than I."

"No, she wasn't," the young girl said under her breath. "She was horrid."

"Yve? Oh, no, Amanda! You must not say such——"

"Oh, madame!" Her voice was suddenly imploring. "I was so afraid you would be like her. Instead you have been good to me and persuaded Mama to let me see Clay. Someone—someone *must* tell you the truth." The young girl's face was paper white with intensity, her dark eyes enormous with remembered hatred.

"What is the truth?" I asked quietly.

"Yve was horrid—to my uncle, to my cousin Andy, to me—to *all* of us. Laura was the only one she didn't dare hurt, because Laura gave as good as she got. Oh, madame,

I have been so fearful you would turn out to be like her."

"In what way like her?" I was bewildered and a touch frightened by the passion in the young girl's voice.

"She used to scream at Uncle Andrew, terrible things, and she never missed a chance to hurt him. And she *beat* Andy. Why, only two days before she took sick, she beat him with her *riding crop*. Terrible welts were all over his little body. Uncle Andrew was in a rage! And she screamed so loudly at him, we could hear her in the schoolroom." Amanda's voice dropped tensely. "She would go along for hours, smooth as cream, then all at once she would say cruel things to everyone. Grandmother—she called her a great cow, who had raised a brood of vixens. She called my mother a *bitch* and a *whore*, words my mother won't even let me say out loud. But Yve——"

I recoiled. "Amanda, Amanda, *c'est vrai?* I cannot believe it!" Hot tears had filled my eyes and I bit my lip to keep it steady.

The young face softened. "Madame—Lilibel, I could not bear you not to know. But you are *not* like her. You love children. I had to tell you the truth, though—for that is why we are not mourning her as you might wish us to do." She hesitated, then said swiftly, "I must get to my lessons. I hope you have a nice ride." And she was gone, running lightly up the stairs.

I stood looking after her dumbly, my eyes burning with tears, my throat aching with unspoken denials. What had changed my sister into a virago? The evidence against her was mounting, and yet in some secret place in my heart I remembered the volatile, impetuous, and charming girl she had been. Something had changed her. *What?*

After a long moment, I slowly took the downward flight, moving blindly to the great hall. Turning, I walked to the rear entrance and out the door. I thought of the changed Yve as I walked slowly down the boxwood-lined gravel walkways, wending my way past and through some of the gardens and finally to the stables adjacent to the carriage house. I was still half-blind with tears when I reached them and called for Noah. It was darker in the stables and I blinked furiously at the moisture in my eyes, trying to summon up excuses for my poor dead sister lying defenseless in the still unmarked grave beyond the red brick church.

I smothered a sob and called once more, "Noah, where are you?"

"He ain't here, ma'am," rumbled a deep voice from the doorway to the feedroom beside me.

I whirled to see Railo towering there, his black face menacing in its total lack of expression. "Railo," I gasped. "You must know that Judith has gone to Richmond with Mistress Laura. What are you doing here?"

"I heard they was comin' back today."

"Tomorrow, Mr. Charles said. He was at the Stuarts' two days ago."

He was silent.

I asked guardedly, "Did you get permission to come over here today, Railo?" I swiftly brushed my wet eyes with my gloved hand.

"No, ma'am," he growled. "An' from the looks o' you, ma'am, you got troubles, too."

"Not the kind you have," I said forthrightly. "I fear for you if Mr. Livingston finds you away from your work."

He laughed shortly. "He'd like to have me killed, but I'm worth too much to him alive."

The memory of Livingston's red face with its cruel hooked nose and crueler mouth rose up before me and I said urgently, "Railo, don't push him too far. Please go back before he finds you gone."

"That's what Judith say. But my peoples will tell him I'm off in the farthest fields. Besides, life without Judith ain't worth much to me, Miss Lilibel."

Noah came running up to the stables carrying a brown wrapped package. He stopped short at the sight of me with the big slave. Railo said, "It's all right, Noah. Miss Lilibel know what I done. Gimme the food an' I'll be on my way back. An' tell Judith fer me I'll come agin—by night, tomorrow."

He took the package Noah handed him and moved lithely and silently out the door. We stood looking after him without speaking for some time. Then I asked, "Noah, what will Jabez Livingston do if he catches Railo running off to see Judith?"

"Beat him within a inch o' his life, ma'am. As near

kill him as he dares an' maybe make him work in chains fer a month."

"Noah, he called me Miss Lilibel. He knows who I am."

"Judith call you Miss Lilibel. Miss Laura tells Judith all about the fambly. I reckon you'd be surprised how much Railo an' me—all the servants, black an' white—knows about you."

"And perhaps some things I do not know," I said bitterly.

"What you mean, ma'am?"

"I mean you must have known my sister as well—no, better than you know me."

He gave me a wary glance and said, "Did you want me to saddle up Dandylion fer you, ma'am?"

"First, tell me about my sister," I said bluntly.

"Miss Lilibel, I didn't know Miss Yve—too well. She a hard person to get to know. She kinda cold like, but a nice lady," he finished hastily.

"Didn't you ever saddle up a horse for her? Didn't she talk to you?"

"Yes'm. I saddled up her big gelding, Jean, she call him, fer her on the day of the hunt—'twas the day she come back with the lung congestion what took her. 'Twas a bitter cold rainy day 'bout a week before Christmas."

"Well?"

"What you want me to say, Miss Lilibel?" He opened his hands appealingly.

"What was she like? Kind? Pleasant? Harsh and cruel?"

"Miss Lilibel, you been upset by somethin'. I kin tell. I'm sorry Miss Yve done took sick an' died."

I let my breath out. It was no use. Noah was not going to tell me the servants' gossip about my sister. He asked hopefully, "Want me to saddle up Dandy now?"

"No," I replied moodily. "I've changed my mind." And I turned to retrace my steps through the winding walkways and the gardens to the house.

When I reached my room and took off the blue velvet riding habit, I looked at it thoughtfully as I hung it once more in the armoire. Running my hands over its velvety folds, I wished with all my heart that it could speak and tell me what had altered my Yve so disastrously. For there was no doubting the passionate sincerity in Amanda Jackson's face when she accused Yve of cruelty.

CHAPTER 6

Laura returned from Richmond at the end of the week. It was evening as the carriage drew up before the visitors' entrance. Charles had ridden horseback beside the carriage and when they entered, I sensed at once the tension between them. Laura flung off his hand as she entered and greeted us. His handsome face flushed darkly, the black eyes bright with rage.

He said curtly, "I shall see your luggage is brought up to your room."

"You needn't bother." Two bright spots of color glowed in her ivory face. "Pepper can see to it."

Without another word, Charles flung back out the door, slamming it behind him, as Laura turned to the gathering family before her with a bright smile.

She began with high spirits to tell us of her adventures in Richmond. We all streamed after her to her room. She had come loaded with small gifts for everyone. When Henry Pepper brought up her portmanteaus and Clementine followed with several interesting boxes, she began to give them to us. There was a gold locket for Mélisse, lengths of silk for Mary, Cornelia, and me, ribbands of all colors for Amanda, and a small, perfect schooner for Timothy.

As she cuddled my nephew close, I caught her whisper among the cries of delight about her: "For you, my darling, the best of all." She burrowed through a valise and came up with a small wooden horse, perfectly carved, its mane flying in the wind, its painted nostrils flaring. It was exquisite, and the little boy was open-mouthed with pleasure.

Laura looked at Mary defiantly. "And I bought him some clothes. A new velvet suit for church. And some little pantaloons like his father's and his Uncle George's—with a matching coat." She pulled forth the beautiful clothing and Mary's large eyes widened.

I felt again the queer revulsion as the strange flaw in Mary's face revealed itself to me. I alone saw it. The others were entranced by their gifts and those she had presented to Andy.

Laura said lovingly, "Your father and Uncle George helped me choose those—only yesterday. And they said to tell you they will be home soon." Andy hugged her when she bent to him and kissed her cheek warmly.

Mary's full red mouth tightened and she said jealously, "We will buy more when we go to Richmond, darling Andy—for you and Timothy"—and to her daughter, who was leaving the room with her ribbands—"and for you, too, Amanda, my precious."

Laura pushed her large portmanteau over to Judith, who began unpacking her dresses. She smiled at Cornelia. "John and Lucy said you must all come to Richmond soon. The social season is in full swing, and it's been ages since we've all been together in the city."

"Mary could do with some new frocks," Cornelia said reflectively, "and our dear Lilibel sorely needs all manner of things."

"But I feel very rich," I protested, "with the two lovely new dresses you and Mary have helped to make."

"Nonsense, my dear, you need a dozen," Cornelia said briskly, walking to the door with her length of silk over her arm. Mary followed and the two boys darted out before them, clutching their new toys.

As I started to leave, Laura said softly, "Wait—I have another present for you, Liliane," and I turned back. Judith stood smiling expectantly.

"I hung it in your armoire, Miss Laura," she said. "I'll get it." And she took from the rack the loveliest dress I had ever seen. It was a delicate pink muslin, gathered full beneath the bosom. The bosom itself was bordered by a band of deeper pink satin. The long, fitted sleeves were cuffed in the same satin. Still deeper pink ribbons hung from the high waist. Over it hung a matching pelisse, banded in the satin.

"Ohh," I breathed. "Laura, *comme c'est jolie*—it is so lovely!"

"I wanted to buy you a ballgown, but Judith and I agreed you most needed a dress for Sunday—to wear to church with us. I guessed your size, but if 'tis too large, we can——" she broke off suddenly.

Charles towered in the open door, holding a large hat-box. "Pepper missed this one." His face was dark with anger as he strode into the room and deposited the box on Laura's high bed.

Judith put the pink dress and pelisse in my hands and slipped silently from the room. Charles glared down into Laura's defiant face and growled, "Little coward!"

"Don't you call me a coward!" she retorted furiously. I turned to follow Judith, but she called pleadingly, "Don't go, Lilibel—please."

"You think I care if Liliane hears me?" Charles raged. "I don't care who hears me! You put on pious airs and insinuate you're too good for me, above my animal desires—after all, I'm a bastard, the housekeeper's son. But you let that drunken sot, Hugh Carleton, fondle you in John Stuart's library—"

"I *told* you! He was only *trying* to kiss me—but you had to burst in and knock him down! You practically challenged him. If he hadn't been a reasonable man, you could have killed each other. And you had no right——"

"You are damn well correct in that, madame. I hadn't the least right to defend your honor." His voice grew bitter. "And I'll tell you something else—I believe *I'm* too good for *you!*"

It was the sort of meaningless accusation a frustrated lover would make, but it had a curious effect on Laura. Her face went paper white and her hand flew up, striking him a stinging blow along his jaw and cheek. For a timeless moment, the three of us were stunned and still as statues. Then Laura's lips quivered and her great blue eyes filled with tears. Charles stared at her stricken face and in one fluid movement gathered her into his arms. She melted to him, turning her lips up to his in a swift gesture of wild hunger. As they stood fused together, I turned and fled.

That night as we all gathered in the dining room for dinner, Laura cast me a quick questioning glance. I smiled reassuringly. Charles favored us both impartially with an impudent grin, while Cornelia held forth about the coming trip to Richmond, for she had determined that we should go.

"And you, Lilibel," she said as we took our seats, "must have at least two new riding habits. We are going to sponsor the last hunt of the season in late March. We have not attended any— Well, it will be three months since we lost Yve by then." She hesitated and there was a moment of awkward silence. Then she said with determined gaiety, "There will be parties in the spring and summer, Lilibel, and you will need some ballgowns as well as tea frocks and riding habits. I think we will go next week. Ladies, do you agree?"

I murmured assent. Mary's moist red mouth spread in a wide smile as she said, "Indeed we do."

"I shall send word to the servants to prepare the town house for us," Cornelia went on, as Pepper and the maids began serving. "With our men stopping off there at brief intervals only, I'll wager they have become very slack."

"This will please Lucy and John, Cornelia," Laura said. I sensed she was making an effort not to look at Charles, who regarded her often, his black eyes shining with wicked enjoyment. She added, "She said she would let me go only on my solemn promise to persuade you all to come to the city for a while."

As the meal progressed and the discussion continued, only the little ones were despondent, for Cornelia had decreed they should stay home and miss no lessons. Our trip would be of fairly short duration, no more than two weeks. This was because she must return in time for the supervision of the hunt breakfast in late March.

Mary said pensively, "I shall be so glad when Andrew returns home—and George, too, of course."

Amanda said suddenly, "I believe I shall stay with the children, Mama. Seton is teaching me the history of the fall of the Roman Empire. 'Tis very interesting."

The always quiet Seton looked up from his plate in surprise, and Charles pretended to choke. He said, coughing, "Feel her forehead, Mistress Mary. She must be ill. To miss a chance for a shopping spree and a session with the seamstresses!"

A dark flush rose on Amanda's fair face and she shot her half-uncle a look of entreaty. It was wasted on him, for he added, "I thought you loathed history, Mistress Amanda." His deferential "Mistress" was mocking.

Mary frowned. "I know that Clay is still at Tulip Grove on leave from the university." Amanda turned her face from her mother, who continued, "Nay. You will accompany us, daughter. All the pretty dresses we shall buy for you will make up for missing your lessons." She turned to me. "Lilibel, will you mind leaving Mélisse in the care of Bibsey and Tina and the others for two weeks? She is so young."

Mary's excessive love for all the children had the effect of making me wish ardently to give them more freedom. "She is near five and very fond of Bibsey and Clementine. I'm sure she will be quite all right." I had not spent a night without my little daughter nearby since she had been born, and I was suddenly assailed by what I told myself were foolish doubts.

Seton spoke up in his gentle voice. "Madame Sevier, Mélisse is very quick and intelligent and she enjoys her lessons a deal more than"—his glance strayed to Timothy, then Andy—"than some others."

"I'll warrant that's true enough," said Charles, running a hand over the black, unruly hair of Timothy, seated next to him.

The boy laughed carelessly, cutting an eye at his tutor. "Aw, Seton—I try hard. It's just I'm not too bright."

"But you are bright, Tim," Seton said gravely. "Much too bright to waste time as you do. You want to go to William and Mary like your uncles, do you not?"

The boy shrugged. "I'd rather go away on the *Tern* with Uncle George and be his cabin boy."

Charles said, eyes twinkling, "Perhaps we can arrange that for you during one summer. You wouldn't miss more than three months of school, making the return trip."

Cornelia said reprovingly, "Don't encourage him in that, Charles."

"Ah, Mistress, surely when he is fourteen——" he broke off.

Mary said decisively, "I'd much prefer he stay near his Uncle Andrew and learn to manage Cloudmont successfully." Her look at her son was possessive and loving.

Charles scrutinized her, then said, "His cousin Andy will be the one to manage Cloudmont."

Mary's eyes sought the small table where her nephew sat with Mélisse. "You forget, Charles, Andrew does not believe in primogeniture. A third of Cloudmont is mine. Timothy and Andy will share their inheritances."

"What of Mr. Jackson's lands on the York River?" Laura asked with faint malice.

"No doubt Timothy will be able to look after them, too, when he grows up," Mary replied serenely. "In the meantime, Andrew is doing that for me."

"Better than he is looking after Landon for me," Laura said coldly.

Mary's eyes flashed with scorn. "You have never given Andrew credit for all he does! I *do.* Jackson's Landing lay fallow and when the time came for its use, Andrew used it—and is using it to its greatest advantage, I have no——"

"Hark!" Charles cut in. Just outside the tall windows there arose a hubbub of barking dogs and the sound of male voices, then running feet on the gravel.

"Hoy!" It was unmistakably Noah's glad cry. The deep, laughing voices must be those of George and Andrew.

"Oh, they're home!" Mary cried joyously, seizing the bell beside her mother. "Louise—Bibsey!" she called, ringing it loudly. "Come set two more places at the table." She jumped up, and her mother rose with her.

They were met at the opening into the great hall by the two brothers, unbuttoning their greatcoats and pulling off their wide-crowned hats to hand them to Clementine, who hovered nearby beaming with pleasure.

Laura and I had turned to observe the meeting and Charles was looking on with an expression of dry humor. Mary had briefly brushed her brother George's cheek and was now in the arms of Andrew. She took his face in her two hands and kissed him repeatedly on the mouth. He was plainly her favorite. I found her obvious partisan feelings a touch repugnant, but I forgot it in the conversation that flowed about the table as the servants hurried in from the pantry and kitchen, bringing fresh plates, glasses, and silverware.

"Mr. George—Mr. Andrew," Henry Pepper said, entering with a tall bottle of spirits on a silver tray. " 'Tis the last bottle of whiskey from the supply you brought up before the New Year's Open House."

"Ah," said Andrew, taking the bottle to pour a pony into his glass. "Then we must make a raid on the cellar again."

The balance of the meal was a merry one, as George and Andrew told us of their errands in Richmond and the ladies told them of the coming trip to Richmond. "Perhaps we can all travel together," George remarked. "Andrew and I must return soon to see about the construction of a second warehouse for our goods. My new venture demands it."

I was wearing my new orchid and lace dress and I was aware of the admiring glances of Andrew and George as we finished the meal. I registered anew the compelling vitality of these two men, who made me intensely aware of my femininity. I was half annoyed at the way they stirred my blood.

After dinner, I left the others and made my way into the little room opposite the great hall from the main drawing room. The room was next to the library and had a pianoforte in it. Having studied music during my childhood and early youth, I had been availing myself of the pleasure of playing recently. At first the household had been intrigued, for Mary played rather poorly and was not too fond of it, so the family often came in and listened as I ran through the music on hand. It afforded me a comforting nostalgia and soothed my tensions when I played.

I had not been there long before Andrew came in to stand behind me, listening. Suddenly he put his warm hands on my shoulders, and I brought the chords to an unmusical halt.

He removed his hands at once. "I did not mean to startle you, Lilibel. I was enjoying the music so."

"That's quite all right, Andrew," I replied hastily, and began to play once more. I was shocked that the man's touch set my heart running like a rabbit. Glancing around, I saw his haunted dark eyes filled with pain.

"Yve played beautifully, even as you do, when first I brought her to Cloudmont as a bride. We were so happy then."

"Didn't she continue to play?" I asked. "She used to love it when we were children."

"No," he said sadly. "She didn't play after Andy was born. She said—she hated it. I missed it, for I enjoy music greatly."

I let my fingers trail away and turned to face him abruptly. "Amanda has told me things about my sister that I find almost incredible."

His face darkened and he muttered, "That little chit. You must not believe her. Like most fifteen-year-olds, she embroiders the truth."

"I can't even repeat to you the terrible things she said."

His dark face was harassed and the lonely brooding in his eyes touched me. "Then she lied," he said flatly.

I wanted to believe him, but I could not. "Were you so unhappy with Yve? Had she changed so?"

"I loved Yve. And I was at fault. I made her unhappy but I could not help myself. I did all I could to make it up to her, but—after a while, we began to grow apart. She seemed to hold it against me that there were no more children after Andy."

I said slowly, my fingers light on the keys so the music was very soft, "It would worry Yve—to have but one child. But it seems unlikely that it would drive her to beat the one she had." I glanced up at him again. "I believe it took something far more terrible to turn my sister into a virago."

His face paled. "You think I haven't thought of that? I've spent many a sleepless night since her death wondering if I drove her to such—insanity." The words were torn from him, and the anguish on the strong features was genuine. I felt my heart going out to him.

I stopped playing and put a hand to his where it hung

by his side. "I believe you, Andrew," I said impulsively. "I know my sister was possessive of all those she loved. It was part of her charm, in a way. Obviously you were —independent of her to a degree, and you cannot blame yourself for that always. You must go on living."

"I do blame myself," he said bitterly. Catching my hand, he pressed his lips to it fervently. "You are so good, so sweet, my dear. You ease the torment in my soul."

I was astonished by the warm flood of sympathy the touch of his lips evoked, and took my hand away swiftly. It had been far too long since I had known masculine tenderness, and I realized my susceptibility. I said, "I grieve for my sister, too. But I had no idea how things stood between you—when I asked to come to her for refuge."

He said quickly and with force, "That must make no difference to you, Liliane. This is your home. You are of our family now." He shook his head, sadness settling over his face. "I had hoped you would never know of the estrangement between Yve and myself. It can only distress you. Amanda should be spanked, fifteen years notwithstanding." He reached for and caught my hand once more, kissing the palm lingeringly, again setting off the chain of tender feeling. "How can I thank you for your words of comfort, dear sister-in-law, for your kindness and understanding?"

And I, who had not intended to comfort him at all, who had been suspicious that he was a villain in my sister's life, rose to stand silent as his compelling charm seemed to flow around me. Suddenly I could understand my sister's passion for the man, but I was not prepared to yield to it.

Slowly, he drew me toward him. I was sure he meant to take me into his arms, when laughter came from the doorway and George entered and said blithely, "Am I interrupting? You both look very intense."

I was annoyed to feel my face heat up under his merry glance, but Andrew was entirely at ease. He said gravely, "Lilibel has been giving me something I've found very little of since the death of Yve. Comfort."

"Bless you, Lilibel," George said soberly. "We have all tried to comfort Andrew, but have met with a singular lack of success. He seems to blame himself for something that could not be helped." He caught my arms and seated me again at the pianoforte. "Do play. The ladies will be in shortly and we all enjoy it so much."

Andrew stirred my sympathy, but contact with George sent a sharply pleasurable shock through me. He was slow to take his hands away even after I seated myself once more, and I carefully concealed the turmoil his touch put me in. I said smoothly, "What would you like to hear?"

"Any—all of the études by Charteris," was the quick response.

When the ladies arrived, I sat and played for all of them, including Charles Alexander, for the better part of an hour. They were reluctant for me to stop, but I said, "Laura has promised to take me to Mincy Delafield's tomorrow, bright and early. I must be ready to go."

I knew it was a long way, for Laura had told me it was past the Reeds' Tulip Grove, past the Chenaults' Rose Hill and the Montagues' Lindens, just between the Livingstons' and the sweeping inland acres of Laura's old home, Landon. I wanted to be well rested. I had been looking forward to meeting Mincy, because she was, with Andrew, the last person to see Yve alive.

My audience was reluctant to let me go, but at my firmness, we went our separate ways to bed. The children had long since been put to bed, including the grown-up Amanda, who retired early, a hangover from her recently departed childhood.

As I crept into the covers beside my Mélisse, I thought of the many questions I would ask Mincy, and slept at last.

The following morning, I rose early, leaving Mélisse sleeping in the big bed alone. I would tell Bibsey to come later and see that she breakfasted before lessons began. I donned the worn blue velvet riding habit and stepped into the hall, where I walked down the long dark passageway to the main structure of the house and rapped quietly on Laura's door.

She came out dressed in a new black riding habit, which contrasted strikingly with her blonde loveliness.

Judith was behind her, tall and willowy. The black girl said, "I've been down and Miz Beady has an early breakfast for you two in the kitchen, Miss Lilibel." She held a tall taper in one slender hand, for the February sun was slow to rise and the windows behind her were only faintly gray.

"Thank you, Judith, for your help. You can go back to sleep if you like," Laura said.

Before she left, I said quickly, "Judith, I saw Railo yesterday at the stables and he said—he told Noah to tell you that he would be over tonight."

The girl's eyes widened and I was struck anew by her dusky beauty. Her lashes were thick as a brush and curly. "He must know that Mr. Livingston will let him off. You mind if I meet him at the stables tonight, Miss Laura?"

"I think you're getting far too serious about him, Judith. I've told you Jabez Livingston will not sell him," Laura said severely. "And I simply can't let you go to Anna Livingston."

The girl shivered. "I don't want to go to Livingston's, ma'am. I couldn't work for that woman." Her eyes were wide and poignant when she added, "Won't you try once more to get Mr. Livingston to sell him to you, Miss Laura?"

Laura's delicate brows drew together sharply and she tapped her chin with the butt of her riding crop. "Well—I will, if you'll promise tonight will be the last time you'll see him until then. Nothing good can come of your association now."

"He's my friend," she murmured inaudibly.

"Friend!" Laura laughed. "Friend is not what Railo wants to be to you and you know it, you sly fox. Come on, Lilibel, let's go. It's a fairly long ride to Aunt Mincy's."

After a large breakfast, just as the sun was rising over the southeastern edge of the fields and forests, Laura and I set out at a good clip in a northwesterly direction. We did not follow the edge of the river as we had done before, but kept back from it on a narrow road with carriage tracks in its sparse gravel bed.

As we trotted along, Laura once again began telling me

of the country around us. "I must take you to see the lake where the cattle graze. 'Tis to the north of us."

"There are cattle on Cloudmont, too?" I asked in surprise.

"Of course, my dear. We have always fresh beef on our table—and butter and milk. Where else would we get them?" She smiled at my ignorance and continued, "And to the west—far to the west and a little north of us is Mary's inheritance, Jackson's Landing, a fine plantation on the Chickahominy River, a tributary of the James. Her brothers see to it that it is well run; and Mary's income is considerable." There was rising anger in the low voice as she continued, "And directly north is Landon country. My father built on the York River. You and I shan't come anywhere near my old home, but it's no loss. It's gone to ruin in the six years since I left there and I can't budge Andrew or George to fix up the house, though Andrew has had the fields plowed and fertilized."

"Why not?"

"They say they haven't time yet, and I guess they haven't. But if they'd spare Charles and some of my people, Ephraim and Joshua, for instance, who are expert carpenters, it could be easily and quickly refurbished."

"Perhaps they will soon, *chérie*," I said comfortingly. "They do seem so terribly busy."

"Oh, they are," she agreed. "They've a finger in many pies, and now George has some new venture he's investing in—I heard him talking to Andrew about it last evening."

"Would that be the new warehouse in Richmond he mentioned at table the other night?"

"I don't know yet—it has to do with shipping. You know how George is about the sea. He should have been a navy man. We'll soon find out, as it's the reason they are accompanying us to Richmond."

"Then they are going with us?"

"Didn't you know? They told Cornelia last night. Here, let us follow this path. It leads us past the back of the Chenaults' Rose Hill and then Tulip Grove, where the Reeds live. If we had time, we'd stop and visit with them all—even the Montagues at the Lindens, which we will pass also. But then we'd never get to Aunt Mincy's," she laughed.

We passed under giant tulip poplars and ash trees and through a thicket of arborvitaes. Laura remarked, "Andrew says these old arborvitaes are a thousand years old. He says they grow an inch every thirty years—and he measured the trunks and says they are well past a thousand years."

"*Alors!* That is astonishing," I replied, eyeing the patriarchs of the forest respectfully.

Laura shrugged. " 'Tis a fact that means little to me." She pointed. "Those are linden trees. There are hundreds of them on the Montague place, which is why he named it Lindens. And those are black walnuts. I think they are the hardest-shelled fruit in the world, but so tasty in Beady's Christmas fruitcakes. Those big bare trees are catalpas and in the spring their blossoms are as beautiful as the dogwoods. Those are sugar maples and those, holly trees," she pointed with her crop.

By the time we passed Lindens and drew near Mincy Delafield's cabin, I had learned a great deal about the flora of tidewater Virginia. We turned away from the narrow pathway into what appeared to be virgin forest. The horses' feet were silent on the thick carpet of leaves that covered the sun-dappled earth. My blue velvet skirt caught suddenly on the extended branches of a holly tree.

With a cry of dismay, I halted Dandylion and attempted to loosen the skirt, but the material tore with a loud ripping noise.

Laura said with finality, "Now you really must have a new riding habit. Thank God, we will soon be in Richmond again, where such things can be bought or made." She turned to watch me as I regained my balance, adding, "You will have to have it for the March hunt, now that the period of mourning is—ah—somewhat past."

"So Cornelia said," I replied shortly. I thought their period of mourning had been a mockery, but I did not say that to Laura. I had been too young to ride to the hounds in France. Then too, the sport was not as popular there as it was in England, and I did not particularly look forward to the prospect of riding with the Madisons and their neighbors. My sympathies lay too often with the hunted animal; especially now in view of my own past experiences.

Laura and I seemed to have wound our way for miles before we came abruptly upon a clearing that held a small log cabin crouched against the wall of pines behind it. Smoke floated lazily from a tall stone chimney. The yard, in sunlight now, was filled with well-kept shrubs. There was an herb garden near the rough small house.

"Aunt Mincy owns five acres in here—a gift from my grandfather to her. Every plantation owner for miles around sends for Aunt Mincy when there is sickness in the family."

We dismounted, tying our horses to a hitching rail which stood outside the yard. As we entered the gate, a lean hunting dog got slowly to his feet and gave a single bark—a spotted butler announcing visitors.

"That's Gypse. George gave him to Aunt Mincy years ago. God knows how old the dog is by now."

I saw a curtain flick at one of the windows as Laura and I walked up the path to the porch of the cabin where Gypse stood slowly wagging his tail. Laura dropped a casual pat on his spotted brown head and the tail moved faster, as she rapped smartly on the planed door with her crop.

The door opened silently and we stepped inside. Even with the four windows in it, the room seemed very dark after the brilliant morning sunlight. Curtains shut out much of its brightness, but I was immediately aware of a pleasantly pungent odor of herbs and spices heavy in the warm air of the room. I was conscious, too, of a bright fire in the fireplace.

"Chile, how you been?" The voice was soft, throaty, and ageless. "Is somebody sick to Cloudmont?"

"No. I've brought Yve's sister to meet you," Laura said, as the two embraced. "She arrived the very day we buried Yve. And Madame Sevier wants to talk to you about her."

I noticed a heavily curtained area at the rear of the room. The cabin consisted of one big room with many cupboards and shelves. There were rough steps leading upward to a loft and I sensed there must be a cellar beneath us, for I was able to perceive a bright rag rug covering a space before the fireplace that probably concealed a trap door.

"Set down." Aunt Mincy motioned to a rocker, still faintly moving back and forth, and a mammy bench with several straight-backed chairs about it. "I'll make some mint tea and give you both a slice of my fresh gingercake." Then directly to me, "I'm glad to meet you, madame."

"Thank you," I said uneasily, for suddenly there was borne in upon me a pressing sense of suspended violence and danger. I seated myself apprehensively in the rocker, conscious of hair at the back of my neck lifting with some primordial instinct.

Mincy Delafield was busily hanging a kettle over the hot fire before us. Then she went to a cupboard and took out three cups of delicate china with matching saucers. " 'Member when your mama give me these, Laurie?"

"Indeed I do. You pulled me through a terrible case of measles and I cried for two hours after you finally left me."

Mincy laughed softly. Putting a sugarbowl beside the cups on a small table, she murmured, "You was a dear, lovin' chile, Laurie."

Moving restlessly, I turned toward the curtained area to the side of me. Did I fancy movement behind those curtains? The aroma of herbs was thick in my nostrils, medicinal and sharp.

"Smells like you've been cooking up a new batch of medicines, Aunt Mincy," Laura remarked, confirming my own conclusions.

"Yes, I been cookin' up some unguents—good fer burns an' wounds and suchlike." She opened a tin of tea and put a generous amount in a silver tea-egg, which she dropped into a small porcelain pot awaiting the water to boil. I saw another pot, pushed back on an iron rack above the fire.

"Smells potent." Laura smiled. "Did you just bake the gingercake, too?"

"No'm. Baked that last night, but it's fresh in my cake tin."

My eyes, accustomed now to the dim light, rested on the thin supple figure of the ageless black woman. Her dark face was a mass of little wrinkles. Her obsidian eyes rested on me and she said slowly, "You a quiet one, ma'am."

"I'm afraid our visit is untimely," I replied tensely. "I fear we have interrupted you." I was certain now of movement behind the curtains at the side of the room. They were thick, rough curtains made of coarse sacking, but clean and attractive despite that. It was what they concealed that put me on edge. Unconsciously I glanced at it once more and, returning my gaze to Mincy, found her black eyes narrowed on me.

"No, ma'am, you ain't interruptin'. I'm always glad to see one of my babies."

Laura laughed. "That's me, Lilibel. I'll be one of Aunt Mincy's babies until I'm old and decrepit."

"You be one of my favorite babies, Laurie, long as I lives." The old lady bent easily and stirred up the fire, sending bright sparks up the sooty chimney.

Convinced now that there were more than three of us in the cabin, I rose abruptly to my feet. "I think we should return at another time, Aunt Mincy, for our visit. Perhaps you would like to set a time for us to come?"

I was truly frightened now. I had always been intuitive and every sense I possessed was humming with the unknown danger that lurked within the warm, spiced abode of Mincy Delafield.

Laura stared at me in disbelief, while Mincy's eyes moved slowly around me, behind me. I whirled to see a towering figure step from the curtains into the room.

"No use to go, Miss Lilibel. An' no use to hide, I tol' you, Aunt Mincy," Railo said. He wore only coarse homespun breeches. His huge muscled chest was bare in the firelight.

CHAPTER 7

There was a stricken silence in the room while Laura and I stared at the big man looming before us.

Swift as a shadow Aunt Mincy went to him and pulled him to a seat near the fire. She made no more pretense about tea, but took the second pot from the rear rack and dipped a hand into it, turning Railo so she could smear the concoction on him.

As she turned him about and I saw his broad back, a gasp escaped me. His back was a mass of red, raw flesh. The man had been near flayed alive. Laura, seeing it as well, drew in a sharp breath and whispered, "My God——"

Mincy, her hand covered with warm salve, touched Railo's back lightly but even so, the big man shrank perceptibly. As I watched the two silent people, the young, strong man and the old, thin woman, I felt the tension that hung in the room.

I said fiercely, "Did Jabez Livingston do that?"

Railo looked up, face contorted with rage and pain. "No, ma'am. He wouldn't touch a slave. He has his overseer, Speers, do it."

"For coming to Cloudmont yesterday?" I asked. "You did not have his permission?"

"No, ma'am. I didn't."

Laura cut in, distressed. "Railo, I told you no good would come of your visits to Judith!"

He gave her a cold, measured glance. "You can tell Judith I'll be there tonight, Miss Laura."

Laura cried, "Railo, he'll kill you if he finds out!"

"No, ma'am. I'm worth too much to him alive. You'll notice he ain't had Speers fix me so I can't work."

"He could put you in chains," Laura said, "make your work ten times as hard. And Jabez would do it, too. You know that."

Railo said nothing, wincing slightly as Aunt Mincy continued to smear the pungent salve on his raw back.

I said thickly, "Is there nothing that can be done to that inhuman man to stop him?"

Railo looked up at me from under his brows. "Yes, ma'am. You could kill him."

The menace I had first felt descended once more like a cold web, imprisoning, chilling. Laura said harshly, "Railo, you must not speak so. You know well that if others not as sympathetic as Lilibel and I were to hear you, nothing would save your neck."

"You goin' to tell Livingston?" he asked.

"Of course not," she replied indignantly. "But I hate to see you take such chances."

I turned to her. "Why don't you talk to Jabez again? You promised Judith you would ask him to let Railo court her. That would surely stop this—beating."

Laura gave me a frustrated glance. "I have asked him to sell me Railo—I even explained it all to George and Andrew and got their permission. But that old devil just laughed at me. Told me he would buy Judith as a maid for Anna, if I made the price right. But Judith doesn't want to work for Anna Livingston. She feels about them much as Railo does."

"I wouldn't let Judith work for them people," Railo burst out violently.

"You see?" Laura looked at me and shrugged. "It's an impasse."

"You ain't goin' to free Judith. She tol' me." Railo did not look at Laura.

"I'll pay her," Laura said defensively, "just like Abigail MacTavish, or Clementine and Bibsey. And I'd pay *you*."

Railo shook his head and said nothing. I moved restively. Aunt Mincy concentrated on her efforts to soothe the big black's wounds. She would have little to say to me about the death of Yvette de Belvoir Madison after this episode.

"Let's go home, Laura," I said uneasily.

"Tea water's bilin'," Aunt Mincy said matter-of-factly. "An' I'm almost through. Livingston know you come to see me?" she asked Railo.

"Nope."

"You lives dangerous, man," Mincy rejoined without expression. "I'm finished. Now git on back before you're missed."

In a moment, she had slipped a white muslin shirt from one of her shelves over the big black man and Railo put on his coarse, heavy jacket and was gone. The gust of cold February air caused the flames to flare in the fireplace as Railo closed the door behind him.

Later, as we sat sipping tea and eating delicious ginger-cake, Aunt Mincy looked at me levelly over her teacup and said, "You wanted to talk about your sister, ma'am. What can I tell you?"

I took a deep breath. "Tell me how it was when she died. Did she not leave some message for me, perhaps?"

"She were a sick chile. When I come in, her fever was 'way high an' she were out of her head. She thought she was a little girl back in France with you an' her papa and mama. Yes, she talked to you—called you Lilibel, but she didn't know it."

"Do you think—she could have been saved?"

Laura's quick glance held a touch of consternation. Aunt Mincy said calmly, "I've seen many a one like her in the winters round here. You can't save nobody with deep pneumonia. They lungs fills up an' they can't breathe."

I hesitated, then plunged on. "Mary has told me how unhappy she was, that she wept a great deal and was very nervous, that she did not like children. Indeed, Amanda told me that she beat her own son unmercifully shortly before she took ill!" I took a deep breath in the silence that greeted my words. "Do you know what was troubling her? Something must have been, to change her so."

Mincy was silent so long, I turned to Laura, who averted her face. I said, "Well?"

"Madame Sevier, nearly everybody got a personal devil

what drives 'em. I treated Andy and he were bad bruised." Her black, impenetrable eyes flicked Laura, then returned to me. "But I don't know what drove Miss Yve to do it."

"Can't you venture a guess?" I asked desperately.

"What good a guess do you, ma'am? That ain't answer your question. It ain't goin' to comfort you neither. Best we all accepts what we can't change."

I had the feeling I was fighting something I could not see, and I knew no more about my sister's death than I had before. Only corroboration of the things told me by others, this time laced with a bit of philosophical advice that comforted me not a whit.

On the way back to Cloudmont my silence seemed to worry Laura. "Don't you feel better, knowing Yve's death couldn't really be helped, Lilibel—that she was desperately and fatally ill?" she asked anxiously.

"Should I?" I asked moodily, thinking of the pool of sweat, the open window with December wind sweeping over my sick sister, of her failing to waken and close it. "The Yve others have described to me is not the Yve I remember." No, I did not feel better, but I had reached a point beyond which I could not peer.

Laura said hesitantly, "People change, Lilibel. We all do——"

"Don't fret, Laura," I interrupted with forced cheerfulness. "I shall get over it eventually."

"Of course you shall." There was great relief in her words. And we chatted inconsequentially until we reached Cloudmont.

The week before we were to leave for Richmond, March blustered in on strong winds and I sensed a gentle stirring of things in the earth. The chief gardener rounded up his workers and when I looked out mornings from my north window, I could see them hoeing, spreading mulch, and clipping at the richly dark green boxwood hedges. The long sweep of lawn that formed the bowling green looked fresh and new. I wanted to raise the window and drink in the sunlit air, but I knew it was cold, for the gardeners' breath made little clouds before their noses.

However, after breakfast when Laura and I went for

our morning ride on our little mares, it seemed quite warm. We talked of the upcoming trip to Richmond and then she regaled me with details about the hunt that would be held at Cloudmont the end of the month.

" 'Twill be informal, compared to the ones in England, for we have made many of our own rules. 'Tis a happy, helter-skelter thing, you'll see."

"Who will come?"

"Oh, the Montagues, the Chenaults, the Livingstons and the Reeds—and their son, Clay, will come up from William and Mary to ride, too."

"Will Amanda be allowed to ride with us?"

"If she is, 'twill be the first time Mary has permitted it."

"*Tiens!* The girl will soon be sixteen! I shall ask Mary myself."

Laura smiled. "You're a good friend to have, Lilibel. I hope you will be so quick to stand by me if the occasion arises."

"You may be sure I shall. Now if only I could persuade you to stand by Judith and get Railo away from that awful Jabez Livingston."

"You are right," Laura said abruptly. "We will go over there this very afternoon. I will make him such an offer, his avaricious soul will be unable to resist it."

My spirits lifted markedly. Early afternoon found both of us ensconced in the polished Madison carriage, with Noah and Henry Pepper acting as coachman and footman, on our way down the long graveled road toward the Livingston plantation.

It was my first trip on the Richmond road. We followed it through the woods, past turns that branched off to Rose Hill and Tulip Grove. As we passed Lindens I remarked to Laura how beautiful the country was.

"Yes, and the homes of our neighbors are beautiful. But none can match Cloudmont. Their kitchens are built away from the house and the servants have to bring food through the weather to the tables. Though the Montagues do have a covered walkway between kitchen and house, 'tis open and the weather blows through."

"It appears the first Thomas Madison was a thoughful builder."

" 'Twas Andrew attached the kitchen to the house by means of the pantry and morning room." There was the usual edge in her voice as she gave Andrew credit. She talked on of the neighbors to the west of Cloudmont until at last, Henry Pepper turned the horses in between two tall brick pillars and down a winding road toward our destination.

I was much impressed by Livingston's plantation, but as Laura had remarked, the kitchen was placed at a goodly distance from the beautiful house. Like Cloudmont, it was Georgian colonial and exquisitely appointed. The Livingstons, though unaware we were coming to visit, welcomed us warmly.

They had a huge staff of black slaves, all quiet, well trained, and unobtrusive as they circled about us. I glanced into their dark, smooth faces as they moved silently, taking our wraps, bringing linen and silver service, fine china and trays laden with a variety of delicious pastries. Their eyes were downcast and they were gravely polite and subservient to Anna Livingston's crisp orders.

Jabez and Anna were childless, and looking into their pale eyes, I could not repress a shudder of relief that it was so.

Gracefully pouring tea, Anna said, "Jabez is just back from Washington and has the most interesting news—or rumors, I suppose I should say."

Laura, who was anxious to put off her reason for coming, asked quickly, "Do tell us?"

"First of all, there is a great to-do amongst the officials in the government." She put on a mysterious smile. "They say the president has embarked upon a venture of such magnitude as to well nigh shake the foundations of our nation."

"Good heavens!" Laura was impressed. "Whatever about? Not war with the French or the English again, surely?"

"Not war," Jabez said portentously, "but the results will be the same without bloodshed possibly."

"Then you know what it is?" I asked.

He frowned. "Not exactly. Only that it will affect the nation tremendously. Of course, if you can trust a man of Jefferson's peculiar habits."

"I thought he was the great egalitarian," I remarked dryly. "Is it not his philosophy that equality and freedom are for all Americans, and is he not adamantly against the rise of any aristocracy in America—such as we, in France, had until ten years ago?"

Anna laughed. "I'm sure Jabez is thinking of Jefferson's private tastes. Surely you read the newspapers?"

"Occasionally," answered Laura, sipping her tea and daintily eating a pastry.

"Then you must know about his Sally at Monticello?" Anna said delicately.

"Don't go any further, Anna dear," Jabez said sternly.

"I don't know what you're talking about," Laura said bluntly.

Jabez rose and went to a tall, gleaming *secrétaire* and took a well-thumbed newspaper from a drawer, coming back to present it to Laura. "I'd rather my wife did not speak of such matters," he said, tucking his mouth about the words with relish. "But you may read for yourself what is common knowledge."

Laura held the paper so that I might read as well. Jabez had circled a portion of an article with a firm quill.

It is well known that the man, whom it delighteth the people to honor, keeps and for many years has kept, as his concubine, one of his slaves. Her name is Sally. The name of her oldest is Tom. His features are said to bear a striking, though sable, resemblance to the president himself. The boy is of ten or twelve years of age.

I glanced at the heading on the paper and saw that it was the *Richmond Recorder*, dated September 2, 1802.

"Of course, Sally Hemings is very beautiful, they say. She is half sister to the president's late wife, Martha Wayles Jefferson," Anna said, her pale little eyes scanning our faces hopefully for signs of shock and outrage.

"I don't believe it," Laura said flatly.

"It's true, all right," Jabez put in. "I've been to Monticello—on business of course—and I had occasion to see this Sally. I must say, she's beautiful, damn near white and with long black hair. They have four other children, I hear." Jabez's colorless eyes held a depth of salacious enjoyment. I noted how quiet the black butler and maid had become. " 'Tis said that the president's own wife—he was widowed at thirty-nine, you know—acknowledged Sally and some of her brothers as her kin. Seems her father, after four daughters by three white wives, took a slave on his plantation, the daughter of an English sea captain and an African slave woman, as his—ah, how to put it? I'll use the editor, Mr. Callender's choice—his 'concubine.' She bore him six children, the youngest being this Sally, who came to Monticello along with Martha Wayles as her inheritance from John Wayles, her own and Sally's father."

I was fascinated by this man's leering enjoyment as he dug into the relations surrounding Thomas Jefferson's life. While I did not approve of Jefferson's ideas regarding the aristocracy, I thought his private life should be his own. Jabez took my still face as being rapt with attention, for he continued his dialogue, while his wife looked on with an insinuating smile.

He said, "Naturally, this sort of behavior revolts me. I was an ardent supporter of Mr. Jefferson during the Revolution and afterward, from the time of my youth onward—until all these sordid details came out about him. I think the siring of mulatto children is vicious and his blatant living with a Negress most repellent."

"I thought you said this girl, Sally, was three-quarters white," I remarked blandly.

He replied with force, "It doesn't matter how small the amount of Negro blood she has—she is tainted and therefore beneath him. Negroes should live only with each other—*only with each other*."

"In that case," I replied smoothly, "you will be happy about the errand that brings us to visit you today."

"Eh? What's that?" He was momentarily taken aback by my abrupt turn of the conversation.

I looked at Laura, who was staring at me fixedly. I glanced back into Jabez's face. "Laura's Judith and your Railo are much in love. We have come to see if we cannot arrange for them to be together at Cloudmont."

"Eh?"

"Of course, you yourself have said they should live only with each other," I prodded. "Believing as you do, I know you will want to sell Railo to Laura."

Anna said swiftly, "It would be better if Laura sold

Judith to me. Railo has a cabin of his own, by himself here at Livingston's. Jabez will gladly buy her."

"Judith has been with me since she was eight years old. I cannot sell her." Laura's face had paled and her lips were set.

Jabez's eyes gleamed. "You know Railo cost me a thousand, and he's the best field hand and foreman I've ever had, even if he is a wayward buck. I won't part with him."

"I'll give you two thousand for him," Laura said in a controlled voice.

Jabez pursed his thin lips and pulled at the beaked nose. The two house slaves had drawn unobtrusively near and I glimpsed three more black faces peering at the door's edge.

"Hmmm. I don't believe I could replace Railo," he said, dropping his hand to his chin and pulling at it thoughtfully.

"I'll give you three thousand," Laura said with sudden desperation, and the room grew very quiet.

I drew a sharp breath. "Surely you can replace him for that amount, Mr. Livingston."

His head came up and his eyes beneath his brows were sharp as rapiers. "I think not, Madame Sevier."

"You must have another reason for keeping him, then, Mr. Livingston," I said coldly. "For even I, inexperienced as I am in such matters, know you could replace him three times over with the amount Laura has offered."

He laughed shortly and Anna's accompanying smile was grim. "Possibly, madame, possibly. Sell him, I will not. But I'll give Laura a thousand for Judith."

Laura put down her teacup with restraint and we both rose to our feet. "If you should change your mind, Jabez," Laura said, "I will have three thousand in gold ready for you at Cloudmont."

"Surely you aren't going to take your leave so summarily," Anna protested.

"We must," Laura said coolly, drawing on her gloves. "We are going to Richmond to visit and do some shopping at this week's end. Lilibel and I must do some packing as the day draws nearer."

"How lovely," Anna said enviously. "It's been months

since I've been to Richmond. Life is so gay there. I've often told Jabez we should build a town house there, as the Madisons did, and remain in Richmond every winter. Summer is the time for the Livingston plantation." She gave Jabez a wounded glance.

They followed us to the door, and one of the maids scurried to inform Noah and Henry Pepper that we were ready to leave.

As we stood in the open door saying our good-bys, Henry and Noah came around the side of the house with the carriage. Each dismounted and stood by to help us ascend into the vehicle.

"Hope you're not offended because I can't come to part with Railo," Jabez said jocularly. "After all, you feel the same way about Judith as I do about my boy."

"Not quite," Laura said, her blue eyes flashing. "I would never beat Judith."

Jabez laughed. "Railo's a better boy for the beatings he gets. It's the only thing slaves understand."

"We disagree," Laura replied, and I felt my lip curl with scorn for this man and his wife.

Anna said, "We have so enjoyed your visit, ladies. You so rarely come calling. To have you, Madame Sevier, is a special treat." She looked at me and there was spite in the smiling eyes. "Since you are of the French aristocracy, I would have thought you more sympathetic to our troubles with the slaves."

I said icily, "My dear Madame Livingston, no decent aristocrat ever took up a sword—or a whip—except in self-defense." I was amused by the slow flood of color in the gossipy woman's face. "Our visit has been most informative," I added, and swept out on the granite square of steps without a backward glance.

Laura and I were silent as we entered the carriage, assisted by Henry Pepper and Noah. We did not speak until we had clattered down the long, graceful drive. Then Laura said with repressed fury, "That terrible man and woman! I'm so glad you had the wit to put her in her place. They're enough to make even *me* believe in abolition."

I said thoughtfully, "The seeds of tragedy are buried in oppession. Believe me, Laura, I know from experience."

"Now you sound like George and Andrew," she said wearily. "The great plantations, which are what this country's economy is based on, depend on slave labor to survive."

"And you sound like Jabez Livingston. You know that Andrew and George have proved that slave labor is not a necessity to a successful plantation."

"Cloudmont is an exception. Not everyone can have tenant farmers and white help."

"Not always white help. Just paid help, from free men."

"Ah, Lilibel, we are poles apart. I cannot make you understand the good that arises from slavery."

"No. You cannot, Laura. No good arises from slavery."

She laughed suddenly. "We'll not quarrel, my dear. I'm much too fond of you, and you may come to see my point of view one day."

I was with Laura when she told Judith of her failure to move Jabez and his wife. Sorrow and frustration, as well as affection for Judith, showed on Laura's face. My throat tightened when I saw Judith's thick-lashed black eyes fill with tears, and I knew I would never see Laura's point of view on slavery.

The following morning, Yve's tombstone arrived from Richmond. It was an elaborate marble stone with an angel whose wings were spread above the stone itself, which was inscribed with her birth and death date and her name. With Seton Cambridge officiating, we had a little ceremony in the churchyard as it was placed at the head of her grave.

I had steeled myself against the moment and though my eyes were dry through the brief service, my heart ached unbearably. It was with sad relief that I followed the others from the small churchyard cemetery, leaving the winged angel to watch over the remains of my beautiful sister.

Cornelia sent Henry Pepper and Abigail to Richmond two days ahead of us loaded with provisions and orders to galvanize the resident servants in the town house into preparations for our arrival.

Andrew and George, who returned later that day from

their morning round of the plantation and tenant farmers, were apprised of the fact that the entourage would take leave of Cloudmont early Saturday morning.

George said with a quick grin, "That will give Andrew and me plenty of time to arrange our affairs with the men building our new warehouse there. We have to leave for Norfolk and Hampton Tuesday."

Cornelia replied severely, "But I want you both back in Richmond for the dinner and dance that we will have on March twentieth."

"We shall try, Mother, but much depends on how things go in Norfolk," Andrew said firmly. Then, with a slight smile at Amanda, "I hear you have prevailed on your mother to let you remain at Cloudmont after all."

Amanda shrugged, lashes veiling her shining eyes. "After all, Clay will be in William and Mary all through March. I shall only have the fall of the Roman Empire to comfort me." She caught Mélisse and Timothy by the hand. "Come along, children—time for lessons!"

Seton Cambridge called to the children in his gentle voice, but his eyes, behind the little round metal-rimmed glasses, were fixed on Laura worshipfully. She was opening a polished humidor for George to fill his pipe. She offered it to Andrew afterward, her glance at him full of the strange dislike she bore him.

"We shall have fun while they are gone," Amanda told Timothy gaily. Her voice was light and happy and I had the feeling she knew something her mother did not.

The thought must have occurred to Mary, for she said sharply, "Amanda, you will mind Louise while we are gone—and not go riding off on your mare to Tulip Grove to see the Reeds. Clay will be at the university, his mother told me so only two days ago." She sounded as if she were reassuring herself.

"Yes, Mother." Amanda paused in the doorway to the great hall. "Whatever mischief could we get into in so short a time? You will all be back by the twenty-second to arrange for the hunt."

I saw my chance and took it swiftly. "I hope you will join us for the hunt, Amanda."

Amanda's eyes grew brilliant with excitement, "Oh,

Mother, I'm really quite old enough! Clay was riding to the hounds when he was but fourteen. He told me——"

"Clay, Clay!" Mary said peevishly, "I've told you, Amanda, you are far too young to have that boy calling on you."

I said smoothly, "Well, he will hardly be calling on her in the melee of a hunt."

Mary was forced to agree, and the issue was settled. Amanda would ride with us for the hunt. She would even have a new riding habit, brought back from Richmond by her reluctant mother. She shot me a grateful glance as she followed Seton into the great hall.

After the youngsters' departure from the drawing room, we spoke of the coming trip while the men sat and drew on their pipes, listening to the conversation and occasionally joining in.

Laura said the Stuarts were planning to hold many galas and entertainments, parties, and dinners for us. It seemed they were anxious to meet me again and glean the latest Paris fashions from me. It appeared my countrymen were having a marked influence on American fashions, kneebreeches slowly giving way to the pantaloons, which fitted the gentlemen's slim hips and legs snugly and attractively. I knew what the fashions were, I thought to myself dryly, but I was a poor example of them in the rather innocuous dresses that I owned.

CHAPTER 8

The chill, brisk morning of March seventh arrived. The carriage was full to overflowing with boxes, portmanteaus, and cases of luggage. We four women were seated comfortably in the spacious interior of the vehicle, but part of the luggage had to be inside with us. Laura had been persuaded to leave Judith behind and make do with Abigail. She complained about it, but I glimpsed Judith's shining eyes and I knew she was thinking of the nights she would meet Railo while we were gone. I also knew intuitively that Clay Reed would find occasion to leave William and Mary and meet with Amanda during our absence, and Mary had nothing to thank for that but her own rigid discipline.

As we made our farewells, Laura embraced Andy fervently. Mary embraced her own children and then spent some time with Andy as well. I clung to Mélisse until she wriggled restively in my arms. I hated to leave her this first time, but she had no qualms at all. During the hubbub of good-bys, the men came trotting up on their stallions from the stables. They would ride alongside the carriage all the way to Richmond and after their business there was transacted, they would go to Norfolk and Hampton. Charles Alexander sat his stallion with easy grace, which was matched by the lithe forms of George and Andrew. Looking at them, I could not help thinking what a handsome trio they were, their kinship undeniable in the set of their firm jaws, long, high-bridged noses, and curved mouths. Their horses pranced restlessly about the carriage, anxious to be off down the long winding road.

At last, with final admonitions to the servants who stood on the granite steps before the rear of the big house, Ephraim snapped his whip. We were on our way. The drive was a fairly long one, some thirty miles or so, taking most of the day, but with a basket of delectables prepared for us by Mrs. Beady, we ate and talked and the time passed swiftly.

As we approached Richmond, evening was falling, and Cornelia and Mary undertook to tell me something of the city. The population was not quite five thousand. Its chief taverns were the Eagle Hotel, on the south side of Main Street between Twelfth and Thirteenth, and Boler's Ordinary, on Main Street. The Eagle had been built in 1798, so it was fairly new. It was a large building forming the four sides of a square with an entrance under a large archway. It was really the chief hotel in the city and much frequented by members of the Legislature, Richmond being the capitol of the Commonwealth of Virginia. The Ordinary was a plain, one-story wooden building, a place of much resort. The Washington, facing the public square, afforded thirsty members of the Legislature an opportunity of imbibing toddies and juleps to help offset the tedium of a dry speaker, or to assist them in their patriotic endeavors to serve the public.

I stared through the twilight at all of the buildings that made up the little city. Actually, it was rough and very much needed improvement, especially the upper part. Main Street was so rugged that carriages could scarcely pass and it formed a disagreeable path for pedestrians, so we bypassed most of it.

The Capitol stood alone on its square, an unenclosed common marked by two deep ravines. The hillsides were covered with galled places and bare of trees or shrubs, with only a few stunted pine bushes scattered here and there. Running through the common between the governor's house and the Capitol and passing down Eleventh Street to Main was a wagon road; all of the country produce was brought into the city on it. Some of the Allegheny members were accustomed, so Mary said, to come down to the Legislature on horseback. A five-gallon bowl of toddy was made daily in the governor's house for their refreshment after they had closed the day's labor in the Capitol. Houses extended up Broad Street and a large pond of water, fed by rains, stood on part of Shocko Hill. Cornelia said it afforded skating ground for the children in winter. Far up the end of Broad Street was the Madison town house, and a very fine edifice it was indeed.

Built of the same red brick as Cloudmont, it was three stories tall, long and narrow, and close beside its neighbors. Smoke was pouring from its several chimneys and the marble stoop looked scrubbed and polished. In one of the front windows, the curtains were drawn back, revealing a table with a glowing lantern beside a vase of dried and painted flowers, adding a gay touch to the darkening evening.

Ephraim and Noah drove the carriage down a graveled drive beside the tall, narrow house in the chill, quiet twilight and we debarked, hurrying in through the rear entrance to the foyer. A bevy of servants, Abigail and Henry Pepper among them, met us at the door and divested us of our cloaks.

The house seemed surprisingly large when entered. The rooms were smaller than those at Cloudmont, but the ceilings were quite as high. Our bedrooms were on the second floor and the servants occupied the rooms on the third floor. Abigail and Henry had done their job well, for there was a blazing fire in each room. Despite the cold weather, it was warm and cozy throughout the house. I shared a room with Laura while Mary and her mother had separate rooms, as did the three men, Andrew, George, and Charles.

The maids brought us hot water in hip baths and we were all able to refresh ourselves before dinner. After dinner we sat and talked over coffee in a large salon. I gathered from the conversation that Richmond was a lively place, more famous for its amusments in racing, drinking, and frolicking generally than for anything of a greater cultural character. Its citizens seemed to have abundant leisure and spent much of their time seeking amusement. Society consisted of the families of the neighboring planters, who left their estates to the management of overseers and spent the larger part of the year in Richmond, returning to their country homes only occasionally during the winter and permanently for the summer. The Madisons, I had observed long ago, though eminently qualified as members of society, did not belong to this idle group.

To this circle of planters were added the better class of merchants, of which John Stuart was one, as well as resident citizens and the state officers with their families. I could see why a woman like Anna Livingston wanted her husband to build a home here and join in the festivities that evidently were continuous in Richmond. It was a city of mixtures, the rough blended with the smooth, when the cultured met with the raw woodsmen who came to town with their wares.

We talked of the ball to be held at the Stuarts' the next evening in our honor, and of the seamstresses the three women knew and patronized in Richmond. It was agreed that the day following the ball, we would make a sortie into town and investigate the stores and shops with a view to acquiring a wardrobe for me and refurbishing the others'.

In the lamp glow about us, I looked at the faces of these people whom I was coming to know so well. Andrew's, brooding, thoughtful—George's, tanned and laugh-lined—Charles's, reckless and friendly. Then I observed the women, Mary with her gaze more often than not turned worshipfully on Andrew, Cornelia serene and disciplined, and Laura's mobile beautiful features concealing from the world an inner turmoil. I thought briefly of Yve among them, and tried to stem the resentment in my heart as I realized she was scarcely missed.

We retired early and as I sank thankfully into the deep feather bed beside Laura, I missed Mélisse dreadfully, but I determined to let myself flow with the current that moved the lives of these people who had made me so welcome.

The following day something of a crisis developed when it was learned that I had no ballgown. Most of the afternoon was spent fitting me with one of the many Laura kept at the Madison town house. She was larger than I, and it took the combined efforts of Abigail, Mary, and myself to take it up and fit me properly. But by four o'clock, an ice-blue satin evening dress that fitted me very well hung in the large armoire of the room Laura and I shared.

Later, as we were dressing for the Stuarts' ball in our honor, Laura remarked, "I should like you to have had a gown to match your remarkable eyes, Lilibel—a sort of honey gold, I think." We were putting the finishing touches to our toilette before going down to join the others.

I adjusted tiny puffed sleeves and the rather startlingly low neckline that arched provocatively, heart shaped, over my breasts. The pale blue satin fell straight to the tops of the pale blue half-slippers that I had laced on my feet. I wondered if my sister had ever danced in the slippers, for they looked almost new.

"I feel favored by fortune to wear this," I told my companion, who was a vision in a pale yellow that almost matched her hair. "You look perfectly beautiful, Laura," I added sincerely.

She gave me a swift, light kiss and said, "You've had a hand in my appearance, darling. This lip salve from Paris is the answer to my pale mouth. You must tell me where to send for it. I shall have the *Tern* bring me back a case of it, I vow."

"I'll be glad to share mine with you until we can order some from France," I replied, following her from the room. I wore a borrowed fur-lined cloak of Laura's, and was very grateful for it, as the air was chill now in the stairwell of the house.

At the bottom of the dark stairs, the English housemaid Mollie took the oil lamp from Laura and stood holding it as the others gathered in the foyer to join us.

"I'm so glad the men are going in the carriage with us," Cornelia said happily. Mary took Andrew's arm possessively and snuggled close to him. I saw Laura's lip curl momentarily in the shimmering light from the lantern held by Henry Pepper. He and Jason Morebridge stood by as coachman and footman.

Charles Alexander, who had attached himself to Laura's side, said with satisfaction, " 'Tis much too cold to be riding horseback tonight. We've had a sharp change in weather."

As Cornelia ascended to sit on the seat beside George and me, Henry took the small, bright lantern and affixed it to a niche beside the carriage door, where it cast flickering light over the interior.

It seemed to me that George took up an uncommonly large space, for his long, hard thigh pressed warmly against mine. He appeared to have difficulty in placing his arms, and finally laid one along the back of the carriage seat, where it brushed me regularly. Though I knew George's intentions were not serious, his touch was pleasurable and I was unwillingly excited by it.

When he leaned his head down, his breath was warm on my cheek as he murmured, "You smell almost as beautiful as you look." I was hard put not to lift my face to his and smile provocatively.

" 'Tis French *parfum*, George," I replied sedately.

"I am finding anything French utterly irresistible." He was flirting with me outrageously under the noses of the rest of his family, who continued to discuss the weather. He murmured *sotto voce*, "You know well you wear that scent to inflame. Are you so cold, knowing that you have made me feel so—warmly toward you?"

I had to smother laughter. "Your feelings are easily stirred, I'll wager."

I could see across from us Charles had finally succeeded in capturing Laura's hand where her fur-lined cape had fallen back. He held it tightly imprisoned between his thigh and her skirts. Mary was engaging her brother and mother with some tale about the children.

George bent his head even nearer mine. "You do me great injustice, madame. I am hard to stir, but you stir me violently."

"Then you are so jaded—so often stirred in the past—that only I can stir you now?" I parried, glancing at him from beneath my lashes.

He drew a quick breath and muttered, "By God, you're a temptation. If we were alone, I'd kiss you until——"

"What are you two plotting?" Andrew asked suddenly. Then lightly, "From the look of you, it can be no less than the downfall of the nation."

George did not move away from me as he said dryly, "When it has just arisen, brother? Hardly."

All eyes were on us now. Mary looked faintly resentful and I felt my own unaccountable animosity for her rise as she said, "You certainly look conspiratorial."

"We are conspiring," I said smoothly. "George has just promised to introduce me to all the eligible bachelors in Richmond."

There was general laughter and under the cover of it, George whispered, "What a charming liar you are, Liliane. And it is with great reluctance that I shall introduce you to any man at all."

For the benefit of the others I laughed gaily, "Why, George, I do believe you would marry me off to any man, when I've only come to Cloudmont."

"He wants only to insure you a merry evening, Lilibel," Mary said, all good humor now.

The others joined in light conversation, and soon our short drive up Broad Street ended before the brightly lit Stuart house.

As we took the steps to the landing of the small porch, we could hear the sound of music and a babble of happy voices. The house was as tall as that of the Madisons, and perhaps a shade wider.

Inside we were enveloped in a merry crowd of greeters, Lucy and John Stuart heading them. Lucy hugged each of us in turn, her face rosy with excitement. In the foyer above us hung a gleaming crystal chandelier with half a hundred tapers, casting a flood of becoming light over the gathering.

Laura called, "Lucy—we are going up to your dressing room and put our hair to rights." She had taken the hood from her curls and I thought them in charming disarray, but I followed her and Mary up the stairs. We passed a series of lighted bedrooms and went into a large one containing the great wall mirror that Laura sought.

An English maid followed us up the stairs and took our cloaks. There was a bright blaze in the fireplace, but the room was chilly and I heard the wind plucking at shutters beyond the windows. The weather had indeed changed; it was much colder.

After a summary patting of curls and adjustment of clothing, the three of us started down the hall lit by long tapers in wall sconces.

"Doesn't Andrew look handsome in his new pantaloons and waistcoat?" Mary asked, her dark eyes bright with excitement.

"Yes," Laura replied shortly, "but you'd think he looked handsome in a towsack, Mary."

Mary laughed. "That's true—I would. But I will add that I think Charles and George look handsome, too."

"Generous," Laura said dryly, as we reached the bottom of the stairs, "and quite true."

Another pretty English maid approached us with a tray of sweetmeats and Laura popped a sugared date into her mouth. "Thank God 'tis warmer down here," she murmured to me. "I vow I near froze when I visited here last month." Mary plunged into the crowd beyond, seeking her brother.

I looked thoughtfully after the maid and around the large ballroom at her counterparts. I murmured in surprise, "All the servants appear to be English."

"Has no one told you about the Stuarts?" Laura gave me an amused smile. "They are even more antislavery than George and Andrew. They are working here in Richmond—and throughout the states—with a group that is raising huge funds to buy up a great tract of land in Africa just for the freed slaves. They plan to buy the freedom of every slave they can and then ship them to this land, where they can make new homes for themselves."

"*Mon Dieu!* So they think that is the solution. Are Andrew and George subscribers to this plan?"

Laura laughed. "They would have been, but they asked our slaves if they wanted to be shipped back to Africa."

"Didn't they?"

"I should say not. Some of them are third generation and think of themselves as Americans. There were Negroes who fought on our side in the Revolution, Lilibel."

"Then they *are* Americans."

"But slaves still."

"And you think that is right?"

Laura shrugged. "For some it is. Come now, Lilibel, let us not get into another of our arguments over this touchy subject. Let's enjoy the ball. Here comes Charles, looking miserably handsome in his new pantaloons, and would you look at that new pin in his cravat. I'd swear it was a diamond! The way he spends the money he earns! Good evening again, Charles."

There was a smile on his handsome face and his black eyes fastened hungrily on Laura's fair face as the orchestra struck up a gay tune. The brightly appareled crowd eddied about us as he took her in his arms to dance.

When Charles claimed Laura, I felt myself caught up in a strong embrace and led out on the polished floor. I looked up into Andrew's white smile with a faint frown.

The smile disappeared. "You think it is too soon after my wife's death to dance with my sister-in-law?" he asked as we swung apart, then together in an old-fashioned minuet.

"Yes," I replied straightforwardly. "But you do things differently here in America. Perhaps it is not too soon according to American standards."

"I'm sorry if we offend you here in Richmond," he said, his face brooding once more. "They say in England that we are crude and lack the manners of our English cousins. Perhaps we are more offensive to the French, who have even better manners than the English."

I looked into his dark eyes and felt my heart softening at the genuine sorrow I saw there. "Traditions differ," I said gently. "I know you mourn my sister."

"More than you know," He said bitterly, swinging me forcefully so that I bumped against his hard thighs. Then, turning skillfully, he moved out of the group and through a double door into a large dining salon. "Would you like a glass of punch?" He gestured to the enormous crystal bowl in the center of the table and I nodded breathlessly. Even as he served me, one of the butlers approached with glasses of brandy on a silver tray.

Andrew took one, saying, "I wish it were warm enough for us to go into the gardens. The Stuarts are famous for their gardens—small, but English-perfect." He sipped his brandy, and I drank the punch slowly.

"When does spring really come to Virginia, Andrew?"

"April is the happiest time. Then all the trees are budding and the first flowers come up."

"It will soon be here. Only three more weeks." The punch was delicious and potent. I looked at Andrew suddenly through my sister's eyes. He was tall and appealing and I resisted a strong urge to touch him. There was something mysterious about Andrew, as if he bore some secret burden that was almost unendurable. It set all my feminine sympathy throbbing. He caught my eyes and the expression in them, for he took my free hand and held it warmly.

"Comfort me, little sister-in-law," he murmured, his eyes holding mine. "I am very lonely."

I took a deep swallow of punch, its warmth exciting me. "You have a wonderful family." I glanced through the doorway into the room in time to see Mary glide by in the arms of some guest, and her eyes rested on Andrew for a flashing instant. I continued, "And they love you dearly. Then, too, you have Yve's little son to comfort you." The dining room was nearly empty but for an occasional servant going in and out through the wide doors.

Andrew set his brandy glass down on the table and, still holding my hand with one of his, tipped my face up. Stooping swiftly, he brushed my lips with his and a sharp thrill cut through me, even as I summoned guilt.

"You remind me so of Yve—when first we married," he said roughly. "I was mad about her. I forgot all other women the moment I saw her. What a pity it—" He broke off, half turning away.

"It did not last," I finished flatly. "You see, others have been talking to me."

His face paled, I thought, and he said in a low voice, "Loose tongues are an abomination, Lilibel. You must not believe——"

"Ah. So here you are!" It was George's deep, laughing voice. "I've been searching for the lady with the extraordinary eyes, to claim her for a dance."

I looked at him with annoyance. I had wanted to continue my conversation with Andrew. "Good evening again, George," I said coolly.

"Finish that punch, madame. The next dance is mine. If you have no objections, brother?" He made a punctilious bow to Andrew, but there was no real question in the words.

In a few moments, I was being recklessly spun about in the thick of the dancers, so breathlessly there was no time for talk. George was an excellent dancer, better even than his brother, who was a good dancer indeed. I found myself thoroughly enjoying our speechless and vigorous activity, and when it was over, my breath was coming fast.

"You're a fine partner in dancing," George said, the twinkling black eyes fastened to mine. "As I imagine you are in every endeavor."

"You shall never have the opportunity to find out," I said coolly. My quick retort seemed to please him, for he threw back his head with whole-hearted laughter, and I noticed others looking at us with varying degrees of amusement and interest.

"I can be very persuasive, dear sister-in-law. And my intentions are never honorable."

"Your intentions, like the rest of you, are of no interest to me," I replied.

"Andrew is more to your taste?"

"Much," I replied without thinking. Damn the man and his sharp insight! I added with composure, "That is to say, he is much more of a gentleman than you, George."

"So Andrew draws you, does he? Ah, well, I haven't the glamor of the recently bereaved. There's no incentive for you to comfort me, darling Lilibel, but I could give you more pleasure, for I have fewer compunctions about the arts of love."

"And all without the benefit of clergy," I replied with an impudence of my own. I turned away indifferently as the music stopped, but he caught my arm.

"Stay. Let me tell you how lovely your golden eyes are, set off by that pale blue dress. How did you find one on such short notice, my dear?"

How observant the man was! "Laura was kind enough to lend it to me."

"You must have sewed somewhat upon it, for our Laura is larger than you— Well, I'll be damned!"

"What is it?" I looked up at him in surprise, to find his eyes riveted across the room.

"Those two charmers, Anna and Jabez Livingston, have just come in."

"I'm sure their servants must be thanking *le bon Dieu* for their absence."

"I perceive we have something in common—a distaste for the Livingstons."

"One of very few," I replied, glancing at the beaming couple as they made their way around the room with the Stuarts.

George's face was sober and he spoke half to himself. "Those two are breeders of trouble—for all of us." Then, with fresh impertinence, "I believe you enjoyed that last dance with me. Shall we dance the next?"

"I think not, George," I answered, drifting away. "I did not get to finish my punch."

His smile deepened knowingly and I felt a strong desire to slap his face soundly. I knew he thought I was going to seek out Andrew once more. For this reason, when our host Stuart approached me, I gave him a dazzling smile and accepted his invitation to dance immediately.

After that, the evening went swiftly. I danced with both handsome and plain, charming men all, and found myself having a very good time. I was even courteous to Anna and Jabez, who were so pleased at having been invited they were not even unpleasant to the servants.

The Reeds, Chenaults, and Montagues were there, all of them having town houses in Richmond as well. Young Clay was not with his parents and when I asked about him, they replied he was at the university. Still, I wondered if Amanda got word to him somehow. I had an intuition that Clay would come calling at Cloudmont—or more dangerous still, the two would arrange to meet away from their homes—while Mary was gone these two weeks.

By the time the evening was over, I had made many new acquaintances and was comfortably tired after having danced the entire evening. It was near two in the morning when the Madison entourage entered the carriage. Despite the hour, when Laura and I reached our room and disrobed, we found we were not too tired to discuss our evening.

"I saw you with Charles," I said, drying my hands on a delicately embroidered towel at the washstand after bathing my face. "You looked to be quarreling."

"We seem to quarrel all the time," Laura sighed, slipping a cambric nightgown over her head. "But there's something about him that I— Well, it's very difficult to stay angry with Charles. He can be so winning when he chooses." Her voice hardened. "But I am angry with him now and I intend to stay so. I shall ignore him after this."

"I can't see why, Laura. He is so in love with you."

"He accuses me of the most outrageous things—of being still in love with Tom—or George—or even Andrew. That I'm too secretive and not open enough. That I have a tight, narrow little mind."

I had slipped into my gown and was brushing my long brown hair when there came a soft rap at our door. I halted the brush midair and looked at Laura, who returned my gaze with some apprehension. I went to the door. When I opened it, Charles Alexander stepped in before I had a chance to protest, closing it firmly behind him. Laura, who had no wrapper over her gown, ran to the armoire and put one on at once.

"Charles Alexander," she hissed, "what do you mean, coming into our bedroom at this hour?"

Charles smiled, which lit up his dark features and intensified his attractiveness. "I couldn't go to sleep on our quarrel, Laura darling. I don't think you can either."

"You assume too much. I shall sleep easily."

"I came to beg your forgiveness for the harsh things I said at the Stuarts'. You are not cold and calculating or narrow-minded, my dear. You know that." Though his words were soothing, his tone was arrogant.

"Whatever will people think if they find you in our bedroom?" Laura spoke softly, but she was very angry.

He strode toward her and she backed away. I stood by the dressing table, transfixed by the emotion that surged between the two.

"No one will be the wiser, Laura," he said, catching her shoulders in two strong hands.

She tried to twist away. "You can't behave like this before Lilibel! You will shock her out of her wits—as you are shocking me!"

He sent a mischievous dark glance at me. "Lilibel is French and the French are justly famous for their sympathy with *l'amour*, eh Lilibel?"

"Our reputation for that is greatly overrated, I think you should leave if Laura wishes you to," I said firmly.

Instead, he swept Laura into his arms and kissed her

slowly, deliberately, and deeply. For a moment her hands pushed against him, then fluttered about his shoulders in surrender. When at last he took his mouth from hers, he said roughly, "You love me and you know it, Laura. All your highflown pride notwithstanding. The sooner you recognize and accept it, the sooner we can find happiness together."

Laura burst into tears. "You don't understand, Charles. I can't tell you—why. But there are many reasons that I cannot love you. You have no name——"

"I certainly have. Alexander. Not Madison."

"You have nothing but your half-brothers' largesse to depend upon."

"I am a very necessary cog in the wheels of Cloudmont. And you and I could renovate and make a fine home out of Landon on the York, as well. I could put that old plantation back on its feet again."

"Oh, Charles," she cried despairingly, "You don't know—you can't understand. I *can't* marry you——"

"There, my darling," he soothed, stroking her tossed curls. "I'll go now." He released her and turned to me. "You are a lovely and understanding woman, Lilibel. It shows in all you do. I know you will keep our tryst a secret."

"If you will only go," I said desperately, "I promise to say nothing."

He gave me his reckless, charming smile and I found myself involuntarily returning it. The door closed silently behind him, and Laura threw herself across the bed in a storm of weeping. I made no move to comfort her, knowing instinctively she needed the release of emotion.

When at last she rose up, she said huskily, "You can stop brushing your hair now, dear, and come to bed. I'm over my tears."

I put down the brush and approached the bed. "Do you love him?" I asked gently.

"I must not love him." Her voice was bitter. "He is a bastard, even though he is a great planter's bastard."

"I do not think of him as a bastard," I said reflectively. "He has made his own identity, and the circumstances of his birth cannot detract from the man he has become." But I was troubled. Some deep inner self told me there was more in Laura's refusal to accept Charles's love than his illegitimacy, unacceptable as that might be.

"I've thought of all that." Her great blue eyes were veiled, secretive. "But the world looks at it differently."

I climbed the steps beside the bed and my fingers snuffed the candle on the nearby table, plunging us into silent darkness.

CHAPTER 9

The following morning George, Andrew, and Charles set out for Norfolk, over a hundred miles to the southeast. They would not return until our visit was almost over, sometime the following week. We did not see them off, for they departed before dawn.

The rest of us had a leisurely and delicious breakfast, which we were just finishing when Lucy Stuart came to the house. Her blue eyes flashed with pleasure as she announced she had her carriage outside and was ready to take us on a tour of the stores and shops in Richmond.

"We can get our seamstress, Betty and Jane Chandler, to make anything we can't find to suit us," she said briskly as we set out in the Stuart carriage. "John has some perfectly delectable materials in our store now—just in from your own country, Lilibel. They will make your mouth water. Silks, satins, muslins, cambric—even cloth of gold and fine laces. Oh, we will have such fun!"

I couldn't help my spirits rising. Just before we left, Cornelia sought me out where I was donning Laura's borrowed cloak. She put a small leather bag in my hand quietly, saying "There's fifty dollars in gold, my dear, for you to buy presents for the children and any small item that strikes your fancy."

I took it reluctantly but gratefully, unable to resist the prospect of returning to Cloudmont bearing gifts for the four young ones remaining there.

It *was* fun, as we went from one shop to another and tried on the lovely frocks and gowns they displayed. Cornelia was determined that I should lack nothing. Though my demurs and remonstrations were steady in the first two shops, she bought morning frocks, afternoon dresses, pelisses, and undergarments.

Then when we approached the third and last dress shop that Richmond boasted, Laura said, "Cornelia dear, you know the hunt is coming up and Lilibel has naught but that old blue riding habit of Yve's, and it's been torn."

Cornelia bustled into the shop, which bore a sign outside the door saying *Chandler Sisters, Ladies' Fine Clothing*. It was a small shop, crowded with displays of garments. A sign over a rear door proclaimed modestly, *Lingerie Shown on Request in This Private Room*.

The two sisters themselves, women of middle years and rather stout, came to serve us.

"I don't see a riding habit on display here," Cornelia said.

"I can do very well with the blue velvet—I've mended that tear so it scarce shows, Cornelia," I protested.

"Lilibel, my dear, do hush. I had completely forgotten the summer ball the Chenaults usually have around the first of August. You must have one more ballgown for that. And certainly you must have at least three riding habits."

Catching the arms of the two gentle sisters, Lucy brought them forward, announcing to me, "This is Betty and this is Jane Chandler. They can make *anything*—beautifully!"

I contracted for a lace-trimmed white silk ballgown and three riding habits, one of dark gold velveteen, one of black twill, and a lightweight summer muslin, to be made by the Chandler sisters of materials supplied from John Stuart's large store.

I returned for fittings during the following three days, between social functions planned by Lucy and Cornelia. There was a tea following the day of our shopping trip, a dinner the night following that, and numerous parties at the homes of various friends and acquaintances.

In the afternoons, we were allowed to nap, a rest much needed if we were to keep up with our busy social schedule. One day, just before the Madison men and Charles Alexander were to return, we attended a horse race, escorted by John Stuart. I was astounded to observe how excited Cornelia and the other ladies became, and even more surprised to see Cornelia lose fifty dollars in a bet with Lucy Stuart. I had heard of such races in France before the Terror, of course, but I was sure only the men bet openly on the horses.

By this time, I had made the acquaintance of several eligible men through the popular Laura, and she and I had been escorted to several social functions. I observed that both Laura and Mary Madison Jackson could easily have been married several times over, because both were attractive widows of substantial means. But they appeared indifferent. Of course, Mary was passionately fond of her family, and there were so many of them that she scarcely seemed to need the attentions of a husband. As for Laura, she was a puzzle. I could not understand her attitude. During our Richmond visit, she flirted outrageously, but veered swiftly away the moment any man became too serious with her.

When Andrew and his brothers returned, they were anxious to go on to Cloudmont, for they had been gone nearly two weeks. However, Lucy had planned another large dinner to be given the night before we left. George and Andrew demurred but they were prevailed upon to stay over one extra night, after Cornelia reminded them of their promise before we had left Cloudmont.

All three men were pleased with their transactions in Norfolk and I learned through Mary that George's new enterprise was the establishment of an importing firm in that city. Through all our social gatherings, there ran a broad streak of politics and much talk of negotiations between France and America; the same mysterious negotiations that Jabez Livingston had mentioned to Laura and me on our unsuccessful visit to their home. Now it appeared there was something quite portentous in the making.

As Laura and I dressed for the final dinner, Mary, who had finished her toilette, came into our room, and we chatted pleasantly.

"George thinks he's so foxy with this importing firm," she said fondly. "It's just a means to get away to sea again. He misses the *Tern* dreadfully—they have sent her off again, loaded to the gunnels, he says, with the last of the tobacco in the Madison warehouse in Norfolk."

"I'm surprised he didn't go with her," Laura said.

"He would have, if Andrew hadn't been so persuasive, I'll vow." Mary smiled. "But they have achieved their most important objective, Andrew says, with the purchase of another vessel—a schooner with more sail than even the *Tern*. 'Tis the *Anemone*, and she's carrying a cargo to England right now—American-made rum and cotton. Oh, my brothers are pleased with themselves!"

"How does Charles feel about it?" Laura asked, rubbing some of my lip salve on her delicately curved mouth.

"He's a bit more conservative in his pleasure. You know how he loves the land—Cloudmont especially. I think he fears the new ventures, importing and the *Anemone*, will take him away from it more."

"Perhaps that might be as well," Laura said moodily.

"Ah, Laura, you take Charles too seriously. You know his reputation with the ladies in Richmond." Mary's laugh was faintly contemptuous, but her eyes were veiled.

Color flooded into Laura's fine textured features, but she said nothing, and we all went down to partake in the final festivities.

The following morning, we set out for Cloudmont with a relieved Henry Pepper and Ephraim on the box, Noah having returned to Cloudmont. I gathered that Henry had not enjoyed his visit too much. He had stayed with Jason Morebridge, the rather supercilious houseman, and made himself useful in the serving of food and waiting table. At Cloudmont he ruled supreme, and satisfaction was etched on his long, mournful face as he took up the reins.

The Chandler sisters had finished my ballgown and all three riding rabits, so I was able to take my entire new wardrobe back with me. The carriage was indeed over-crowded with baggage and the new clothing all four of us women had acquired. For that reason, Andrew, George, and Charles had set out for home before dawn, leaving us to make the trip at a more leisurely pace.

Cornelia told us that Anna had prevailed upon Jabez Livingston to remain at the Eagle Hotel for another week for a series of parties that were to be given by the resident planters. Thinking of Judith and Railo, I rejoiced, for I knew it meant he could come to see her without fear of detection and punishment for another week at least.

When we reached Cloudmont that evening, I was met by a disaster that sent every thought but terror flying from my mind. Clementine met me at the rear visitors' entrance bursting with it.

"Oh, madame, thank God you've come! Little Mélisse is took bad sick. She can scarce breathe. Judith's been putting poultices——"

"*Bon Dieu*—let me go to her——" I brushed past Clementine and raced to the steps, flinging my reticule and the box containing presents to a chair in the great hall. Lifting my long skirt, I flew up the stairs. Another instant and I was in my room. The heavy drapes were drawn and a hot fire burned in the fireplace. Judith sat beside the bed, a pan of water on a small table beside her, a cloth draped over it.

Looking up, she said, "I been bathin' her face, she's so hot. I'm so glad you're home at last." The woman looked very fatigued and there were dark circles beneath her eyes.

Clementine, behind me, murmured, "Judith's been stayin' up ever night since she come down with this sickness."

I stooped over my child, putting my cheek to hers. It was fiery hot to touch. Her face was flushed and I could see that her fever was very high. My heart beat fast and heavily with dread, as I put my cool hands to each of her pink cheeks. The black crescents of her lashes did not move. She slept the deep stuporlike slumber that comes with high temperature.

"Doesn't seem like she can get a good breath, madame," Judith said in an exhausted voice. "When she coughs it's all rattly-like."

My heart took a sickening downward plunge. Like Yve's last illness! An involuntary groan escaped me before I realized the rest of the family had come quietly into the room.

I heard Mary hiss, "Clemmie—what of the other children? Have they been ill?"

"Timothy had a cold, but he's over it now." At that moment the boy and Andy burst into the room behind them, and were immediately shushed by Mary.

"How long has she been like this?" I asked, controlling a quiver in my voice by sheer will.

"She'd took sick two days ago, but just today it got so much worse."

Cornelia put out her hand to take mine. "Dear, do not be so frightened. We will send for Mincy."

"That's what you did for Yve, but she died just the same," I said a touch wildly, catching one of Mélisse's hot little hands that lay upon the cover.

George said, "I will ride to fetch Mincy immediately, Liliane. Mélisse is not Yve. She is young and she will recover." He was gone instantly.

Laura came to me. "Give me your cape, Lilibel. 'Tis too warm in here for it." She slipped the garment from my shoulders, adding "Judith, you look dead for sleep. Go to bed now."

Cornelia put in, "We will look after Mélisse now."

"You'll call me, Mistress Madison, if"—she let the sentence hang as I took her chair beside the bed, then finished with determined cheerfulness—"if you need me for anything."

"Of course," Mary said as she came to stand beside me. "Lilibel, do you not think we should bathe her face until the fever breaks?"

I looked up to see that Mary was quite pale with worry. She reached out to stroke one of Mélisse's hands, her face drawn and sorrowful. I wanted to scream at her to get out and stay out. She was like some great, grim, full-bosomed bird, hovering over my sick child. "You should go rest too, Mary," I said roughly. "It has been a long, tiring ride from Richmond."

"I will stay with you," she said doggedly, "until the fever has broken. It is bound to break, you know."

I made no reply, but laid the cool cloth on Mélisse's forehead. I felt I could not bear to have this woman with me through the long night ahead.

"Mama," Tim whispered, "what did you bring us?"

"Amanda," Mary said, not taking her great dark eyes

from Mélisse, "go with Clementine and she will open my portmanteau. There is something for all of you."

Andrew came and put a hand on my shoulder tenderly. "My dear, she will recover. When George returns with Aunt Mincy, she will know what to do." His dark face was full of compassion and worry, for he was genuinely fond of Mélisse.

I murmured a response, then said, "Cornelia, would you have Pepper bring up a lantern? 'Tis too dark in here for my liking." There would be no sweeping March wind to blow across my Mélisse when this fever broke—for I would not leave her for an instant.

It was after midnight when Aunt Mincy came into the room. She brought with her a basket of herbs and equipment. She came straight to the bed and laid her black head gently on Mélisse's chest, which rattled ominously with each labored breath she drew. Sometimes she coughed thickly.

"This child got a bad case of croup," Aunt Mincy. "Could go inter pneumonia, but Mincy got here in time, I thinks."

I could not help but draw comfort from the competent movements of the remarkable old black woman as she made ready her treatments. She removed the pan of water from the nearby table and replaced it with a brazier. She kindled a hot fire which burned rapidly to coals, and over this she set a strange kind of kettle with a large spout. She poured water and herbs into this vessel and in a short while a great gust of steam issued from the spout. The steam poured over and around Mélisse. Then Mincy took a bottle and poured a dark liquid into a teaspoon. Raising Mélisse slightly, she murmured, "Here, my lamb—take this fer o'l Aunt Mincy. Come 'long an' open your little mouth." Mélisse whimpered, and without opening her eyes, did as she was bid. "Now drink all this water—come 'long, lamb—you can do it."

"Mincy," Mary said sharply, "she should not be given water with fever!"

"Ma'am, I knows what I'm doin'," the old woman said tartly. Then to my vast relief, she added, "You go 'long to bed, Mistress Mary. You looks tired, and this chile don't need so many peoples breathin' in this room."

"But Lilibel is here! There are only three of us. Surely——"

"No'm. It ain't good for so many peoples to be in here. Her mama got to stay."

"But she is *my* niece. I shan't sleep a wink——"

With sudden ruthlessness I said, "Mary, I would prefer you to leave." Then at the sight of her stricken face, I added, "I will come and get you if she should worsen."

Without a word, Mary turned and lift the room.

It was a long and terrible night, for Mélisse's cough seemed to come more often, and it was heavy, labored, and thick. Toward dawn, Aunt Mincy caught her up during one severe coughing fit and held her head over a basin. I was terrified when Mélisse gagged and coughed up thick lumps of mucus, and I began to weep silently. After Aunt Mincy had persuaded Mélisse to drink more water, she looked at me.

"Madame Sevier, that's a sign she gettin' rid o' this here thing. The steam is loosening that phlegm. She's gettin' better."

I drew a long shuddering breath. "She's never been so sick."

"I done seen lots o' this in early spring. Croup's a common ailment, but your little girl has 'bout the worst case I ever seen. It's been touch an' go this whole night, but she better now."

Still the silent tears streamed down my face as we watched by lantern light the steam pouring over that still, small form. Terrified and heartsick as I was, I could see that her breathing was easier.

"Don't you want to get a little sleep, Miss Lilibel?" Aunt Mincy asked kindly. She seemed less reserved with me after our long vigil and used my first name in its diminutive now. "You kin lie down right there beside Mélisse, if you wants."

"No, I'll sit up. I want to watch her." I dried my eyes with the heel of my hand and straightened my shoulders.

The next three days crawled by, with Mincy's kettle over the brazier sending its herb-scented steam over my

Mélisse. I slept but little and was thankful when at last I was able to spoon a little broth into my child. At the end of the fourth day, she was sitting up, listening to fascinating stories Mincy spun out for her about animals who talked and lived like people. She had taken some solid food and I allowed myself to sleep deeply at last.

When I woke, it was to find Mincy readying herself to leave. She had packed up the brazier, the kettle, all her bottles and herbs in a great heavy sack.

"Aunt Mincy, I don't want you to leave," Mélisse said tearfully. "I love you." A bond had sprung up between the old black woman and the child during those frightening days of extreme illness, and now Mincy's obsidian eyes looked with frank longing at Mélisse.

"There, chile. You'll come to see ol' Aunt Mincy in her house in the woods one day." The dark lids fell over her eyes, but I had seen the love and warmth in them and my heart suddenly went out to this woman who gave so much of herself to others.

"How can I thank you, Aunt Mincy?" I asked impulsively, brushing her cheek in a swift kiss.

"Seein' this baby gettin' well is my thanks."

Mary, who had come into the room with her mother, said brusquely, "We have prepared a sack of supplies for you, Aunt Mincy. A ham, a smoked turkey—flour and sugar, coffee and meal. It's in the kitchen."

"And here is a five-dollar gold piece, Aunt Mincy," Cornelia added, putting the coin into Mincy's hand.

"I thanks you all," the old lady replied with dignity and she left the room. I took Mélisse up into my arms to comfort her.

Cornelia said, "Mélisse looks wonderful now. I do hope you'll accompany us on the hunt. In another four days, she should be herself entirely."

"We'll see, Cornelia," I replied evasively. Mélisse looked pale and hollow-eyed to me and she had lost some of her becoming plumpness.

"I don't blame you for being cautious, Lilibel," Mary said broodingly. "She has had a narrow time of it."

"She is going to get stronger very fast now," Cornelia said cheerfully, "or Mincy would never have left her."

Cornelia proved to be correct. Mélisse was much improved and taking her meals hungrily by the time the day of the hunt arrived. I was so relieved, I allowed myself to be persuaded to join the crowd of riders in the rear courtyard.

The whole countryside had turned out for it, the Reeds, Chenaults, Montagues, and Livingstons, each family arriving with its entourage of hounds and whippers-in. It was a threatening day, clouds boiling darkly above, but there was as yet no rain. As Laura had warned me, nothing stopped these enthusiasts when a hunt was planned. I felt very elegant in my new gold velveteen riding habit, and I couldn't help being a touch prideful about it.

As I rode on Dandylion, I thought I had never seen so colorful a gathering. Most of the men wore scarlet coats and the ladies were all sporting new riding habits. Amanda, her face pink with excitement, was mounted beside young Clay and the two exchanged glances and low-keyed conversation, oblivious to the hubbub about them. I was sure they had met—and often—while we were in Richmond.

In the kitchen of Cloudmont, a great breakfast was being prepared for later, when the huntsmen would return triumphant and hungry. For two days, Mrs. Beady and her helpers had been baking breads and meats and pastries and stewing fruits. It was to be a sumptuous spread, such as Cornelia and the family reveled in.

Excitement was almost tangible in the air as the horses moved restively and we got ready to take to the field. I had seen Josiah, one of Laura's slaves, with a barred, wooden box containing the fox he had trapped the day before for this event. It had scuttled frantically about the cage, bright, panic-stricken eyes imploring behind the bars. It was beautiful, its thick red and white fur, black trimmed, a vivid target for the hounds. Pity welled up in me and I found myself wishing devoutly that it would escape hounds and hunters alike.

Sensing my distress, Cornelia eased her horse alongside Dandylion and said matter-of-factly, "The reason that cocky fox Josiah has for this hunt is so fat and beautiful is that he's full of Cloudmont chickens."

Cornelia Madison sat her horse like a young woman,

erect and graceful. I found myself admiring her profoundly, and hoping I would age as pleasantly.

We all began moving out toward the fields running to the west. In a short time, the hounds were baying and all of us set our horses to follow at a gallop.

These Virginians did not cling together in a group as the smaller hunting parties did in France. Each struck out on his own, shouting, "View, halloa," as they sighted their quarry darting in and out of the brush and skimming over the meadows. Some of the men were intrepidly leaping hedges and brush, but most of the women went around the obstacles, though I watched Cornelia take two hedges before I lost sight of her.

I stopped trying to keep up and looked at the threatening sky. It was the only thing to mar the day for the hunters. Rain appeared imminent and the wind was moist and chilly on my face. Then men had expressed the belief that it would clear up before noon, but it did not look so to me. Indeed, I heard a distant roll of thunder. The sky appeared to be lowering even as I watched most of the others vanish into a stand of trees and brush far down the meadow. A lone horseman, looking back, saw me and turned his horse, galloping back. After a few moments, I discerned that it was George Madison.

As he drew abreast, he said, "I don't think your heart is in the hunt, Lilibel."

"I saw the fox before Josiah turned him loose. He looked so pitiful, I keep hoping he escapes."

He threw back his dark head and laughed. "What a tender heart you have, my dear. Foxes are predators and cause all the planters nothing but trouble. My indomitable mother is usually in on the kill, and I'll wager she returns with the trophies, brush, pads, and mask."

I shivered. The hunters would dismember their prey, taking his tail, his paws, and his narrow little face for trophies and cutting up the remainder for the dogs. I was feeling less and less like pursuing the others, when a large drop of rain struck me forcibly on the forehead. Startled, I cried, "*Alors!* It is going to rain *certainement!*"

"And hard, too," George added squinting up at the rolling dark clouds. "That won't deter the hunt. Avid is the word for all of us. The sport is what is important."

"It deters me," I said with annoyance, looking down at my beautiful gold velveteen riding habit that was making its first appearance in such weather. I adjusted the small black hat on my head and looked longingly back the way we had come.

"We're too far from the house to make it back now," George said, following my eyes, "but we aren't so far from Aunt Mincy's cabin. Want to go there and wait it out?"

I scanned the trees to our left. Their outlines were vaguely familiar. I said hesitantly, "I would rather not get my new riding habit wet."

"Then follow me." George led off at a gallop toward the woods. The rain was increasing now, with great fat drops and I hastened after him. Once in the forest, the trees broke the fall of rain, but a roll of thunder served notice that a cloudburst was pending.

I followed George through the trackless woods for what seemed an interminable time, when suddenly we broke into the little clearing where Mincy's cabin stood. The rain began coming down in earnest and we tethered the horses beneath a tree and ran pell-mell toward the cabin porch. As we stood shaking drops from our clothing, George rapped smartly on the door. There was no answer.

He called, "Aunt Mincy!" and received no reply. "She never locks her door," he said, as we stood on the small porch with the rain pelting down beyond the narrow overhang. With those words, he lifted the wooden latch and we entered the dark, spicy confines of the little one-room cabin. "She must be nursing someone," George added, as we brushed at our dampened garments.

Thunder cracked so loudly about the cabin, that I winced, and restrained a desire to clap my hands over my ears. "Won't the others miss us?" I asked uneasily.

"To be sure. But they're all widely scattered themselves. Often we stir up as many as three foxes and everyone pursues the nearest. They'll eventually come back, drenched I'm sure, but probably with two sets of trophies hanging at the saddles of the ones who happen to be in on the kills."

The storm broke in full fury over the house and it was very dark inside. Taking up a flint from a table nearby, George struck a spark to the candle that stood there.

"Aunt Mincy won't mind our sheltering here until this blows over. I think it's a typical spring storm. It will probably clear up with a bright sun in less than an hour."

I was suddenly nervous. The cabin seemed very small and George's big, hard body seemed to fill it. He towered up, his six feet three inches putting his head near the low ceiling of the dim fragrant room. He peeled off his dampened scarlet coat, his muscular shoulders outlined beneath a white fitted cambric shirt, ruffled down the front.

"Would you like to take off your coat—give it a chance to dry out?"

"No. It isn't really very wet," I replied.

He smiled and shrugged. I had the feeling that he was aware of my reluctance to uncover myself in his presence. Remembrance of the night in the library lay heavy and warm between us. I was acutely aware of an unsettling and defenseless sensation. He pulled one of the little straight-backed chairs over close to mine, straddling it and folding his strong arms along the back.

He asked, "Shall I build a fire? We'd probably dry out the quicker." He gestured to logs neatly stacked beside the fireplace where dying coals burned redly. His eyes on me were alert and watchful.

"We won't be here that long, I'm sure," I replied with a shake of my head.

He was silent a long moment, then, "I think you and I have some unfinished business between us."

I made no pretense of misunderstanding. "I think not. What happened before will not happen again."

"Ah, Liliane," he laughed softly, "every time I'm near you I get a message. And you are a dangerously beautiful woman."

"You're quite safe with me, George," I replied with studied coolness.

"But are you safe with me?" There was rising heat in the black eyes looking into mine. The light from the windows grew dimmer as the storm boiled directly over us. "There's no one here but the two of us. No one can prevent us from doing—whatever we desire this time."

A great flash of lightning lit the room brightly, followed by an earsplitting crack of thunder, and involuntarily I shrank in my chair, covering my face with my hands. George was up and at my side at once, his arms encircling me.

"You're afraid of the storm," he said, surprised.

He pulled me from the chair and held me pressed closely against his long, tough body while the rain drummed a wild tattoo on the roof and windows. I struggled only faintly, for there was great comfort and security in the man's body warming against mine.

With my face in his shoulder, I could not see the lightning either. We stood silently for what seemed an interminable time, a fierce urgency communicating itself from him to me. Tipping my face upward, he slowly put his mouth over mine.

During that sweet, hungry kiss, once again something deep within turned slowly, then awakened with a wild leap of my pulses. I tried vainly to reason with my fervent response. I had been too long without male companionship—the darkened privacy of this small dwelling invited intimacy and George Madison was an exceptionally attractive man.

As his mouth grew more and more demanding I forced myself to twist from his embrace. "You are taking advantage of my terror," I said huskily.

"Better that than play the gentleman and miss that kiss," he laughed, his black eyes twinkling. "I warned you long ago, madame, that my intentions are always on the dark side of propriety."

I said stiffly, "We must return to Cloudmont at once."

"Not until this cloudburst is over," he said calmly. "It won't last much longer."

"I cannot trust you, George."

"Or yourself, Liliane?" His dark eyes were brimming with laughter, for I had responded to his caress hotly.

"You overestimate your charm, monsieur."

"I do not think so," he said soberly, leaning forward to put a strong finger lightly at the base of my throat. "There is a little pulse there that says you are a liar."

With his words, the vulnerability of my position struck home forcibly and my hard French practicality asserted itself. George offered me nothing but the immediate satisfaction of my passion. No matter how I burned for him,

I could not risk taking what he offered.

"I am leaving," I said, turning away from him.

Swift as I was, he was swifter, and stood leaning against the door before me. I looked up into his lean, tanned face and felt a new terror at the eager ferocity in it.

"Not so fast, my dear," he drawled, his stance blocking my exit. But as my eyes widened with fright, his face changed subtly and filled with odd tenderness. He came to me where I stood frozen and took my face gently in his two big hands.

"Don't be so afraid of me," he whispered, kissing my forehead with light, warm lips. "I will not force you." His arms went about me and I melted against him with relief.

Lifting me as easily as I would lift Mélisse, he carried me back to the chair and sat me upright. Then, with his face inches from mine, he said teasingly, "What a brute you must think me, to wear such a look of fear."

I gave a shaky laugh. "You looked so—fierce."

"I am fierce. A very fierce man to be sure," he laughed. "And you are an innocent, Lilibel, despite your sophisticated French manners and for all that you've had a child."

I ruffled, then wilted. "I suppose you're right. I misjudged you, George."

"You did not misjudge me," he said curtly. "I had every intention of ravishing you, but your look of innocent terror is a great deterrent to brute force."

My eyes followed him as he turned and went to the window, and I was forced to admit to myself with bitter honesty that his desires and mine had been the same. Yet I was glad that my fierce pride made me demand better than he offered.

Watching him as he looked out the window, I noted, in some detached compartment of my brain that was still functioning clearly, that his profile was not the same as his brother's. The jawline was stronger, the high-bridged nose was larger, the line of the mouth more sharply cut. It was a reckless and wilful face. Even so, there was great strength in it, and obstinacy, but not a trace of cruelty.

I rose abruptly and went to stand at the other window, curtained in butternut homespun. Surely the rain was slackening! I waited, feeling the presence and restlessness of the man near me. I was tense with fear that at any moment he might lose his concern for my terror and force me. And worse, I would respond with the wantonness that boiled up in me at the thought of his mouth on mine. Mincy's bed in the far corner of the room, with a bright patchwork cover, was dangerously propitious. I looked away from it quickly.

Thunder trailed off in the distance and the rain was thinning even as I watched. The sky began to brighten.

I started at the sound of George's voice at my shoulder. "You see, I told you it was only a spring storm. The sun will be out in another moment. It's been less than an hour."

It had seemed much longer than that. I had the curious feeling that something had happened between us, some intimacy more potent than a kiss.

He donned his coat and stood at the door, holding it open for me. As I went through he said mockingly, "I shall savor that kiss tonight in my lonely bed."

I thought unhappily, *So shall I*. But I could not let him know that. I moved swiftly out the door, down the path through Mincy's garden of herbs and through the narrow gate of the little fence of saplings that bordered her yard. I looked about for the dog Gypse, but he was not to be seen. He must have followed his mistress wherever she had gone. Clouds were parting and a warming sun shone through, imparting a washed cleanliness to forests and meadows. Birds were setting up a chorus in the trees where our horses were tethered leisurely cropping the early spring grass.

George took a snowy handkerchief from his pocket and wiped my wet saddle carefully, then his own. He looked at me with an open smile, saying, " 'Twould be a shame to spoil that new riding habit. It matches your eyes, Lilibel, almost exactly."

I felt constraint between us. "Do hurry, George. The others will think we've had an accident."

"We shall never catch the others now, my dear. They probably cornered more than one fox and by now are on their way back to Cloudmont. We will take the route home by the river."

Together we set off at a leisurely canter, Dandylion slightly behind his big stallion. The trees were still dripping and occasional drops struck us lightly. All about was the clean-washed smell of growing things, an indefinable fragrance that set my blood tingling and made me long to break into a gallop. My feeling of euphoria was touched faintly with regret, which puzzled me, and I was worrying the fact like a dog with a bone when suddenly we rode silently into a small clearing.

We halted, astonished to see a circle of more than a hundred seated black men, who looked at us with equal astonishment. For a moment it was a frozen tableau.

Then the men rose to their feet as one and, without a sound, began to melt into the woods with a speed I would not have thought possible.

A great sinewy black I had never seen before came directly toward us, a machete in his huge hand. It was a great razor-sharp, semicircular blade of the kind I had seen the slaves use to cut away the reeds and cattails that choked the edges of the James River.

The man passed threateningly near, and George rose tensely in his saddle, alert to the attack that seemed imminent. But with a glance of distilled hatred, the black passed us and he, too, vanished in the thick woods.

I looked back at the clearing in time to see a last and somehow familiar form disappear into the woods beyond. "Wasn't that Railo?" I asked, as the last figure vanished.

"I think so," George replied grimly. "Most of them looked to be from Livingston's. But there were others from Reed's and Montague's that I recognized—but not that big buck that passed us so closely with the knife. Perhaps I should have seen one or two from Cloudmont, had I had time."

"What were they doing?" I asked, alarm growing. "What does it mean?"

"It means, my dear, that they took advantage of the hunt and the weather to get together."

"What for?"

His eyes were somber. "Either to air their grievances to one another, or to plan an insurrection."

"An insurrection!" I echoed, chilled.

"Lilibel, how would you feel if you were in slavery to

someone like Anna and Jabez Livingston—or if you were bought and sold, body and soul, by any individual?"

"I should hate it."

"They are no different from us. They hate it, and sometimes they are desperate enough to risk their lives to escape. And in doing so, others may die as well."

"I know. Laura told me there had been insurrections."

"With bloody and tragic results. Slavery is an evil institution and no good can ever come of it. There is great danger in what we have just seen."

I cried, "But you aren't going to tell Jabez about seeing Railo!" I could envisage the fury on that cruel face and the terrible punishment he would mete out to Railo.

"I must tell all the planters what we have seen. But I shall name no names. Only that we happened on the meeting and they scattered before we could recognize any."

"Oh, why? It will only cause trouble for the poor slaves."

"My dear, the planters are greatly outnumbered by their slaves. They must be alerted or they could all be found dead in their beds of a morning." His face was set in grim lines as he added, "They are fools, keeping a captured race by force. Perhaps one day they will see the folly of it and turn, as we have, to other sources of labor."

We continued our way steadily through the dripping forest until we came upon the rolling lawns that swept to the banks of the James River. At the James we turned sharply left and followed the outskirts of Cloudmont's burgeoning gardens to the graveled road around to the visitors' entrance. The broad area before the stables and kennels was empty, as were the long path beside the smokehouse, washhouse, and quarters.

Noah could be seen inside the stable with a shovel in hand. George shrugged. "I was mistaken. The hunters are still out—and no doubt this bright sun will whet their appetites for the chase." He laughed suddenly, "I'll make you a wager. Their clothing will dry on them before they return."

As Noah looked up and saw us, a grin split his young face. Ephraim appeared behind him, holding a rake. In answer to George I said wryly, "I won't take that wager.

I saw their faces and I know how eager they are for the sport."

"You back soon, Cap'n George—Miss Lilibel," Noah said.

"We sat out the rain in Aunt Mincy's cabin and decided it was too late to find the others," George replied.

Ephraim took the reins to Dandylion and said, "Aunt Mincy over to the Reeds. They got sick chillun." I marveled at how these black people knew everything about the countryside and its inhabitants. It was as if they had secret means of swift communication. As George swung himself down and handed his reins to Noah, Ephraim said, "We'll give Dandylion and the Count a good rubdown, Mister George."

George said casually, "What was the meeting in the woods near the river about, Ephraim?"

Noah and Ephraim were very still. Then Noah quickly led Dandylion toward the open stable door and Ephraim said blandly, "What meetin', Mister George?" Ephraim and his wife and two children were one of the two slave families that were to be sent to Boston at the end of the summer.

George's eyes narrowed. "Then it's to be a secret, eh? That makes me think the worst, you know."

"I don't know nothin' 'bout no meetin', Mister George," Ephraim said quietly. "Them as works elsewhere don't tell me everything. They knows me and Belle an' our young 'uns gonna be free peoples come next summertime."

George glanced down toward the quarters and asked, "Then there were no Cloudmont people at that meeting?"

"Don't know 'bout no meetin'," Ephraim repeated stubbornly, and moved with George's stallion toward the stable where Noah had disappeared.

George sighed. "You're a good man, Ephraim. I'm glad you weren't among them."

The big black man made no response, and George and I struck out toward the house. It was a long walk up the garden paths to the broad graveled courtyard at the rear entrance to Cloudmont. As we passed the kitchen wing, the savory fragrance of roasting meat floated to our nostrils, reminding me suddenly that I had not had breakfast, and I was very hungry.

George revealed a similar feeling by growling, "I'm hungry enough to eat a leg of beef," as we entered the rear door to the great hall.

"We must wait for the others," I remarked, but my mind had veered back to that circle of black faces we had looked into when we reached the clearing in the forest. Uneasiness slipped over me like a veil and I could not throw it off. I was suddenly anxious to go up and find Mélisse, make sure she was still mending, and more—that she was still *safe*.

As we reached the staircase, I said, "I shall go up to see about Mélisse."

"And I shall have a tot of brandy in the library while awaiting the arrival of the triumphant hunters," George replied as we parted.

I went into my room to find Mélisse gone, but Clementine was there tidying up. She had a broom and a dustpan in her hands and looked up as I said anxiously, "Where is Mélisse?"

"She's playin' upstairs in the nursery with Andy and Tim," and at my sigh of relief, she added, "Mistress, how come you're back a'ready?"

"I returned with Mr. George because of the rain."

"Lor', the rain don't stop a hunt here, Miss Lilibel."

"So I've heard," I replied with some acerbity. "Is Mélisse feeling all right?"

"Right enough to eat two poached eggs and a thick slice o' toast and ham." Then as an afterthought, "Maybe you're smart, though, Miss Lilibel, not to ride in the rain, for you might've took cold like Miss Yve done, had you rode on in the weather."

I went to the short chest of drawers to get my brush and comb. Taking off my hat, I began to rearrange my hair.

"Noah told me Yve became ill on the hunt. Was she taking something for it—before she——"

"Not fer the cold," Clementine answered, sweeping a little pile of lint into the dustpan. "Only laudanum, perscribed by the doctor in Richmond, fer her nerves, her not bein' able to sleep well an' all."

"How much did she take?" I kept my voice casual.

Clementine's brow wrinkled and she looked down at the pan. "Now that's strange you should ask—because it worrit me. Miss Yve must'a been turrible restless with that cold, fer the mornin' when I come in an' couldn't wake her, afore Mister Andrew got back with Aunt Mincy, I noticed she had took an awful big dose. The bottle were more'n half empty."

"She took it by herself, you think? With no water to wash it down?"

Clementine's brow cleared. "Oh, no'm. The whole pitcher o'water by her bed were empty. She must of drunk lots of water with it, sweatin' like she done. I refilled it right away," she said importantly. "Mr. Andrew had sent fer me and Abigail when he lit out fer Aunt Mincy. We was to change her nightgown—it were so wet—an' put fresh dry linen on the bed—which we done." She gave me an ingenuous smile and added, "Miss Yve were a strong-minded lady and she dosed herself as she pleased."

"No wonder she slept through the night in the wind," I murmured. "Half a bottle of laudanum!"

"That's what Abby an' me thought, Miss Lilibel. But we didn't say nothin'. The poor little thing sort of brung it on herself in a way." Then at the door, "Anything I can do fer you, madame?"

"No, thank you, Clementine," I replied. *You have already done something.*

The girl went out, closing the door softly behind her, and I flung myself down on the sofa before the freshly fed fire. It warmed my chilled body, but it could not warm my heart.

In my brain a macabre picture rose up like smoke. A nebulous figure hovered over my sister, cajoling her into an overdose of laudanum and returning to pour water from the pitcher over her drugged form. Then, since the household would have been asleep for the night, the figure could have stealthily opened the window directly on Yve's still body lying in a pool of "sweat." Those few hours between midnight and dawn would have been enough to bring on a quick death.

Suddenly from outside my north window I heard the stamping of horses, the clink of bridles and bits, the babble of voices, some high and excited. The hunt was over. I went to look out and saw the colorful panorama of the sportsmen below. Some were still trotting up to join the milling crowd that had drawn up in the broad graveled courtyard. Several slaves appeared to take the reins as the riders began dismounting. The hounds, still excited, were moving in and out among the people. Noah was trying vainly to separate Cloudmont hounds from the visitors' and get them into their pen.

I went into the hall and down the stairs as the colorful hunters poured in through the visitors' entrance to the great hall. Joining the crowd, I saw that, true to George's prediction, Cornelia had been in on the kill of not one but three foxes, and had the masks as trophies. She was in high spirits, and when we all trooped into the enormous dining room to partake of the mouthwatering foods prepared by Mrs. Beady and the girls, her laughter sounded young and gay.

We made our way past the sideboard, filling our plates before taking a place at the long table. Clayton Reed, just behind me, spoke to George beside him. "Grace and I are certainly grateful to you, George, for sending Ephraim after Aunt Mincy for us so early this morning. I fear Grace would never have made it to the hunt, with the twins down with summer complaint."

I froze with shock. George Madison had known that Mincy was not in her cabin. He had deliberately taken me there for the very purpose he so nearly achieved. I turned to glare at him, my fury rising like a flame, only to meet his wickedly laughing eyes as his trickery was found out. Oh, would I tell him a thing or two when the opportunity presented itself!

When we were all seated, I was in such a rage I could scarcely eat or join the merry conversation around us. Cornelia seemed to notice my silence, and said warmly, "Lilibel, we missed you and George—whatever happened to you?"

George said easily, "Lilibel is not the enthusiast you are, Mother, so we sat the rain out. When it was over, it was too late to rejoin you."

"You mean you came all the way back—but surely not!"

"We sheltered in Aunt Mincy's cabin. 'Twas nearby."

There was a sudden silence, and I glanced up to find several pairs of interested eyes on me. Andrew's dark gaze fixed on my face with peculiar intensity. Even Mary looked at me with closer than usual attention.

As the awkward silence spun out, I plunged in unthinkingly, "And when we left, we came upon the strangest thing. There was a large group of black men in a clearing in the forest—they were sitting as if in conference."

My hope had been to take their minds from the fact that I had spent an hour alone in that intimate cabin with George Madison. My purpose was achieved with a thoroughness I had not counted on.

The silence at the table became fraught with anxiety. Every man and woman fixed his eyes upon me with varying degrees of shock and fear.

"A hundred, you say?" It was Jabez Livingston, and I saw that a white line had formed about the thin, cruel lips.

"I had meant to wait until breakfast was over before telling you all," George replied, his tanned face sober now. "But there were well over a hundred. And some were armed—machetes, hatchets, even an ax or two."

"My God," Vance Chenault muttered. "They must be planning an insurrection." Everyone seemed to have lost interest in their plates. The women's faces were pale.

"It's possible," George said. "But then again, you know how they gather to talk among themselves. It's also possible they were merely airing their grievances.

"That could be," Evan Montague said soothingly to his wife. "You know how Jethro and his brothers never go into the woods without a weapon, my dear. They always hope to get a rabbit or a squirrel or two for roasting."

"I think we should go home," Grace Reed said abruptly. "I am concerned for the twins. I should never have left them—even with Mincy. 'Tis a very bad time of year for colds and fever."

Jabez said harshly, "Did you see my buck, Railo, among them?"

"I recognized none," George said evenly. "When we came upon them, they vanished like shadows into the thickest woods. You know how quick they can be."

"I'll wager he was among them. By God, I'll arm Speers and I'll carry a gun myself now. There'll be no uprising at my plantation.

Everyone was pushing away from the table now, leaving their half-finished breakfasts cooling on the plates. The merry hunt was over; fear hung in the air like a miasma.

"Did you recognize none?" Helen Montague beseeched. "If we only knew from which of our plantations they came——"

"None," George said. "They were so swiftly gone I can only estimate their numbers."

In a few moments, the guests had gathered themselves and mounted their horses. Cornelia and the rest of the family went out into the courtyard to see them off. It was a grim and distrait crowd of riders who trotted swiftly away from Cloudmont in the bright sunlight of that last day in March.

PART TWO

CHAPTER 10

Tension spread across the land with April. Nevertheless, I reveled in the glories of the season. The flowerbeds were full of tender green shoots and the perennials were burgeoning. Pink and white dogwood starred the forests and azaleas rioted in luscious bouquets from snowy white to fuchsia. And, to my great relief, Mélisse recovered fully.

After my daughter was once more herself and attending lessions with the other children, Laura and I, in the face of Cornelia's protests, resumed our rides along the river, enjoying the beauty of spring around us.

As the days grew longer and nothing happened, talk of an uprising among the slaves cooled. Our neighbors relaxed and we all went calling. We took our young ones to Tulip Grove, where they played with the Reeds' seven-year-old twins Jane and Anne. Tim, Andy, and Mélisse liked to go to the Chenaults' at Rose Hill best, for they had two small daughters, Elizabeth and Amelia, and three sons, the oldest, Donald, just thirteen. Often we made an entire day of our visit, staying for supper and driving home in the cool, sweet spring evenings.

During those first busy weeks, Andrew and George paid me scant attention, whether because of George's and my brief and dangerous sojourn in Mincy's cabin or because of the pressure of their duties, I did not know and frankly did not care. I was extremely angry with George for having deliberately taken me there, knowing full well we would be alone. And I suspected that Andrew might be shocked and upset at our behavior. For some reason that disturbed me greatly.

I put these worries from me as we visited our neighbors, who were always so gracious that it was with regret we took our departure. All of them were slave owners, but Laura made a point of assuring me their slaves were treated well. Still, I could not stem the feeling of leashed violence that crept upon me even as these quiet, impassive black people served us coffee and cake or sumptuous meals in the great homes of those who owned them.

On the surface it appeared that these Virginia planters had nothing on their minds but the pursuit of pleasure. But that was a false impression, for Cloudmont was a beehive of activity, and I knew it was the same across the land. By now, the fields of Cloudmont had been plowed and planted with tobacco and cotton. George, Andrew, and Charles, attending to their many interests, often made it back barely in time to attend one of Cornelia's evening parties.

On such an occasion near May I found myself seated beside Andrew on a damask couch near the windows. The others were playing loo, but Amanda, who had been allowed to come to this party, could scarcely take her eyes from young Clay. The young couple held hands whenever Mary's sharp glance could be avoided.

I was a little uncomfortable, fearing Andrew might mention my unwilling tryst with George during the hunt, but my fears proved groundless. He remarked, " 'Tis wonderful to see how your little Mélisse has come out of her illness."

"Yes," I said with relief, "she has put on the weight she lost, as well. I owe Aunt Mincy a great deal."

"She has saved many young lives," he said gravely, a shadow crossing his face. His clean-cut profile was like a gold coin against the dark window behind him.

"But not Yve's," I said involuntarily. At the twisting pain that crossed his face, I added hastily, "I know that was hard on you, who loved her so much."

His sigh touched my heart. "I loved her deeply, and I miss her." Then abruptly he turned the conversation to me. "Have you thought of remarriage, Lilibel?" His brilliant black eyes probed mine.

"No," I replied shortly. I was shaken by my utterly insane notion that he was about to propose marriage to me.

"You are young and beautiful and you have much to offer. You should give it some thought." He was smiling faintly now at my obvious flutter. He added slowly, "You will be besieged by offers before the summer is over, I have no doubt. You should have heard the compliments that came to my ears in Richmond when you were there."

I let my breath out slowly. So that was it. The men I had met in Richmond. I smiled at him demurely and turned the talk to his plantings and his efforts to revitalize the soil, which brought an enthusiastic response.

Later that night, as I lay beside the sleeping Mélisse, I thought about Andrew. I knew that unlike his brother George, Andrew was a marrying man.

The sweet-scented days of May flew by on silken wings. Each morning Laura and I went for our rides along the sparkling James. Sometimes Amanda, who was fond of riding alone, would instead ride with us, full of talk about Clay Reed. Because her mother was so strict with her, she was bottled up most of the time, and full to bursting by the time she was away with us. Her youthful praises of her beloved brought smiles to our faces as we accorded her our sympathetic attention. Several times Cornelia herself accompanied us when her household duties permitted, and each time, I was impressed by her steely grace in the saddle. She was a much better rider than either Laura or I.

George, Andrew, and Charles were busier than ever, riding the farflung acres, supervising and organizing tenant labor, overseeing repairs to the barns in which crops of cotton and tobacco would be stored. Occasionally they went to oversee the properties of Laura and Mary, but these were brief jaunts, as the Landon acres were still lying fallow. When not out on horseback, they were in the big plantation office, going over and adding to the entries kept in their spidery well-educated handwriting. Only occasionally now did they go to Hampton, Norfolk, or Richmond.

On their return from a trip to Richmond, late in May, the three of them rode in with startling news. Jefferson had purchased the whole of Louisiana, more than doubling the size of the United States. Everyone was agog—even the president's severest critics were speechless at the magnitude of the acquisition.

At dinner that night, George said with a grin, "He is said to have paid fifteen million dollars for eight hundred and twenty-eight thousand square miles. That's a little less than three cents an acre, my dears."

There was a babble of conversation, then Andrew's voice rose over the rest. "For land-hungry Americans, the purchase of the Louisiana territory from Napoleon is a great blessing. I imagine there will be an exodus west now, the like of which we have never seen."

"It makes me want to pack up and go out to claim a homestead myself," George said. "I have heard how rich and fertile it is beyond the mountains. There'll be many a fortune made by enterprising settlers."

"If they can survive the Indians," said Mary quietly. "I have heard terrible tales of murder and torture of those who have ventured beyond the mountains."

"Mary, old girl, anything worth having is worth a risk," George said irrepressibly. "There'll be enough settlers to hold their own with the Indians."

Andrew smiled, adding, "We saw Jabez in town. The Livingstons are going to have a ball celebrating the acquisition of the territory the first of June. You ladies can begin planning what you will wear to the festivities."

"So they truly are going to have it," Laura laughed. "Jabez has hinted around about this land purchase—though I don't believe he knew exactly what it would be—and Anna's certainly talked of having a ball long enough." And she and Mary fell to discussing ballgowns.

But I sat quietly thinking. How like the tyrant who ruled France to sell off her richest possession for money that would surely be used to fuel his further wars of aggression. And how like Jabez and Anna to celebrate Thomas Jefferson's wisdom and foresight with a ball, while whispering calumny behind his back.

The day of the Livingston ball dawned bright and clear. It was the first day of June and it was very warm. After a morning spent in Laura's room trying to help her decide which of eight ballgowns she should wear, both of us descended to the cool salon, where we were joined by Mary and her mother for tall glasses of iced tea. The children, released early by Seton Cambridge, found us there.

Amanda immediately fell to arguing with her mother. It no longer amazed me that Mary, who was so obsessed with her family, was resentful of allowing Amanda the pleasures of growing up. It was as if she wished to keep her a small child forever.

When the quarrel had run most of its course, Laura and I put in a mild defense on behalf of the tearful Amanda, whose well-formed bosom was heaving stormily. To our surprise Mary sighed resignedly.

"Very well, you may go to the ball, Amanda." Then, almost spitefully, "If you have anything to wear."

Amanda's face was suddenly stricken. "Oh, dear," she wailed. "I have nothing but those silly short party dresses you make me wear. Oh, Grandmother, why didn't you buy me a ballgown in Richmond?"

Laura put down her empty tea glass and caught Amanda's hand. "Come along, Amanda. You and I are near enough of size that, with a very few alterations, one of my more modest gowns should be made to do. Will you join us Lilibel? Your French taste is unerring and we need your advice."

Two hours later, a dazed and ecstatic Amanda left Laura and me, clutching her remodeled treasure to her breast. We had tightened the hip and breast lines in a pale yellow taffeta gown. The matching pelisse that was part of the ensemble was exactly right, for which we fervently thanked God.

"A little more and I swear I should be too tired to go to the ball tonight," Laura said. "Judith," she called, and as the slender black girl came into the room, she ordered, "I want you to press my green silk for the ball tonight—and don't worry, dear. I shall take you with me and you shall see Railo. Old Jabez can't object to that."

Warmed by the brilliant smile that lit Judith's face, I smiled myself as I left them to begin my own preparations for the coming festivities.

It was dusk when we all gathered at the carriage, which Henry Pepper and Noah had brought to the rear entrance. The big carriage easily accommodated the six of us. Cornelia and Mary, with a subdued and self-consciously dignified Amanda, occupied one seat, while Laura, Judith, and I took the other. We talked inconsequentially as we covered the few miles that lay between the Livingston plantation and Cloudmont. I had no inkling of how the evening was to change my life.

The carriage lamps had been lit before we left, for it was dark by the time the carriage pulled up to take its place among the others that lined the drive. The mansion was ablaze with light. The huge chandelier in the ballroom, containing near a hundred tapers in its crystal holders, cast diamondlike brightness over those beneath it. The tall windows were all open and the delicate June night sent tendrils of cool air into the room, dispersing heat from the many candles and lamps that filled the house.

Anna and Jabez greeted us with a great show of affection, and Jabez said, "Ah, so you brought Judith. Railo would have been glad of that, but unfortunately, I am punishing him for impudence. He is in the stockade right now."

"Surely you will release him to visit with Judith while she is here?" Laura's voice rose indignantly.

"Ah, my dear, I cannot do that and maintain any sort of discipline," Jabez said piously. "And we could scarcely permit Judith to go into the stockade and visit with him, you know."

A sudden, appalling, and ungovernable rage shook me. I said softly, "*Nom de Dieu, monsieur*. If you do not let Railo out to be with Judith I shall return to Cloudmont at once."

Jabez laughed uneasily. "What a little firebrand you are, Madame Sevier. You surely do not mean that."

Judith, who stood just behind Laura, was looking at me with wide, terrified eyes. "I never meant anything more in my life," I replied, drawing the white taffeta pelisse about me.

Laura caught fire from my anger and added, "I shall leave as well. And I imagine Cornelia, Amanda, and Mary will not want to stay where we do not feel welcome."

The men had gathered about us now and I was awarded

an amused and admiring glance from George, as well as a troubled one from Andrew. Charles watched the scene alertly as George said with easy good humor, "I think we would have to accompany the ladies back to Cloudmont in that event, Jabez. Surely you can bend your rules a little to accommodate our French rebel?"

Jabez Livingston, who had paled before our onslaught, recovered his poise and said with poor grace, "Well, I cannot have so charming a group of ladies leave when the ball has scarcely begun." He called over his shoulder, and a tall black man in butler's uniform came at once. "Cully, you will take Judith out to the gardens and release Railo so that they may visit during the evening. But mind, he's to be locked up as soon as the guests leave."

Judith, still frightened, cast a backward appealing glance at Laura and me, as she followed Cully from the foyer.

"Now do come in and let Rustis take your wraps, ladies," Jabez said, and we allowed another short, impeccably clad slave to take our pelisses and carry them up the long circular staircase.

We entered the ballroom, where the sound of merriment struck us pleasantly. Amanda was big-eyed and quiet, but her face was pink with pleasure. I knew she was searching the crowd for young Clay, and her face changed magically when her eyes fell upon him across the room. The tall, broad-shouldered young man seemed to sense her arrival, for I saw their eyes meet, and the spark that flew between them warmed me.

Mary whispered warningly, "Amanda, I *will* not have you spending the entire evening with young Clay! You dance with the other young men, too, you understand?"

"Yes, Mama," Amanda said dreamily, already drifting toward Clay, who was hastening toward her.

There were many people I had never seen before, and soon introductions were being made. There were more men than women in the crowd that filled the big room. A group of musicians was seated at the end of the ballroom, surrounded by potted ferns and palms. Glancing through a broad double door off the ballroom, I could see the table in the dining hall laden with food, and I marveled anew at the opulent mode of living indulged in by these

Americans. There were black house-slaves everywhere, serving drinks and filling plates with food for those who requested it. The musicians had been playing at our arival, but at the moment were taking an intermission, sipping tall, cool drinks.

"Young Edward Cholmondeley is here from England," Anna whispered to us. "His father is the duke, you know. I think he plans to buy land and remain here. He is the youngest son, but well endowed, and would like to make his fortune here." She gestured toward a tall, rangy young man with a shock of sandy red hair. "And those two over yonder are Roger Essex and Adam Manderwell, very eligible bachelors, my dear Laura and Mary—and you too, Madame Sevier. Oh, I know you are very choosy ladies, but you might pay them a little more mind than usual. They are very wealthy young men."

She chattered on, naming guests and giving their backgrounds. Some of them came from as far away as Washington. Among the many guests, I greeted our old friends, the Reeds, Chenaults, Montagues, and Stuarts. Before long, the music was struck up once more and I found myself spinning about the room in the arms of first one man, then another. They seemed to be quite as complimentary to a penniless French refugee as they were to the wealthy Laura and Mary.

At last, Andrew claimed me for a dance. As we moved together, he murmured, "I would so like to talk to you—alone, Lilibel. You have had such a swarm of men about you—I knew it would be that way. I didn't get to show you the Stuart gardens, but later we will go out and I shall show you the Livingston gardens. Though, for all their use of the lash and the stockade, they have not equaled Cloudmont's.

I looked up into his lean face with the peak of black hair in the middle of his forehead and thought once more that my sister's passion for him was quite understandable. I murmured, "I should like to see them. I love to dance, but one must rest occasionally, too." And as we looked into each other's eyes and smiled, I wondered anew what had turned Yve into a shrew with him. Yve had been too instinctively wise in the ways of men not to know that such behavior would alienate a man like Andrew Madison.

Something had driven wisdom from her and replaced it with cruelty, and that puzzled me deeply.

"I see that Edward Cholmondeley is bearing down upon you, my dear," Andrew said with asperity, and at that moment, the man tapped his shoulder.

"Sir, may I have the next dance with this charming lady?"

"Of course," replied Andrew courteously, "if she agrees."

"I should like it very much," I replied, smiling warmly at the lanky, sandy-haired man, who responded by blushing furiously.

As a matter of fact, he blushed throughout our dance together, his naturally ruddy face glowing with an endearing warmth. He appeared quite taken with me. Indeed, after our dance, he took me to one side of the room and began a flowery series of compliments. He told me he had been watching me with admiration all evening.

Andrew and Mary drew near us, just as Edward Cholmondeley said, "My dear Madame Sevier—may I call you Liliane?" At my nod he continued, "My dear Liliane, please do not think me forward, but I am compelled to tell you that you have captured my heart. Please tell me that I may call on you at Cloudmont?"

I glimpsed Andrew's face around Edward's shoulder. His black brows were drawn in a thundercloud of disapproval.

When I agreed to let Edward call soon, he appeared quite ready to take his stand by my side for the entire evening. George Madison prevented this by stepping up smoothly to take my arm as the next dance began and, with a casual nod of dismissal to the duke's son, spun me away into the crowd. Along with a fine new suit and ruffled cravat, George wore his usual mocking smile.

"You are the belle of the evening, my dear Madame Sevier, and I do believe all the gentlemen have honorable intentions toward you."

"You wouldn't know an honorable intention if it sat upon you," I retorted. I was still angry with him for having lured me to Mincy's cabin. And worse, he had let Andrew find out about it.

He threw back his head and laughed so heartily that I

pinched his arm and whispered, "Do hush! Everyone's looking at us."

Still laughing, he said, "I know honorable intentions well, Lilibel, but I refuse to harbor them. They are dangerous to a man's freedom."

"I feel very fortunate to have escaped your intentions," I said coolly.

"You haven't escaped them, my dear," he said, eyes glinting, "Your bedroom is only a few steps from mine. How do you know that I won't come quietly in some hot dark summer night and have my wicked way with you?"

"Alors!" I couldn't help but laugh. "You are an audacious rascal!" This man had the power to stir me, and my heart beat faster.

"And you are an allurement I cannot resist. What would you do if I rapped softly on your door about three this morning?"

"I should have to defend myself," I replied, smothering my laughter. "Possibly I should shoot you."

"Ah, Lilibel, surely a man so filled with love and desire for you as to flout convention would not meet with so bloody a welcome."

"Indeed, I shall bolt my door tightly tonight when we return home. You have properly frightened me, George."

He put on a long face. "I am sorry for that," he said, but his eyes were still merry. "Suppose I promise to be very polite and circumspect now. Would that return me to your good graces?"

I looked up at him from under my thick black lashes. "Let us see how polite and circumspect you are, before I commit myself."

The music stopped and he bowed to kiss my hand, murmuring, "I shall be the soul of decorum. You shall see." But the buried laughter in his voice belied his words, and I felt something like regret to see Andrew wending his way through the halted dancers.

"George, I have promised to show Lilibel the Livingston gardens by moonlight. You will excuse us, of course?" Andrew asked courteously.

"Of course," George bowed deeply. "I'm only sorry I didn't think to offer that service myself." And, with an irrepressible grin, he left us.

Andrew led me to the dining salon, where we were served glasses of champagne. We took them with us as we made our way through the ballroom, then out through French doors that opened onto the gardens. The moon was brilliant and the gardens were beautiful, bathed in silvery light. Far down the rolling central lawn, the James River could be seen, sparkling like a satin ribbon. The fragrance of roses was carried faintly on the warm June air, as we walked down a graveled path beside the rose gardens. The statue of a small boy stood amid a rushing spring in a marble pool at the center of a circular span of grass.

"How beautiful it is," I murmured appreciatively, sipping my champagne.

"Yes," Andrew agreed dryly. "Too bad the Livingstons are so unlovely."

"They are truly dreadful, I think," I said honestly. "I can find no redeeming virtues in either of them."

"I agree. But I did not bring you out here to discuss our unpleasant host and hostess. I have something most important to—ask you."

Once again a curious intimation swept over me, and I chided myself for being a fool. My sister had been dead scarcely five months and this attractive man had made no moves to indicate other than a friendly interest and affection for me. Nevertheless, my heartbeat stepped up and my breath quickened.

We strolled in silence to a marble bench, beyond the fountain, under a treelike crepe myrtle whose thick blooms were silvered by moonlight. There Andrew seated me and, as we finished the champagne, he took both glasses in one hand and set them down on the grass.

As he seated himself beside me, he said huskily, "I scarcely know how to begin, my dear, for what I have to ask you is highly inappropriate at this time." He took one of my hands and held it between his two big warm ones. "But I find I can wait no longer. Out of all those eligible bachelors hovering about you, I fear you might find one to your liking—and feeling yourself a stranger still at Cloudmont, you might be tempted to accept one of them."

I looked at his face, the even planes of it in sharp black and white relief under the brilliant moon. I could not see his eyes, but I knew unerringly now that my instinct was correct. Andrew Madison was on the verge of a declaration.

"I have felt most welcome at Cloudmont," I said quietly, "but nevertheless, it is true I am there on your charitable kindness."

"I feared you felt that way." He hesitated and drew a long breath, then continued, "Please, I beg of you, do not think me callous or forgetful of my Yve, but I must confess to you that in these past months you have endeared yourself to me so greatly, that I feel I cannot bear to lose you." He lifted my hand to his lips and his kiss in the palm was lingering and tender. My heart was beating wildly by now.

I said breathlessly, "Andrew, I am mindful of the fact that my sister has been dead but five months——"

"I know, I know," he cut in hastily, "but I cannot risk losing you, my dear. You are so beautiful, so kind and so loving—all the things that would make my life complete. I know we cannot be married until a year has passed, but I want to ask you now to be my wife. At least we can be betrothed—even if it must be secretly—while we wait." He paused, then added quickly, "Your status in the house would change immediately, Lilibel. You will be future mistress of Cloudmont. You need no longer feel an object of charity—though you have never been that!—for your future would be assured." He paused again, then asked humbly, "Is it possible that you might come to care for me?"

I drew a trembling breath. "I think you are a very fine man, Andrew. I can understand why Yve loved you so greatly. Indeed, I think coming to love you might not only be very easy but most pleasurable." He was so solid, so strong and capable. He was steady and reliable, all the attributes I admired in a man.

With my words, he took me firmly in his arms and began kissing me, first my forehead, then my eyelids and cheeks, and finally my parted lips. Lifting his head, he said, "Then you will become my affianced, Lilibel? With the wedding set for December?"

"Yes, Andrew," I replied weakly. A sudden memory of George's eager mouth, urgent, wildly exciting, intruded, and I tried to shut it out. Andrew was kind, considerate and a gentleman—totally different from his brother. As Andrew's affianced, I would be beyond George's dangerous attractiveness. Surely he would not make forbidden love to his brother's intended wife.

"You have made me very happy," he said softly, "and I must tell you that I do not love Yve the less, but I cannot live in the past. You understand, my dear?"

"Yes," I replied, a faint bud of uneasiness deep within me. He had loved Yve—I knew it. But I found the old specter of her death rising like a vapor in my mind. Though I could not imagine Andrew having anything to do with it. His was not the ghostly figure I visualized hovering over my sister's drugged form.

"I know you loved Yve, Andrew, despite the way she had changed. Oh, yes, I know she had changed! Too many have told me too much."

'You must not think of that, Lilibel. My affection for her was unaltered." Flinging his arms about me in a sudden excess of joy, he murmured into my hair, "We must tell the family, Lilibel. You know how close we are and I cannot keep secrets from them. But we will wait the prescribed length of time. Is that satisfactory to you?"

"Yes," I whispered, thinking of the security that would be mine and Mélisse's now. No longer waifs, cast adrift in a hard world to either accept charity or make our own way. Now we would be loved and cherished by a man of unimpeachable integrity. "We must go back. Andrew," I murmured, "or there will be those who will suspect long before any announcement on our part."

He pulled me to my feet, stooped, and caught up the champagne glasses. He took my hand in his free one, and we started back. As we passed a wide hedge, our footsteps silent on thick grass, a hoarse young voice said clearly, passionately, "You're not too young, Amanda, and you know it! I say the hell with your mother's obstinacy—I love you, my darling! I love you!"

Andrew had slowed and was listening, a scowl on his handsome face. I tugged at his hand, wishing to protect the privacy of the young lovers beyond the heavy boxwood hedge.

"Clay, darling—you know I love you with all my heart!"

"Then you must let me go to your mother—or your uncles. I'll wager George would be sympathetic to us."

I tugged harder at Andrew's hand, and still he hung back. I seized his arm as Amanda was saying, "No, darling, let me talk with Mother first——"

As we drew away, I whispered fiercely, "Andrew, that was a private moment. We shouldn't eavesdrop on two young lovers!"

Andrew's voice was troubled. "It might be wise to listen to them. After all, Amanda's father is dead, and I have a grave responsibility to her and her mother."

"Ah, but they are so in love, Andrew!"

"All the more reason to be careful, my dear. I shall have a talk with Mary before the night's over."

"Oh, Andrew, please do not! Give Amanda a chance to talk to her mother. *Mon cher*, you heard her say she was going to talk to her mother first!" I realized suddenly I was very close to quarreling with the man I had just promised to marry. I added, "I cannot understand why Mary will not permit the young ones to be together under adult supervision."

"Because it leads to what you have just overheard, Lilibel. They are too young to be turned loose with their passions. Mary has reason on her side." There was an undercurrent of annoyance in his voice.

"I did not mean to imply that Mary should not supervise her daughter. It's simply that she's overly protective. Amanda will soon be sixteen, and if she is allowed a little freedom she will be much less likely to take too much."

"We will not argue about it, my dear," Andrew said shortly, covering my hand. His voice lightened. "I shall tell each of the family of our betrothal—adjuring each to secrecy, for I realize well enough that conventions must be observed." He added hastily, "Though you and I know that I shall mourn Yve the rest of my life."

"Yes," I replied calmly, refusing to allow misgivings about my dead sister to add to my uneasiness. "We both shall." Then with sudden strength, "Little Andy needs a mother's love and care—and I fear Mary and Laura have made him an object of rivalry, with both trying to mother him too much."

As we neared the house, Andrew spoke with an uneasiness of his own. "I hope you will not deny either of them—Mary especially—an aunt's love of a nephew."

I looked at him in the reflected light from the open French doors. "I'm his aunt, too," I said slowly. "And Mary's love seems so—overpowering. . . ." I trailed off, envisioning her ardent, loyal eyes on Andrew, her fierce embraces and hot loyalties to all whose blood she shared.

"Mary cannot help that," Andrew replied. " 'Tis her nature to be loyal and affectionate with the family." There was a tender, sorrowful note in his voice, and something else that I could not name.

In the great ballroom of the Livingstons' home, the first person I noticed was George Madison, who leaned against a wall, sipping his bourbon and water. His eyes were on his brother's face and their expression was unreadable. Yet I thought, *He knows.* Then sharp on the heels of that thought came another: *He expected it.* And I wondered at the odd disquiet that stirred in my breast.

The music was gay and light and the dancing in full swing, but many were seated about the big room, and like George, several of the men were merely watching the dancers. Mary, in the arms of young Cholmondeley, kept glancing anxiously about. When her eyes lit on her brother Andrew, some of the anxiety left them. But they swung back to the French doors quickly, giving Amanda her full attention now that her brother was accounted for. I wondered with sudden curiosity what Mary's reaction to our betrothal would be.

Laura, her lovely face pink with exertion, was dancing with Charles Alexander, to the obvious annoyance of the several bachelors who had been invited down for the ball by the Livingstons. They hovered near, waiting to claim her as soon as the music stopped.

Andrew and I had made our way past those seated around the room, nodding and returning greetings as we progressed to the dining salon. "Wouldn't it be lovely if Laura and Mary found—what we have found here tonight?" I remarked as we entered the salon.

Andrew, holding out the empty champagne glasses to a

tall slave in a red waistcoat, smiled at me. "My dear, Mary loves her family much too much to leave it again for any man. As for Laura"—he shrugged, and his voice was tinged with the strange bitterness he reserved for her—"who knows? It seems to me she already favors Charles."

Taking a fresh glass of champagne from the servant, I brought it to my lips thoughtfully. What Andrew said had an unfortunate ring of truth. Still, it was a great pity about Mary. She was, I suspected, a passionate woman, having thirsts and hungers within that voluptuous body, and yet I could not escape the feeling that those appetites were often satisfied in some manner I could not fathom. For, at times, she wore the look of a woman whose desires were richly fulfilled.

I saw with relief that Amanda and Clay had returned and were dancing decorously.

After the second glass of wine, Andrew and I danced again, and this time I was conscious of eyes following us. I thought, *They all suspect that there is an attraction between us*, and that added somehow to my uneasiness.

When George claimed me once more, I braced myself to meet his mockery. As we whirled about, there was little breath left for conversation, but he did whisper as we swung together, "I take it you have removed my brother from the list of eligible bachelors."

"I don't know what you mean," I lied.

"I think you do."

I said with annoyance, "And I think you are an impertinent, inquisitive man."

"And you and Andrew will live happily ever after."

"He's told you——" I broke off.

He shook his head, his cynical smile white in the tanned face. "It was plain to see on your faces when you came in from the gardens. I'm sure, however, he has agreed to wait a decorous length of time before the wedding."

I was infuriated that this man could read me so well and that he had tricked me into admission. I took refuge in blandness. "Andrew and I merely talked of the future at Cloudmont."

"I'm sure you did. With you as his bride."

"George, you're impossible."

"You don't deny it, eh? Ah, my brother has a penchant for beautiful refugee French noblewomen, has he not?" Swinging away from the other dancers, we came to a stop in a small alcove and I met him head on in the quarrel.

"Andrew wanted to tell you," I said angrily. "Yes, I have agreed to marry him and we will wait a proper length of time—until next December, if you must know. But it is to be a secret." I added coldly, "I do hope you will respect our desire for that."

He looked at me for a long moment before asking, "Do you love him?" His eyes were piercing.

"Of course," I blurted hastily, though now it occurred to me I had not declared my love for Andrew. But I admired him greatly and I was attracted to him; he stirred me. The white-hot passions of extreme youth would naturally be in abeyance. We were adults and love was understood.

"I think you are making a mistake," he said as the music stopped. He was smiling, and I was suddenly enraged.

"How dare you!"

"I know my brother well, and I dare suggest that he might well take from you by persuasion that which you feared I would take by force."

"You *are* a cad!" I whispered furiously and walked away, my bosom heaving beneath the new white brocade ballgown.

It was a long time before my anger cooled, but I put on a serene face as the evening wore on and the buffet was served.

Clay never once left Amanda's side and Mary was ever watchful, so much so that her dancing during the balance of the evening was desultory.

There was little dancing after the buffet anyway, for the men gathered in groups and talked politics, while the women formed their own circles and spoke of households, children, and the latest fashions. I did not dance with Andrew again, but his mother approached and whispered her pleasure over our engagement.

Mary followed soon after but her good wishes were cold and reluctant. She said, "I think you and Andrew are acting precipitately. Yve has been dead less than six months." Her eyes met mine, and I was shocked to see the violent emotion in their glittering depths. She added, "I hope you will be—kinder to my brother than your sister was." She paused. "I congratulate you and wish you well." She brushed my cheek in a fleeting, perfunctory kiss.

The near hatred that lay in Mary's cool voice disturbed me.

Amanda left Clay just long enough to hug me and whisper, "Perhaps—just perhaps I will have the same kind of announcement to the family myself soon."

She looked so hopeful, cheeks aglow and eyes brilliant, that I found myself whispering back to her, "Amanda, *chérie*, it warms me to see you so happy!" After squeezing my hand, she went back again to Clay. She seemed to float as she reached him.

It was near the end of the evening before the last member of the Madison clan approached me. Laura's blue eyes were oddly veiled as she took my arm and said, "Ah, my dear Lilibel! I do wish you happiness with all my heart." There was something curiously sympathetic in her murmured congratulations that set my teeth on edge.

"You sound as if there were some doubt that I shall be happy, Laura," I responded with unusual sharpness that made me half ashamed.

Laura took it calmly. "Isn't there always some doubt? As adults we should be able to meet that knowledge. Blind passion is for those"—her eyes strayed across the room—"as young as Amanda and Clay." Her voice grew more cheerful. "But Andrew will bring you financial security such as you have not known since your childhood, and he will make Mélisse a wonderful father."

I restrained a wince. She had so surely hit upon my own most positive thoughts in accepting Andrew's proposal. "That's a very cold-blooded approach to marriage," I replied.

"Well, you know how I feel about Andrew, Lilibel," she said with a shrug.

At that moment I caught Andrew's eyes from across the room where he stood with a group of men. He smiled. In the tender glow of candles and lamps, all the people in the room seemed charming, civilized and genteel—even

Anna and Jabez. At that moment, I found it hard to realize that the Livingstons kept a stockade behind their slave quarters where the rebellious were chained and beaten. As for Andrew, so tall, so courtly and urbane, I felt a sharp thrill of relief that this man would make me his wife and keep Mélisse and myself far from the harms that filled an uncertain world.

Laura, who had observed me closely, was smiling now, a faintly cynical smile. "Believe me, dear Lilibel, I do wish you the best of everything. I am sure you will get most of it."

I squared my shoulders and said soberly, "I shall probably get what I deserve."

"Then you will, indeed, get the best of everything," she said, and this time there was only friendship and pleasure in the brilliant smile she gave me.

As we left the ball, the other women stepped into the waiting carriage with assistance from Henry Pepper and Noah. But Andrew himself waited to assist me up the narrow steps with a hand so strong, warm and tender that I felt new confidence flowing into me. Once in the carriage with the others, there ensued much chatter about my betrothal. The ladies, enforced by convention to silence at the ball, were full to bursting with it. Over the babble, Laura said firmly, "No, Judith, I don't want you telling any one of the other servants—not even Railo—about Miss Lilibel's engagement. 'Tis a secret, remember."

"Yes'm." In the dim light from the small lamp that swung beside the carriage window, she turned large dark eyes on me. "I wishes you much happiness, madame."

" 'Twill be a secret for less than a week, I'll wager." Cornelia chuckled. "Henry, Abigail, and the others will sniff it out in no time at all. And I shall be so glad to turn the reins of domestic Cloudmont over to you. Of course, child, I shall be there to help you—and so will Mary, in any way we can. But I have a feeling that you will manage beautifully."

"Did Yve—do well managing Cloudmont?"

There was a momentary silence, then Cornelia said kindly, "My dear, your sister did not like keeping the household accounts and supervising the larder, or overseeing the servants—she was happy to let me continue doing it.

"I see," I murmured. My poor Yve. Her shortcomings mounted up at every turn, and I wondered anew what could have brought about such a change in her. Or had she always been as these people implied, cruel, careless, and jealous? I loved her so, my mind rejected it even as I was forced to admit that the evidence was overwhelming.

We were all still in a state of excitement when we reached Cloudmont, but we dispersed to our rooms immediately. I held the candle and looked down at my sleeping child, my heart filled with love for her. Now she would have a father, a big, kind father to whom she could turn for comfort and strength. Andrew loved children. It was one of the characteristics that endeared him to me. All these people seemed to have an abiding love for children. Even George was extraordinarily tender and winning with the young ones, and his pockets on his return trips from the city were filled with small treasures for them. If the Madisons had one outstanding trait, it was devotion to their children and to each other.

I had donned my long cambric nightgown and was ready to blow out the candle by the bed when a soft rap came on my door. I knew it must be well past two in the morning, and my heartbeat stepped up involuntarily.

Who would be rapping at my door at such an hour?

CHAPTER 11

Going to the portal, I opened it a fraction and Andrew whispered, "Let me in, darling. I want to talk with you." I opened it wider to permit him entry. He wore a wine-red dressing gown belted about his narrow waist, and his black hair tumbled over his forehead. His eyes were brilliant.

"What has happened?" I asked, obscurely frightened, as a gust of summer wind caused the candle by the bed to gutter, then flare up again.

"Nothing but the most wonderful moment of my life. I couldn't sleep, knowing you were so near. I had to come —talk with you. Kiss you again." With that he took me in his arms and kissed my forehead, my eyelids, and at last my mouth, tenderly at first, then with growing fervor.

"Andrew, dear!" I pulled away uneasily. "This is most unseemly."

He took my arm and led me to the couch, pulling me down upon his knees. "Little love, it's most seemly. We are to be married. What harm in tasting a few of the sweets before the ceremony?" He began kissing me once more, his big warm hands moving gently, over my body, all too vulnerable under the thin, gathered cambric. He cupped my breast and bent to kiss it through the material and I felt his breath, hot and stirring against my skin.

He pressed his mouth to the hollow at the base of my throat, murmuring endearments as his hand crept along my thigh. Memory, sharp as a razor, pierced the smoky acquiescence that was fogging my brain. *I dare suggest that my brother might well take from you by persuasion that which you feared I would take by force.*

Andrew's hands were stronger, more persuasively tender as he eased my slender body to the couch beneath him, pulling my gown upward. Suddenly I wrenched from his grasp.

"Andrew, I cannot do—what you wish," I gasped.

"But my darling, who is to know? And we will soon be married——" He tried to pull me down as I reared upward and away.

"We will not be married until December—we must wait until then for these intimacies."

"You mean I can't kiss you, caress you until then?" he asked, as if that were all he had in mind.

"Of course, but not like this."

"I thought you loved me," he said reproachfully.

I had still not told Andrew I loved him. I thought I loved him. I was sure I did until this moment. Now he leaned forward and, lifting my hair, kissed my shoulders, gently.

He said, "If anything happened—if you were to get with child, I should marry you immediately and the devil take a proper waiting period."

"I do not choose to risk that, Andrew," I said clearly, the physical passion he had stirred ebbing rapidly. "I hope you understand." I had no intention of becoming another Louise Alexander in this household. I came dangerously close to succumbing, but now I was determined to wait until we were wed.

In the dim light of the candle, his handsome face wore a scowl. "I do not believe you love me as I love you," he said, his anger rising on the words.

"Then perhaps we have made a mistake," I replied coolly.

He seized me, holding me fast against his broad chest. "Don't say that! Don't ever say that. I will wait for you, if I must, but have you I will. You stir me as no woman ever has before." At my brief expostulation, he went on ruthlessly, "Yes, my darling, more than Yve, for you are more woman than Yve. More than"—he hesitated—"than anyone I have ever known."

"Then please do not come to my bedchamber in the

night again, Andrew. We will wait the proper period before we marry."

"Very well, Liliane—but one last kiss before I go," and his mouth came down on mine voraciously. I felt as if I were being absorbed into him, as if he possessed some terrible power to render me helpless against his desires. So overpowering was his passion, I felt drowned in it, and found myself pushing feebly against his broad shoulders.

"Andrew, let me go!" I insisted. George's deep and cynical voice mocked in my brain.

He released me reluctantly. "Let that be a measure of my longing for you, Lilibel. I love you—deeply." His voice was shaken. He rose abruptly and, tying the wine robe about his waist, strode to the door. Over his shoulder he said, "I will try to respect your wishes."

For a long time after the door closed behind him, I sat on the couch, bruised lips throbbing. My thoughts were a strange mixture of relief that I had not yielded and fear that this might happen again before the wedding. George had been right—and somewhere deep inside I felt a grudging respect for him, who made no pretense at seduction, but laid his desires openly before me.

What had really restrained Andrew? A small niggling voice replied, *the fear of my rousing the household with cries*. Then shame for him mingled with the first doubts about my betrothal. Andrew had said he would try to respect my wishes. I made a silent vow then. He *would* respect them. I would be a full and legitimate member of the Madison household—or I would be none at all!

Sleep came slowly that night and my dreams were uneasy and shadowed with uncertainty.

The following morning I would have slept late, but Mélisse was awake with the birds that twittered cheerily outside our windows in the towering tulip poplars.

"Maman, do wake up," she said, shaking my shoulder. "All the birds are up and I can smell Beady's biscuits baking."

"You smell what you hope for," I said, tousling her black hair with a loving hand.

"Andy says I have a tremenjus good smeller," she said, laughing, "and we are right above the kitchen."

I flung back the sheet and said, "I'll wager I can dress before you do—after we wash the sleep from our eyes!"

She beat me by several minutes in dressing and darted to the door that opened on the hall stairs leading down to the morning room.

"No, darling. You know Aunt Cornelia likes us to take the central stairs and go to breakfast with the rest of the family."

"I know," she said disappointedly, "but I hoped Beady would give me a hot biscuit before."

"*Alors!* You *are* hungry, *chérie*," I replied as we made our way into the dark paneled hall. "But Aunt Cornelia will be up—you'll see. And breakfast will soon be served."

As we made our way toward the front stairs, the sound of an angry young voice came to us.

"Oh, oh," Mélisse said, as we slowed. "That's Amanda, and she sounds tremenjus angry."

The argument was coming from Mary's bedroom and Amanda sounded near tears. As we reached the staircase, she suddenly burst out of Mary's room, fleeing blindly in our direction. Catching sight of us, she cried, "Oh, Aunt Lilibel! Please come talk to Mother! She is so cruel!"

Reluctantly, I turned to Mélisse. "Go downstairs, dear, and persuade Beady to give you that hot biscuit. I will be along soon." Mélisse skipped down the polished stairs.

I approached Amanda hesitantly, but she caught my hand and pulled me quickly into Mary's spacious bedroom. Cornelia was sitting on the couch and Mary's face beside her was flushed, her eyes wet.

I said warmly, "My dears, you all look so distressed. Whatever is the matter?"

Before her mother could speak, Amanda burst out, "Clay wants to marry me, but to hear mother, that's a fate not to be borne!"

"But Amanda—I agree to your marrying Clay! He's a fine boy, but only a boy. And you, dear, are but a child, not quite sixteen——"

"You'd keep me a baby forever! You were married at fifteen. How you can say sixteen is too young confounds me." Amanda's voice was harsh and accusing and she dashed her hand across her freshly wet cheeks as she turned to me. "Lilibel, do they not marry at fifteen and sixteen in France?"

"Sometimes," I replied with a compassionate look at the stricken Mary. Cornelia, as always, was in complete control of herself, but said nothing. I added gently, "But Amanda, they consider their parents' wishes before they marry in France. Indeed, most marriages are arranged by the parents."

Mary looked at me gratefully, and said, "There is so much responsibility that Amanda does not take into consideration—and there are the babies. She is not ready to be a mother. She is so young!"

"I *will* marry him!" Amanda's voice rose passionately. "I will—if I must slip away with him in the night. I swear it!"

"But Amanda, he has three more years at William and Mary before he graduates," Mary cried. "Can't you wait just three years?"

"No! His mother would welcome me at Tulip Grove. And I could be with him on holidays. He's *seventeen!* Aunt Lilibel, don't you think we would be happy?" Because I had helped her achieve permission to go to the hunt and the ball, the young girl looked at me as if I could arrange her marriage by the stroke of one sentence.

Caught between Amanda and her mother, I chose my words carefully. "Yes, I think you and Clay are ideally suited and I think you would be very happy—*if* you would wait a little longer, *chérie.*"

Amanda's face closed against me. "You're just like mother and grandmother! I thought you'd be on my side!"

In truth, I was. I could see no reason for the quarrel other than Mary's possessive love for her daughter. I said quietly, "I am on your side. But we must not consider our own wishes only, but the wishes of those who love us. Your mother deserves your consideration, Amanda."

"She'd keep me with her until I'm old and feeble. Mother never lets go of those she loves."

Cornelia said abruptly, "That's enough. We will discuss this later, Amanda, with your uncles' advice. Let us go to breakfast."

The finality in her low voice was indisputable, and we were a silent quartet descending the stairs.

Laura came out of her room as we started down and hurried to join us. "I thought I'd be the early bird, but I see you have bested me." Then, as no one replied, she said quickly, "Such a silent group! Has something happened?"

"Only Amanda," Mary said wearily. "She approached me this morning with plans for an immediate wedding to Clay. She even tried to get Lilibel to persuade me to it."

There was a momentary silence, then Laura said shortly, "You hold too tight a rein on Amanda, Mary. You will regret it."

Mary gave her a cold, level look. "That is easy for you to say, with no child of your own."

Laura's face paled slowly and she said, "I know you can smother a child with love. The Chenaults come close to it with their five. You come close to it with Andy."

"Andy is of *my* blood—not yours," Mary said in the same cold voice.

"I—I love Andy as if he were my own," Laura said in a low, trembling voice and I felt a flood of pity for her. Mary seemed so much more the mistress of herself in all ways—all except in dealing with her immediate family. Laura was an emotional, highly strung woman, unable to hold her own with a woman of Mary's stern nature. I wondered fleetingly how she had done so with Yve.

Cornelia spoke with sudden compassion. "Laura, you have a perfect right to feel that you are truly Andy's aunt—you were married to his uncle."

Mary shrugged as we reached the last step. "But the fact is, you are not. So kindly do not sit in judgment of my relationships with my children and my nephew."

I held back my perverse desire to shout, *he is my nephew too and I shall soon be his stepmother*. Mary had such a talent for drawing a circle about herself and those she loved, closing out others.

Laura, however, made no reply to Mary, and Amanda was stubbornly silent as we made our way through the great hall into the library, where the men were enjoying a pipe before breakfast.

Charles looked very spruce in a new cravat and pantaloons, and his eyes kindled as they rested on the pale, unresponsive Laura. He went to her and began talking in low tones.

George and Andrew were hearty and teased us about being late as we made our way into the dining salon. The children were already there, squabbling over the spaniel, Domino, who was thoroughly enjoying being pulled back and forth.

It was easy to see from Amanda's glum face as we took our chairs that she expected no more encouragement from her uncles than she had received from me or her grandmother. However, nothing further was said about her problem and the conversation about the table was, as usual, of Cloudmont and crops. Neither Amanda nor her mother spoke to the men of the quarrel between them.

As June wore on, Andrew was as good as his word and made no more nocturnal visits to my bedchamber. But he found occasion to be alone with me more often and his kisses and caresses were as fervent as they had been the night of our betrothal. I was responsive, but careful not to be too much so. I felt that with any encouragement at all, I could find myself again in the position of resisting outright seduction. He was a difficult man to keep at arm's length, so smooth and polished was his approach.

On cool mornings, when the sun was barely over the horizon, we would sometimes go riding in the fields together. The cotton plants were a luscious green, the small bushes well up above the dark brown loam and the bolls forming nicely. The tobacco shoots were healthy and sturdy in long unbroken rows, as the men worked among them, chopping out weeds.

Most of these men were sun-burned tenant farmers who tipped their old straw hats to us as we rode by. They would, I knew, go back to their own acres and work during the long summer afternoon. But there were many of Laura's people scattered among them in the fields and working in the huge barns, readying them for the storage of cotton and restringing the cords on which the tobacco would be hung and cured.

The vegetable gardens near these great barns were full to bursting. Beans, peas, tomatoes, okra, eggplants like great purple teardrops grew there, as well as other vegetables such as carrots, beets, and potatoes, a great many of which would find their way into the root cellar near the icehouse. The table at Cloudmont these days was laden with the fruits of these gardens and the orchards beyond them.

The tempo of life at Cloudmont in summer was leisurely, but steadily one of business. My status in the household was subtly changed after my engagement to Andrew. Cornelia consulted with me often and initiated me into the household accounts, which she kept in the large *secrétaire* in the morning room.

"Andrew and George, of course, keep the plantation accounts, and Charles enters my tabulations in a ledger that carries all our records, including George's new venture in shipping and importing," she told me.

I had always been good at figures and had kept accounts for Tante Genèvre in the small milliner's shop in Paris. These were far higher figures and there were more of them, but I knew I should be able to handle them.

True to Cornelia's prediction, the servants became aware of my engagement to Andrew quickly and treated me with a touch of awe. There was but one in the household who apparently viewed my coming marriage without favor. Louise Alexander's smiles were strange, and she had said no word of congratulation or well-wishing. I could even sense disapproval.

I mentioned this to Laura, who laughed and said, "I think you are just now becoming aware of Louise. She is always a touch thorny with all of us. How would you react to the family you were part of only because you bore the master a charming but illegitimate son?" There was a curious quality in Laura's voice and the blue eyes were luminous with a unnamable emotion.

"Much as Louise feels, I expect," I replied uneasily, recalling that I might well be in Louise's position if I let my guard down with Andrew. Still, Louise's dark eyes haunted me, and her faint look of reproof drove me to speak of it to her.

She had come into my room with fresh bed linen one morning, which it was her duty to distribute from the linen chests for all the maids to use in changing our beds once a week.

As she was leaving, I spoke. "Louise, I——" I hesitated.

"Yes, madame?"

"I have the feeling you do not look kindly on my betrothal to Andrew, and it distresses me."

Her face softened somewhat. "Why, madame, should you care what a common servant thinks?" Then mockingly, "Especially one with a bastard son?"

"I like your son," I replied with a touch of heat. "I do not think the unfortunate circumstance of his birth has hindered him. He is a very worthy person."

Louise's face altered with dark emotion. Rage or frustration, or both? I wondered. There was a thickness in her words. "My son is not the only Madison born on the wrong side of the blanket, but others are more adroit in covering their tracks than I. Or luckier, perhaps."

"Louise, do you mean to say there are other sons—children of Thomas Madison——"

"I've said too much." Her eyes became remote. "If you are going to marry into this family, the less you know, the happier you will be, madame."

"But you must tell me what you are implying!" I was acutely disturbed. Louise had, in one short sentence, spun another fine strand pulling me into the web of intrigue of which I was becoming more and more aware.

"I've said too much," she repeated. Then, under her breath, "More than I ever have before. Forgive me, madame! I am a bitter woman and possibly a great fool as well." She turned and left me in the chaos she had created.

After that, I found myself looking at each member of the family with renewed and reluctant doubt. I had tried to lay my sister's ghost to rest, and during these warm summer days I had almost succeeded. Now a new specter had risen. Louise Alexander had certainly implied that one among them was illegitimate. Knowing how Cornelia worshipped her children, I was certain that each one must be her own, surely.

That left only Amanda and Timothy, for Mincy had

delivered my sister of Andy, with Andrew present. Mary, with that voluptuous and sensual body, was, I felt, quite capable of indulging in an illicit affair, and she had had a much older husband.

I finally concluded that Louise was indeed a bitter woman, who found a measure of comfort in distressing me. So I buried my doubts as Laura, Cornelia, and I, with Mary hiding her reluctance from all but me, began preparing a trousseau. The three of them were enthusiastic about the prospect of a wedding at Cloudmont and determined to outfit me in the best for becoming a bride.

Andrew, George, and Charles brought lengths of fine materials back from Norfolk and Richmond, and the four of us cut patterns and sewed a great deal of the time. The Chandler sisters had my measurements and Cornelia sent them elaborate instructions through Charles, along with rich materials from George's importing firm. Even Abigail and Clementine volunteered to help, and I was rapidly acquiring day dresses, Sunday dresses, ballgowns, and a chest of lingerie made of silk and laces.

Another thing that brought me great joy during that halcyon month of June was the complete flowering of my little daughter. Mélisse, with the loving camaraderie of the other three young people in the house, had become a bubbly, merry child. She had put on needed weight and was dimpled and beautiful and healthy as a young colt. She adored her cousin Andy and he reciprocated fully. Even the prickly and sometimes sullen Amanda forgot her frustrated love for Clay and romped joyously with the two young boys and Mélisse. It was such pleasure to watch them in the third-floor nursery and schoolroom, where Amanda forgot her newfound dignity and laughed as abandonedly as if she had never put her air up or worn a ballgown.

Laura and I did not give up our rides together, though they were not so frequent now, since I often rode in the mornings with Andrew. When he was away, however, I rode with her often and Charles would sometimes accompany us, sparring with her as we rode along. Though Laura was often short with him—and he gave us good as he took—the undercurrent of attraction between them was undeniable. Still, there was something in it that made me uneasy, as if these two were star-crossed. It was in their voices, in their exchanged glances, as if their love were shadowed by a dark secret. Laura, however, did not confide in me. Indeed, it seemed as if this emotional, sensitive young woman fought always against some heavy cloud, as if she carried some sorrow she could never escape. And often I surprised a disillusioned and haunted look in her light blue eyes. I wondered if it were only her unwilling attraction to the penniless, illegitimate, but compelling Charles Alexander that put the secret pain in those beautiful eyes.

During these long, sweet days I was aware of Judith going about the house with a drawn and frightened look about her. If Railo were coming to see her now, it was by stealth and at night, for we never saw him at the stables waiting for her, as he had done in the winter and early spring. Once, I essayed to comfort her.

"Judith, I feel that one of these days, Mr. Livingston is going to sell Railo to Laura. Then you two can be married and live here—as free people, with pay for your services." I did not have any real hope that the malignant Jabez would do any such thing, but the girl appeared so forlorn and miserable, I felt compelled to comfort her.

She looked into my eyes and said slowly, "No, madame. He ain't going to do that. Railo and me are going to have to take our happiness as we can. I love him and he loves me and in the sight of God we are already married."

"We will make it official one of these days, Judith. Do not despair, *ma chérie*." A sudden feeling of rage made me wish with all my heart that Jabez would fall ill and die. I crossed myself hurriedly and silently asked God to forgive me. Judith watched me with a faint smile.

"You're kind, Miss Lilibel, but I know ol' Livingston will never let Railo go and Railo won't let me come to him, even were Miss Laura willing, which she ain't. Railo says the Livingstons would make my life a hell—like his."

"I wish to heaven there was something I could do, some power I had to force that man to an act of kindness," I said, my voice hard.

"I know, madame, and I thank you." Her big black eyes were fixed on some point beyond me. Her face was a beautiful, dark mask, concealing the torment that must be with her constantly.

"Don't give up hope," I said firmly. "Things will work out for you in spite of Jabez and Anna Livingston."

"That's what Railo——" she broke off. Then, "Railo won't give up hope either, madame. I hope you're both right." There was something in her voice that chilled me. I could not place the emotion. There was implacability in it and finality, and as we parted, I had a swift precognition of disaster, which left me singularly apprehensive.

Still, all through that month, while I took rides with Andrew and with Laura and Amanda, sewed and chatted with the women of the house as we worked on my trousseau, and learned about managing the domestic side of the big house under Cornelia's expert tutelage, a certain peace came to me, a sense of belonging, and there was great comfort in it. And then one day, as June drew to its end, that was all destroyed.

July Fourth was just five days away. Preparations for a great celebration were already under way, and everyone in the house was in high spirits. On that last day in June, I found myself alone midmorning, and looking for Mélisse, could not find her.

Abigail, coming from the kitchen, said, "I think the little ones are all out in the children's garden playing, Miss Lilibel. Miss Mary's out there, too."

I knew Cornelia was in the morning room with the end-of-the-month accounts, and I had no desire to go over them with her. I opened the rear door of the great hall and stepped out onto the square granite stoop, then crossed the graveled courtyard and took the path between the boxwood hedges that lead through the gardens on either side of the bowling green. The flower beds, so dark and sere when I had arrived six months ago, were a riot of exotic colors and scents. There were blue perennial flax and belladonna lilies, Canterbury bells and clove pinks, periwinkles and day lilies, and over it all hung the strong, sweet fragrance of roses under a hot sun. It was the lush beauty of June's final fling before the fiercer love of July took the gardens in its heated embrace.

I turned a corner and embarked on the longer path that led to the children's playground. After a moment, I heard voices beyond a lacy lilac hedge. Mary, with her back to me, sat on a wrought-iron bench and, just in front of her, Andy was industriously digging at the earth. Then before I could circle the thick shrub, I was caught by the conversation between the little boy and his aunt. Mary was embroidering something—for my trousseau, no doubt.

"What is that great hole you're digging, darling?" Mary asked.

"It's a hole to put dead people in," was the unexpected reply. "Like the one in the churchyard where they put *her*."

Through the green and lavender lace of flowering limbs, I saw Mary drop her handwork and catch the little boy in her arms.

"Forget her, my darling. You are safe with your Aunt Mary now." Then fiercely, "Did you think no one would save you, my precious, after that terrible beating she gave you? No, no! Your Aunt Mary will never let anyone do that to her little love again. Never!"

I stood hypnotized, silent as the boy, before he spoke again. "When Aunt Lilibel marries Papa, she'll be my new Mamma, won't she?"

Hesitantly, Mary said, "Yes—but she's not like your mamma. Lilibel is gentle and kind. She loves you and she would never beat you, darling."

"But what if she does?" he asked curiously.

Mary said slowly, "Then your papa would—Grandmother or Aunt Mary would have to——" She broke off. Her voice was not Mary's voice at all, but that of a steely stranger, when she said quietly, "No one shall ever beat you with a riding crop again, Andy. We will see to that."

I turned and moved silently down the path until I was some distance away. As I turned back to retrace my steps, I began to call gaily, "Mélisse? Andy? Children, where are you?"

When I reached the spot where I had listened to that chilling conversation, Mary called, "Here, dear. Come join us." By the time I reached her side, Andy was helping Mélisse build a sand castle in the sandbox a few feet away. Mary's face wore a welcoming smile. "Amanda was here until half an hour ago, building a sand castle too—like any five-year-old. But she decided to go in for a morning snack. I told her to tell Bibsey to bring us a cold pitcher of lemonade."

"I didn't see her," I said idly, seating myself beside her. "Lemonade will be nice. How lovely that is," I added, gesturing to the delicate pink roses on sheer white lawn of the garment she held.

" 'Tis a petticoat—for you," she said, with a touch of acidity, "to wear next winter with that fine pale blue wool that Cornelia is about to finish up."

"You are all too good to me," I said automatically. The conversation between my nephew and his aunt had disinterred all my fears regarding Yve's death choking off the last of my hard-won trust and comfort.

Though we talked on in the wary, cautious way we had with each other, drinking the cool lemonade Bibsey brought, I knew my peace of mind had fled, and this time it would not return.

That night, as I climbed the three steps into the wide soft bed beside my child, my old enemy, fear, began gnawing insidiously at me. I had lived so long with it in France, first through the Terror, then while Napoleon's soldiers sought Mélisse and me, that I had thought to greet it as an old familiar. But I was in the heart of a big American family, bound by ties of blood through my daughter and her cousin Andy, bound by betrothal to the titular head of that family. And one of them had *saved* Andy from his mother. If in the future I made any member of the family too unhappy, they too would need to be *saved*. With a sinking heart, I concluded that such love was only a step away from madness.

I lay tense, examining from all sides the idea of breaking my engagement to Andrew. I weighed what I would be giving up, which was everything, against what I would gain, which was nothing. Except escape perhaps. And from what? No one had threatened me. There was only the implication I had drawn from Mary's avowed determination to protect our small nephew from harm.

Toward dawn, I finally resolved that I would never do anything that the Madisons could construe as harm to

Andy—an easy conviction, for I loved the child more each day. And I reasoned myself into thinking the morning would scatter my fears as the rising sun scattered night shadows.

I was almost right, for the next four days were merry with anticipation of the celebration of the Fourth and the house was abustle with preparations for the picnic on the banks of the James River. Everyone for miles around would come, including slaves.

The republic of the United States was already officially twenty-eight years old, and I was astonished at the tradition and warmth with which these people greeted this fact. They made a greater to-do about it than the peasantry at home made over Bastille Day, which was only twelve years gone by.

Mélisse and I woke early that hot, bright morning and hastened to join the others at the breakfast table. The preparations, of which today was the culmination, had begun nearly a week in advance. George and Andrew had come home from Richmond with a pack mule loaded with fireworks, among other purchases. Mrs. Beady, with the help of the other servants, had two great smoked turkeys, deviled eggs, fruits, innumerable pies and cakes and great jugs of tea, lemonade, and cider in enormous hampers. Henry Pepper had brought in large chunks of ice from the icehouse and had put it with a variety of wines and champagnes in a large wooden tub.

The Reeds, Montagues, and Chenaults would join with us, bringing food and all their families to celebrate the occasion and enjoy the fireworks in the late evening. Even Jabez and Anna Livingston would be part of the group. This made Judith happy, for we knew that Railo would be part of the Livingston entourage, helping to load and unload the hampers of food and drink they would bring.

The weather was exceedingly warm, and all the ladies wore light summer dresses with short puffed sleeves and low, square-cut necks. I wore one of my new frocks, a delicate pink muslin, with pale blue satin ribbons threaded through an embroidered band just below my breast. Everyone was very complimentary as Mélisse and I came to breakfast.

Afterward, we went into the salon, where we milled about chatting as the carriage was brought around to the rear drive. It was followed by three wagons, loaded with food, quilts, and picnic supplies of dishes and silverware and drinking glasses. Straw was placed on the beds of these wagons. The servants would ride in them.

There was much laughter and talk as we waited for everything to be ready. Timothy was chasing Mélisse and Andy, with Domino barking and darting among them as they circled the room. Mary remonstrated, "We shall leave you here all alone, Timothy, if you do not behave." But the boy only laughed and plunged after the two squealing children and the wildly excited dog. Catching Mélisse, he touseled her hair and tickled her ribs until she shouted with laughter and protest. Andy, coming to her rescue, pummeled Timothy, who replied in kind. At that point, Cornelia interceded, giving Timothy a sharp slap on his small buttocks. After that he calmed down momentarily.

Amanda, excited over the prospect of nearly a whole day in the company of Clay Reed, looked at her brother loftily. "You certainly don't act ten years old. More like two!"

"Aw, you think you're so old—because Clay thinks you're grown up. Well, you aren't!" He flung himself on a rosewood sofa and stared at his sister belligerently.

"I'm old enough to be married," Amanda said, shooting a quick, angry glance at her mother, whose mouth firmed.

"Mother says you aren't," Timothy said triumphantly, catching Domino and wrestling the spaniel until he barked.

"We'll have no more talk about this, children," Mary said in a cold voice. "Do not aggravate the dog, Timmy."

"See!" Timothy cried. "She called us 'children'!"

Mary looked at him with exasperation. "Timothy, I don't often do it, I know, but I shall take you upstairs and use the hairbrush on you—and you know it."

A bit sullenly Timothy went to the window to watch the activity about the carriage and wagons. In less than an hour, we were all ensconced in the vehicles. Timothy and Mélisse and Andy were delighted to be riding with the servants in an open wagon. Domino was with them, his stubby tail frantic with glee, his paws on the wagon sideboards. Mrs. Beady and the other women wore large bonnets against the bright morning sun; the men wore straw hats with broad brims.

Andrew, George, and Charles, accompanied by the thin, bookish Seton Cambridge, rode horseback beside the carriage in which the women were seated. Henry Pepper was alone on the box, for Noah, Ephraim and Joshua drove the wagons that contained the servants and supplies. Laura's people were in two of the wagons, with supplies of food their women had cooked for the occasion, and everyone seemed in high good spirits as we set off for the shaded banks that had been chosen for the picnic at a point where the corners of Cloudmont and Rose Hill met.

The carriage and wagons bumped over the country road until it dwindled into untilled meadow before we came to the James. We were laughing merrily among ourselves and the wagons filled with the servants strung out behind us were melodic. They sang hymns taught them by Seton Cambridge, who now rode beside them and led the music with his clear, precise tenor. None of us had any presentiment of the tragedy that was soon to strike.

"I love this spot we're going to," Mary said, her face glowing. "The river is shallow there at the edge, where some small boulders make such happy sounds as the water pours over them."

"Mary's my poet," Cornelia said smiling, her eyes warm on her daughter. "She used to wade there as a child and make rhymes about it."

"I loved to wade at the edge of the York River, as a little girl," Laura remarked, then put her head out the window to look back at those behind us. She added, "I do wish Andy would sit down. He's always trying to outdo Timothy."

Mary said anxiously, "Then call to him to sit down, Laura."

Laura lifted her voice sternly, "Andy dear, sit down or Aunt Laura will stop the wagon and make you ride in the carriage with us."

There was a loud cry of indignation, but apparently the little boy complied, for Laura drew her head in and said, "He's a bit too much like his father. Headstrong."

When at last we drew up beneath the tall, spreading

arbor vitae, maples, and tulip poplars, everyone poured from the vehicles, and there was a great cacophony of voices as we saw the Montagues approaching in four open wagons. His wife, the two married daughters and four grandchildren occupied the first, as Evan and his two sons-in-law rode horseback beside it. The last three wagons contained all their slaves, who were grinning and calling to their friends in our group.

"Go on, all of you," Laura told her people, laughing. "You all should set up your picnic place before the others arrive." She turned to me. "They always celebrate in that thicket of pines over there," she said, gesturing toward a stand of tall pines beyond us. "And we shoot off the fireworks in the meadow behind us— Oh, Judith, I see the Livingstons coming! Railo will soon be here."

Judith, who had been helping unload the quilts, stopped and looked eagerly where Laura pointed. We could just see the carriage, followed by two wagons. But as they drew up and greeted us, I did not see Railo among them. He was such a giant of a man, he would tower above the other blacks.

Jabez was full of flowery compliments for the ladies, and as usual it irritated me beyond all endurance. I said sharply, "Where is Railo?"

Anna avoided my eyes and Jabez, catching sight of the eager Judith, wore a sudden look of specious sorrow. "Ah, Judith, I see you were looking for him, and I so wanted to bring him. But my dear ladies, Railo is a very obstinate slave, and impudent too. I had to punish him today with a good whipping and he is in the stockade at home. You can't know how it grieves me when I must do that—but Railo must be taught his place."

Judith turned away silently and went back to help the others spread out quilts. I was boiling with anger, so much so that I did not trust myself to speak, but Laura said coldly, "I'm sure it does distress you, Jabez. Certainly it should. It seems to me you could have made an exception on this day, of all days."

"I took that into consideration, my dear," he said sadly, "but if you let them get away with insubordination even once, you invite disaster."

I turned away, sickened by the deceitful reasonableness in his voice, and looked on the happy confusion that was all about us. The slaves seemed full of good fellowship, not only with one another, but their attitude toward their owners was one of courtesy and apparent fondness. It was hard to imagine an insurrection among them in this moment of camaraderie. But Jabez always made me feel that rebellion among the slaves was only a whisper away. My hatred for him and for Anna was almost physically apparent as I stared at them with loathing.

In the hubbub, the Reeds and Chenaults arrived, adding to the noise and bustle. Their servants mingled with the others in unloading the supplies and food and helping to set up the picnic area, which was growing steadily larger.

As hampers and boxes were brought forth, I thought for the hundredth time I had never seen so much good food in my life, and I wondered how we would manage to do away with it. Our English servants mingled with the few of their kind who served the Montagues, Chenaults, and Reeds, and found their own place a hundred yards from us under a large oak tree.

We were only a few yards from the river. The children, including the sometimes grown-up Amanda, with Clay in close and adoring attendance, were begging to be allowed to wade.

Cornelia took a firm stand on this. "You cannot go wade in the river until we have eaten and we can stop and watch you."

Domino was plunging into the river, then out again, in a frenzy of delight, stopping long enough to shake water over all those nearest him.

"Then let Clay and me sit on the bank and dangle our feet in, Grandmother," Amanda coaxed. "We'll watch the little ones—"

"I'm *not* a little one," Timothy said hoarsely, still angry at his older sister.

"Clay and I will watch them, Grandmother, and we'll just trail our feet. It's so hot!"

"Do let them, Mother. They have my permission," Mary put in, fighting to hold down a corner of the tablecloth in a sudden light breeze. George came up and put a flat rock on it and she said, "Thank you, dear."

The youngsters went bounding down to the river's edge,

where they peeled off their shoes and stockings amid squeals and laughter and put their feet into the shallow pool of water.

The men had all gathered under one huge tree as the women and servants put down the hampers of food, and already I could hear politics being argued. Only Seton Cambridge, his gentle eyes holding his heart, hung about, hoping to do some small service for Laura. To her credit, she was kind to him, though I knew she did not even consider him other than the teacher and preacher that he was.

The wind was hot off the meadow. Even our nearness to the river did not cool it, and we were fanning ourselves and murmuring about the heat. The fragrant smoke from the pipes of the men seated beneath a big linden tree came comfortingly to our noses. They were all coatless, their frilled white shirts open at the throat and the full sleeves rolled up past their elbows. They looked lazy and comfortable and relaxed. I envied them briefly for their easy confidence, their certainty that they could shape their lives to suit themselves. Under their casual bantering attitudes, each man was powerful in the community of the commonwealth, and the destiny of Virginia was in the hands of these men and men like them. It was a destiny they would help fulfill, a rich and fruitful destiny. I knew a swift dart of pride in Andrew—and George, almost unwillingly—as their drawling voices, authoritative and final, rose above the others.

Much later, after we had sated our appetites whetted by the out-of-doors, all the children importuned to be allowed to wade once more. Amanda and Clay had gone hand in hand for a walk along the sandy bank of the James and were out of sight, to Mary's keen distress. She kept looking after them.

But the parents and grandparents were weary of the younger ones running about and, calling among themselves, agreed to let them go. Amid cautionings not to wade out into the stream beyond the shallows, the youngsters went caroling down to the river's edge, put their shoes and stockings neatly on the bank, and stepped in.

Seton Cambridge had detached himself from the men and was sitting worshipfully at Laura's feet, talking earnestly to her as she stifled a yawn and tried to look interested. Charles, with the group under the tree, glanced over occasionally with an amused expression. Seton's thinning hair was damp with the heat and curled limply over his high forehead, and he repeatedly wiped his small, gold-rimmed glasses with his handkerchief.

I was in the middle of the women, listening to the two married Montague sisters discuss the raising of children. The subject seemed to have endless variety, and everyone was having a wonderful time as the somnolent afternoon wore on. While they talked, some of them still munching small pastries the Livingstons had brought, I became aware of increasing shrillness from the children at the river's edge. Amanda and Clay had not reappeared from the trees that bordered the riverbank. I felt a touch of anxiety as I saw my small Mélisse, holding Andy's hand, venture gingerly out farther from the bank.

Suddenly releasing her hand, Andy moved boldly forward and called, "See, Tim? I'm not either afraid. 'Tis shallow out here."

Timothy ran past him, farther into the shallow water and very near a bolder where the current looked swift and deep to me. Mélisse moved back, watching with fascination as the boys ventured further. I decided to go down and call them back. The other women, even Mary, were so engrossed in their conversation they had not noticed the two boys' daring. Now the Montague grandchildren, the Reeds, and the Chenault youngsters yelled, urging Timothy and Andy to greater rivalry.

Before I could get to my feet, Andy, enraged by his cousin's enterprise, plunged forward, overtaking the other boy and forging ahead. At that moment, I saw him disappear in the water. An involuntary cry went up from the children and my own echoed it, drawing the attention of those around me.

"*Mon Dieu!* Quickly!" I cried picking up my skirts and starting to run. "Andy has fallen into the river!"

A little scream escaped Mary and Laura's face went white. Cornelia was beside me as we sped toward the river. I did not see Andy's head bob up for what seemed an eternity. But when I did, Seton Cambridge was already at the river's edge. Without stripping off coat or shoes, he plunged in and began swimming toward Andy. Timothy reached shore, his face white and terrified.

By the time we reached the riverbank, Seton was already fighting the current as Andy's small head appeared and disappeared in the late afternoon sunlight. The tide was going out and the river's flow toward the sea was strong. The little boy had not once cried out, which was frightening in itself; we did not know if his silence was because he was drowning, or because he was fighting the current too hard to give cry for help.

The other children and Mélisse had climbed from the shallow water and stood awed and stricken by the imminent tragedy. Mary clutched my arm, crying, "I can't swim—dear God—I can't swim!"

I glanced behind to see Cornelia, then the many servants and slaves running to congregate on the banks. At that moment, I saw George and Andrew plunge into the river. Both had paused long enough to shed their knee-boots.

Cornelia and Mrs. Montague were physically restraining Laura from entering the river. She was crying, "But I can swim—and he needs me!" She tore loose from them and ran into the shallows, but Vance Chenault and Evan Montague caught her there and pulled her to shore.

"Enough are already there to save him, Laura," Evan said compassionately. "Too many would be as bad as not enough."

Out in the river, I saw Seton begin to falter and his head went under. Then he and Andy, several yards farther downstream, cried out in unison. The sound was faint in my ears as the volume of sound around me rose.

Cornelia turned on those about us and cried, "Be silent! We must not distract them."

George, swimming strongly, was two yards ahead of Andrew. Seton Cambridge had sunk once more and when he rose, his voice was strangled and faint. George, some distance from him, shouted to his brother, "Andrew, help him! I'll get Andy," and he put his head down, using powerful strokes toward the small bobbing head, which went down at that moment. I waited for it to reappear, but it did not.

A groan was wrung from Laura. "Ah, God—he is gone—gone!"

I turned, caught her arm tightly. "George is almost there! He will get him in time." I spoke with much more assurance than I felt. Mary had bitten through her soft lower lip, and a scarlet thread of blood ran down her white chin. Only Cornelia was in control of herself, her colorless face drawn, and I thought for the first time that she looked her full age.

Andy's head did not reappear, nor did Seton's, and I saw George's black, dripping head go under deeply as he searched for the small boy. Andrew was diving for Seton, apparently also in vain. The current in the center of the river was deep and treacherously swift on its way to the sea.

Mary, whose arm I had been holding, abruptly tore from my grasp and lunged toward the river, but I caught her hard. *"Mais non, non!"* I cried. "Already four are in danger, Mary. We must not make it more."

By now, the other men on shore had ceased shouting words of encouragement. A deathly pall of silence settled over us as the two men in the river continued to be swept farther downstream, plunging repeatedly beneath the surface in vain efforts to find Seton and my nephew.

It seemed to me that Andy and the teacher had been beneath the water for hours, when George's dark head suddenly broke the surface and he shouted, "I've got him!" His voice came to us faintly, for he was far downstream by now. We saw him raise the upper half of the boy from the water. Andy's head rolled with terrifying limpness. George struck out for shore with powerful, grim strokes, bearing his unconscious nephew.

As one, we all began to run along the riverbank to the spot where he would emerge. Tripping over debris cast up by the current on the narrow sandy shores, I watched Andrew's head still appearing above the water, only to sink once more in his desperate search for Seton.

As we ran, we saw Amanda and Clay approaching, their faces flushed with happiness. As they drew near, their expressions changed to alarm. When the others told them hastily what had transpired, they joined us with pale faces and wide eyes to wait for George to reach the shore with his limp burden.

"Give him room," bellowed Evan Montague, his graying leonine head rising above the welter of black and white spectators. George was nearing the shore now. A spot cleared as we all backed away and George, reaching the shallows, staggered to his feet. He stumbled forward with Andy dangling from his arms.

"He's full of water," he said hoarsely. "Got to get it out of him quick!"

Clayton Reed stepped forward. "I've done that before," he said quietly as George deposited his unconscious burden on the flat stretch of ground beside the river's edge. Clayton bent over the small figure. I could no longer see for those taller than I crowding forward.

I stepped back so I could see the river once more and I watched as Andrew's dripping dark head came up, only to sink once more. All the time Clayton worked over Andy, Andrew kept diving beneath the clear, dark waters of the James, seeking the teacher without success.

Clayton Reed worked steadily over the small boy while Andrew drifted farther downstream. At last Vance Chenault cupped his hands to his mouth and shouted, "Andrew! It's been too long. You can't save him now. Come back, man, before we have to send someone for you."

Andrew plunged once more and was out of sight for a long time, so long that I grew uneasy before he popped to the surface, flinging water from his face. I saw then with relief that he was making for shore at last. The river curved very slightly and trees near the edge obscured my view of him. Turning my attention to the group before me I saw that they were silent, intent, and their desperation made itself felt. Peering between the others, I could see Clayton Reed moving rhythmically over Andy's small form, and I heard Cornelia murmur, "At least they've got some of the water out of him—"

"He's breathing!" Laura's cry was ecstatic.

I moved away, my legs suddenly weak. I had not realized how much I had come to love this bright child of my sister until this moment, when we might lose him. I went to a large fallen tree, a giant the river had washed loose from its dead root system but had failed to carry to the sea. Louise Alexander sat there, her dark eyes lifted to mine as I took a seat beside her.

" 'Twill break his mother's heart if he dies," she murmured, her eyes measuring me.

"Seton's mother?" I asked.

"Andy's."

"He'll be with his mother if he dies," I replied, giving her an astonished glance.

Her little smile was enigmatic. "No, madame. Have you not yet come to realize that Andy is not your sister's child? I would have thought your intuition would have told you."

CHAPTER 12

I stared at Louise Alexander. I was stupefied. "You're mad. Everyone saw Yve pregnant. Andrew and Mincy Delafield were with her when she was delivered."

"Yve's privacy was closely guarded—by Yve. We saw her grow bigger, apparently with child, but she allowed no one near her during labor until Andrew and Mincy arrived. I think Andrew forced your sister into the deception as his price for staying with her. Now his bastard is in his house, enjoying all the fruits of legitimacy."

"You're lying," I said flatly, the curious sickness of belief taking hold of me even as I spoke. "Why would you tell me—such a monstrous thing?"

"You're her sister. Her closest kin. Can you not understand why your sister hated the child—hated the family? All but her adored Andrew, of course, poor girl." There was grim satisfaction in her voice. " 'Twas very smoothly done. I was in the shadows in the great hall that July night when Andrew and Mincy came in. He wore his greatcoat, oddly and conveniently, large enough to conceal a baby beneath. And Mincy herself carried a large covered basket, which I'm sure she told them all held only her equipment for midwifery— Ah, but I heard a baby's small cry as they hurried up the stairs," she finished triumphantly.

"You're lying," I repeated stubbornly, "or you are demented."

"Not so loud, madame. It is my opinion that none of the rest of the family knows of the deception."

"Then why haven't you told them—as you have me?"

Her eyes went to the group around the child on the ground, where Cornelia, George, Mary, and Laura stood with servants, slaves, and friends. Her smile was wintry. "I've enjoyed seeing them deceived. It pleases me to watch Cornelia make a fool of herself over her son's bastard. And I've delighted in seeing a bastard receive the respect of the community—something my son has never enjoyed." Her smile grew and thawed. "Besides, I'm fond of the cheeky little rascal. Why should I destroy his world for him?"

A glad cry rose from those around the boy. As they fell back, I glimpsed Andy sitting up, his back against Laura, whose head was bent to his and whose shoulders shook with sobs of relief. Tears streamed down the cheeks of Mary, who crowded down to kiss the child, and Cornelia was unashamedly wiping her eyes with her hands.

"If what you say is true, who is his mother?" I asked woodenly.

"Can't you guess?"

"I still think you're lying. If Yve wasn't pregnant it would be impossible to fool everyone into thinking she was.

She shrugged, " 'Tis your affair. I only told you so that you might understand why none of them have a good word for your sister."

The others were dispersing now, discussing the best methods for trying to recover the body of Seton Cambridge. Andrew had come up to his son and was kneeling before him, holding his small hands and speaking with love and gratitude to the boy. I looked at them, too sick at heart to join them. Mary succeeded in taking Andy, and held him to her breast. He was pale and limp, but he was breathing regularly. The rest of the men and more than a dozen of the black men were fanning out along the shore beyond, searching the swift water.

I went up to Mary and took one of Andy's hands in mine. It was warming now. I kissed his pale cheek and murmured. "Thanks to *le bon Dieu.*"

Beside me, Andrew said wearily, "Indeed we can thank God—and George." He looked after his brother, who was far down the river's edge now, his eyes searching the water for some sign of Seton. Andrew added, "They'll not find him for miles. Perhaps never, if his body is carried to the sea."

I looked up at Andrew, at his thin, high-bridged nose above the curved, clean-cut mouth. His wet black hair curled over the high forehead, clung, persistently curling, along the back of his neck. Something of contempt turned over deep within me, like a living thing in my vitals. My feelings for Andrew were undergoing a change and I was not yet sure of the outcome.

I moved away, following Cornelia, Laura, and Mary. The servants and several of the slaves were still about them where Mary held the child. Laura was still crying, but her sobs had lessened and she wiped her eyes repeatedly. Something of her agony penetrated my numbness as I saw Amanda lift Mélisse to her hip. Timothy was staring at his cousin Andy with open admiration and envy at his being the center of so much attention.

Andrew, following me, said in a strained voice, "You are all right? This hasn't been too much of a shock to you?"

"I was terribly afraid for Andy—and I'm grieved for Seton," I said with forced calmness.

"It has been a terrible ordeal," he agreed. Following me to the women, he said, "My dears, we must get my boy home where he can be ministered to—I've already sent Noah to fetch Aunt Mincy to the house."

I put a gentle hand on Laura's shoulder. "I'm so glad he's all right," I murmured, and she looked at me with tear-filled eyes.

Andrew took his son from his sister. "Come," he said to us, swinging the slight figure easily into his arms. "Pepper has hitched up the carriage. I've told the rest of our people they may stay for the fireworks tonight. Evan will set off the display—and those who wish to return with us may do so."

I looked around for George as the other men returned to the scene of the picnic. Clayton Reed informed us, as we mounted the carriage, "George and Vance and a dozen of the servants are going to cover another mile downstream before giving up, Andrew. But I think they're wasting their time. Poor old Seton's halfway to Chesapeake Bay by now."

"I think you're right," Andrew replied grimly, "but I'm going to get my boy home and in bed, where Mincy can nurse him, as soon as I can." At his father's words, Andy opened his eyes briefly and swallowed hard, then closed them again.

A wagonload of Laura's people had elected to return with us, declaring they would not enjoy seeing any display of celebration until they could be sure the small Andy would recover satisfactorily. Louise Alexander and the English servants felt the same and followed in a second wagon.

We were a silent, crowded group in the carriage, for Andrew had elected to ride inside with Andy. We had little to say to each other on the way back to Cloudmont.

I was concerned for Andy, but I found myself looking at those about me with strange clarity. Laura sat next to Andrew, who held his son in his arms. Both looked uncomfortable, as Mary kept craning to look at the little boy, crowding them close together. Amanda, beside her mother, wore a worried and slightly sullen air. Timothy, his grandmother, Mélisse, and I occupied the seat across from them. Slowly my suspicion began to focus on Laura.

It seemed to me now I could see resemblance in the fair hair and curve of lip. I had seen only the characteristics of his father while I sought Yve in Andy's face. If I were to believe Louise, I would never find Yve there.

On that long ride home, I decided I would go to Laura after the house was quiet and the others sleeping. She might give the lie to Louise Alexander. I could then put it down to an embittered servant's desire to revenge herself by lying about a family to which she could never belong.

After Andy had been put in his father's bed, as Andrew demanded, I took Mélisse and went downstairs through the great hall and out to the gardens at the rear. She had clung to me like a small shadow since the accident, and I wanted to get her out of the house and away from the distraught atmosphere. Amanda trailed disconsolately after us, grieved at having to leave Clay at the picnic, shaken at the sudden violent death of her teacher. Timothy remained with Mary, Laura, and Cornelia, who would not leave the bedroom where Andy lay.

Amanda said abruptly, "I shall miss old Seton."

"Yes," I replied, "he will be missed by all of us."

"Uncle Andrew and Uncle George will get someone to take his place and I'll bet we won't like him. Come on, Mélisse, I'll swing you." She took my daughter by the hand and went to the hickory tree in the children's garden where the swing hung. In a few minutes, my child was laughing happily as Amanda pushed her higher and higher.

I sat on a wrought-iron bench and watched them, but my mind went back to Andrew and Laura. In my heart, I was sure Laura was Andy's mother, and I could not understand why Andrew had asked me to marry him, when he could have had the true mother of his son. Fleetingly I thought of Laura's flirtation with Charles. Was it done merely to pique Andrew, for all she seemed so hostile to him? But no. There had been genuine emotion between Charles and Laura, I thought, recalling the scene in the bedroom at Richmond.

Suddenly I heard Noah's voice beyond the flowering hedges and the disciplined boxwood. Amanda, hearing, caught the swing and halted its impetus.

"It's Aunt Mincy!" Mélisse cried, jumping down and running around the hedges.

It was late evening now and I followed the children to find Aunt Mincy. She had just ridden into the stableyard on her horse, her sack of herbs and medicines slung over the rump of the animal. Mélisse flew to her outstretched arms when Mincy dismounted and kissed her lined black cheek, crying, "Aunt Mincy, you must help my cousin Andy—he is so sick from falling in the river."

"I know, honey," was the soothing reply. "Noah told me. Mincy's goin' to fix him up fine. You'll see."

Mélisse's small face cleared at once. With her hand tucked into Mincy's, she accompanied her to the big house. Amanda and I followed after.

Noah, falling in beside us, said, "Do you reckon Mr.

Andrew would mind if I come in, too? I been powerful worrit about the little feller."

"Of course not, Noah," Amanda said. "You know that!"

In a few minutes we were with the rest of the family in Andrew's spacious room. Laura and Mary were sitting as near the bed as they could and both looked up with immense relief as Mincy entered, carrying her sack of medicines.

Andrew said, "Aunt Mincy, I put him in here because I thought I'd sleep with him tonight. I don't want him to wake up and be alone."

"Best put him in his own bed, Mister Andrew. I'll stay up with him through the night."

No one demurred and there was a general exodus to the third floor, where Andy's room lay between Amanda's and Timothy's. As his father carried him, the boy opened his eyes and said weakly, "Aunt Mincy, can you make my tummy feel better? I swallowed so much water and I feel so bad." Mincy's very presence was comforting to all of us.

" 'Course Aunt Mincy can fix you up, lamb. I got somethin' here in my sack gonna make you feel like your old self, Andy." Even her voice was comforting. Everyone began to feel better. I could sense a lightening of spirit among us.

"You all go 'long now," Mincy said kindly to all of us. "Leave ol' Mincy with this boy and he be good as new termorrow." Noah was the last to leave the room.

Much later, well after darkness had settled over the countryside, George returned to Cloudmont. I had put Mélisse to bed and reluctantly joined the women in the library, where Cornelia was determinedly doing fancy work on a pillowslip by the light of oil lamps lit about the room. Laura and Mary made no pretense at occupying themselves, their minds on Andy to the exclusion of everything else. I was in a fever to confront Laura with Louise's statements, but I knew I must wait.

Cornelia looked up as I entered. "Ah, Lilibel. Would you pour us all a glass of wine to ease our nerves?"

As she spoke, George came into the room. His clothes,

ruined by river water, had long ago dried on him, giving his big frame a curiously pleated look.

Cornelia put down her embroidery and said with relief, "My dear! I am so glad to see you—and did you find Seton?"

"No," he said shortly. Then to me, "I'll have a brandy when you get the wine."

I went to the liquor cabinet and, opening the finely carved doors, selected the wines from an array of bottles and glasses. While I poured the liquid, George said, "We covered ten miles of riverbank, but there was no sign of him. Perhaps he will wash ashore farther down the James in the next day or so. Word will come to us, if he does."

Mary said morosely, "He may be swept out to sea and we shall never be able to give him a proper burial. As it was with the Chenaults' guest five years ago—remember Mr. Buford? He was never found."

Laura said thickly, "I thank God, and you, George, for saving Andy."

"It was a near thing," he replied gravely. "I was afraid for a while he wouldn't make it even after we got to shore."

I approached with a silver tray, holding four glasses of wine and a stiff tot of brandy in a crystal snifter, which George took gratefully and tossed off in one gulp. Then he asked, "Is Aunt Mincy with him?"

"Yes," replied Cornelia. "She seems to think he will be quite all right by tomorrow. But he was so pale, I was terrified."

We talked desultorily about the tragedy of Seton and the near tragedy of Andy until we finished our wine. George sprawled comfortably in a great wingback chair, obviously exhausted from his strenuous efforts of the afternoon.

Finally, to my great relief, Cornelia put aside her work and said firmly, "It's time we were all in bed. This has been a bad day." She got to her feet. "Come, my dears, we will look in on Andy once more and then retire."

From his chair, George said, "Fetch me one more brandy, Lilibel, before you go, please."

The others went out and I stepped to the cabinet once

more, where I splashed fresh brandy in the snifter he handed me. This time he sipped it slowly, looking at me steadily over the rim. I turned to go, but he said, "Wait."

I turned back, brows lifted, and for another interminable moment he did not speak, heightening my impatience. Then with total unexpectedness, he asked, "What has happened to you?"

"Why, you know well enough what has——"

"I don't mean the accident at the river, Lilibel. I mean what has happened to *you*?"

"Nothing."

"You're lying," he said flatly. "It's in your face, in your eyes. Something is disturbing you greatly—more than the death of Seton and the narrow squeak for Andy."

For an instant, I had a powerful urge to blurt out my problem, but I checked it. "You really don't know me well at all, George," I said coolly. "You mistake my concern over Andy and Seton for something else. What it is, I cannot imagine."

He laughed softly. "I know you better than you think—and I know you are lying, my dear. But so be it. Keep your secrets." He added softly, "Somehow I cannot see you wedded to Andrew."

I bit my tongue on the words, *Nor will you see me wed to him.* Instead I smiled and said, "*Tiens*—you have a wayward tongue, George."

"Have I? Your eyes tell me that you are not happy here now, Lilibel. How do I know? Have you looked into my own? We've a kindred problem, you and I, madame. Cloudmont is not for us."

I shrugged. "Then why do you stay?"

"For the best of reasons. For the worst of reasons. For love." He paused, then asked grimly, "Why do you stay?"

I could feel the blood leaving my face. "My reasons are much like yours," I replied evasively, thinking of Mélisse and what being in the midst of a big, warm family had meant to her. What could she know of the fierce undercurrents just beneath the surface? Since my conversation with Louise Alexander, I had scarcely dared touch on what it had done to my feeling for Andrew. Now it began to force itself up under George's mocking smile.

He asked, "You mean for love of my brother?"

"*No*——" It burst from me involuntarily and my hand flew to my lips.

"I thought as much," he said cynically. "You stay then for love of comfort—for the happy child that your little daughter has become. Why spoil it all by marrying Andrew? You don't have to, you know, in order to stay." He put the empty brandy glass on the table beside him and got slowly to his feet, moving lithely forward. He stood looking down into my white face. "Or has the need for marriage passed already? Andrew is an expert in seduction——"

"So you have said," I flashed. "He has been unsuccessful with me."

He smiled. "Ah. Then he has tried."

Color flooded back. I felt it burning in my cheeks. "What an impertinent blackguard you are!"

"No, Lilibel. Do not confuse honesty with impertinence." He added broodingly, "I know my brother well—too well." His big hand was suddenly cool and rough against my cheek.

"Then Louise must be wrong. You must know about ——" I broke off, but too late, for his eyes were wary and alert.

"Know about what?" he pounced.

"Ah—about—" I began, trying to improvise. "That he tried," I finished miserably.

"Then Louise Alexander knows about that also?"

"Oh, no!" I cried in a panic, fearing this arrogant, inquisitive man might well question the servant. "No one knows about that." I gave him a bitter glance. "But you, now."

"Then you and Louise share another secret," he said with swift insight, "and that is what has changed you." He lifted his hand. "No. Don't bother to deny it. I shall question you no further." His voice was suddenly weary. "God, I'm tired. I shall look in on Andy now myself—then I hope to sleep for twelve hours." He brushed past me and disappeared into the great hall.

I stood there a long time, pondering my narrow escape, terribly aware of the momentous secret Louise had imparted. If what she said was true, she and I held the small boy's future in our hands. If such a thing were whispered about, his life could be ruined. What I could not understand was the source of hostility between Andrew and Laura.

Oh, I must seek out Laura! I would find a way to make her tell me if Louise had lied. I waited a few minutes longer before I left the room.

Making my way slowly up the long broad flight of stairs, I thought, *I can never marry Andrew now.* In my mind, I saw him locked in Laura's arms while my sister's heart broke in her lonely room—while she played out the charade of motherhood to please the dark-eyed, willful man I had promised to marry. No wonder she had become embittered—though I still shrank from the stories of her treatment of Andy. Andrew's unfaithfulness was not enough to account for that. Beating a child with her riding crop would take greater provocation than his father's unfaithfulness. Yes, something had driven Yve to the brink of insanity.

I took the third flight of stairs, to look in once more on my nephew—*my nephew*, I thought mirthlessly. Ah, well, I would guard his secret. I traversed the hall and came to Andy's room where the door stood open. One candle glimmered on the washstand and the three women, Cornelia, Mary, and Laura, were seated around the high bed where the child slept peacefully. Aunt Mincy crouched over her brazier, and a spicy, herbal scent hung in the air. The two great windows on the south were open and a gentle evening breeze fluttered the curtains. Despite the brazier, the room was cool and comfortable.

"He's been asleep for over an hour," Mary whispered joyfully to me. "Look at his cheeks. His color has returned." I nodded and she went on, "George has just been in to see him. That poor dear is nigh dead from his search for Seton. He and Andrew have gone to bed."

Aunt Mincy said quietly, "You ladies go to bed too. Ol' Mincy see to it this boy get well. He's goin' to sleep all night now. Termorrow he be hisself again."

"I'm so glad." I spoke with deep relief. "I had feared so for him."

"He jus' need sleep," Mincy reiterated, stirring the pot over the brazier.

Mary rose reluctantly to her feet, as did Cornelia. "I hate to leave him," she said, her great dark eyes lingering on the still form. "But you're right, Aunt Mincy."

Laura, the last to rise, went to the bed and leaned over the small boy. There was a poignancy in her body, a yearning that knifed me to the heart. Louise Alexander had not lied.

When I reached our room on the second floor, I could see Mélisse's small rounded form. She slept in the pale darkness of the room without cover. The night was very warm, but the breeze was sweetly cool, fragrant and refreshing as it came from across the broad river to the south. I sat in darkness on the couch before the fireplace, now hidden behind a painted screen and two large pots of what Cornelia called Boston fern. I waited impatiently for the household to settle for the night.

After a while, I rose restlessly and, going to the armoire, took my cambric gown from a hook beside the open mirrored door.

After I donned it, I could wait no longer, and my breath grew short as I went into the wide hall without a candle. It was very dark, but I knew my way well as I moved silently to the northeast bedroom door, directly across from Cornelia's. I stood a moment before the door and drew a long, silent breath.

Then I rapped, ever so gently, and tried the brass handle slowly. It gave and I stepped inside. In the dim light from the great north windows, I saw a pale figure rise up in the tall bed.

"Who is it?" Laura whispered hoarsely, half accusation, half question.

"Lilibel," I whispered back, hastening to close the door behind me.

"Oh—" There was relief in the sound, and I saw her bend to the table by the bed. In an instant, a spark flared from the flint, a candle bloomed into fire and giant, ragged shadows staggered about the room. She looked at me, her short curls in disarray, blue eyes enormous with apprehension. It was as if she knew my mission and would ward it off. "Lilibel, whatever brings you here in the dark—and so late?"

I came to the bed and climbed the three wooden steps to sink down beside her in the soft depths of the mattress, but I remained sitting and so did she.

"Is something wrong?" she asked anxiously.

"Yes," I said slowly. "Is Andy your son?"

I heard her sharp intake of breath, and the silence spun out before she said coldly, "What in the world are you talking about? Andy is Yve Madison's son and you know it."

"Ah, Laura, do not dissemble. Louise Alexander has told me Andy is illegitimate. She was in the great hall the night Andy was born. When Andrew and Mincy came to the house—she heard a baby's cry from the basket Mincy carried—before Andy was supposedly delivered. She says they brought him with them and Yve's pregnancy was a deception."

In the light of the candle, flickering wildly in the breeze that coursed past and down the crystal chimney, her face whitened. She swallowed twice before she said huskily, "Louise is a liar. I'm surprised you'd let her take you in with such a tale."

"I have watched you with Andy. I have seen the resemblance between you. Do not lie to me. It is so important that I know. Please tell me the truth."

There was again silence. Laura sat carved of stone, and I said slowly, "I cannot marry Andrew—not knowing."

She drew a long breath and her voice shook, "But you *must* marry Andrew. You are strong enough, gentle enough to change him." She halted, then her words came jerkily, "You have the strength to keep Mary from smothering Andy with an overpossessive love that could ruin him. Ah, Liliane, with you as Andy's mother, I could leave Cloudmont!"

"Then you are his mother."

"Yes, yes!" Now words poured from her in a tide. "No one knows—we were so careful. I thought I loved Andrew for years, even when I married Thomas. Then after Thomas was killed, Andrew came to me. We were lovers until——" She hesitated and began crying softly. "Then when I found myself pregnant, I moved back to Landon on the York and stayed, hiding myself from nigh onto everyone, supposedly trying to live on my own—an independent widow. Many do. Then Andrew persuaded Yve to pretend pregnancy in order that he might have his child." She looked at me with large, pleading eyes. "He is very paternal, you know, and Yve did not seem able—to conceive. He dearly loves his family."

"I know."

"Oh, how could we know that Louise would be where she could see them arrive that night! I'll wager she never heard Andy at all. She just put two and two together—that cruel, vindictive woman! Ah, Lilibel, say you will keep your promise to marry Andrew?" She was crying hard now. "I would be so relieved to know my Andy had a—a mother he could claim. You would take precedence over Mary in decisions, then."

"I cannot understand," I replied slowly, "why Andrew does not marry *you*. Then Andy could claim his own mother."

In the glimmering candlelight, Laura's eyes were suddenly veiled, her voice husky. "Andrew and I discovered long ago that we did not love each other."

"The strong animosity you share would indicate you do."

"That's the opposite of love!"

"*Au contraire*, it is very close to love," I replied. "Hatred and love are kin. Sometimes hatred is love in disguise."

"It is not hatred I feel for Andrew," she said, panic creeping into her voice. "I could never marry him because of——"

"Because of what?"

"Of all that has gone—before. There has been too much that has gone before." Her voice was controlled now, but there was a curious emotion in it that unnerved me. "And you forget, Andrew loves *you*. He has said so. And I tell you now that my feeling for him is not love."

"What is your feeling for him?" I felt I must know—there was something that made it imperative that I know.

For a long moment, she did not answer. Then she said

slowly, "If I told you friendly affection, you would know I lied. So I will tell you the truth. I do not even like Andrew, but that is because I am the way I am—and he is the way he is. He is a kind man and in many ways a good one. You know that, Lilibel."

"Yes, I know that. You must have a reason for not liking him."

"Not I." She laughed shortly. "I can like or dislike, hate or love, without too much reason, my dear."

"That also is a lie."

"All right, then," she said desperately. "The truth is that Andrew used me to bear him a son, when he loved Yve. I think he planned the whole thing. But you see, he loves children. He longs for them and that is a good thing, even if what he did to me was not!" As she caught my two hands in hers, I was shocked at how cold hers were to the touch. "Darling Lilibel, can't you see how much Andrew needs you? You are twice the woman I am—for I am light and unstable. Ah, yes, I know it well. And my Andy needs you terribly." She waited, her lips trembling.

I was silent.

"Please, Lilibel, for God's sake do not let this stop your marriage to Andrew. Cloudmont needs you. Cornelia needs another daughter-in-law. And my Andy—oh, my Andy needs you most of all! Please tell me you will not break your betrothal vows. *Please.*" There was genuine anguish in the pale, beautiful face.

"I cannot promise you that, Laura." My words were dredged up from the depths of my being.

"Why? Surely you will not destroy my child's life by revealing his birth?"

"Of course not," I replied swiftly. "No one shall ever know from me."

"It will do no good to tell you how much joy you would bring to this great house if you married Andrew next December. Please think long before you deny my son a mother who will rear him to be a man."

I began to slide from the bed. "It grows late, dear Laura," I said, my feet touching the cool wooden steps to the bed. "I promise you that I will give it much serious thought."

She leaned toward me as I reached the floor. "If you really love Andrew—and believe me, you do not know how much he needs your love—this sad secret will not change you."

"That is true," I replied, looking into the beseeching face under the tousled mass of gold curls. "I swear to you I will give it much thought. And whatever decision I reach, you may be sure it will be for what I feel is the best." I moved away.

"Good night, Lilibel," Laura said quietly. "You are a dear and wonderful person. I shall pray hard tonight—that you may become my son's mother. I could trust your care. Mary could not reach him—— Good night."

"Good night," I echoed, opening the door silently and entering the dark hall.

When I reached my room and climbed up into bed beside Mélisse, I found it hard to relax. Every muscle in my body was tense and my mind a millrace. Despite Laura's convincing plea for marriage, I found I was consumed by a powerful urge to escape my betrothal to Andrew. Feverishly, as I lay there in the late darkness, I went through scene after scene in which I told him I could not marry him. There was hardly any way to do it without revealing that I knew he had foisted off his illegitimate son on my sister. And I was determined to keep my promise to Laura. Besides, loving little Andy as I did, I could not see myself making such statements. With piercing regret, I realized now I had never really loved Andrew. It had been his security, the comfort he offered me, that had passed for love. Suddenly, those things were as ephemeral as smoke alongside these revelations of his character and the strange unwholesomeness I instinctively felt in him. This unwholesomeness was something Laura had somehow confirmed, yet I could not name it.

Withal, in some cold, clear corner of my mind I argued with myself. Could I not come to love Andrew in time? The love he gave Andy, he would give freely—was giving freely—to Mélisse even now. Wealth would be mine, and security, insofar as it could be provided in this uncertain life. I fell asleep at last with nothing resolved.

After the second day, Aunt Mincy left her charge fully recovered. But we, who loved him so dearly, could not lose so quickly the fears engendered by his narrow escape. It was a rare moment in the two days that followed when Mary and Laura were not with him. Mary was especially overcareful, supervising his food, his play, and all his activities.

Seton Cambridge was sorely missed, and Cornelia undertook the sad chore of writing to his widowed mother in Boston.

On the fifth day, after breakfast, George and Andrew stated it was their intention to teach Andy and Timothy to swim in the pasture lake beyond the tobacco fields. It provoked a genuine quarrel with Mary, who was adamant in her belief it was too dangerous, that the boys would double their chances of drowning as they would want to swim too often.

George was furious. "Nonsense," he fumed. "Andrew, Charles, Thomas—I—all learned to swim in that lake, and by God, it's saved my life more than once on the *Tern* when I've been knocked into the sea!"

He turned to ask Laura her opinion, but before she could answer, Mary said coldly, "Laura's no judge—no kin of Andy's. Only an aunt by marriage with no children of her own. You cannot consider her opinion."

They wrangled on until Andrew, jaw hardening, turned to me. "Lilibel, surely you do not agree with Mary and Mother—to keep my son a weakling!"

"No," I said abruptly. "I agree with you and George. I would like you to teach Mélisse while you are about it."

The following three mornings Laura and I accompanied the children and the men to the lake each morning. After the first day, Mary chose not to go. "I suppose they'll be as safe as can be expected with my brothers and Charles," she said grudgingly, "and I hate that ride in the sun."

She had been having an altercation with Amanda, who elected these mornings to go for solitary rides on her mare. Amanda was angry with her mother, because Mary had once again refused to let young Clay come to call.

On the fourth day, we had a picnic birthday party by the lake for Andy and Mélisse. Even the morose Amanda attended, and found herself joining in the hilarity. Beady and Louise had prepared a large wicker basket full of delicious food—fried chicken, tender roast-beef sandwiches, deviled eggs, a staggering array of sweetmeats, and great jugs of cider and lemonade.

Everyone had a small gift for the children, George and Andrew having brought toys back from their trips some time ago, to lay up against this day. The birthday party was a wholly satisfying event and we all straggled homeward late in the afternoon. Even Domino, stuffed with tidbits handed him by the children as they ate, appeared surfeited and languid.

I noted the children were becoming a golden brown from the early hours spent in the sunlit lake, and I took great satisfaction in the fact that my daughter was becoming as good a swimmer as the two boys, Andrew was so unfailingly kind and patient with the children that I found myself warming toward him again.

Laura and I had spoken no word about our midnight tryst, but I often saw the question in her eyes, though she was far too discreet to ask me. I was doing as she had begged me, considering my decision seriously.

After all, the entire family would be shocked and dismayed if I broke my betrothal vow. There was that enormous trousseau, which kept growing like a giant mushroom. My room was filled with it, in chests and in the armoire, in long broad boxes—and each garment was another strand binding me to Andrew. I kept reminding myself that his longing for his child had driven him to force Yve to deception—and I realized that, loving Mélisse as I did, I would probably do anything to keep from losing her.

These things made my decision increasingly hard, for Andrew never missed an opportunity to corner me alone. His kisses on these occasions were hungrily rapacious and I found them increasingly repulsive. He had come no more to my bedroom at night, but I lived with the knowledge that he longed to do so, and I found myself behaving toward him with a coldness that he ignored.

As those days slipped by, we found we missed Seton

more and more. There were no lessons for the children, and church services had not been held since the tragedy of his loss. The slaves and the lease-holding farmers, whose children had benefited from Seton's gentle instructions, mourned his loss as deeply as we did.

The second week after we had given up hope of finding his body, George saddled up his horse on a Friday and rode into Richmond, returning a day later with a young man to replace Seton.

He was tall and slender as Seton had been, but his hair was thick and curling and bright blue eyes twinkled merrily above a wide, friendly mouth. His name was John Seabury and his education, as a graduate of William and Mary, was impeccable. Further, he was an ordained minister.

He arrived on Saturday, and Sunday morning he preached a stirring sermon to an overflowing congregation in the Cloudmont church. By Monday, he was firmly ensconced, teaching the children, the slaves, the farmers' children with aplomb. He came from a large family in Richmond and seemed far better adjusted to family life than his quiet and unfortunate predecessor.

After two weeks, John held a service for Seton Cambridge in the little church and we all attended. Some of the slaves wept unashamedly, for Seton had been a good teacher and they had a deep affection for him.

It was late July and heat was unrelenting. A fleet of gardeners hauled water in huge casks from the river to water the gardens. The orangerie was full of ripe fruit and we had fresh oranges, lemons, and pears on the table often. They were a rare delicacy and enjoyed by all of us.

The flowerbeds were a riot of color and scent. I often walked among them in the mornings, drinking in the many fragrances that filled the warm air, before I went to the stables and had Noah saddle Dandylion for me.

Sometimes Laura went with me on these rides and sometimes not. On one occasion, Charles accompanied us, and his sparring with Laura was provocative as ever. He seemed to take my presence for granted.

He was as outspoken as ever. In response one day to Laura's bantering refusal to marry him, he said with sudden cruelty, "Laura, you're a vain—no, a vicious little snob to let my low birth stand between us and the happiness we could share!"

She whitened and her curved mouth twisted. "Snob, eh? And what are you but a snob? You take *pride* in your low birth—you revel in it—flinging it on every occasion into the teeth of polite society!"

I put heels to Dandylion and rode ahead of them, wishing to give them privacy. I knew Laura's true reasons for hesitating. Charles's bastardy was but one of them. She lived in fear for Andy under the supervision of Mary's suffocating love. Further, she could not bear the thought of giving up her small son entirely, which marriage to Charles and a return to Landon plantation would surely mean.

Suddenly behind me on the pine-needled earth came the thud of hooves and Laura burst into view pursued by Charles. Tears coursed down her pale cheeks and her lower lip was caught between her teeth. I moved Dandylion swiftly out of their path and, as she flashed by, Charles thundered up beside her. He reached over, lifted her easily from Missy's saddle and brought his horse to a halt.

Before my astonished eyes, he slipped to the ground, still holding the struggling Laura. Her small booted feet tangled with his, throwing them both to the ground, where Charles rolled over to pin Laura beneath him. As he bent and put his mouth to hers in a passionate kiss, Laura's arms twined themselves about his neck and she pressed her body to his.

I turned Dandylion swiftly to retrace our steps. I rode slowly down the curve of the path, reflecting on what my own feelings would be if Andrew were to pursue such a course with me. I was constrained to admit to a touch of panic. Ah, but if it were George . . .

As I made my way back to Cloudmont I faced the fact squarely that I was betrothed to the wrong man, but for all the right reasons. George offered me nothing but the fleeting joys of a physical alliance with him, and every fiber of my practical French soul warned me against such a course. Andrew offered me the worldly security for which I had longed through more than ten interminable years.

As the days drifted by, Laura made no reference to the scene I had witnessed. However, I was thankful that Andrew was too busy to accompany me on my rides along the James. After the swimming lessons with the children, his business took him over Cloudmont's acres with his brother and half-brother, supervising and co-ordinating the work. Then, too, he and George went frequently to Richmond and Norfolk.

George had undertaken to build himself a home in Norfolk, to his mother's great distress. But he liked the city and his importing business was flourishing.

The nights were oppressive, often without a breeze from the James to stir the curtains. And slowly it was borne in on me that the oppressiveness was not the weather. It stirred old apprehensions and, while I worried over my predicament in the Madison house, I recognized that something else had intruded into my consciousness.

It brooded in the summer evenings and was reflected in Noah's somber face when he saddled Dandylion for me or when he and Henry Pepper took us in the carriage to call on our neighbors. I seemed to sense it in their homes as well. I felt it mostly in Anna and Jabez Livingston's house.

Once when we came for afternoon tea, Jabez, who always made it a point to join us, remarked on it in a vague way. The house slaves had brought in the silver service with the steaming tea and pastries and silently left. Jabez turned to us, smiling, and said, "Surly devils, aren't they? I suppose 'tis the weather. It has us all on edge. But my stockade is full. Impudent rascals—you should be glad I didn't sell you Railo, Miss Laura. He spends almost as much time in the stockade as he does in the fields these days."

"And why is that, Jabez?" Laura asked coolly.

"For one thing, he disappears for hours at a time. I've decided to chain him now, even as he works. I expect you know well enough where he goes—probably to see your Judith. You should sell her to us."

"I shall never sell her to anyone. Judith is like a sister to me."

"Sister, eh? You aren't too particular then, are you, miss?"

"On the contrary, I am very particular. Judith is far superior to many white women I know." Color was bright in Laura's face, and I knew she was holding her temper in check.

Cornelia recognized it and said, "Let us discuss pleasanter things, my dears. We want you both to come to dinner at Cloudmont tomorrow night, Jabez. Andrew and George have just returned from Richmond and are full of political talk and the latest activities of our President Jefferson. I know they would enjoy discussing it all with you. The Montagues are coming as well as the Reeds and Chenaults."

The corner of Jabez's mouth went up as he accepted the invitation, and we did not discuss the slaves again. Still, I was glad when we left the place. I could not describe what I felt in the air. I only knew that it was dangerous and depressing and I was glad to be out of it.

The dinner Cornelia planned came and went like others before it, a pleasant evening with after-dinner liqueurs, topping off a superlative meal. Cornelia especially enjoyed the company of the Montagues, who were of her generation. She and Helen Montague spent most of the evening with their heads together.

The Reeds had left their small children at home, but young Clay came and he and Amanda spent a decorous evening, sitting side by side on a couch and talking. As I observed them, the yearning in those young, vital bodies was almost tangible. The desire to touch, to hold, to embrace was evident in every move, in the bend of their heads to each other. If they could only be allowed to see each other in the welcoming drawing rooms of their own homes, much of that pressure would be relieved. As it was, there was a touch of desperation in their soft half-whispers that boded ill. I wanted to tell Mary this, but the prospect of her reception of my interference made me hesitant. It was one more burden on my already heavy heart.

Judith was a silent wraith these days. She rarely smiled. I felt sure that she and Railo were finding it almost impossible to meet, and the girl was wilting under it. My lack of ability to do anything about it was extremely frustrating.

I stopped her in the hall the morning after the dinner to ask about Railo. Her face wore the shuttered look that had become part of her.

"Railo can't get away so often, Miss Lilibel. We have to be terrible careful. Ol' Livingston's getting meaner and meaner." The girl's beautiful face looked pinched and her usual vitality was dimmed. More, there was about her a secrecy that disturbed me, and she did not meet my eyes.

"Please don't give up hope, Judith," I said gently. "Sometimes things that are so dark turn suddenly for the best."

Judith's smile was mirthless. "You're a strong woman, madame. I wish I could feel as you do."

"It takes courage to hope—I know. But you have that courage, Judith."

"Yes, madame," she replied, and glided away from me down the hall. There was something in her demeanor that was extremely disquieting. I could not explain it, but it heightened my intuitive fears.

Already the morning was very hot, the July sun rising higher, and I pressed my perfumed handkerchief against the moisture on my brow. I told myself that I was a fool for letting the secrets I guarded flavor my relations with everyone, even Judith, little dreaming that I was soon to add another dark secret to those that troubled me already.

CHAPTER 13

The following morning after breakfast, George announced, "Well, dear ladies, I'm off to Norfolk. I must check on the construction of my new home there—and the *Tern* is due in port any day now, with the merchandise from France."

As the family streamed from the dining room toward the library, Cornelia said to her younger son, "George, I do not see why you want a house in Norfolk—an old bachelor of twenty-nine now, whose duty is clearly at Cloudmont."

George bent to kiss her cheek lightly. "Dear Mother, I like being an old bachelor and I shall like having a house to be one in even better."

"But Cloudmont needs you, Andrew needs you——"

"That's true," Andrew said quietly, as we all reached the library, "but then he knows we need him here."

Mary's eyes were on her younger brother reproachfully as well. But Laura's eyes were approving.

"I have told you all," George said, his voice hardening, "that I mean to divide my attentions between Cloudmont and the importing business. I shall be away at least half the time. Now where is Amanda, so I can make my farewells to her as well?"

Mary said wearily, "She's still furious with me because I won't let Clay call. She got up at dawn and snatched a bite to eat and went off on her mare to brood."

"You hold too tight a rein on her, Mary," George said, a touch of asperity in his voice.

"Andrew and I do not think so," Mary said coldly. "She's a headstrong, wilful girl and needs at least another year in which to mature."

Cornelia said, "Bibsey will bring out coffee in a few moments, George. Will you not wait to have it with us?"

"No, thank you, Mother. I must be off as soon as possible." He left as the women seated themselves to wait for coffee.

I, too, excused myself, after checking to see if anyone cared to join me for a ride. I could not persuade even the usually dependable Laura to come along, so I went off to the stables alone. There, Noah saddled Dandylion for me with unusual silence. He seemed preoccupied and I remarked on it to him, asking if something was worrying him.

"Oh, no, ma'am. I just got the summer megrims, I guess." His white grin was fleeting. Being troubled myself seemed to make me hypersensitive to the moods of others.

I trotted Dandylion around to the front of the house and cantered off into the woods along the river. The sun was hot when I chanced to ride from under the trees, but the wind from the river was blessedly cool and refreshing. I determined I would ride until I grew tired, if it took me three hours.

For a long time I followed the riverbank, then moved back into the woods. The birds made the air musical and I glimpsed squirrels leaping gracefully from branch to branch. I had passed Rose Hill and was approaching Tulip Grove when a sound came to me that caused me to halt Dandylion. Listening, I recognized laughter, joyous and unrestrained, coming from a copse of sweetgums and lindens. The voice was familiar and I turned Dandylion toward the sound. Then I recognized it as Amanda's. Ah, I thought—she and I can ride together.

I approached the copse slowly, for the trees were thick. Suddenly I came upon a little clearing. As I reached the edge I halted the mare, transfixed by what met my eyes.

There in the dappled sunlight and shadow, I saw Amanda's horse and another, tethered to nearby trees; but it was Amanda herself who held my eyes. She was beautiful to see, standing nude before young Clay, her young body pale in the golden sunlight, her slender legs perfect in their symmetry. Her clothing lay in a little heap near where she stood.

Clay had stripped too and his muscular torso was tanned, no doubt from work in his father's fields, for Clayton had often remarked that his sons should know all phases of a planter's enterprise.

A quilt had been spread upon the thick green grass and in that moment, Clay swept Amanda into his arms and laid her gently upon it. As he bent to kiss her high, pointed breasts, his dark tumbled hair was outlined cleanly against her white flesh.

I turned my horse as quietly as I could, but I knew they would hear nothing, so caught up were they in their own turbulent passions. When Dandylion and I were some distance away, I drew rein and sat staring thoughtfully over the gleaming water of the James River.

Mary's harsh discipline had borne the fruit I feared, and Amanda was risking her future because of it. The sun was seeking its zenith and burned hotly across my shoulders. It was a day for love and it was becoming still and fragrant with the scent of wild growing things, with only a faint stir of air from the James.

I sat there a long time, letting the sun beat down upon me, my heart aching for the two young lovers who were forced to consummate their love secretly. Had Mary only allowed them to meet more often in the conventional and beautiful rooms of Cloudmont, they might have restrained their wilder passions. Convention might have held them in check until a wedding day—had they been allowed to look forward to a wedding day. Now the future stretched out dismally before them like eternity. I remembered all too clearly how far away the future had looked to me at sixteen.

Sadly, I turned Dandylion toward Cloudmont, but we did not hurry. I let the mare walk easily under the thickly leaved hickorys and tulip poplars. I looked at the huge trunks and recalled George saying to me that this native wood was well adapted to turning of the lathe and it was of high durability. Many pieces of exquisite furniture in Cloudmont had been made from the wood of these trees. Some of the rooms were paneled in hickory. I kept my mind on these desultory things and the gracious house to which I was returning, veering away from what I had seen in the glade.

The house seemed almost like another person to me now, a person filled with currents and undercurrents, hatreds and loves, joys and sorrows. I was filled with the urge to talk to Mary once more about Amanda. I would not reveal what I had seen in the glade, but I must make one last effort to persuade Mary to let them meet under their own roofs—and to set a wedding date. How I could prevail on that strong-willed woman to see the merit in this, I did not know. But I could not rest until I had tried.

Trotting by the church, my eyes involuntarily sought the marble angel where Yve lay beneath the ground. It was still white and new and, as always, my heart ached in memory of her gay, laughing face when we were young girls in the château outside Paris. Her loss had become more real to me, but I turned resolutely from the suspicion that had plagued me since my coming to Cloudmont. I realized with sorrow that now I would probably never know the truth of her death, and must accept the story told me. At least, I knew in part the reasons for her feelings toward Andy—though I knew that was not all of it. It had taken some terrible knowledge, some incomprehensible blow to her heart to make her beat a child so young.

On my way to the stables, I passed Ephraim's smithy. He was busy, pounding on a shoe for a big gelding, which stood patiently, held by Ephraim's brother, Ezekiel. I spoke cheerfully and they returned my greeting, though Ezekiel appeared sullen. That was understandable, for Ezekiel was slow to learn, and when his brother and wife and their two children left for Boston, Ezekiel would have to wait until later to join them.

Reaching the stables, I called to Noah, who came out and helped me to dismount. He said, "Miss Amanda been gone a long time. You see her, Miss Lilibel?"

"No," I lied. "She will probably be along shortly. I know I'm late for lunch, but the day was so perfect and riding such a pleasure."

"Miz Beady'll fix you somethin', Miss Lilibel." He still had not smiled, which was completely unlike the joyous young boy, but I did not remark upon it.

After I had finished the sandwich Beady prepared for me in the big kitchen, I went from the pantry to the morning room where I found a tearful Mary in Andrew's arms. Her head was pressed against his broad chest and her shoulders shook.

They looked up as I entered, and Mary wiped her eyes with Andrew's handkerchief, but did not move from the protective circle of his arms.

Andrew said courteously, "Come in, my love. You must forgive us. Mary is very distraught about Amanda. She did not return for the noonday meal."

"I can't talk to her any more," Mary said, turning her tear-stained face to me. "She goes off alone like this and stays for hours—as if she can't stand to be home. There seems to be no happiness in her when she speaks to me."

The brother and sister clung to each other for comfort, and Andrew dropped a light kiss on Mary's forehead, murmuring, "My dear, it will all work out. Amanda is so young. She's mercurial at sixteen, up one day and down the next."

Mary moved away slowly, shaking her head. "I cannot stand by and see her ruin her life by marrying too young." She cast me a glance filled with strange, unnamable emotion and added, "I know whereof I speak. I was married too young, had children too young; I was miserable my entire life with Mr. Jackson."

"I'm so sorry, Mary," I murmured. Now was not the time to advise Mary to let her daughter marry Clay. But all the same my determination hardened to have a private conversation with her.

"I must go to the office—the ledgers need bringing up to date, for there are but few days left in this month. Lilibel, try to comfort my sister."

After Andrew left. I thought it would be easy to win him to my views quickly, for he seemed to regard my opinions very highly despite my coolness to his amorous intentions. His deference to my wishes was one more tie to my betrothal, and I was slowly coming to face the fact that I could find no way to break it, even if I were imprudent enough to do so. Despite Andrew's promise of secrecy, too many people were aware of it now. It was widely known even among the neighbors that I was affianced to Andrew, and nearly all of them had quietly offered congratulations, expressing great pleasure in our coming union.

"Mary, dear," I said, taking her hand and pulling her to a seat beside me on the couch, "Andrew is right. Young girls are often mercurial. Don't you recall how you liked to be alone and brood——"

"I was a mother at sixteen," she said bitterly. "I had no time to spend growing up."

Cornelia entered, her eyes flying to Mary's tear-stained face, and she at once took her into her arms. There ensued a lengthy conversation, in which her mother and I essayed to comfort Mary. Most of the time, I sat and listened, frustrated by the fact that I could not persuade Mary to realize that Amanda had made up her mind.

The day wore on and, as evening approached, Amanda's lengthy absence put a damper on all of us. The fact that only I knew she was lying in Clay's arms made me restless as we sat together in the library sewing. Mary was uncomfortably silent.

She finally spoke. "If she is not home within the hour I shall send Andrew and some of the slaves to look for her."

The wind became cooler and the silken drapes belled inward with gentle, swinging motions. Laura and Cornelia had tried hard to talk brightly of the social events that were filling this summer for us, but Mary's lack of response had brought us all to this waiting silence. Amanda had been gone eight hours.

Suddenly, voices were heard and high young laughter. The children had trooped in from their play under Clementine's supervision. Amanda's voice rose in cheerful banter with her brother Timothy and they all burst into the drawing room, followed by Domino.

In the midst of the children's clamor for lemonade and cookies, Mary half rose and sank down again, her eyes clinging to her daughter. Relief fought with anger and won. "Amanda, darling—I have been so worried. You have been gone far too long."

Cornelia shushed the young ones, telling them they might have tea, but it was too near the dinner hour for cookies. They scampered out to the kitchen to ask Beady for tea.

Amanda's face was closed. Her riding habit was neat and tidy and unwrinkled. It looked as fresh as if she had just donned it. Her flushed face was beautiful, but her full lips firmed. "Sorry, Mother. I love to ride—I forgot the time."

"You forgot to eat, too," Mary said with irony. "Did you not become hungry?"

"Oh, yes," was the casual response, "but it doesn't hurt to miss a meal. The river is beautiful this time of the year and the woods are full of wild honeysuckle."

"Well—'tis nice you are getting so much exercise," Mary said, trying to warm her daughter. "You look exceptionally lovely."

"Thank you," replied Amanda, uncompromisingly remote. "Will you ladies excuse me? I've told Abby to bring hot water to my room. I should like to bathe before dinner."

"Of course, dear," Mary said quietly, but her eyes were filled with hurt and a little muscle along her jaw quivered momentarily.

When Amanda had gone, Cornelia rang and Bibsey came. "Bring us a glass of iced tea, Bibsey," she said. Her eyes on Mary held a touch of pity as well as distress. After we were served, Cornelia again brought up the dinners and teas among our neighbors, remarking pleasantly on the Chenaults' ball to be held mid-August. Mary joined in with visible effort, trying to ignore the contretemps with her daughter, as we discussed what to wear.

"Lilibel, do wear your new white silk," she said.

Cornelia chimed in, "After all, my dear, you have so many now! And the white silk sets off your dark hair and lovely skin. You will look like an angel—and a bride-to-be, as well."

"The white silk is one of my favorites," I agreed, a heaviness descending on me at the mention of being a bride. The white silk did fit my figure most flatteringly. It clung to my long slender thighs when I walked, outlined my bosom seductively. It was altogether the right dress for a bride-to-be, I thought, depressed.

Laura, who had been exceptionally quiet, looked at me searchingly. "And it would please Andrew. He loves you so much, you know."

At dinner that evening, the parties that would be held were still the topic of conversation. I missed George's wit and comment at the table. Charles, who had accompanied him that morning to Norfolk, left another vacant chair. Andrew seemed unusually silent and I saw Mary's dark eyes going to him frequently. There was anxiety and love in her glance.

Domino, despite Cornelia's protests, was first under our table, then the children's, and as usual nearly all of us surreptitiously slipped him tidbits. I even suspected Cornelia, for all her arguments that he should be an outside pet. His girth was showing our indulgence; he was a fat rascal, despite his dashing about after the children.

Amanda made no pretense of secrecy as she held out a bit of roast beef, making him stand to reach it. She was very untalkative at the table, but I was aware of her shining eyes and her abstracted expression. Mary had given up trying to draw her out, and I felt a sudden, sharp sympathy for her, as I thought of Mélisse at some future time, looking at me as Amanda looked at her mother. Hastily, I promised myself that I would never give Mélisse cause to look at me thus.

Then it came to me suddenly, the solution to my dilemma over Amanda and Clay. I would go to Mary's room tonight, after the house was quiet, and we could have a long, intimate talk. Such a talk had proven successful with Laura. Why not with Mary? I would use all my powers of persuasion to get her to divert her present restrictive course. It was not too late, if that was the first time Amanda and Clay had met in the glade. My heart lifted magically.

Much later in the great hall as I stood beside the staircase, Andrew came up to me and said, "My darling, will you accompany me on my inspection tour of the tobacco crop in the morning? It will have to be quite early, but

Beady will fix us a quick breakfast before we go. It's been some time since we've had a ride together."

"I would like that very much, Andrew," I replied readily, for the very early mornings were like wine, cool, sweet, and invigorating.

He smiled his disarming and handsome smile. "Will you wake up early enough, or shall I have Pepper send Abby to wake you?"

"Have Abby come," I replied, laughing as I took the carved newel-post in my hand, my foot upon the first step. "I've become a sleepyhead." And if my plans went as they should, I would be up late trying to move Mary to a more lenient course with her rebellious daughter and Clay Reed.

I, too, had planned a bath, and Bibsey and Clementine had already poured the carved wooden tub full of steaming water when I reached my room. Mélisse was sitting up in bed, where they had put her in her nightdress, full of chatter about her day with the boys.

We talked as I undressed and sank thankfully into the warm water. It was so refreshing, I lingered until the water was tepid before stepping out and toweling myself. Then Clementine and Bibsey came and took the tub out as we exchanged good nights. Mélisse had curled up in bed, no longer interested in my ablutions, and spoke sleepily.

"Maman, I love Andy and he loves me very much. He says so when Timothy can't hear."

"That's nice, darling. Cousins should love each other very much," I replied; regret that Andy was not truly her cousin was sharp as a knife in my breast. Slipping into my thin gown, I came to bed and climbed the steps to lie beside her.

She talked on drowsily of Domino, then of Timothy being bossy with Andy, until suddenly she was quiet and her even breathing told me she was asleep. I moved restlessly, my mind a millrace of arguments for Amanda and Clay. At last, I could endure it no longer and climbed down from the bed.

At the table beside the bed, I took up flint and struck a spark to the candle there. The flame wavered wildly in the night air that blew in from the river. It was going to be a while before I could go to Mary. I heard the tall clock in the great hall strike ten distantly. The sound was faint and hollow outside my door to the central hall.

I sat down in a chair beside the washstand and began to brush my long thick hair. I had wanted to have it cut in Richmond, but Cornelia had been so outraged and wounded that I had refrained. Though I felt terribly out of fashion, even Andrew remarked his pleasure that I had not cut it.

George had been maddeningly casual. "Hair grows," he said shortly, overhearing the conversation between Cornelia, Andrew, and me. "Long or short, it's a feminine foible."

George was an impossible man, I told myself severely, running the brush over my dark mass of hair. Yet there was something about his long, hard body that drew me. He was bigger than Andrew, and tougher, too. Ruder and more arrogant, added another small voice. But his black eyes rose up before me now, warm ardor behind their glinting merriment. I could see his firm mouth laughing at my resistance, and suddenly such a gust of desire swept me that my knees grew weak with it. I realized with a touch of despair that I was coming to love the elusive George Madison, and I must take care to keep out of the man's reach.

The night dragged on and again I heard the clock in the great hall, dimly striking eleven. When at last silence enveloped the house, I tiptoed from my room, barefoot on the cool, polished wooden floors.

I snuffed out the candle before I left, and now felt my way carefully past the two dressing rooms next to mine, past Laura's and Cornelia's closed doors, past the empty room that had been Yve's.

It was then I caught a glimmer of light spilling into the dark hall. It came from Mary's room, which was directly across from Andrew's. With a touch of relief, I thought, *She's not in bed yet.* She would not be too sleepy to talk, and the late hour would invite confidences. My feet were silent on the cool flooring and I slowed as I heard low voices coming from the open door. Drawing near, I peered from the blackness of the hall into the room.

Mary and Andrew stood clasped in a desperate embrace. Andrew, his voice muffled against her hair, said, "Mary, Mary, you know each woman I've held in my arms, I pretended was you— God help me, why couldn't we have been born in ancient times, when brothers and sisters wed?"

"Don't, my darling. We know it's hopeless, and your marriage to Liliane is—she is strong." There was a faint condemnation in her voice on the last word. It cleared as she added, "And she is beautiful and kind and she will bear you many children. We both know that is most important."

"But Mary—" Andrew's tortured voice was husky. "You know it's you I love—you I want and shall always want. I am not a whole man, nor ever shall be, without you."

She drew a long, trembling breath. "I know, my darling, and I would do anything for your happiness—and have done it always. When I saw how miserable Yve was making your life, how cruel she was to Andy, it was I who recognized the blessing her death would be." Then as he jerked his head back to look at her, she said, "You know *I* did not kill her, my love—I merely made it possible for her to die of the disease."

"Don't speak of it again!" His voice was muffled. "You know I loved Yve—in the only way I could. Don't ever say it again!" he cried in sudden, hushed agony.

"Only to you, my dearest, to give you a measure of my love. Besides, she would have died anyway—I only helped the disease along."

I was paralyzed with horror as I stared from the darkness at this brother and sister locked together like drowning swimmers.

Mary said thickly, "And I shall be here—always. I shall never marry again. You know that. You can come to me as often as you like and we can be together. Though our moments must be stolen, we shall be together always."

Andrew's hands slid down her back, cupped themselves about her buttocks, and jerked her roughly against his narrow waist and hips. He went to her face, his kiss on her mouth deep and hungry. At the sight of his passionate movements, my paralysis broke, and I turned and fled back down the inky corridors. I could not put enough distance between me and what I had witnessed. Gone were my hopes of a conversation with Mary about her daughter. Gone was my belief that Andrew bore a real love for me. When I reached my room, I shut the door hard, as if to shut out the sordid scene I had just witnessed.

Meddler, I told myself bitterly. Meddlers get what they deserve, yet this was almost beyond belief. I crept into bed beside Mélisse, and despite the warmth of the night, lay rigid and shivering. So many pieces of the puzzle were falling into place. The ghostly figure who dosed Yve with laudanum and opened the window on her drenched body in the December wind had a face now, a face of passion, of sensuality, of perverted love, belonging to Mary Madison Jackson.

The strangely veiled look that Laura wore when she said she did not love Andrew—*could not* love him—was explained now. She had known the relationship between Andrew and his sister and it had killed her love for him.

Looking back, I called myself a fool for not having seen the signs long ago—Mary's proprietary air with Andrew, her welcoming kisses directly on his mouth when he returned from any journey, no matter how short. The thousand and one gestures she made for him, her defense of him at every turn, all pointed to their relationship.

And oh, most heartbreaking of all, this was what had driven my sister to insanity. How could she face up to the fact that her husband was in love with his sister? Poor Yve! Yet she had loved him desperately, had been reluctant to give him up, even pretended motherhood of his bastard to keep him by her side.

And Mary had taken the opportunity of her illness to end her life. With a sudden hardening of my heart, I named it. Mary could dissemble all she chose, but what she had done was murder.

A surprising, sharp relief swept me. How narrow had been my own escape. What Mary had done to Yve could be so easily repeated if a new wife threatened her brother's happiness. The revulsion I felt toward Andrew was touched with pity, making it all the more terrible in my mind. What could I say to Andrew when I told him I would not marry him? For now, trousseau, neighbors, family and friends notwithstanding, I could never marry Andrew. The children he craved must be borne by other than I.

The thought of his touch on my body was repellent, and I shivered anew in the feather bed as the breeze from the James River poured, fragrant and cool, over my still shaking limbs.

At last, worn out, I slept.

CHAPTER 14

The following morning I woke with the first sound of birds, stiffening as memory of the night before flooded back into mind. Mélisse lay sleeping quietly. It was not long before there came the softest of raps on my door. Then Abby, her freshly starched dress and apron making faint rustling sounds, tiptoed to the bed. I closed my eyes and in a moment her gentle touch was on my shoulder. A faint clean fragrance of soap and fresh clothing hung about her.

"Madame, Master Andrew asked that I waken you. 'Twill soon be six of the clock. He will be waiting for you in the dining room in thirty minutes."

My first thought was to sigh and whisper I could not go, pleading a headache. But some hard core of honesty deep within refused. Andrew must be faced eventually, no matter how distasteful that might be. The only times I had ever run away was to save my life and the life of my child.

"I shall dress immediately and join him," I replied.

"May I help you, madame?"

"No, thank you, Abby. 'Twill take me only a few moments to dress and I can do that myself. If you will look to Mélisse when she wakens—see that she bathes. Heat the water first."

"Yes, madame," Abby replied, smiling with pleasure at the thought of tending Mélisse. It was a wonder the way my daughter had won the entire household.

When she was gone, I dressed swiftly and silently in

the cool morning air. The wind from across the river was heavy with scents, all of them pleasant. I felt something within me rise to meet the ordeal I was facing. I knew I could not blurt out what I had seen and heard last night to Andrew. Like Andy's birth, it was so raw it did not bear touching. I had determined last night I would make other excuses not to marry him. Security for Mélisse, for myself, the luxury that was Cloudmont, and the prestige that would be mine as Mrs. Andrew Madison meant nothing to me now.

I reflected on these things as I stood before the mirror over the chest of drawers patting my face lightly with rice powder and rubbing the pink salve on my lips. There was no color in my cheeks but I did not bother with the rouge pot. My eyes looked enormous, clear and golden, but shadowed in the glass. I was thinner, I knew, because the rich foods had not appealed to me in the agony of indecision over the past weeks. I had not decided yet how I would break my betrothal, what excuse I would make to Andrew.

I joined him in the dining room, where Beady had set two places side by side at the vast mahogany table. I greeted him gravely. "Good morning, Andrew."

"My dear," he said solicitously, "you look pale. Are you well?"

"Yes," I replied. "I do not think I am fully acclimated to Virginia yet, Andrew, for I do not sleep well these warm nights, and my appetite has suffered."

Henry Pepper came in with the sterling pot of steaming coffee and filled the cups beside our plates. Shortly after that, Bibsey, sleepy-eyed, came in with a platter containing crisp bacon and shirred eggs. Abby followed with a plate of piping hot biscuits.

"You must eat well this morning, darling, for it is cool. You are so slender—beautifully so—but I would see you looking rosier," Andrew said, helping himself generously to the platter, then the biscuits.

I took small portions. It was all I could do to swallow them down, and when at last we were through and on our way, I was relieved. Noah had saddled a big bay, named Lucifer, for Andrew, while I mounted my pet,

Dandylion. I slipped her an apple I had filched from Bibsey and she munched it contentedly.

Noah was silent as he held his hand for my foot and I mounted.

Andrew said kindly, "Noah, is something troubling you?"

The young Negro looked up at him, startled. "No, sir."

"You're mighty quiet these days. Have you fallen in love with someone off Cloudmont?" Andrew smiled.

Noah's return smile was faint. "Not yet, Master Andrew."

"You act like a man in love."

"Guess I got the summer megrims, Master Andrew." It was the same excuse he had given me.

"You can look forward to being your own man soon, Noah. That should cheer you. You will follow soon after Joshua and Ephraim and their families, to work in the Boston shipyards, as a free man."

"I know, sir. But I got a feelin' I'll miss Cloudmont. It's been home so long."

Andrew's horse shifted restlessly and he said, "Well, then stay. We will pay you a salary and you will still be your own man—free."

"I know, sir. You been mighty kind to me and I appreciates it. Reckon I'll make up my mind one of these days what I wants to do."

"Cloudmont would miss you, Noah," I put in, as we began to urge our horses forward.

"Have a good ride, madame—an' Master Andrew." He waved to us as we trotted away.

"Something is on his mind," Andrew said, when we were out of earshot. "He's had a falling out with some of his kinsmen, or he is in love with a girl on another plantation. I hope to God it's not one of Jabez Livingston's wenches."

I shuddered, thinking of the man. "I hope not, too. Jabez would take such pleasure in frustrating their love."

" 'Tis certain he'd not be selling me the girl, if he knew Noah wanted her."

"Why is the man like that?"

"Lilibel, there are people who wallow in their power

to rule others' lives, and Jabez is one of them. He pleasures in domination over his slaves. He gives the whole planter system a bad odor, despite his currying political favor and having once been invited to Monticello."

"I think he and Anna are beasts," I said coldly. "There is nothing likable about them."

"You mustn't be too hard on them, my dear. None of us is perfect."

I said nothing. I was only too well aware that none of us was perfect. The flaws in Andrew appalled me, and not one of them could I mention to him. I had it in my power to wreck his life with revelations, but I could not do it. I glanced at his profile as he sat his horse. It was classic and beautiful and manly. His back was straight and strong. He looked to be a perfect mate. How could I broach the subject of our betrothal? I looked away as we cantered past the smithy, where Ephraim had a wide smile for us as he stoked his forge. The contrast between his expression and Noah's was remarkable, and Andrew spoke of it.

"Something is very definitely troubling Noah," he said thoughtfully, "and it troubles me as well."

"Why?" I asked, faintly alarmed at his tone.

"I don't know. But I have a feeling I should."

He continued to frown as we rode past the quarters and outbuildings, past the church beside the cemetery where ornate and neat white headstones stood. Beyond it, we rode through a heavy stand of trees and into the border of a sweeping field of tobacco. The leaves were richly green and a faint but pleasant aroma floated up from them as the sun rose higher.

Andrew spoke in his low, drawling voice of nutrients and fertilizers of his own devising that had been plowed into this field, accounting for the excellent, meaty grade of the plants.

"This will be the finest tobacco Cloudmont has ever turned out, and 'twill bring a fancy price in England next winter, you may be sure." He waved to two sunburned men with hoes as we approached.

They removed their straw hats as we drew near and one of them spoke. "Good morning, Master Madison. You and your lady are out early."

I restrained a wince. *Your lady*. Even the farmers knew of our betrothal. It would make a fine scandal when the wedding failed to come about. The Madisons might even array themselves against me for my defection and turn Mélisse and me out, despite the tie of blood they thought existed. Well, that would be better than wedding this man of twisted desires.

Andrew's mood changed to one of quiet pleasure as we continued our ride about the fields and he discussed the crops and their conditions with the men who worked them. I had met his foreman, or overseer, Jacob Worth, who had a small brick house beside that of the gardener's at the rear of Cloudmont. Now he greeted me warmly as we came upon him near the long tobacco and cotton storage barns.

"Good morning, madame. You are well, I trust."

"Very, thank you, Mr. Worth."

" 'Tis good to see you and the master riding so early of a morning."

I nodded. Another one who knew of our intended wedding. A faint touch of panic bloomed. I must tell Andrew and soon. Today. Before we returned to the house. The first moment we were alone.

As we rode away after a short conference with Jacob Worth, Andrew said, "Let me inspect the work done in the barns, my dear, and after that we shall head for home."

At the tobacco barn, he dismounted and reached up to help me down from Dandylion. He looped the reins to both horses over a nearby hitching rack. We stepped into the gloomy interior of the building. Though there were broad openings on all four sides of the cypress structure, it was so huge that it took a moment for my eyes to adjust to the gloom. Years of hanging tobacco leaves along the racks near the ceiling had left the place impregnated with their scent. It was pleasant, and I drew a long breath. It was very quiet about us as Andrew scrutinized the repairs to the building. A door had been rehung where we had entered and many of the long heavy strings that were strung row on row near the ceiling had been replaced.

Andrew said, "Darling, look up at the roof. Did you

know those are cypress shingles, sawed, rived, and drawn from virgin cypress of the lower tidewater? They are like the ones on Cloudmont itself. They will last forever. Andy—and our sons—will make use of them in their present state—and our grandchildren for generations to come."

Our sons. I said abruptly, "Andrew, my dear—I cannot marry you."

In the scented shadows he looked at me incredulously. "What did you say?"

"I find I cannot marry you," I repeated, feeling my face pale and my eyes widen with the enormity of the step I was taking.

"But we are betrothed," he said, bewildered. "Everyone for miles around knows, and you have an entire trousseau near finished!" He took a step nearer to me, but I drew back. "Lilibel, for God's sake, why?"

"My feeling for you is one of affection," I blurted, for this at least had been true. "But I have come to realize that I do not love you—in the way you would have me love you."

His face darkened and suddenly he swept me into his arms. "But you must love me! My darling, love such as mine for you cannot go unrequited."

I struggled in his embrace as he drew me fiercely nearer. Catching my face in his muscular hand, he forced it upward and his mouth came down on mine, forcing my lips apart even as I twisted against his embrace. I could not breathe for a moment and I flailed out with my legs against his, my arms being pinioned to my sides. When he took his lips away, I shrieked "Andrew—let me go!"

He put his hand over my mouth, but did not release me as he whispered, "For God's sake hush—you'll bring Jacob Worth riding back."

"Then release me this instant," I said icily, and I remained stiff as a post in his arms.

Slowly, he loosened his grasp, his face puzzled and hurt. "Lilibel, I do not understand. When I kissed you in the gardens last, you returned my kisses—there was love in your touch."

"No," I replied, still cool. " 'Twas infatuation. You

have so much to offer in the way of security and luxury, I mistook gratitude for love."

"I cannot believe that," he replied. "I *will* not believe that."

I thought, *Won't one woman do as well as another to breed your sons, since your heart can never be given, belonging as it does to your sister?*

He stepped to me, his hands reaching down and catching mine. As I tensed and moved warily away, he said, "No. Don't do that. I shall not attempt to kiss you again, Lilibel." His hands were cool and hard and he held mine lightly as he went on, "I would ask you a favor, since you say you bear me an affection."

"I bear all of the Madisons an affection. Everyone has been so kind to me since I came to Cloudmont. I would be a beast not to return your affection." *All but the one responsible for my sister's death. I can feel nothing but loathing for her, loathing without a trace of pity.* Then I added calmly, "Andrew, if you want Mélisse and me to leave Cloudmont after—this decision of mine, we will. I would ask only that you lend me money to live on until I can find employment in Richmond or Norfolk. I will repay you."

His expression was so dismayed that I found some comfort in it. "No, indeed! Your home is Cloudmont. You are my wife's sister and Mélisse my son's first cousin. Nothing should persuade you to leave Cloudmont!"

"I only thought perhaps—you would rather not see me since I have so disappointed you."

We were silent for a long moment as he scrutinized my closed face, then he said, "You are so beautiful, my dear—and bearing an affection for all of us as you say you do, the favor I would ask is that you say nothing of this sudden decision to call off our wedding, at least for one month. Just give me one month to win your heart once again." He smiled at me suddenly, such a young, eager, and winning smile that I found myself unwillingly returning it.

I realized with abrupt clarity that Andrew Madison had a monumental conceit. He could not conceive of any woman failing to respond to him. I sensed that over the years his conquests must have been many, his abnormal passion for his sister notwithstanding. He wanted my silence for a month purely to assuage his own pride. He actually believed he could win my love in that time.

I said uneasily, "Andrew, that seems a mistake. I feel that the sooner we make our break public, the better."

"We will make it quite public, darling Lilibel—if you want to after a month. But you will come to know me better by then and I shall prove to you that my love for you is so strong that it must be returned." He spoke confidently. "You will see how devoted and charming a lover I can be."

"I cannot give you encouragement on that, Andrew," I said uncomfortably. "I am sure my affection for you"—I stumbled over the word—"is more that of a sister."

Again that engaging smile, creating two deep clefts in his cheeks, the black eyes shining and alert. "Let me take that chance. Will you give me your promise, Lilibel? I won't force attentions on you, little love. Trust me, but give me the right to court you in a mannerly fashion."

I hesitated. To be courted by this man was the last thing I desired. Yet his hospitality, his warmth and friendship for me and Mélisse, made our lives so easy. When I thought of going to millinery and dress shops in Richmond, seeking employment, or approaching wealthy families with a plea to tutor their children in French, unhappiness swept me.

I looked up at Andrew in the shadowed light of the tobacco barn, the fragrance of tobacco all about us, and he seemed so strong and normal. The cold voice within me said, *He is not normal and you are a fool.* But fool or not, one more month would give me that much more time to plan a course of action. Yet that inner voice whispered it would become increasingly hard to remain at Cloudmont after the break. I doubted very much if I could stay, even if Cornelia and the others insisted.

Still holding my hands in a light, firm grip, Andrew said persuasively, "I will not try to make love to you. I shall win you in other ways, with thoughtfulness and gentleness. Is it a bargain, Lilibel?"

"Very well," I replied reluctantly. "I will say nothing until the end of August."

He gave my hands a slight squeeze and let them drop. "Thank you, my dear." Then briskly. "Let us inspect the cotton storage barn and we will return to the house in time for lunch."

I sat my horse while he dismounted and went into the barn, which unlike the tobacco barn had cypress flooring, and only one broad double door at the side. He returned shortly, saying everything was in order, and they would store the cotton there in September before hauling it to Hampton to that new miracle, the gin.

He said with satisfaction, "The *Tern* and the *Anemone* will have good cargoes this fall. We should realize rich financial rewards this year—did you notice how good the wheat field looked? That is something new I am trying. There will be a good market for that right here in the States."

"You are a very shrewd and knowledgeable man, Andrew. I congratulate you."

"Thank you, dear. That means a great deal to me. I want to stand well in your opinion."

I looked away from his smile. I could not sort out my feelings. They were a tangled mass of pity, revulsion, and sorrow. Though Andrew was innocent of my sister's death, it was he who had precipitated it. And my decision was rock hard that I would never put myself in the way of Mary's lethal and obsessive love for her brother.

When we reached Cloudmont, Noah took our horses. His smile was strained and I suggested that he might find release from his megrims if he went to the lake and fished during the afternoon. Andrew seconded the suggestion.

Noah's smile grew warmer then and he said, "Thankee, sir. I'll do that after I eats."

But when we left him, I knew again that prickle of uneasiness. There was something Noah was not telling us, and I smelled danger as clearly as if it were a smoke in the air, stinging my nostrils.

CHAPTER 15

The last few days of July slipped by, hot but pleasant. I found keeping my promise to Andrew easier than I had thought, for he no longer sought to caress me at every opportunity. Still, I felt his eyes, alert and watchful. To my distress, he presented me with a diamond necklace and several lengths of silk on his return trip from Hampton, the first of August. There was even a bottle of French perfume, which he said he had to plead with the *Tern*'s captain to get, for the captain had brought it home for his wife.

He was complimentary to the point of embarrassment. George was present during some of these exchanges and his cynical looks at his brother were unnerving. I had the feeling that George knew about Mary and Andrew and guarded his knowledge as closely as I did.

But life went on at its leisurely pace. On Sundays we attended church, which was always filled to overflowing. John Seabury preached a much better sermon than poor Seton. I no longer dozed under a droning voice, but listened to religion being related to everyday life and came away strengthened.

That first week we attended two dinners, one at Lindens and one at Tulip Grove, to Amanda's delight. The other immediate neighbors were there as well, including the obnoxious Livingstons. After dinner we talked and played loo. Before midnight, we entered our carriages and returned home, satiated with good food and drink.

August was a week old when Cornelia gathered us about her to tell us that she was going to have a dinner party. "Andrew and George and Charles will be back from Norfolk next weekend and I feel we should repay the entertainment we have enjoyed," she stated, beginning a list of the guests. "We shall have dancing and games, too. It makes for such a pleasant evening. I shall invite the Stuarts from Richmond and several others, so it will be a large affair, but the last of its size we will have before Thanksgiving."

" 'Tis very close to the Chenaults' ball. That's but two weeks away, you know," Mary said.

"I know, but the summer will soon be over, and I enjoy entertaining at the height of the season. Of course the Chenaults will have refreshments, but it will be strictly a ball. Now—Lilibel, will you consult with me about the list of foods we shall prepare?"

"Of course," I said obediently, pulling up a small chair beside her desk in the morning room.

"I'm glad you're inviting the Stuarts," Laura said languidly. "I just didn't feel up to going to Richmond in this heat—I hope it didn't offend Lucy and John."

"I'm sure it didn't, dear," Cornelia said, quill in hand and paper before her. "We'll have two great beef roasts, a roast goose, and three smoked turkeys," she muttered, her quill busy. The four of us lingered in the morning room, planning the dinner with enthusiasm.

Under the cover of our chatter, my mind was busy with the strange relationships among us. I found maintaining my attitude of friendly unawareness with Mary the most difficult problem I had. I feared that she might look into my eyes and see the pity, contempt, and bitterness that must surely be there. It seemed astonishing to me that no one could see the estrangement between Andrew and me, but apparently I was a better actress than I realized, for on the surface life at Cloudmont was smooth and pleasant.

Amanda went often on her long morning rides, always returning neat and tidy as if she never dismounted during the entire morning, but she never stayed eight hours again. Her mother seemed to be easier about her absences now, and made every effort to be friendly. Amanda did not help things by treating Mary coldly and politely but always distantly. Mary had arranged with Andrew to call on the Chandler sisters some time ago and have them make up two new ballgowns for her daughter, in an effort to please her. She meant to surprise Amanda with them when the men returned on the weekend.

The day before the dinner and dance, Andrew, George, and Charles returned, laden with the purchases they had been asked to make by the various women of the household. However, Jacob Worth met them and they left immediately to arbitrate some disagreement between two of the farmers who lived on the periphery of Madison lands. After that, they were to ride over to the old Landon plantation on the York River and see about the house. One of Laura's slaves had checked on the house at her request and found that it had been broken into. Laura was very disturbed, despite Charles's repeated assurances that they would take two carpenters from among her people to see that it was repaired and boarded up.

Now we were once again in the morning room, where Cornelia and I were arranging flowers in tall vases, as Bibsey and Henry Pepper brought them in to us.

"I'm glad you didn't go riding this morning, and stayed with us instead," Mary said gratefully to Amanda as she came into the room.

"You were so kind to order those ballgowns for me, Mother," Amanda replied with more warmth than she had exhibited in days. "I just tried them on again—I can't decide which is my favorite. Oh, Bibsey," she called to the girl as she started from the room. "Tell Abigail to bring iced tea for all of us. It's so very warm."

Pepper came in with a great basket of Damascus and French roses. I had never seen such gorgeous blooms in my life. Their fragrance filled the room. Cornelia and I took our glasses of iced tea absently as we worked with the flowers. After a while, Bibsey returned with two baskets, one on each arm. One was filled with large snapdragons, larkspur, and Madagascar periwinkles. In the other was a wild profusion of moon daisies, phlox, peach-leaved bellflowers, and peonies. I had learned a great deal about flowers this summer at Cloudmont.

"Mistress Madison," Bibsey said, "there are beautiful yellow alyssum and day lilies and sweet Williams. Would you like some of those?"

"No, Bibsey. I think we have quite enough to decorate for the dinner and dance tomorrow. We will prepare the centerpiece for the dining table tomorrow morning."

The girl put her baskets on the long table where we were working. "Mistress, is there anything else you need?"

"Yes, Bibsey, get two more tall vases—those two on the mantel in the library. The French porcelain."

As the maid trotted out obediently, Amanda said hesitantly, "The only thing, Mother—the gowns are a little tight across my bosom and in the waist. I think I must still be growing."

"I know, darling," Mary said fondly. "Haven't I told you often enough you're still a little girl? You have two more years to grow at least. Come along and we'll let them out a bit." She put down her tea and the two went companionably out the door into the drawing room, greeting Laura, who was coming to join us.

"Are you leaving?" Laura asked, pausing in the doorway.

"Only mother and I, Aunt Laura," Amanda said, pleasured at the prospect of trying on her two new ballgowns again.

"How lovely the flowers are," Laura said, sinking down on the large Duncan Phyfe sofa against the north wall. The couch, which I admired, had been shipped on the *Tern* from Albany, New York, where the cabinetmaker Phyfe had made it to Cornelia's order.

Laura fanned herself with the small silk fan she carried on her wrist these hot mornings. " 'Tis beastly warm," she sighed. "I don't blame the Stuarts and the Follisons for begging off. Imagine riding all the way from Richmond in this heat."

" 'Tis warm," Cornelia agreed, taking the two vases from Bibsey, who had followed Laura into the room. "What will you wear tomorrow night?"

"A new pale blue silk. 'Tis one the sisters made some time ago."

"It sounds lovely," I said, stepping back to view my handiwork on long-stemmed scarlet roses in a tall crystal vase. "You look so lovely in blue."

"Will you wear the bridal white, Lilibel?" she asked.

"No—I'm going to wear that to the Chenaults' ball," I replied. The customary heaviness descended on me at the word "bridal." For a brief while, with the warm, enchanted perfume of roses in my nostrils, I had forgotten they all considered me betrothed. I said with forced gaiety, "I shall wear that sheer India muslin of lemon yellow that Mary helped me make."

"Ah, yes, the one embroidered with silver thread in diagnoal stripes," Laura said.

"Now that is becoming to you, my dear," Cornelia beamed, tucking a last drooping and luscious snapdragon into a bowl of larkspur. "Pepper!" she called, and he appeared in the door to the wide, broad pantry. "Pepper, you may place the flowers. Get some cracked ice and put it in the water of each bowl and vase. 'Twill give the flowers new life and keep them fresh until tomorrow evening." As he carefully picked up two of the flower arrangements, she asked, "Has Louise polished the crystal chandelier in the drawing room, and made sure the candles are fresh in the sterling one over the table?"

"Yes, mistress. The silverware is polished as well—the good china from France is laid out and ready, as are your handcut crystal punch and wineglasses."

"That's good," Cornelia sighed. "I do like to get everything ready so I have at least eighteen hours to relax before the guests start arriving."

It all seemed so lovely and well ordered that I could not imagine any problems arising; but I failed to consider fate, or man's inhumanity to man.

The morning of the dinner dawned bright and lovely, as had all the long August days, and we were all up early. Laura had Judith prepare a paste of alum and egg whites, which she then smeared over Laura's face. I saw her ghostly mask when I went to her room to ask if she would like to borrow my lip salve. The *Tern* had brought back some lip salve three months before, but it was a strange orchid shade which neither of us liked.

"It makes the skin white and very smooth," Laura said, explaining her appearance. "I try to do it always before a party."

Judith stood by with the bowl of paste in her hand. Laura said, "Now you can do up my hair for me, Judith, dear." Obediently, Judith moved to Laura's little dressing table and took up a bowl full of strips of cotton cloth. While Laura and I talked, she expertly rolled the golden curls over the cloth and tied them.

Now Laura sat, her lovely face dead white, her hair in tightly tied ringlets, and laughed at my expression. "I look like a demon, I know. 'Tis the price one pays for hoped-for beauty. Yes, darling Lilibel, I will come to your room tonight and salve my pale lips generously—and hope to heaven that on its return the *Anemone* will bring us the right color."

"Abby has said she wants to curl my hair for the evening," I said, looking at Laura's corseted locks. "So I shall endure that operation shortly."

Laura and I never mentioned Andrew. He was a subject we carefully avoided.

"Sometimes I wish I had not cut mine," Laura said. "Long like yours, it was very easy to curl and then pin into a great puff at the back of my head."

I looked out the north window of her room absently and remarked, "It looks as though clouds are gathering, Laura. I hope it doesn't rain."

"Tis so dry, we could use a little rain. I noticed the gardeners are having to bring up casks of water from the James again, to keep the flower beds moist."

Going to the window, I saw a long, curving line of blue-black clouds, startling against the brilliance of the summer sky. "It doesn't look like a gentle, needed rain—it looks unpleasant."

"You're a worrier, darling. Forget about it," Laura said from the mirror, where she was peering at her whitened features.

I shrugged and went to my room to wait for Abby. Soon after, she came, bringing with her the cotton strips and a determination to make my coiffure the outstanding creation at dinner tonight.

I spent the better part of the day in my room, looking

as though my head were sprouting cotton twigs and buffing my nails. Mélisse was a frequent visitor to my room, excited by the atmosphere of anticipation in the house and entranced by my strange-looking head. The weather continued to deteriorate. It was exceptionally hot and still, with a long, low bank of clouds rising steadily and slowly.

Mélisse made another visit, this time accompanied by Andy and Domino. "See, Andy," she said, pointing to my head. " 'Tis as if Maman had cloth hair."

I laughed. "But when Abby takes it down this evening my hair will be very curly and lovely. Wait and see." The dog came up to me and put his cold nose against my hand and I rubbed his ears absently.

" 'Tis going to rain, Aunt Lilibel," Andy said importantly. "Ephraim told me it looks like a summer hurricane blowing in right off the ocean.

"*Alors*! I hope not, Andy. 'Twould put a damper on our party."

The boy said confidently, "They'll all come anyway—the carriages will keep 'em dry. Nobody misses a party at Cloudmont."

Andy was right. Of all the plantations along the James River, Cloudmont was the most admired and the most emulated. No one knows what festers in this beautiful household, I thought, sad that it could not be what it seemed.

But when Abby came to remove my curling strips and comb my hair into a most enchanting style with soft waves and curls about my face, with a high peak of hair twisted up the back of my head, my spirits lifted, and I found myself looking forward to the evening. The wind had risen slightly and dark mushrooming clouds spread over the sky. There was a suggestion of violence in the air.

It was near dark, and the completely overcast sky made it darker as I dressed. Mélisse—by now an admirer—stood watching as I put on the new trousseau dress of lemon India muslin. When Abby had adjusted it, she cried, "Oh, Maman, you look like a gold angel lady."

Abby beamed with pleasure. "So she does. Madame is the most beautiful lady I ever saw."

"You are too kind, Abby," I said, knowing her penchant for exaggeration.

I dawdled over my toilette and Abbey did not rush me. I could hear faintly the sound of greetings as guests arrived, and I knew spirits were high despite the threatening weather. Laura had long ago flashed into the room, borrowed the lip salve, and gone.

Now at last Abby said, "Madame, I must get down to the kitchen to help with serving." I bade her go, but still I lingered.

Mélisse and the boys had been fed and Bibsey would come soon to see that they went to bed. "Are you going up to play with Andy and Tim until bedtime, darling?" I asked Mélisse.

She nodded. "When you go downstairs, I'll go up."

"Bibsey will see that you all get to bed on time. Be a good girl and don't give her any argument about the hour."

Mélisse made a face. "I hate going to bed so early. 'Twill be so nice when I'm grown up and can stay up all night."

"Come, *chérie*, you will not want to stay up all night even then," I laughed, holding her small candle, and I began my descent. At the landing, I paused. Under the brilliant chandelier below, Henry Pepper was taking Anna Livingston's pelisse.

I hated to start my evening by greeting those dreadful people, so I lingered in the shadows above.

Jabez said peremptorily, "Pepper, go fetch that black wench of Laura's. I have a little gift for her from Railo."

I thought incredulously, *Is this man going to do some kindness after all?*

After depositing Anna's pelisse in the library, where the wraps of guests were placed, Pepper hurried to the kitchen. In a moment Judith appeared. Her dusky face was wreathed with pleasure, eagerness in every line of her body.

Jabez said pleasantly, "I have a little gift for you from Railo, Judith," and he passed a small white box to her.

With swift fingers, she opened it as I looked down from my shadowy place on the stairs. They were directly below me. Then I heard her gasp of terror, and slowly she slid to the floor in a faint, the box falling from her hand.

An object rolled out upon the floor. It looked to be

a cigar, or a small black tube of some sort, and a shiver of premonitory horror swept me.

I flew down the stairs as Jabez began slapping Judith's face hard, saying, "Here, wench, get up. You will receive a gift like this every time Railo sneaks out to meet you, and by and by you may have all of him."

By then I was at his side, crying, "What have you done? What is the matter?"

"Nothing, madame. I have brought Judith a token from her lover. And she shall receive more as time goes by if he does not become more amenable." He was still slapping Judith's face in an effort to rouse her from her faint.

I looked at the object on the floor. It was a man's finger, chopped neatly off at the joint. It was big, and I remembered Railo's great capable hands as he stood before us in Aunt Mincy's cabin. My stomach churned and a touch of nausea swept me.

"You beast!" I whispered. "Get out of here at once."

"Madame, you are not mistress of this house yet," he said insolently. "My wife and I have been invited and we shall stay."

"Then get out of this room, or I shall start shrieking that you have harmed both Judith and me."

He laughed scornfully, "No one would believe you." By now Anna had drawn close, and there was undisguised hostility in her colorless eyes.

I said softly, "They'll believe this severed finger, and not a man here but will hold you in contempt for it!"

By now, Judith had risen to her feet, clutching the box Jabez forced back into her hand after he replaced its grisly contents. I put my arm around her shoulders as she swayed on her feet.

Jabez said, "A man must keep discipline among his slaves, and Railo needs it more than most. I mean to tame him."

"Are you not afraid you will ruin his usefulness to you if you continue to sever parts of his body?" I asked hotly.

"That's a chance I must take, madame," he replied with a grim smile, "but I'll wager it will make him less impudent and arrogant, less ready to run off to Cloudmont at night to see this wench."

I said nothing. I could not trust myself to speak again to the man. I began to lead the stunned Judith from the room. She still clutched the little box in her hand. We went through the dining room and pantry to the kitchen.

I said to Beady, "Have you any brandy in here? Judith has had a severe shock." Samantha Beady went immediately to an open shelf and taking down a bottle of brandy she kept for cooking purposes, poured a large dollop in a glass.

"Poor lamb," Beady said, looking at Judith's ravaged face. The great liquid eyes were terrified and her mouth quivered uncontrollably. She was clutching the box so tightly that her knuckles were taut across her hand, which shook slightly. Beady refrained from questioning us, as did the others, while Judith sipped the brandy slowly. Gradually, her hand stopped shaking. I spoke soothingly to her.

"Dear, I shall take this up with Andrew and George immediately. There must be something in the laws of Virginia that forbids this kind of treatment to slaves."

The haunted eyes sought mine. "No, ma'am. Livingston can do what he pleases with his slaves. 'Tis the law, I'm told."

"Then we shall bring social pressure to bear on him—forbid him the hospitality of people's homes, make him an outcast until he mends his ways."

A little smile twisted her mouth. "Miss Lilibel, there ain't anything can be done to Jabez Livingston to change him. And I don't think I can keep Railo from coming over here. He's a determined man." She shuddered. "Even after this, I fear he'll come again."

"If he does, you must discourage him, for his sake. Tell him that we will do *something*—and just to wait until then. That beast will do as he says and cut off little pieces of Railo until he kills him, or dies himself in the attempt."

"If only he *would* die!" she groaned. "If only lightning could strike him dead right now." She glanced out the kitchen windows as lightning knifed across the black sky.

"That would be God's own mercy," I echoed fervently. "Now, Judith dear, go up to your room and rest until you're over this shock. We can get along without you after this terrible thing." I could see the servants in the kitchen were bursting with curiosity as to what had happened.

"No, ma'am," she replied steadily. "I'll feel better if I work with the maids. Maybe it will keep me from thinking—God, if I only *could* stop thinking!"

"Then stay here and finish the brandy slowly, dear, and don't do anything you don't feel like doing." I gestered to the box she still held. "What are you going to do with—that?"

"Keep it," she said violently. "It's part of him—and it will remind me of Jabez Livingston—and give me strength through hate."

As I left, the servants were clustering around her to find the reason for her distress. I made my way slowly into the great drawing room, where the sound of merriment was loud. All were having wines and whiskey and engaging in lively conversation before dinner. The small orchestra Cornelia had imported from Williamsburg was playing very softly. The whole scene was one to bring joy to a heart, but mine was far too heavy to lift with it.

Andrew met me with a winning smile. "My dear, what took you so long? Everyone's been asking after you—all our guests are here now."

"Andrew, I must speak with you and George about Jabez Livingston."

"Surely not now, dear! Can't it wait? I know you abhor the man and his wife. Has he given you new cause for worry?"

"Indeed he has. It is something that all the men in the community should take up. Something must be done about him. He's a beast, without any human attributes of mercy or kindness."

"My, you are in a temper!" He smiled again. "Surely it can't be so bad as all that."

"It's revolting. I must tell you about it right away."

"They were last to arrive—I can't imagine what he has done already to put you in such a pet," Andrew said reasonably. The growling thunder outside made itself felt within, and the people around us exclaimed that it appeared we would have a real storm.

Cornelia hurried over, saying, "Andrew, you and George must see to it that the shutters are drawn. That wind is strong enough to break the glass in the windows."

"We shall certainly be warm in here when we close all the windows and shutters, Mother," Andrew replied, looking at the windows where the curtains were whipping inward with the wind. The candles around the room and in the chandeliers fluttered wildly, and for a moment it appeared they would be extinguished by the gale sweeping into the room. "I shall see Pepper and Noah and have them close both windows and shutters." Then to me, "Darling, let us put off talking about the unsavory Jabez and enjoy the evening. We can speak of him tomorrow."

After that, I drank three glasses of champagne rather quickly, hoping the wine would take the edge off my fury. It lifted my spirits not at all; the evening had been ruined for me. Everywhere I looked, I saw Railo's mutilated finger and Judith's fainting form. I could not bear to glance at Jabez and Anna, who stood drinking and conversing with the Chenaults near the dining-room door.

As Pepper and Noah closed the windows and shutters, the candles steadied. Large as the drawing room was, it became oppressively hot. Ladies began using their fans enthusiastically, but nothing seemed to deter their merry spirits.

The first drops of rain began to fall as we all sat down at the enormous dining table. The table was extended its full length and it seemed a great distance from where I sat at the foot beside Cornelia to where Andrew sat at the head. Evan and Helen Montague's two daughters and their sons-in-law were present, as they had come to spend the last two summer months with their parents.

Young Clay and Amanda were seated side by side, and their clean, shining hair as they bent their heads to each other was beautiful in the candlelight. They had been very sedate and polite with each other in the beginning, a concession to Mary, no doubt. But I could see it was difficult for them not to touch each other except with their eyes.

Vance and Sara Chenault were in very good spirits, exchanging anecdotes with Clayton and Grace Reed. The

Livingstons were trying eagerly to participate in their conversation. Only the Stuarts were absent, John and Lucy, and the Follisons, who had sent their regrets. I knew they must all be relieved not to be driving in this violent weather.

The table was sumptuously laden and the maids and Henry Pepper came in and out the pantry door from the kitchen with heavy platters of smoking food. Noah, in charge of the decanters, kept filling the wineglasses steadily. His face was expressionless, but I noticed the stiffness, the aura of hatred, deep and black, when he stood by Jabez and Anna Livingston to serve them. Judith had obviously told the servants, for even Henry and the maids wore a strange and strained expression as they served the two Livingstons.

Driven, I turned to Cornelia and said quietly, "When Jabez arrived, he made a present of Railo's severed finger to Judith, as a warning that he must stop seeing her."

Cornelia stared at me as though I had lost my mind. I went on rapidly, "I tried to tell Andrew, but he wouldn't allow me to—and something should be done about it before the Livingstons leave here," I finished in a rush.

Cornelia's face paled and she looked at my plate of untouched food. "Say nothing until the evening is over, my dear," she murmured under her breath.

"But it will be too late by then—the Livingstons will be gone." I looked at her steadily. "Something should be done *now*."

"I beg of you, Lilibel, our guests would be so distressed. It would ruin their evening, as obviously it has ruined yours." She looked at me pleadingly.

I said stubbornly, "Something must be done!"

"Then please wait until after the meal. I don't believe I can eat another bite."

Picking at my plate, I looked down the table at Andrew. I felt that his reaction would be much like his mother's, and I determined to go to George. Dinner seemed interminable. My glances at George were so intense that he began to regard me with lifted brows. I stared directly into his eyes, leaving my rich dessert of a creamy pudding and cake untouched. And when at last we rose and went back into the drawing room, he sought me out.

"My dear Lilibel, you cannot regard a man with such emotion in those great golden eyes of yours without stirring him to some response, you know."

"I hope to stir you to a response," I said fervently, and launched into a vivid description of what I had witnessed from the stairs. I finished, "He reminded me that I was not mistress of the house and that he and Anna had been invited here. He also remarked that no one would believe me."

"I believe you," George's face was tight as he sought Jabez across the room. He spoke between his teeth, "The bastard—he's counting on being our guest, being under our roof, to save his hide."

"Will it?" I asked coolly.

"Not this time, I think." And he turned and left me. I watched his tall, lithe figure cross to Jabez. When he reached him, his head inclined courteously as though he were passing the time of day. In a moment, Jabez said something to Grace Reed and departed the room with George.

They were gone a long time. The orchestra of two violinists and a man at the pianoforte began to play for dancing. Cornelia and the Montagues had set up a game of loo in the corner and were deep in the game before George came back alone.

I had been watching for him and, walking over to him quietly, I asked, "What did you do?"

"I have persuaded him that he is unwelcome here," he replied grimly. "But he reiterated his intention to make further presents to Judith if Railo persists in leaving the plantation to come see her."

"Can't you and Andrew threaten him with physical harm if he should further mutilate Railo?" I asked, feeling heat in my face.

"I not only threatened him with physical harm, my dear Lilibel, I *did* him physical harm. But ingrained cruelty in a man cannot be so easily wiped out."

Beyond him, I saw Jabez returning to the drawing room. He held a bloodstained handkerchief to his nose and his right eye was swelling. He came directly toward us, passing us and going to Anna, who sat nearby idly fanning herself and watching the dancers. George and I listened unashamedly.

"Jabez, dear, what's happened to you?" she asked in alarm.

"I took a bad fall in the great hall, Anna, and I'm not at all well. We must leave immediately, so my bleeding nose and my eye can be treated."

"In this weather, Jabez? The storm's at its height. Listen!"

The hard drum of rain upon the shutters was a humming background to the music being played. Anna said, "Surely Cornelia can give you a poultice. Are you in pain?"

"What do you think?" he asked sarcastically, "that this nose and eye are numb? I wouldn't care if there was a typhoon out there. I'm going to summon our carriage and leave this house."

By now, others were looking at Jabez. Cornelia left her game of loo with Evan Montague and hastened to them. Still George and I stood by, making no effort to speak. Cornelia cast a troubled glance.

"Jabez, you're hurt!" she said, drawing up to him.

"Yes, mistress, I took a bad fall a few moments ago. Tripped in the great hall and fell, injuring my nose and my eye. I will leave as soon as possible." He glared at George, who now sauntered over to him.

"Jabez, why not tell the truth? Or are you ashamed of what precipitated our exchange?" George's smile was cryptic.

"Exchange? What exchange?" Anna looked confused, and Cornelia viewed her son with disfavor.

"My dear Cornelia," Jabez said, as Andrew and Evan, Clayton and Vance drew up to the little group we had formed, "your son has struck me viciously, and I can no longer remain in your house."

Anna gave George and Andrew a shocked look. "Which one, Jabez?" she asked bewilderedly.

"I, madam," George said with a courteous bow. "I felt he deserved a present in exchange for the one he made Judith earlier. Though I must say my gift was not as ingenious as his, and he deserved a far worse beating."

Andrew said, "Please tell me why you struck a guest, George."

"Gladly, brother. Jabez has made Judith a present of one of Railo's fingers in a box—and if Railo continues to see her, he promises to send other such gifts."

"My God!" Vance Chenault burst out. "You mean you severed one of Railo's fingers, man?" By now the ladies had come to join the crowd and a smothered gasp went up.

"It was only meant to be a warning." Jabez paled slightly, and added, "I wouldn't need to do it again, you know. But he spends so much time running over here to see that black wench, I can't get any work out of him."

Evan Montague said quietly, "But to cut off a man's finger! Jabez, don't you feel you overstepped the mark of decency?"

"If you had to cope with that big bast— black, you'd understand my problem. He's impudent and insubordinate. Beating him does no good. Now if you'll be so kind, Andrew, have one of your men send for my carriage. After all, I owe none of you any explanation of how I discipline my slaves."

I noticed with satisfaction that his great beak of a nose was still bleeding profusely and had swelled appreciably. I was glad that everyone had been told of Jabez's grisly gift to Judith, for now all of the guests were viewing the Livingstons with shocked disfavor.

Jabez turned on me furiously. "And you, Madame Sevier, are responsible for this fracas—for your eavesdropping, and interference during my interview with Judith, and your clacking tongue."

"My overhearing and witnessing your brutality was an accident, but I'm grateful for the opportunity of exposing it," I said clearly. "Men like you were responsible for guillotining my mother and father and hundreds of innocents like them. You are a beast, sir, and I shall be happy to see the last of you."

There was a faint *Ohhh* from the ladies as I lashed out at the man. Andrew, looking pained, said, "My darling, remember Jabez is a neighbor, an old friend and a guest in our home."

"He is no friend of mine, and he is *your* guest," I replied coldly.

"Bravo, Lilibel," George said, his eyes crinkling with enjoyment.

"Send for our carriage please, Andrew," Anna said huffily. "We shall leave immediately."

"But the weather is so inclement. Do stay until it's over," Cornelia said placatingly, and Anna looked at her gratefully.

"Jabez and I know that you would not have had this happen to a guest, Cornelia," Anna said, then with a baleful look at me, "but others are not so considerate. I really feel it would be better if we left so that tempers might cool."

"That's a very good thought, Anna," George said agreeably. "And it will give us some time to adjust to the fact that Jabez has become a butcher."

Anna gasped and rose, and Jabez's look at George and me was filled with venom. "You owe me an apology, sir. And you, madame, I will overlook your insufferable attitude because you are a foreigner among us and your ignorance is to be expected."

Pepper, who had unobtrusively joined the gathering, said gingerly, "I have sent for your carriage, Mr. Livingston. And I have your wrap, madam." He had Anna's mauve pelisse over an arm. "I will see you to the carriage with a covering for your heads."

After they had gone, I realized that the evening was indeed spoiled for everyone. There was little laughter and much discussion of Jabez and Anna. Though Pepper and Noah carried their trays of tall crystal wineglasses filled to the brim, most drinks were refused, and the musicians played on unnoticed as the guests talked among themselves.

I said to George, "You were quite wonderful. Thank you for doing something about it."

His quick smile was white in the sun-burned face. "I would slay a dragon for an accolade like that from you."

"You may have slain our friendship with the Livingstons," Andrew said dryly. " 'Tis no easy thing to have bad blood between neighbors."

George shrugged. "Ending friendship with the Livingstons would be no loss."

"My feelings exactly," I put in.

Andrew took my hand in his. "My darling, you must come to realize that these people do need a certain amount of disciplining—now, now, not the way Jabez does it, to be sure. And it's why I want none of them on the place."

George gave him a strange look. "And I had thought our giving them freedom stemmed from less selfish interests, brother."

There was a little silence as Cornelia joined us, fanning rapidly. The rain was still heavy but the wind seemed to have abated. "This thing has ruined our dinner and the festivities. Everyone is too polite to say so, but they are all anxious to return home as soon as the rain lets up."

Only Clay and Amanda seemed untouched by the events. They now sat boldly on a rosewood couch, holding hands openly, their heads close together as they talked in low voices. I thought of them in the copse, so beautiful with their bare symmetrical young bodies and their unrestrained joy in coming together. I wondered if, as Amanda threatened, they were planning to elope to Williamsburg or Richmond.

The Chenaults joined us, expressing doubt that the Livingstons would attend their ball to be held next week. But George put in with amusement, "They'll be there all right. Jabez has the nerve of a brass monkey, and I expect all will be glossed over by then. But I'll tell you this, if he mutilates Railo again, I shall hunt him up." He paused, and his quiet voice cut like a whip. "I may possibly kill him."

Andrew said quickly, "George, you were always too ready for trouble. It's really none of our business. I deplore his action, of course, but I can't see personally involving myself in it."

Mary had drawn up as close to Andrew as possible. She said, "Andrew's right, George. You should abide by his advice."

George laughed easily. "Dear sister, I am two years younger than Andrew, but I have been my own man for many years. Involving myself personally is one of the things at which I learned to excel while commanding the *Tern.*"

There came a lull in the rain and everyone began talking of leaving. "The storm might return worse a hundredfold," Grace Reed said, "and I think we should leave before it does. It has been a lovely party, Cornelia—Andrew."

Helen Montague chimed in, "Our daughters are anxious to get back and see about the children. This storm must have frightened them out of their wits—their mammy is afraid of storms herself."

So one by one, they took their leave, and long before midnight, Cloudmont was empty of guests.

Before the family went up to their chambers, Andrew said to me before the others, "My dear, you must remember that we planters must stick together and present a united front to the slaves. We cannot afford to feud with the Livingstons. We have been friends too long and live too near to them."

"And the Livingstons have powerful friends in Washington, Lilibel. Jabez's influence is widely felt," Mary put in.

"And now that he's made his point," Cornelia said calmly, "I'm sure he would not mutilate Railo further. Really, Laura, you should sell Judith to the Livingstons. It would solve this whole problem."

Laura, who had been very quiet during the entire incident, said in a small, still voice, "Judith does not want to be sold to the Livingstons and Railo has begged me not to do it. Jabez beats all his slaves at one time or another. I will not have Judith subjected to that."

Cornelia shrugged. "Well, the whole thing is a tempest in a teapot. By the time we go to the Chenaults' ball, I'll wager it will all have blown over."

As we moved out of the drawing room, George came up to me and walking casually near, whispered, "Do you feel guilty for precipitating a fight and the ruination of Mother's little tea party?"

I flashed him a brilliant smile. "Not in the least."

He threw back his head and laughed. The others looked at us with reproach as we started up the stairs, but he said to me quite clearly, "I do admire you, Lilibel."

The following morning found the skies still overcast, and there was intermittent rain.

"It's obviously the end of an early Atlantic hurricane," Andrew said with satisfaction, as he lit his pipe in the library after breakfast. "And not a moment too soon. This will do the crops tremendous good. It has been far too dry this month."

Breakfast had been rather strained. Evidently Mary and Cornelia had joined together in a pact to be silent on my part in last night's fiasco. No one mentioned it but Amanda, who remarked pertly that she thought "Old Jabez got what was jolly well coming to him." She was rewarded by her Uncle George's dry smile and her mother's frigid glance.

After that, the subject had not been mentioned at all. Most of the talk among the ladies was about the coming ball at Rose Hill, a well-worn topic by now. The men ignored us, and George regaled Charles with details about his new house being constructed in Norfolk and the importing trade, which was flourishing. Even Andrew permitted himself to express satisfaction over the money to be made in importing.

Most of the windows were up but a fraction, because the wind still came in erratic gusts, sweeping the rain before it. It made the house somewhat stuffy despite the coolness of the air. Before coffee was served, Amanda came and perched on the arm of the satinwood chair in which I was sitting. I greeted her presence warmly, as I had been feeling something of a pariah since my participation in the chastisement of Jabez Livingston the night before.

"Aunt Lilibel," she said softly, "when it clears up—as it will later today—will you go riding with me?"

I hid my surprise and said I would be delighted to do so. Her mother, who had been watching sharply, asked, "What is it you're planning, Amanda?"

The young girl started, then said casually, "I just asked Aunt Lilibel to go riding with me if it clears up later."

I bit my tongue on the words, *If you don't mind, of course, Madame Mary*. I was finding it increasingly hard to hide my hostility to Mary, knowing her love of family to be in truth a devouring monster.

Instead I said pleasantly, " 'Twill be nice, riding after a rain. The air always seems so fresh and clean, don't you think?"

"I suppose so," Mary said, losing interest.

"Lucy and John have sent word they hope we will all come to Richmond in September," Laura announced. "The trappers all come into town from the mountains early in the month, with their furs from the winter and summer catches. Lucy thinks we would enjoy choosing among them for our winter cloaks."

George was saying to his brother and Charles, "Let's make the rounds, men. 'Tis but a light rain and our capes will keep it off us."

In a few moments, the men were gone to see how the crops had fared in the hard rain. Much of the vitality and excitement in the room went with them.

Mary felt it too, for I saw her look longingly at the empty door through which her brothers had departed. But I knew the longing was for one, more than the other, and I felt anew the churning nausea that struck when I came too close to the unnatural relationship between Andrew and Mary. I began to talk somewhat hurriedly to Amanda, still perched beside my chair, about the merits of Dandylion.

We did not get to ride until well after lunch. I had almost given up on the idea when a straggling sun came forth and the wet foliage of the garden gleamed under its hot rays.

We left Laura composing another letter to Lucy Stuart, and made our way down the wet graveled pathways to the stables. The sky was clearing of soft white clouds slowly, for there was little wind, and the sun, when it came forth, was steamy hot.

"We had better stay in the woods as much as possible," I said, glancing upward, "for it promises to be hotter than ever as the day wears on."

Amanda said cheerfully, "We can take off our jackets and the breeze we stir will cool us."

I smiled. "Your mother would take a dim view of removing our jackets to ride in our blouses."

"Mother takes a dim view of everything that's any fun," Amanda said casually.

I made no reply. In truth, I felt Amanda was right. Mary's mind was such an intricate maze of overpowering and forbidden passions that I felt she would never see her daughter's normal affections for Clay Reed with any clarity at all.

Noah was not to be found, despite our repeated calls. Finally Joshua appeared with two other young black men, Jupiter and Ezekiel, the sullen younger brother of Ephraim. They greeted us courteously and Joshua said, "Miz Lilibel, Noah gone on an errand fer Judith——"

"Oh, that is all right," I said, for I felt sure she was sending word to Railo not to come again to Cloudmont until some way could be found to restrain Jabez Livingston.

Joshua's little smile was unrevealing and he asked politely, "You ladies goin' fer a ride?"

"Yes, Joshua," Amanda replied. "Would you and the men saddle up my gelding Boyo and Madame Lilibel's mare for us?"

Jupiter and Ezekiel went silently into the stables, to return shortly without the horses. Joshua, who had taken our saddles from the tack room, looked at them inquiringly.

"Noah must 'a put 'em in the pasture early. They ain't in the stalls. None of 'em in there cept'n Miss Mary's ol' roan and Miz Cornelia's stallion." They did not glance at us, and I had a strange presentiment as Joshua told them shortly to fetch the horses from the pasture. He put the saddles over the fence that enclosed the stableyard and looked after them, a certain tension about his shoulders.

"Is something troubling Ezekiel and Jupiter?" I asked.

Joshua hesitated, then said, "No'm. They just put out 'bout the storm last night. It done beat down our gardens a little."

I had the feeling he was not telling me the truth, for the storm had brought only welcome rain, despite the strong winds. But I said no more. The two younger men silently brought the horses to the stable and helped

Joshua saddle them. Finally, we rode off down the long broad path past the church and into the woods.

"You don't want to ride by the river?" I asked my quiet companion.

"Not this time," she said, angling off to the west.

"Are we going to meet Clay?" I asked bluntly.

She shot me a swift glance of surprise. "No. But I asked you to ride with me for a reason."

"It has to do with Clay?"

"Everything I do has to do with Clay," she said simply. "We mean to marry each other—and soon."

"And you want my help."

She turned a blazing smile on me. "Oh, Aunt Lilibel—if you only would!"

"How?" What could be wrong with helping this girl escape the confines of her mother's asphyxiating and twisted love?

"We thought we would elope before dawn—the morning after the Chenaults' ball next weekend. You could help by keeping my things in your room, where Mother would never think to look." Her brows drew together as we rode further into the woods. "She has been snooping about my room ever since I threatened to elope with Clay weeks ago."

"All right."

She looked at me in astonishment. "You aren't going to try to argue me out of it?"

I shook my head. "And if anyone should be disturbed by any noise that morning, I shall be up—with candle lit—making my way to the kitchen for a bite to eat. I shall be very sorry to have wakened anyone."

"Oh, Lilibel, you *are* a love! I am so grateful!" She rode near and put out a hand to me.

I clasped it, saying, "Darling Amanda, I hope you will be successful. And I shall do everything I can to help."

"I have planned to slip out the kitchen door a good hour before Beady arises. Clay will bring two horses and we shall ride to Williamsburg, where he will have his minister waiting for us at ten of the clock."

"Do his parents know of your plan?"

She shook her head and sent me a worried look. "I

know his mother and father approve of our marriage, though. They told me they did, and expressed their sorrow that Mother was so against our wedding now." She said pleadingly, "We are afraid to tell them for fear they will feel beholden to tell Mother, rather than risk her anger. You do not feel we should tell them?"

I shook my head. "I think you are probably right. Elopement seems the best answer."

She gave me another bright smile. "I do not see how you and Uncle Andrew can bear to wait—but I suppose when I am twenty-five I shall be more patient."

I laughed aloud. "No. You will be wiser and have better control of your desires—but no more patient, my dear."

I thought of my own impatience regarding Andrew and my burning desire to break with him. It was like a slow fire within me, day and night, but I controlled it fiercely. The promised time would be over soon enough. Less than three weeks now. I was glad Amanda would not be there when I broke with her uncle.

So we laid our plans, Amanda vocally, I in the silence of my own mind. Neither of us dreamed that our little schemes would be rent by violence and drowned in blood.

CHAPTER 16

The evening of the Chenaults' ball came and with it, mid-August's fiery breath. Even inside huge, high-ceilinged Cloudmont, the air was stiflingly hot and oppressive. I dressed slowly with Abigail's help as she fanned us both vigorously with a broad palm fan, one of many that had come on the *Anemone* on a run with molasses and rum from the Caribbean.

She put down the fan and began looping buttons at the back of the white silk gown. There was a rather revealing lace insert over the bosom and small cap sleeves of the lace, which was repeated at the bottom of the skirt. Under it was a petticoat of the same silk with rows of lace inset.

"You are lucky, madame, to be so slender that you do not need the long corselet with those binding stays," Abby remarked, hooking the last loop and adjusting the skirt. "Now sit down and let me put up your hair."

Mélisse, who was always an interested spectator at these affairs, said from her seat in the middle of the great bed, "Now this time you look like a white angel, Maman." Abby lifted my heavy hair and began coiling it atop my head. She pinned it loosely and took down the small curls she had tied earlier in strips of cloth, leaving small curls at my cheeks.

"Looks can be very deceptive, *ma petite*," I told Mélisse, thinking of the elopement I would help Amanda achieve in a few hours.

"You are very quiet, madame," Abigail said, working swiftly with the mass of hair, tucking pins in rapidly.

"I am rather tired, to be truthful, Abby. There is much entertainment in this country. More even than we had when we visited in Paris when I was very young."

"Yes, 'tis true, madame. I was amazed meself, when I first come over here from Scotland. These people live better than royalty in the old country." Then with sudden humility, "I, meself, live better than any I knew in Edinburgh or Glasgow. I've no complaints about me life."

Later, I descended the stairs to join the others, still thinking of the problems that beset me. I shrugged. They would be over and I would have an entirely new set of them after the next two weeks. If my part in the elopement came out and I then broke with Andrew, Mélisse and I would soon be in a carriage on our way to Richmond, with the life of a small shopkeeper's helper in store for me. The future looked dismal—but not as miserable as a life with Andrew.

I saw that Henry Pepper was on the box alone and asked, "Where is Noah this evening?"

"I don't know," Cornelia said, a touch of worry in her voice. "Pepper said he had not seen him since early in the afternoon. 'Tis not like the youngster to go off without saying where."

"Andrew and I think possibly he is in love with one of the girls on another plantation," I said, to still my own uneasiness as much as Cornelia's.

Laura said, "I've noticed he's been very quiet for near a month now." As the carriage started forward at Pepper's cry to the horses, she added teasingly, "Almost as quiet as you, my dear Amanda."

"And for the same reason, probably," Mary said dryly.

"I'm thinking," Amanda said. There was a wild excitement deep in her voice that only I could detect.

"We know," Mary said, somewhat coldly. "And you shall be with him tonight and dance to your heart's content."

Outside, we could hear the deep voices of the men and the clatter of their horses as they rode alongside the carriage.

I reflected on the curious attraction George held for

me. He was different from any man I had ever known, very unlike Jacques and certainly unlike his brother, Andrew. He put me in mind of Robert LeCompte, son of the Duc de Chalet, who had courted me briefly before the Terror, a devil-take-the-hindmost heart if there ever was one. One of Tante Genèvre's customers said that she had seen him guillotined and he had been laughing as the blade fell.

Robert had probably seduced most of the daughters of the nobility, and had very nearly succeeded in seducing me. If it had not been for the untimely appearance of our *sommelier*, he should very likely have succeeded.

I almost laughed aloud remembering. Nothing like the timely arrival of the butler for the safety of a maiden's chastity. I had been barely fourteen then, and very curious. I recalled that all the preliminaries had been most pleasant. I had never known a desire so powerful, not with Jacques, certainly not with Andrew.

But I had known it with George Madison in Mincy's cabin that cold, rainy day of the hunt.

"You haven't said a word for two miles, Lilibel," Mary remarked. "What are *you* thinking of—your wedding?"

"No," I replied truthfully. "I had gone back a long time. I was thinking of parties I went to before the Terror in France."

"They must have been very gay," Laura said enviously. "Much more so than ours here in America."

"As a matter of fact, yours here in America are quite as elegant, and the food is even better."

"How tactful you are, my dear," Cornelia said, but her voice was pleased.

"And you were much younger than I then," Amanda said without envy. She knew that by this time tomorrow night, she would be in the arms of her beloved.

"Yes." I replied, laughing, "I was barely fourteen."

Rose Hill was bright with lamps and candles, as we drove up the serpentine lane to the front of the house. The brilliant moon made the James beyond a river of silver light, and I sniffed the hundred and one fragrances that filled the hot night air.

John Seabury, who was usually invited to these balls

and dinners out of courtesy, had left for Richmond the day before to buy new books for the fall for lessons for the children and to visit his large family, so he was not among the men who rode with the carriage.

Vance and Sara Chenault met us at the door, their faces flushed with pleasure at hosting their own ball. The great hall was full of flowers, fresh from their gardens, bunches of fragrant peonies like great pink and white clouds anchored to vases and cabbage roses as perfect as those at Cloudmont.

When we entered the drawing room, we saw that Sara had the same three-piece orchestra that Cornelia had hired from Williamsburg to play for the previous weekend. The music was sweet and rhythmical and the house slaves were making the rounds with refreshments, filling glasses, taking empty ones away, passing trays of sweetmeats and tiny sandwiches. Though this was a ball, it was in truth also a dinner, for the refreshments were many and varied. Dancing had not yet begun and everyone was visiting, chatting and laughing with each other.

All the neighbors had arrived, the Montagues with their daughters and sons-in-law, the Reeds and their son Clay, and two couples from Richmond whose acquaintance I made for the first time. They were houseguests of the Chenaults. Only the Livingstons had yet to arrive.

Clay came at once to Amanda, helping her out of her light pelisse and handing it to the tall, impassive black butler. Looking into the dark face, so blank, so still, so unreadable, I felt a renewal of my earlier uneasiness.

It grew as I watched the slaves watching their masters. Taking a small meat sandwich from a tray held by a young black girl, I felt a distinct shock of fear. For a moment her eyes were on mine, and they held such a depth of hatred that I could scarce believe I had witnessed it. She looked down at the plate and murmured, "Thankee, ma'am. May I fetch you some wine?"

George came over to me and in his low, husky voice said, "The Livingstons haven't put in an appearance yet." There was amusement in the words. "Do you suppose they were so offended by my actions last week that they will stay away?

"That would be too good to be true," I said pessimistically. "I think they're just a bit late." The black girl drew up with a glass of champagne on a tray and I thanked her courteously.

When she had gone, I said, "George, do you feel that something is not quite right?"

"What do you mean?" he asked alertly.

"I am probably a fool, but I have the feeling that all is not well—that something is about to happen. I can't explain it, but I feel I must get home to Mélisse at once. It's as if she were ill and needing me."

"You French and your intuition— No, no, far be it from me to discount it, Lilibel," he laughed.

"I had this feeling before, just before Jacques rode up to our *pension* mortally wounded. And I had it before I saw Maman and Papa on their way to the guillotine."

"Perhaps you have a second sight," he said. "Perhaps you are gifted in that way."

I shook my head and turned my troubled eyes to his black ones. He caught his breath and said low, "My dear Liliane, have you the faintest conception of how beautiful you are? You stir my blood as no one else has ever done."

"But you want no ties, George. For you, there are many women."

"No one like you. I have never met a woman like you."

"I shall take that as a compliment," I replied with a faint smile. "Though knowing you, it could have an entirely different meaning."

His big shoulders lifted and fell, but his eyes were still compelling mine to his, and I knew once more that sharp thrill that he alone provoked. "Your prospective marriage to Andrew seems a farce to me. Do you love him very much?"

I wanted to cry out, *No!* Instead I said evasively, "Andrew is a kind and charming man. Any woman should be proud to be his wife."

"Are you sure this feeling you have—of something not being quite right—does not stem from your promise to marry my brother? Had you thought of that?"

I looked away from him quickly, fearing he might see the truth in my eyes. He could be right, yet I had already made up my mind there would be no wedding. Why should it still nag me? No, my feeling of—what? danger?—was more immediate.

"George, could we leave a little early, do you suppose? Could you ask the others? I want to get back to Mélisse." I lied suddenly. "She hasn't been feeling too well."

"But we've only just arrived."

"I know. But if we could leave by eleven—instead of after midnight. I'm worried about my little daughter."

He took a whiskey and water, tinkling with ice, from a tray proffered him by one of the impassive servants. "I will speak to the others, my dear, and see if I can persuade them. It will disappoint Vance and Sara, for they have been looking forward to this soirée for weeks."

"Then perhaps *you* could take me home early." I knew I sounded distraught and I tried hard to sort out my tangled senses at the moment. But I was so aware of menace in the air that I could scarce bring myself to sip the champagne I held. I must get hold of myself, I thought with a touch of panic.

He laughed. "My brother might well call me out if I escorted you home alone."

"Yes, yes, that's true. I will stop worrying. Abby will care for Mélisse. I will put it out of my mind until later."

The dancing began shortly after that and everyone was filled with high spirits, with one exception—myself. It seemed to me the evening dragged interminably as I danced first with Andrew and then the other men.

After another hour, the Livingstons' absence was being remarked on by others. As I stood talking with Vance and Sara, Vance said, "Perhaps old Jabez took George's chastisement seriously this time. Maybe he doesn't want to face him again."

"No," Sara said with concern. "I had Anna to tea just yesterday and she said she and Jabez were looking forward to our ball with great anticipation. Do you suppose one of them took sick?"

"I would think they would send word in that case," Vance said. "But I place my money on Jabez's pride. He knows George is here and I think he's a touch embarrassed by his butchery of Railo, and the beating George administered him." Vance laughed with sudden heartiness. "I can't grieve for their absence, my dear ladies. I think it's a better gathering without them."

"I, too," I said coolly.

Sara laughed indulgently. "We all know of your feud with Jabez over Railo and Judith, Liliane. And our sympathies are with you, but we planters must stick together. We are greatly outnumbered by our slaves, you know."

"All the more reason you should keep relations with them on a human and friendly basis. Men like Jabez should be restrained from such brutalities. Had he performed such an atrocity on one of us, he would be thrown into jail," I replied.

Vance's face hardened. "Ah, you are right. Of course, Jabez could even have remained home to see that some of his slaves were properly punished. He never misses a chance to assert his power over them. I propose we stop worrying about them and enjoy ourselves. May I have the next dance, Miss Lilibel?"

As the orchestra struck up once more, I swung out upon the gleaming floor with Vance Chenault's arms about me. My conversation with him was scant, for my mind was on my part in Amanda's elopement in a few hours. She had made several quiet and unobserved trips to my room during the last few days. Under my high bed, where the quilted spread hung down to hide them, were a portmanteau and two small valises. "We shall both have horses. Clay is bringing one from Tulip Grove for me," she had said breathlessly on her trip with underthings for the valise. "Clay says we can easily strap these behind us and ride like the wind."

I knew some of my apprehension came from the fear that Amanda might be discovered, and the uproar that would follow. No doubt Mary would invoke the assistance of Andrew and, between the two of them, they might well frustrate the young lovers. In that case, I promised myself firmly, I would cast my unwanted advice in their faces, and tell them plainly that I thought the two should be married as soon as possible. I might as well be hung for a horse as a flea.

"You are certainly preoccupied this evening, my dear," Vance said, as the music drew to a close. "But I suppose a prospective bride has much to think about, eh?" His smile was warm and friendly. I knew both he and Sara sincerely liked me.

"Yes," I replied, "I have much to think about—but mainly, at the moment, I'm worried about my Mélisse. She seemed feverish when I left this evening." I was laying the groundwork for an early departure.

Still the evening dragged on. By eleven, I saw George conversing with Andrew. Charles came up and stood listening, then glanced in my direction. Andrew looked my way and pulled at his ear thoughtfully, nodding his head to George. Relief and gratitude to George swept over me when the men seemed to agree. Even so, I felt the women would try to dissuade me, for they were so obviously enjoying themselves. Cornelia, laughing with Helen Montague as the two of them exchanged confidences, had danced with nearly every man at the ball. Laura, of course, had been monopolized by Charles, while Mary had sedately spread her dances equally among the men. But I had twice seen her dance with Andrew and, the way their bodies flowed together, I marveled that everyone could not recognize the strange, unnatural love between them.

Vance and Sara were vocal in their disappointment at our early departure. But, after much distressing conference and regret we were on our way home at last. Only Amanda did not appear disappointed at leaving before the ball was over, a fact that Mary remarked on rather acrimoniously.

Amanda replied demurely, "Well, Mother, you don't want me to see too much of Clay, so I suppose 'tis best we leave early." In the dark I could not see Mary's expression, but I was sure it must be one of astonishment.

With every beat of the horses' hooves I felt a touch of relief. I was quiet, wrestling with my strange, premonitory sense of danger, and the others undertook to comfort me about Mélisse's supposed fever. Cornelia said, "My dear, 'tis the summer complaint, I'm sure. All young children have it sooner or later. I'm relieved that Andy and Tim have escaped so far. Do not fear."

Mary patted my hand, adding, "In a day or two she will be quite herself. You really should have told us earlier today. We could have sent for Aunt Mincy."

As we came upon the narrow road to Cloudmont, I strained my eyes out the open windows, seeking the lights that always showed at the great house, welcoming strangers and friends alike. When they came into sight, a flood of comfort suffused me and I leaned back against the leather cushions with a sigh of relief. It did not last long, however, for as we drew up before the broad door at the rear of the great hall, I found I had anchored my unfounded fears in Mélisse after all, and I could hardly wait to get to my room.

I sped down the hall, shifting my candle from one hand to the other as I pulled out of my light white pelisse, and entered my room a bit breathlessly. I shut the door quietly behind me so as not to wake her, then turned and looked toward the bed. It was neatly made. Mélisse was not in it.

Stifling a scream, I looked wildly around the room before reason asserted itself. Abby must have her in her room. She had taken her to bed with her on several occasions when I had been out for the evening and Mélisse had a particularly bad nightmare.

I hastened to the door and on my way to the central stairs I encountered Laura, who was yawning as she made her way to her room, bearing a candelabrum containing three candles. Observing my wide eyes and pale face, she exclaimed, "My dear, you look as though you had seen a ghost!"

"Mélisse is not in my room—but I'm sure she's with Abby. I'm on my way to get her."

"Of course she'd be with Abby if she's feverish. Abby wouldn't leave her alone in that big bed of yours." She smiled at me reassuringly. "You should let her spend the night there, rather than disturbing her, Lilibel."

"Yes," I replied, forcing calmness into my voice. "But I must see that she's no worse than when I left." My lie was taking on a nightmarish veracity, and my heart pounded heavily. As Laura went on down the hall, I took the stairs to the third floor and hurried to Abby's room. After knocking softly and receiving no response, I tried the knob. It turned easily and I stepped silently inside, the candlelight sending shadows flaring about the room. It was cozy with the furniture that Abby had been given and there was a small grate over a piece of marble on the floor, where she had her winter fire. Seeing a large mound in the bed, I peered closely to find the smaller one beside it. I did not. There was no one in the bed but Abigail.

I fought down renewed panic as I shook Abby's shoulder and whispered, "Abby—Abby, do wake up!"

She rolled over and said groggily, "Ma'am? Who is it? What——"

"Abby," I said forcefully, "where is Mélisse? She is not in her bed, and I left you in charge of her!"

Abby sat up with a start. Her red hair was tied with what looked to be hundreds of strips of cloth, against tomorrow when she would prepare her own elaborate coiffure. She looked bewildered. "Why, madame, ye know Mincy took her. She said ye sent Noah fer her to come and fetch her because she was a touch feverish with the summer complaint."

"Bon Dieu!" I cried. "She had no fever. You know that, Abby! She was bright as a bird while I dressed."

"But madame—Mincy wouldn't do that without ye asked her to—an' she wanted to take Timmy an' Andy as a special treat, but they was asleep an' I told Mincy they didn't need to be woke up." Now Abby's face drew up with fear in the light of my candle. "Miss Lilibel, Mélisse was still awake in me own bed here an' she was happy as a lark to be goin' with Mincy. I thought—ye mean ye *didn't* send for Mincy?" She was more bewildered than ever.

"Never mind, Abby," I said quietly. "I'm sure it's quite all right. Go back to sleep, dear, and so shall I."

I couldn't have the house in a turmoil, but panic was sweeping me in black waves. I had never been so terrified. Surely my lie about Mélisse's health would not punish me by suddenly becoming reality. Abby sighed and lay back down as I bade her good night.

I fled down the hall, extinguishing my candle in my precipitous flight, and had to negotiate the stairs in complete blackness. Only when I reached the second floor did the palest of light filter in from the moonlit window at the end of the west wing. I felt my way along to my room. Now that I knew where my child was, I was filled with anguish to see her. Aunt Mincy loved Mélisse, and surely she would see she came to no harm. But she was *mine*, my baby, and I must be with her if she was ill.

My mind was chaotic, but the house about me was still as I made my way to my room once more. I dared not rouse the family, for they would argue that I leave Mélisse with Mincy—that Mincy could care for her better than I. Since I had so carefully laid the premise of her illness, they would be relieved that Mélisse was with the old woman.

In my room, I struck flint and relit the candle, then flung out of my ballgown. I did not bother to put on a riding habit. No long, binding garments for this ride! But I did stamp on my riding boots, then changed to a thin, pink cambric dress, without donning a petticoat between it and my scanty chemise. I would ride astride and make better time.

I would not call Noah at the stables, nor any of the slaves to help me. I would slip in quietly and put the bridle and bit on Dandylion and be off. My hair was loose but I wasted no time with putting it up. I fled my room in darkness this time, with hair hanging loose to my waist.

I tiptoed through the great hall, for I could hear the deep murmur of the men in the library, still imbibing their nightcaps, and slipped out the rear door without a sound. I could not bear the thought of that long, dark ride in the company of Andrew, and he would insist on accompanying me, I knew. Though I would have welcomed George, I thought fleetingly as I sped down the path. He might have tried to reason against my panic.

The moon washed the gardens, gilding the flowers and trees, making the bowling green a carpet touched by silver as I made my way to the stables. The doors were open, allowing the breeze to course through the stalls and cool the horses.

I was struck by an eerie sensation that the quarters were all empty, but I told myself I was a fool. The hour was late and everyone was abed. I felt my way through the dark lane of stalls, the sandy soil soft beneath my boots. Which one was Dandylion's—the third or fourth?

The horses, sensing my presence and probably my agitation, began to move restively, blowing through their noses with soft, velvety sounds in the night. I heard a nicker, and recognized it as Dandylion's. She was in the fourth stall and I fumbled with the gate. She followed me out and stood patiently while I darted into the dark tack room. Inside, the windows admitted enough of the brilliant moonlight for me to see to pluck a bridle and bit from a peg on the wall.

I had a little difficulty in putting it on her, mainly because of my nerves and panic. It would take nearly an hour riding through the forest to reach Mincy's. I pulled Dandy close to the stable fence and climbed up on it to mount her bareback, my skirt hiked up about my thighs as on that long-ago May night in France. I remembered all too well my wild flight from Paris and my terror, but I had Mélisse with me then. Looking back, it seemed not nearly so terrifying as this moonlit night, with the fears that now peopled my mind.

I dug my heels into Dandy's flanks and we set off, past the ominously silent slave quarters and into the thick woods beyond. The moonlight helped, but I knew the way so well by now that I could have found the path without it. The night was deathly quiet and there was not a vestige of breeze. It was dry and hot and I felt perspiration gather on my upper lip, even as I rode at a brisk canter. My hands were slippery with moisture on the reins. I tried not to go too fast, but Dandylion seemed to have a feel for the path and we made better time than I hoped. It was a long way to Mincy's cabin, where it lay between the Livingston plantation and the Lindens, the two houses farthest west.

I was consumed with desire to reach my child and I had thought it would put all other fears out of my head, but I found myself tense as I rode through the silver dappled forest. The moon scarcely penetrated some parts of the thick foliage of the trees, and often I could not see where we were going and had to trust to Dandylion. The ride seemed interminable, but at last I felt sure I was drawing near Mincy's.

Looking ahead at some distance, I saw an orange glow in the sky and wondered momentarily what phenomenon of nature would cause such a sight. Fire? I put it from my mind. It was a trick of the moonlight. I urged

Dandylion onward. Her feet were silent on the leaf-padded floor of the forest, and slowly, slowly, I became aware of a faint murmur in the distance. I was almost at Mincy's and I was mystified by the dim sound.

Then as we rode on, I strained to look ahead and I saw pinpoints of light in the depths of the forest. I became aware of an occasional shrill cry, rising among the murmurs, that chilled my blood. I drew rein tautly and sat narrow-eyed, watching. I sat a long time, for I felt that something terrible was abroad in the night and I was riding to meet it. As I sat silently, the flickering lights multiplied, the murmur and cries grew louder.

They were coming—it must be people—from the direction of Aunt Mincy's cabin, directly in my line of travel. The old tension with which I had lived so long in France clamped a familiar hold on my vitals. I drew back stealthily, backing Dandylion off the path and into the heavily shrubbed undergrowth. There was menace in those approaching lights and in that low, growling murmur.

My startled heart gave a great bound as a night bird perched in one of the trees above me let out a piercing cry and there was a flutter of wings as he took flight. It was borne in on me afresh that the night was excessively still and the August heat like a furnace. I felt new perspiration gather on my brow and upper lip, and it trickled slowly down between my breasts. I determined to wait until these nocturnal prowlers passed me by. I slipped down from the barebacked Dandylion, and prayed that she would not nicker as they drew nearer.

It seemed hours before I could discern that the lights I saw were pitchpine torches held high in many hands. And slowly, slowly, the mass of people approached. I do not know the exact moment it dawned on me that it was a vast number of slaves, their black bodies gleaming in the torchlight. Their murmur had settled into a chant. "We gonna be free—we gonna be free—we gonna be free tonight!"

CHAPTER 17

As they drew ever nearer, I saw they were strung out in a long narrow file to accommodate to the pathway. The central group carried three long poles, saplings that had been cut and trimmed. I restrained a scream, then a retch, as I saw what was on top of those poles.

On the first, plainly visible in the torchlight, was the bleeding head of Jabez Livingston. Just behind it, another slave carried a pole bearing the head of Anna. The head of their overseer Speers was on the third. The eyes in the severed heads were wide open and the light from the fiery torches reflected in them as if they were watching the proceedings with expressionless faces. Blood dripped down the poles, and occasionally the slaves carrying them would wipe their hands on their clothing.

I had seen many severed heads in France during the Terror but somehow none of them seemed so horrible a sight as these grisly Livingston heads in the light of the pitchpine torches.

Tearing my eyes from the poles, I looked at the slaves marching by, and recognized many of them from the Livingston plantation. Then with horror I saw two that I recognized from Cloudmont. Behind them came Ezekiel, Ephraim's brother.

That would explain the eerie silence, the emptiness I had sensed when passing the quarters as I left the big house. Now I saw the weapons in their hands as well—machetes, scythes, axes, even hoes and pitchforks. I recognized their leader—it was Railo, his right hand bearing a startling white bandage where Jabez had wreaked his fury on the black. By his side strode Judith, her head high and her beautiful features resolute.

The Livingstons' absence at the ball was all too understandable now. I was witnessing firsthand a slave insurrection, the thing Mary had said "we try not to think about." I knew now—had known then—that the human spirit can bear only so much oppression before death becomes preferable. Even Cloudmont slaves, promised freedom and escape only months away, had joined the embattled mass of men and women.

With scalding suddenness I thought, *Is Mincy with them?* Dear heaven! What would they do with my little Mélisse? Frantically I searched the faces that passed, but I did not see Mincy.

I huddled there, pressed close to Dandylion as they marched past, scarcely daring to breathe and thanking *le bon Dieu* for my silent horse. I knew if they found me there, nothing could save me, for these people had stood too much too long from their oppressors—and I knew they would count me as one of the oppressors.

The orange light in the distance grew and I realized it must be Livingston's house, burning while its former owner had found his place atop a pole. I could scrape up no sorrow for Jabez and Anna. Indeed, I condemned them, for they had precipitated their slaughter and thereby ours. We would all pay for Jabez's cruelty now.

When the last light was a good distance down the pathway toward the Lindens, I hastily remounted Dandylion and urged her to a near gallop through the dark forest toward Mincy's cabin. I did not notice when I brushed against a tree or was bruised by a low-hanging limb; I crouched low over the horse's mane and frantically urged her onward.

In a pool of moonlight, I saw that Mincy's cabin was dark when I reached it. I flung myself from the mare and ran to the door. I beat upon it, sobbing for breath and calling out, "Mincy! Mincy—are you there?" The old dog Gypse came around the side of the house and stood looking at me calmly.

The door opened swiftly under my fevered knocking and Mincy drew me into the cabin. "Jes' a minute, madame," she said, and I heard her moving about in the blackness.

I could not wait. "Where is Mélisse?" I sobbed.

Mincy said, "Shhh! She's asleep," and there was a scraping sound as she struck a flint and lit a candle. It wavered in the open door and the room sprang into shadowed view.

Weak with relief, I looked uncertainly about me. Then I discerned my sleeping child on a cot near Mincy's rough wooden bed, which was still neatly made. The old woman had obviously been sitting up, watchful in the darkness.

I breathed, "Aunt Mincy, you've given me such a fright! Why did you take Mélisse without telling me?"

In the flickering light her eyes held a veiled look. "My peoples is on the rampage. I didn't want my little Mélisse cut up or burned. I tried to get Tim an' Andy, too, but that ol' Abigail wouldn't let 'em come."

The flesh on my arms crawled and I blurted, "I saw them in the woods—Railo and Judith and God knows how many others. I hid in the brush as they went by."

"They on they way to the Montagues an' Reeds an' Chenaults. They'll save Cloudmont for last—it bein' the biggest and finest—an' the last in line."

"I saw—Anna and Jabez Livingston and their overseer, Speers." I gulped. "Their heads were stuck on poles."

"Livingstons bad people," Mincy said with a calm shrug.

"But the Madisons have always been kind—have been their friends and plan to free them," I protested. "Yet I saw Cloudmont slaves in their midst."

Mincy gave me an inscrutable glance. "Railo say no white man is their friend. They gonna wipe them out and march on to Richmond, gatherin' more as they go. He swears there'll be enough of 'em to kill all the mens in Richmond by the time they reach it. Then with all the guns in the Richmond arsenal, they'll set up they own free state."

"Dear God!" I whispered. "I must get back to warn them at Cloudmont—to run—to leave. I cannot believe Judith would be party to the slaughter of Laura and the family!"

Mincy shrugged again. "Judith loves Railo. She do what he say. Laura done used Judith all her life. Railo say they all got to die to make a free black state of Virginia."

I shrank from the thought of the Madisons decapitated, their heads impaled on saplings. "I must warn them," I repeated, still stunned.

Mincy's eyes were hard. "You gone take this innocent little girl an' run the risk of them killin' her? She safe here with me, you know." She did not offer to harbor me in her small dwelling.

We were startled by a fierce pounding on the door, and my heart began to race anew. A man's voice cried, "Mincy—is Liliane in there with you—and Mélisse?"

It was George. My heart, still beating wildly, knew a sudden relief. Mincy removed the bar to the door and opened it. George's big body loomed up in the shadows, his vitality filling the room. As his eyes fell on us, he said, "Thank God, I'm in time. Lilibel, there is a slave rebellion—they are marching on all the plantations."

"I know," I whispered, "I saw them in the forest and hid. They had Anna and Jabez Livingston's heads on poles—and Speers's too. How did you know about it?"

"Lucky you hid, or you'd have been on a pole too," he said bluntly. "And lucky that Noah was with them at Livingston's. He meant to be part of it, but when he saw what they did to the Livingstons, he was—he couldn't face murdering us, and slipped away to warn us. We've sent him now to alert Lindens, Tulip Grove, and Rose Hill. Charles is on his way to Williamsburg to get the militia, but God knows if he will be in time. I believe all our tenant farmers have got wind of it and fled. Livingston's house is burning to the ground—it can be seen for miles."

"I know," I replied numbly. "I saw it."

"You folks got a little time to get away from Cloudmont," Mincy said calmly. "Railo done tol' me Cloudmont would be last to go. But I 'vise you all leave for Williamsburg yourselfs. Can't all of us feel like Noah and me does."

"Mincy, can you keep Lilibel and Mélisse safe from harm in your cabin until it's over?" George asked rapidly.

The old Negress shook her head. "I kin keep my Mélisse safe. She a baby—but Railo done tol' me if'n he found one white person in my cabin, he'd burn me to the ground too, no matter how long our friendship. But I'm free—I ain't no part of no rebellion." Her jaw set stubbornly.

George turned to me. "Then you'd best leave Mélisse here, Liliane, for I cannot guarantee that I can persuade my brother and mother and sister to leave Cloudmont unprotected and flee to Williamsburg. Come with me. I will protect you."

The statement was so simple and so firm that panic lessened its grip on me. If George said he would protect me, he would do so. He continued, "Mincy, we will leave Mélisse with you. And Lilibel, we must hurry back to Cloudmont. There's no telling how much time we have left, as they will make short shrift of our friends and neighbors unless Noah reaches them in time. We do not want to risk meeting them in the forest alone. Come!" He caught my cold hand in his big warm one. I saw then that he had two dueling pistols thrust in his waistband.

I pulled back for one more look at my peacefully sleeping child. "Oh, Aunt Mincy," I whispered, swallowing hard, "please take care of her. Don't let anything happen to her."

"I dies, before I let them harm a hair of her head. An' all my peoples knows me. They ain't goin' to come near my place. Ain't I held my tongue these months while Railo been plannin' this? They trusts me."

Stooping swiftly, I touched Mélisse's cheek in a butterfly's kiss, closing off the voice inside me that screamed, *What will become of her if you are killed?*

In bright moonlight, George lifted me swiftly to Dandylion's bare back. I heard his low laughter as I swung my legs over the horse, baring my thighs brazenly. I made an effort to pull the narrow muslin skirt over them without success.

"Don't you dare laugh at me, George Madison," I said in quick fury. "I'll not go bumping along sitting sideways at a time like this."

"You misunderstand. I always enjoy it when I see a lady flout a stupid convention." We both struck out across the short meadow toward the trees.

The ride back to Cloudmont seemed to take forever, though George kept up a brisk pace, even in the depths of the woods. I crouched low over Dandylion's mane, wishing devoutly that I had taken time to tie my tangled hair up before leaving Cloudmont. I took one hand from the reins and gathered up the mass of hair, attempting to shove it down the back of the muslin dress and succeeding in a random sort of way. After that I felt easier as we brushed against small limbs and twigs.

George seemed to be following a track I could not see, and I knew he was taking short-cuts that only a native could know. Though every sense was alert for it, I saw no twinkling torches in the blackness of the forest about us, heard no distant chant, no faint murmur. At least the wind against me was cooling, despite the dry heat of August.

When at last we came upon the narrow path that broadened into the roadway leading to Cloudmont, George drew up and fell back beside me. His eyes searched the sky around us.

"Doesn't look as though they've fired the Lindens yet," he said softly. "That means they've got three to go before they reach us—Lindens, Tulip Grove, and Rose Hill."

"Will they burn them all—and Cloudmont?"

He shrugged. "Who knows? Railo is a shrewd and intelligent man. If he thinks burning the plantations will encourage his people, burn them he will."

"I can understand burning Livingston's. Yes—even killing them," I said bitterly. "But not the rest of us."

"Well," George drawled evenly, "he'll play hell killing us at Cloudmont. We'll not be caught sleeping in our beds, thanks to Noah."

"There are no lights in the house!" I said, alarmed. "Can they have already——"

"No, Lilibel. See yonder? There is a candle moving in that window. Railo thinks he has the heavy sleeping hours to fall upon Cloudmont."

We passed the church, then the silent and empty quarters, then the cold forge in the smithy and the yard where Noah kept the hunting dogs. They rose up and one barked sharply, then fell silent, having caught our scent. Two or three whined pleadingly as we rode by, then all was silent again. At the stable I drew rein, but

George spoke, "No. Let us ride to the house and tether our horses at the door. I shall try to persuade my family to leave Cloudmont."

At the house George dismounted and, taking the reins from both horses, looped them about the hitching post nearby. He came to stand beside me where I sat Dandylion and suddenly he put one hand on my bare thigh. A tingling shock spread through me and I was still as the hot night about us.

He slipped his hand slowly upward beneath my chemise until it met my hip and still I could not move, could not cry out to him, *Stop!* for my blood was pulsing hotly and my lips had parted to give my quick, warm breath better vent.

He said slowly, "I cannot believe you will wed my brother." His hand slid over my stomach and downward to touch me gently.

Swiftly I swung my other leg over the horse and slipped down into his arms. Holding me, he reached behind and gathered up my long hair, releasing it from the binding hold of my dress. His fingers slid along the back of my head as he forced my face upward.

His lips on mine were cool and firm and very tender at first. His other hand found the small of my back and pressed me forward with a sudden, fierce movement, against his hardening body. Kissing me, his mouth grew demanding and bruising.

My arms were about his broad shoulders, my lips parting under his. I had never felt such overwhelming desire as I did then at his touch.

A cry sounded from the door behind us and I tore loose, to hear Mary's agitated voice. "I heard you come up the road——" The candle in her hand wavered in the light night air. "That is you, isn't it, George? Have you Mélisse—and Lilibel with you?"

"I have Lilibel," George said huskily, as we both turned to her.

Her voice sharpened with hysteria, as it always did when one of the children might be in danger. "But the baby! Where—what has happened to Mélisse?"

"We left her with Aunt Mincy. She will be far safer

there than with us, Mary." George had released me, but now took my hand and pulled me to the granite steps and into the rear of the great hall.

Mary's candle flame danced crazily as she slammed the door and bolted it behind us. "But you know Aunt Mincy must have known Railo was planning this thing—and she never said a word! My God, George, you must be out of your mind to have left the child there!"

"I made the decision to leave my daughter there," I said with sudden coldness.

She turned on me. "Then *you* must be out of your mind!"

My reply was stopped by the appearance at the drawing room door of Andrew, his mother, and Laura.

"Thank God, George reached you, my dear!" Andrew cried. "I couldn't leave Mary—or Mother and Laura unprotected. Mary is so terrified." He put an arm about her, drawing her near, and finished, "So George undertook the dangerous ride— But where is Mélisse?"

Abigail pushed from behind them, jostling Cornelia and pushing Bibsey aside. "Beggin' yer pardon, mistress—madame, did you not find Mélisse there? Ah, sweet Lord, surely *they* haven't got her?" She looked imploringly into my face.

"Aunt Mincy has her," I said reassuringly. "I felt it best to leave her there. She will be far safer with her than with us."

Clementine gave a little shriek from behind Laura. "Oh, Lor'lumme, she'll be killed! We're all goin' to be killed!"

"Now, Clementine," Andrew said firmly, "we'll have no more of your hysterics."

Whimpering, she turned back into the drawing room. Cornelia came to put an arm about my shoulders, murmuring that she felt I had made the wisest decision. As Laura kissed my cheek lightly, I looked beyond her and saw Amanda. She was leaning against the door frame, her face paper white and her blue eyes enormous with fear.

"Clay's going to be all right," I said to her, trying to believe it myself. "I'm sure Noah reached Tulip Grove in plenty of time. All the Reeds are probably on their way to Williamsburg by now. Who knows, Clay may even stop here and take you with him."

"Don't put such ideas into the child's head, Liliane," Mary said sharply. "Andrew doesn't choose to run to Williamsburg and leave Cloudmont to be burned by a pack of savages."

We had moved by then into the drawing room and I saw Joshua and Ephraim Landon, the two slaves who had chosen not to join the insurrection, with their wives and four small children. All the servants clustered about, Samantha Beady, Bibsey, Henry Pepper, Abigail, and now Clementine, who was weeping quietly on Beady's shoulder. I thought how lucky for John Seabury, the tutor-pastor, that he had chosen this time to go to Richmond.

George and Andrew behind me were arguing quietly. I strained to hear them over the muted talk of the servants.

"If we're not here, I doubt if they will burn Cloudmont, Andrew. It will be far safer if we all leave."

"No! Cloudmont is the fruit of many lifetimes. I cannot abandon it so easily. Charles will return with the militia soon."

"I love my home, too," George responded, "but I have sense enough to know what moves Railo. He wants to be free and as long as we stand in his way, he will be destructive. Cloudmont will be safer," he repeated, "without us in it."

I looked about the room. Derringers, dueling pistols, and flintlock muskets lay neatly in rows on the floor, bags of powder and bullets beside them. I had not realized that Cloudmont possessed such an arsenal.

"I shall defend Cloudmont," Andrew said.

George said evenly, "Then you want to risk the lives of the women and children by staying here. There are *hundreds* of slaves, Andrew. Lilibel saw them on her way to Aunt Mincy's. She will bear me out. And more are joining them as they go."

"I have told Mother and Laura—all the women may go, but they are as reluctant to leave our home to the mercy of Railo's followers as I am," Andrew retorted.

Cornelia put a hand on George's arm. "My son, I

would rather die in Cloudmont than leave it. Mary feels the same."

George lifted his shoulders. "I feared you were of that mind." His voice hardened. "In that case we all stay to the end."

"I'll man the front windows from the servants' room on the third floor," came Louise Alexander's quiet, firm voice behind us. She had just entered from the great hall.

We turned and looked at her. I was astonished to see she wore strange, softly fitting breeches. On her feet were something the Cloudmont slaves often wore called moccasins. She wore a fringed leather weskit over a soft, coarse white shirt. In her hand she carried a polished and worn-looking flintlock. Standing there in my thin long-skirted dress, I envied her freedom from skirts from the bottom of my heart.

She smiled thinly at my open-eyed admiration at her garb. "I haven't worn these buckskins in over twenty years, madame. I was a sharpshooter in our war for independence from England. 'Twas then I met—the Madisons." She looked very straight and slim and beautiful, with her graying hair coiled neatly on the back of her head.

Cornelia looked at her oddly and said, "Thank God, there is one of us women who knows how to be useful."

"I expect you to be quite as useful, Mother," Andrew said shortly. "As I remember, you are something of a marksman yourself."

"Not as good as Louise," Cornelia said wryly, "but I shall do my best."

There ensued a course in handling the flintlocks, derringers, and dueling pistols, with George and Andrew showing Ephraim, Joshua, and Henry Pepper how to load and fire all the weapons. They were appallingly ignorant, but seemed to be grasping the instructions. I had some experience with muskets in France with Jacques, but very little.

Amanda said, "I can load and keep a flintlock ready for the men to fire."

"You will take care of Tim and Andy in a room near

your Uncle Andrew and me," said Mary, with a sob in her voice, "and leave the guns to us."

"There are so few of us," I whispered to Cornelia.

"The gardeners all fled the moment the news of the rebellion came. Even Jacob Worth took his wife and ran. They must be halfway to Williamsburg by now. If only a few of them had stayed! If Laura's slaves had stood by us, we would have more to man guns at the windows. At least the slaves have no firearms—and if they captured any at the Livingstons' they do not know how to use them." Cornelia picked up a flintlock and two bags of ammunition.

Andrew spoke out clearly. "My dears, I believe that Charles will return from Williamsburg with the militia before the slaves reach Cloudmont, but in any event we will be able to hold them off until the militia can arrive."

I murmured to Cornelia, "When I saw them in the forest, they were armed with pitchforks, scythes, and axes—even machetes."

"Our guns will keep them at a distance from the house. They will not be able to use them on us," she replied.

I thought she was overly optimistic, but I said nothing. The plan was that we would take positions at windows about the house. Andrew positioned each of us, the servants and the two slaves, Joshua and Ephraim, and their families.

He kept me with him, saying, "My darling, you can keep a fresh musket loaded as I fire. They'll come up from the rear and from the front as well. We shall stay here in the main drawing room, looking out toward the James. Perhaps they will parley with us, if I can call to Railo and get him to talk. They could even bypass Cloudmont and return to Richmond."

I thought Andrew a fool. After the terrible oppression Railo had suffered, he would be in no mood to bypass any plantation or any white man or woman. He would draw the line nowhere, for he felt us all in league against him.

At last, nearly everyone had a flintlock or pistol, even Beady, who was surprisingly sharp in understanding

George's instructions. Ephraim and Joshua were showing some ease and lack of fear in handling the weapons now.

Staring out the drawing-room window, George said, "My guess is they'll try to storm the house from every side. Poor devils."

Laura, on the point of leaving with Pepper, turned on him. "How can you pity them? They are bloodthirsty savages, bent on murdering every one of us!"

George laughed shortly. "I am thinking how I would feel if I were in their place—and my dear Laura, I must confess my feelings would be to destroy those who would keep me enslaved."

"You and Andrew," Laura said scornfully. "They are no better than savages. And my Judith—I loved her so—she is among them, with my death on her mind, no doubt."

"We are all savages, Laura," George replied. "The veneer that covers you and me is only a shade thicker than the one that covered Railo before this began. The tragedy lies in the fact that we feel we must kill each other in order to survive."

Andrew asked hopefully, "Do you think they're putting up a fight at Lindens? It could delay them—give Charles a chance——"

"They are if they can," George replied.

Mary, her full bosom heaving, came running into the room as Laura and Pepper left. She held her flintlock in one shaking hand, powderhorn and bag of bullets in the other. "Andrew," she said tremulously, "I can use this flintlock, but I am so afraid—alone in the upstairs bedroom." She ignored the rest of us, looking at him pleadingly in the candlelight. "Could you not come up there with me? I am so alone. Lilibel can help George."

Andrew's look was one of tortured and driven love. He turned to me as an afterthought, asking, "Would you mind staying here with George?"

"Go with Mary, Andrew," I replied quickly, relieved of the prospect of being alone in the dim light with him for the terror-filled moments before Railo and his hundreds fell upon us.

He went with her, and George and I were left silently observing each other as we seated ourselves on the rosewood couch before the broad open window. Beyond it, the

James glittered in the moonlight and lawns, blackgreen, rolled to the river's edge.

"If we survive this, are you still going to marry him?" George asked.

I shook my head slowly. "I cannot tell you why, but I can never marry Andrew. I told him so nearly a month ago, but he begged me to wait a month, thinking I might change my mind. But I shall not."

"Bravo," he said quietly. "I would hate to see you in Yve's trap."

"Then you know about——" I stopped short. I was not really surprised.

"I have for years. Only Mother and the children are unaware of it. Andrew does not know you have learned his and our sister's secret?"

"I told him only that I did not love him—that it had been an infatuation and I could not hold him to his proposal."

George's laugh was low and amused. "How kind you are to spare the feelings of others as you do, Lilibel. I wonder if you know how remarkable you are?"

I said nothing, for I was remembering instead my feelings as George's hand had touched my bare flesh. With remembrance came the breathlessness, the fast-beating heart. He was looking at me intently in the golden light from the candle on the table beside us.

He loves the sea, I reminded myself. He has no use for marriage. A flood of anger swept me at my own folly, for in that instant I knew I had made the mistake of coming to love George Madison. I loved him for his sense of humor, his ability to laugh at himself, his quick wit and his unexpected tenderness and gallantry. I loved him for his hatred of cruelty in Jabez Livingston, for his courage in the face of the present danger—for he sat with the flintlock across his knees, easy and relaxed.

He desired me and had been honest enough to admit it, but that was the end of it. Certainly he had made that clear from the beginning.

He reached out suddenly and put a thumb over the candle flame. "The moonlight is bright enough," he said in response to my unspoken objection. "We don't want to present a target, Lilibel."

He rose, went to the window, then turned. "I'm going upstairs to look out toward Lindens."

"Then I'm coming, too. I'm not very brave in the dark."

Together we took the stairs, making our way swiftly down the long dark hall. Behind those dark open doors the rest of our small company waited, guns in hand, hearts heavy with apprehension. Reaching the west window, we looked out across the tree tops and saw a second orange light in the sky.

"Lindens is gone," George murmured. "That leaves only Tulip Grove and Rose Hill before they reach us."

"Is it possible Charles could be back with the militia before they do?"

"I don't know," was the grim rejoinder. "The hour is late and it will take them time in Williamsburg to assemble, arm, and mount up. Then there is the twenty-five miles to cover between here and there."

"Do you think we can hold them off?" I asked bluntly.

"No." He faced me and I could see the square planes of his face, the dark shadows that held his eyes. There was no fear on his features. "There are too many of them, and they are driven by the stronger force—hatred."

"Then you think we shall all die as the Livingstons died."

Shrugging, he turned from the window. I followed. "There is always the chance of escape. The *Tern* was once nearly captured by Barbary pirates, which would have meant death by torture for every man aboard, but a last-minute storm at sea saved us. Escape is always possible. I have cheated death many times in my short life."

"I, too," I said calmly. "Madame Guillotine would have claimed me twice and I beat her both times."

As we walked back down the hall, he laughed softly. "Perhaps that explains why you are such a remarkable woman. I admire you very much, Liliane—which only adds to my desire to possess you."

"Perhaps, George, I am not of a mood to be married," I said, pretending to misunderstand.

"If you mean that, coming together should be the easiest of accomplishments for us. My town house in Norfolk will need a mistress——"

"I shall be no man's mistress—and aren't you something of a fool, making plans when neither of us knows if we shall live until morning?"

He laughed aloud then, and from Andrew's darkened room, his brother called, "Is that you, George?"

"Yes. I've just checked the west window. Lindens is burning. Lilibel and I are returning to the drawing room."

Andrew came to the door and looked at us in the dim light. "How long do you think we have?" he asked his brother.

"Who knows?" George shrugged. "If Railo decides to divide his forces, we could be attacked at any moment."

"We have to hold them off," Andrew said tautly. "I will not see Cloudmont burned. I will die first."

"I know," George responded dryly, "and everyone else here as well."

"Then leave!" Andrew blazed suddenly. "Take the women with you, coward. Mary and Mother and I will beat them off!" Mary, coming up behind him, struck a flint to the candle she held. As light bloomed I could see her full, trembling lips.

"What is the matter, dear?" she asked Andrew.

"George wants to abandon Cloudmont—to run to Williamsburg." There was a suggestion of hysteria in his voice that shocked me.

"Where we can organize a stand against the slaves," George said levelly.

"And I say, let him go—let them all go! I want no half-hearted help. George has always been too partial to the slaves, anyway." Andrew's voice rose dangerously, and Mary gripped his arm in a tight hand.

"I have sympathized with them, even as you have, brother, and you know I will not leave you to face this alone," George said quietly.

Andrew seemed to come to himself. "I know," he said with sudden contrition. "I apologize, George, but I am certain with Ephraim, Joshua, Pepper, and the girls manning the other sides—though Mother is in her room alone, she can handle a flintlock well—and Louise is more than capable—we can hold out until help arrives." His voice was stronger, calmer. Then he added hesitantly,

"Lilibel, would you like to stay up here with Mary and me?"

"No," I replied quickly. "I will go where I can help George when the time comes."

"Good," he said, and I detected relief. "Keep two guns going, as Mary and I plan to do."

Leaving them, we passed Mary's room, where Amanda and the two little boys sat frozen on the bed, their eyes enormous with terror by the light of one flickering candle. Domino was crouched against them, infected with the fear that was strong as a smell in this great, silent house.

As Amanda looked up and saw us, I said, "Tulip Grove is still dark—no fire. The Reeds must have escaped, Amanda. Why don't you and the boys try to sleep?"

The boys shook their heads, strain etching itself on their small features. "Aunt Lilibel, we can't sleep," Amanda sobbed piteously. "Do you really think Clay has got away?"

"I'm sure he has," I replied, but I had no real hope.

Her face cheered momentarily at my words as George and I moved on down the hall. When we had reached our window facing the James, he said, "My dear, I don't think you should fill Amanda with false hope."

"How do you know it's false?" I challenged. "It could well be true."

"Noah has not returned. If the slaves catch him now, it means a quick death for him, for they will know what he has been doing. Railo, like all good generals, will allow no traitors in his midst. They could even have caught him as he tried to reach Lindens."

"*Bon Dieu!* I had not thought of that. Dear Noah—I pray he is safe!"

"If he is, he should return at any time, for he has had time to make it to all three of the plantations."

We lapsed again into silence. Despite my anxiety, I was acutely aware of George's big, muscled body close to mine. I loved him for that, too, I thought with honesty. He stirred me physically as no man had ever stirred me before, and I had to make a conscious effort to keep from touching him. He did not help me in this, for it seemed to me he brushed against me often.

Now he caught my small hands in his big ones and

said, "Let me show you how to fire the flintlock, Lilibel."

Though Jacques had instructed me, I had never fired one. George and I had two of them now, with powder-horn and bullets beside us, and I knew I could fire one if I must. But as George reached for me, he put the flintlock aside.

He said huskily, "Lilibel, we have such a little time left. Would you send this sailor into battle without love from you?" And as he said it, he pulled me against him, and through the thin muslin dress I gloried in the feel of him.

The desperate situation we were in, the hot, dangerous night, lent impact to my emotions. I strained against him as he kissed me slowly and with increasing fervor.

Taking his lips from mine, he murmured, "Will you give me your love, Liliane? It may be our last and only chance to be together."

At that moment, there came a pounding on the rear door of the great hall, muffled but with desperate urgency in it. We broke apart and ran through the drawing room to the door, which George unbolted.

Noah rushed inside. He was gasping for breath, and I glimpsed his lathered horse in the moonlight beside George's and mine.

"Did you reach them in time, Noah?" George asked quickly, as he closed and bolted the door.

Noah burst out, "Mister George, they had killed them all at Lindens when I got there and was burnin' the house. An' you know how many slaves Mister Reed got at Tulip Grove. I 'spect they done killed all the Reeds soon's they come in from the ball at Rose Hill." The youngster paused, breathing hard. "They was settin' fire to it when I rode up—they's just waitin' fer Railo an' the rest to ketch up to go to Rose Hill. They near ketched me at Tulip Grove an' they knew I was runnin' away—but I *did* get to warn the Chenaults. If they kin run inter the woods, they might can make it."

He began to shake as we stood silent under the enormity of his revelations. "I'm feared it ain't done no good to try to warn 'em—an' it ain't gone be no time before they gets here, Mister George."

George said slowly, "At least you tried. You're a brave and loyal man, Noah."

For a long moment we did not speak, looking out the windows as we entered the drawing room, into the sinister night. Then, still trembling, Noah said, "Railo gone kill me, if he catch me. He don't let nobody go, who traitors him. An' I done traitor him. But before God, Mister George—you all been too good to me, an' I can't stand by and see you butchered!"

George said grimly, "You'll be a free man the minute I can get papers on it—if we live through this. Let me give you a flintlock and you can stand guard in the west drawing room windows."

The youth's hand shook as he reached for the musket and George muttered for him to wait. Going swiftly into the kitchen, he returned with a bottle of brandy and gave Noah a stiff drink, which seemed to calm him.

"They comin' fast, Mister George," he said, "an' they ain't leavin' nobody behind alive."

I touched his hand and murmured, "Noah, thank you for your help."

Noah gave me an uncertain smile and, taking the flintlock, powderhorn, and bag of bullets, made his way determinedly across the great hall to the second drawing room to take up his vigil.

As Noah disappeared, George murmured, "Helen and Evan—their daughters and grandchildren—their sons-in-law, all dead."

"How well Railo timed it," I replied numbly.

"He's been planning it for months, I'll wager. You remember when we came upon them in the forest during the hunt last March. I warned the planters, but they passed it off."

"Vance and Sara and their children—perhaps they'll get away! Do you really think the Reeds and young Clay——" I broke off, fighting back tears. Poor little Amanda. She would never be married to Clay now.

"And all because of the damnable practice of slavery!" George said furiously.

"Perhaps this tragedy will make them change it—free them all," I said, swallowing a sob.

"This has happened before. Nothing will change them. It's gone too far—too many have become too rich from the fruits of slavery."

"Someday they will change it, even if the change is bathed in blood. I lived through such a change in France." I shuddered at the memory and George caught me to him, pressing my shaking body against his firm, warm one.

"Do not be afraid, Lilibel," he whispered into my hair. "Death can come but once and we both have cheated it often. We shall cheat it again!"

His words were comforting but I knew our chances were slim. There must be over three hundred slaves with Railo now. It was an army, one that would grow as it rolled over the Tidewater plantations, swelling until it would sweep over Virginia and make it their own.

Releasing me, George pulled the heavy rosewood sofa nearer to the window. In the dim reflected light of the brilliant moon, he began loading the two flintlocks. He poured the coarse black gunpowder down the barrel, then in swift succession placed a small piece of cloth over the muzzle, carefully positioned the ball over the cloth, seated it in the muzzle, and rammed it home. I was astonished at how swiftly he opened the flash pan and half-cocked the gun, priming with fine powder from the priming flask. Last he snapped the pan cover shut, tilted the gun to the left for a second, and tapped it lightly to ensure that a few grains of priming had entered the touchhole.

"You know to pull the cocks to full cock when ready to shoot, Lilibel?"

"Yes," I replied. Americans astonished me constantly. George had loaded and primed two guns in half the time it would have taken Jacques, I thought.

He leaned them gently against the sofa and took a seat beside me. The house was so quiet, the night noises beyond the opened windows were magnified. Crickets, cicadas, and tree frogs were giving forth their mating calls; their cries of satisfaction, their sounds of joy, made the darkness alive with sound. But nothing human was to be heard. Time went by slowly and the towering clock in the great hall struck three.

George laughed suddenly and low. Startled, I turned to him. "How can you laugh when we are in such danger?"

"I am laughing at myself, my dear Lilibel."

"And why should you do that?"

"Because while I should be worrying about my own skin, I am thinking of yours and how smooth it is to touch and how much I want to touch it."

"You are a fool, George," I said, frightened by the powerful gust of desire that swept me at his words.

"Indeed I am," George replied equably, "but I must confess such thoughts are much pleasanter than those of Railo and his long knife. Don't you agree?" His low drawling voice was as soft and sweet as his caress had been earlier.

"You should be thinking how to save all of us," I protested weakly.

"I have thought of that and made my decision. Now I'm thinking of you and the sweets you could bestow upon me." His hand came up and touched my breast where it strained against the thin muslin of my frock.

"Don't," I said, without any real spirit of defiance, but at least I was able to move my hand to his in a feeble effort to pull it away. He imprisoned my hand then, in his own. And I gave up the hypocrisy of resistance and let it remain.

"That's better," he murmured, pressing my fingers apart until my soft palm was open to him. He brought it up slowly to his mouth. At the feel of his warm breath and his mouth, I thought I would swoon with delight. I wanted to catch that dark head and bring it to my bosom, to cover him with kisses and give myself to him in rich abandon, to know his firmness against my softness. Without thought, I leaned toward him.

As we came together, a distant murmur came to our ears.

Locked in each other's arms, we froze into immobility and George slowly released me. As one, we went to the south windows, straining our ears.

Far down the banks of the James, we glimpsed the twinkle of fire. It sparkled dimly through the many trees that separated Cloudmont and the forest. The murmur grew into a chant, throaty and sinister. Death was marching toward us.

"They have come," George said quietly.

CHAPTER 18

We stood without words until the marchers reached the paths that ran alongside the sweeping front lawns of Cloudmont. Their ranks had been swelled by more slaves from the plantations they had sacked before reaching us. Their ebony faces gleamed in the torchlight and the murmurous chant struck terror into my heart.

They streamed up the paths and spread out across the bright moonlit lawns like a black tide. There looked to be hundreds of them, crudely armed, some dressed in finery from the homes they had stormed, all of them exhilarated and eager. At their center, coming toward the dark and silent Cloudmont, I recognized the figures of Railo and Judith.

Railo never looked so tall and strong. Disdaining any of the clothing from the planters' homes, he stood naked to his waist, still clad in the coarse breeches in which he had worked Livingston soil. His bandaged hand clasped a musket, one I knew must have come from the small arsenal of a neighboring plantation.

I saw a few other guns, but from the way they were carried, it was obvious that their new owners knew little about how to handle them. Many of the slaves were mounted on fine horses, having stripped the stables of the other plantations.

As they spilled into the yard, they began to yell savagely, their faces contorted in torchlight. George caught up one of the flintlock muskets and fired. His shot rang out above them loudly, stilling the roaring slaves.

His voice carried clearly on the still, hot air, as though he strode the deck of the *Tern*, commanding his seamen. "Railo! Hold them back while we talk, or the next shot will find a mark."

"Time for talk is over," Railo cried. "You can't hold out against us—we outnumber you twenty to one."

"We'll kill many a man and woman before you take us. It's better to talk. By God, man, you know the Madisons have never borne you ill will, nor treated your people badly."

"I know you got that trash Noah an' them Landon niggers in there," Railo said contemptuously.

"You and I must talk!" George repeated.

Railo hesitated, and Judith's face lifted imploringly to his. Then he called stubbornly, "Talk ain't goin' to do no good."

The great mass of slaves had fallen back and formed a solid phalanx behind Railo and Judith. I saw the heads of Anna and Jabez once more, still mounted on poles, still looking for all the world as though their owners were observing events through glittering eyes that reflected torchlight.

Andrew's voice rang out from above us. "Railo, we are well armed and determined to defend our home. But let us talk together, you and George and I."

"Ain't no use," Railo said with finality. "No use."

"You know we are freeing our slaves! We'll bargain with you," Andrew said persuasively. "We'll go to the capital in Richmond and work for freedom for all of you."

Railo's gleaming black face was impassive. His eyes in the darkness of his visage flashed whitely and his voice was heavy with sarcasm. "Sure—you're goin' to set all of us free. Send us off to a strange land to make our way alone among strangers. Them in the North ain't so different from you planters. I've heard tell how hard it is for free Negroes in the North! You can save your breath. We gone clean this state out—make a free black nation out of Virginia. Then your government can negotiate with the black free state!"

A great roar of triumph went up from the gathered

slaves as Railo turned and melted among them, Judith clinging to his arm.

George handed me one of the two flintlocks. "It will be better if we both fire. They mean to kill us all, but we shall give them a fight for it."

Before our eyes, the slaves fanned out around the house, surrounding it. They planned to rush it from every angle. But Joshua and Ephraim manned the east end and Pepper with Beady and one of the girls manned the west. Now the crack of musket fire could be heard from the rear and sides of the house, then from the front above. I saw two blacks fall. Those with muskets made no move to use them, proving my guess about their ignorance of firearms correct. At least that gave us a small measure of time.

From the third story, shots rang out steadily and with deadly accuracy, and I felt a new respect for Louise Alexander.

There was a fusillade from the windows just above us as George and I raised our muskets to fire again. I shot into the line of men advancing toward the house. The women hung back, urging their men forward. At such point-blank range, I could not fail, and one of the men clutched his leg and fell to the ground. I saw another fall as George fired.

We turned to pour powder and bullet and ram it home. I knew that every five or so shots, we would have to clean the touchhole of carbon—and again I was surprised at how fast George and I were able to do this, though he got in two shots to my one.

Slowly, the toll of the wounded grew and the advancing slaves fell back. Railo called out to them, drawing them up around him, and others from behind the house returned to gather about him. He lifted his clenched fist and spoke in a powerful voice, but we could not distinguish his words, as the army of men and women were too far from the house. Judith could be seen speaking with him, a pleading arch to her lithe body. Railo made a short fierce gesture that silenced her.

He spoke for some time longer and then, as quickly as they had gathered, the slaves dispersed in all directions, carrying their torches and lighting fresh ones from those they carried, until there were more than I could count.

George said tersely, "Keep firing, Lilibel. It's our only hope."

With steady fingers, I did as he bade, watching as flint struck fire to powder and explosion drove the ball into a shadowy leaping figure, who fell with a scream.

Then to my horror, one dark figure approached our window, creeping forward and bent low, and hurled his fiery torch through the opening.

"George, they mean to burn us out!" I cried. Racing to the torch, I caught it up and flung it back outside. The carpet was smoldering and one of the drapes showed a small, bright red flame. I seized the heavy brocaded material and beat it out, then went to stamp furiously at the smoking carpet.

Turning back, I saw George hastily loading his musket as another torch came flying through the window before him. He flung himself aside just in time. As the burning object rolled far into the room, it bathed in lurid brightness the beautiful furniture, the paintings on the ivory walls, the rich materials that hung at the windows. I watched with fresh dread as George threw down his musket and ran to pick up the torch and hurl it back into the night, beating out the smoldering carpet with his feet.

From the shrill cries that floated through the halls, I knew the others who manned the downstairs windows were meeting the same fiery danger as George and I. As another torch came flying through the window beyond me, I felt sure we were fighting a losing battle. It was only a question of time before we were overrun and cut down, for most of us were too occupied with fighting fire to man the guns now.

Then, as I hurled out another burning torch and beat out the flames, the excited cries of the slaves dimmed. I looked out the window; they were falling back at Railo's powerful cry. Judith stood beside him. I could see her beautiful face turned imploringly to his once more clearly in the torchlight. They stood for a moment, talking together, the great mass of slaves and Railo. Suddenly, they melted into the woods, and a silence infinitely more terrifying than the screams of triumph fell upon the night.

"George," I cried, "what is it? Why are they silent now?"

He had torn off his coat to beat out flames and his shirt had ripped, revealing his broad chest covered with thick, dark hair. He looked up at me, face wet with sweat. "God knows what they have in mind, but you can be sure they aren't giving up to leave us alive. They know a few more torches would set Cloudmont burning beyond repair."

Andrew and Mary ran in from the great hall, carrying their guns and a pair of candles. Laura came in, followed by Cornelia and then, one by one, the weary servants. All of us were worried about the sudden respite we had been afforded, making conjectures as to the slaves' next move. Noah at last came and joined the rest of us.

"Noah, do you have any idea what Railo is planning now? In your meetings with them during the planning—and there must have been many—did he never discuss his plans for taking a planter's home when there was resistance?" George asked, lighting another candle from one carried by Andrew.

"No, Mister George. We talked a lot, but everybody was s'posed to be in bed asleep by the time we got here. We—he didn't count on no resistance."

The men went to the windows on the south and peered out. George said, "I can see their torches in the woods beyond." Then he walked swiftly to the dining room on the north and returned. "They surround us both north and south. Do they fancy we will think they are gone and come out?"

On the heels of his words there came a knock on the rear door to the great hall, and a faint cry. We all poured out into the hall. George, who seemed to have taken command, led us to the door, where he demanded, "Who is it?"

" 'Tis me, Judith, Mister George—I want to talk to you all. Let me in, please, sir."

George shot the bolt back on the great door and Judith slipped in like a night shadow. Laura ran forward to put her hands on the girl's shoulders, her eyes streaming. She cried, "Judith, how could you be part of this awful thing—when I have loved you and treated you like a sister all these years!"

"Don't cry, Miss Laura." Judith took her hands and held them in her own. "I ain't goin' to stand by and let them kill you, without I try to save you. I been tryin' all night. I been arguin' with my Railo."

The black men, Joshua and Ephraim, stood quietly by now, their wives beside them, each holding a baby in her arms and another small one by the hand. All of us were silent while Judith spoke.

At that moment, Louise, in her leather buckskins, came down the stairs, followed by the terrified Bibsey and Beady, whose blue eyes seemed about to pop from her head.

Judith said slowly, "I'm s'posed to be a Judas goat an' lead you all out this door, with a promise of free passage to Williamsburg, but Railo says he gone kill you then—an' I ain't goin' to do it." Her great liquid eyes looked beseechingly into Laura's tear-streaked face.

"What do you propose to do, Judith?" George asked curiously.

"Come with me—quickly. Is this all of you?"

George glanced around the room to check. Looking up, I saw Amanda and the two little boys descend the stairs, Domino with his nose glued to Andy's heels. Amanda said, "Uncle George, why is it so quiet? Why are all the slaves waiting in the woods? Oh, Judith! What are you doing here?"

"We are all here—there are twenty-four of us. You make twenty-five, Judith," George cut in quickly.

"Come, little Amanda—I hope to save you all," Judith said, running into the large drawing room off the great hall. She darted across the broad floor directly toward a beautiful escritoire, pulled back the small carved desk chair, and lifted a hand-hooked rug.

I could see nothing in the dim candlelight, so cleverly concealed was a small brass ring set into the polished wood and so carefully fitted were the edges of the trap door to the floor about it.

A black hole opened up before Judith as she flung open the trap door.

Cornelia gave a little cry. "Judith, that has not been used for over twenty years—How did you find it?"

"Mistress Madison, I knew about this fer many a long month. 'Tis the way I slip out at night to meet Railo. But he don't know. Nobody knows but me, 'cause I knew 'twas your secret."

Andrew recoiled suddenly. "You want us to leave Cloudmont undefended—let them come in and pillage and destroy it?"

"Mister Andrew, Railo ain't goin' to destroy Cloudmont, once you're out of it. He wants to use it as his headquarters. That's why I'm to persuade you to come out. We all will rest here awhile and march on Richmond later. He fancies it to live in when we wins our freedom and Virginia." She looked at Andrew with pity. "'Tis the most beautiful plantation on the James. Railo just wants to destroy all of you—but he *will* burn it if he can't get you out no other way."

George had been right when he said Railo would not burn the house. We had lost all this precious time we could have used to escape. I looked with contempt at Andrew's fallen face. His lips were trembling and he could scarcely bring himself to speak. "You mean he will resume throwing those torches until the house is afire? Just to kill us?"

"He give me a few minutes to persuade you all to come out the door with me—but he don't aim to let you go. He and the others will kill you all. But I'm goin' to take you through this tunnel. It leads close to the river and comes out not too far from the Williamsburg road. You can all make a run for it, because they'll be lookin' through the house to find you."

George caught up his flintlock and mine. Slinging the ammunition pouches over his shoulder, he said, "Come on, Judith—we'll follow."

And we did, down a narrow black stairs of native stone. An oil lantern carried by Louise was the brightest light, though most of us carried candles. Beady carried one in each trembling hand. There were rough boards beside us as we wound our way down into what I expected to be the cellars.

Just behind me, Cornelia said dismally, "I had this

boarded off from the cellars after the war. I can't believe Judith found it. Servants are so curious."

What a fool she was for fretting over so minor a thing, I thought, when it meant possible escape for all of us. As we wound down, a strange, pervasive, unpleasant odor came to my nostrils, dark and decayed. As we angled off from the cellars into a huge tunnel toward the river, the stench grew until I put a hand instinctively to my nose.

Then suddenly in the light from the candles and the lantern, I shrank from the sight before me—bones, some bleached white, some with mummified flesh still clinging to them, and some with decaying red coats and rusting swords and sabers. We had come upon the bones of many British soldiers stretched out down the dank tunnel as far as the light shone. As we passed them Laura muttered, "How ever did you drag them all down here, Cornelia—so many?"

"They weren't dragged here, they were killed here by my husband and his men. They were part of Colonel Banastre Tarleton's bloodthirsty crew—the man who gave no quarter to the Americans in the battle of Waxhaw Creek in South Carolina. We gave them no quarter here." After a small silence, she added in a voice hard as granite, "They thought to make Cloudmont their headquarters, too." Judith turned to look back at her with frightened eyes.

"Why did you never bury them?" Laura asked.

"They were buried here," was Cornelia's cold retort. "Had it not been for Judith, their grave would have remained undisturbed."

Andy began to cry a little and his father picked him up, saying, "You have been so brave, my son. Be brave a little longer." The child smothered his tears. Domino whined and looked at the boy longingly.

One of the little black babies began to whimper in its mother's arms and I saw her pull a large brown breast from her low-cut dress and put the nipple in its mouth. Silence, but for our passage, reigned once more.

It seemed to me that tunnel was miles long, and its ancient odors were so oppressive I feared I would become nauseated. In my heart, I thanked *le bon Dieu* that I had left my Mélisse with Aunt Mincy, for I knew not what waited for us at the end of this long underground passageway.

"We're almost there," Judith said. "Most of Railo's men are on the Richmond side of the house. I think if you hurry, you can get well on your way before they realize you're not in the house. I'll go back through the passage and out the door and tell them I couldn't find you. It will give you a little more time to get further down the Williamsburg Road."

Noah spoke up. "Judith, you know how Railo feels about traitorin' him—an' you traitorin' him. He'll kill you. Ain't you afraid?"

Judith gave him an inscrutable look. "Railo ain't goin' to kill me. I been carryin' his son under my heart for three months now. He'll be mad as a hornet, but he ain't goin' to kill me." She looked at all of us and said, "My advice to you all is to board the first vessel you can find in Norfolk and leave Virginia. Railo got runners out to every plantation in the country and they all goin' to join him. You can go back to England, or up to Massachusetts, but you ought to get out of Virginia as fast as you can."

George smiled grimly. "We appreciate your advice, Judith, but Virginia is our home, too, and I'm afraid it won't be that easy. We'll stop and make a stand when the odds are more in our favor."

The girl shrugged, "There's more of us than you, Mister George, and Railo goin' to teach them how to use guns. I don't think you'll be able to stay in Virginia. And I love you for your many kindnesses, so that's why I'd like to see you leave before the fighting gets real bad. Railo says he ain't goin' to leave one white man alive in Virginia."

Suddenly a dim reflection of moonlight filtered in through a great mass of brush and branches at the end of the tunnel. Judith began pulling them away. Andrew put Andy on his feet as he and George fell to helping her. We extinguished our candles and, in a matter of minutes, we were all out in a small copse of woods. We could see the James glittering to our left under a fast-setting moon. Louise still held her lantern, which cast bright light in a small circle.

Judith pointed to the east. "The road to Williamsburg's just a little way beyond that. Better put out that lantern—some of our men might be prowling about."

No sooner had the words left her mouth than there came a shrill cry and the pounding of hooves. I looked up and to my horror saw a slave on horseback bearing down on us, swinging a great razor-sharp scythe. He rode directly toward Andrew, who was trying vainly to pull his pistol from his waistband.

Mary, seeing the danger to her brother, screamed, "Andrew! My darling!" and flung herself protectively over him, clasping her arms about his neck.

The scythe swept down, striking brother and sister at the waist, cutting them almost in two.

At that moment, Ephraim lifted the dueling pistol and, just as the horseman pulled his scythe loose, threw the gun at the man's head. The big black toppled slowly from the horse and fell directly onto the curved knife. The horse, frightened by the commotion, bolted off into the dense forest.

Ephraim's face in the pale reflection of the lantern was a study in anguish. He moaned, "That was Ezekiel! God, I done killed my own brother!"

I looked down at the fallen figures of Mary and Andrew with horror. I had wanted to be free of Andrew, but not like this—never like this! My heart was torn with pity, with regret and sorrow. In the lantern light I saw they were very nearly cut clean in two and the rich, dark blood they shared was mingling now, as they had mingled their relationship in life.

If things had been different, I might have been Andrew's wife. My throat ached with unshed tears as we all stood a moment, struck dumb by the tragedy before us. Then Cornelia was on her knees beside her two stricken children, a low cry torn from deep within her. Louise swiftly extinguished the lantern.

"My chicks—my babes—they are gone, gone——" In the fading moonlight filtering through the trees, Cornelia's shoulders shook silently. Andy began to cry where he stood beside Amanda. Domino whined, and the blacks stood silent and fearful. Louise moved toward the grieving Cornelia, but George was ahead of her. He lifted his mother tenderly to her feet.

"Dear Mother, come now, we must leave immediately, for there may be other stragglers around the edges of Cloudmont. We must hasten to Williamsburg."

"You mean to *leave* them here?" she asked incredulously. Andy began to cry noisily and Timothy choked back his sobs. Amanda shushed them, her voice thick with unshed tears.

"Unless you wish to see the rest of us, including your grandchildren, meet the same fate." George's voice was hard.

Cornelia leaned against him like an old woman, and I remembered how she had said to me, "I would give my life for any one of my children, gladly." My heart ached for her, for I felt the same love for my Mélisse.

Judith said with finality, "I'm sorry, Mistress Madison. I would have stopped him if I could. But I done all I can." And she turned to make her way back to the tunnel mouth, pulling the brush after her. I prayed that she would keep the secret of our whereabouts from Railo and his men.

George said grimly, "Follow me, all of you." We hesitated at leaving Mary and Andrew in the welter of their blood, but time was running out for us. Cornelia clung to her stalwart son, refusing to look back at the three fallen bodies, and we all followed as George lead us through thickets of trees and heavy underbrush toward the Williamsburg road.

There was no pathway here, for it was virgin forest. We walked fast, servant and master alike, at a pace set by George in an attempt to put as much distance between Cloudmont and us as possible. We were all so weary from the long, wakeful night and the terrors we had endured, I wondered if we could possibly make the twenty-five miles to Williamsburg on foot with all the children in our entourage.

The sky was growing lighter and, to the east, the first faint pink tinge betokening sunrise streaked the horizon. It would soon be daylight and our danger would be doubled. If Railo realized Judith's betrayal and our destination, he might well take out after us at daybreak.

Suddenly we broke out of the woods and came upon a narrow dirt road bordered by deep gullies and straggling blackberry bushes. "We've hit the Williamsburg road at last! Let us make haste," George said. He stepped up his pace.

I stumbled and clutched at my long skirt, tearing a rent in the side of it on a blackberry bush. The thorn pierced my leg as well, leaving a long scratch. Laura gave me a silent glance of sympathy as she helped me steady myself.

Amanda picked up Andy and put him upon her shoulders, and George paused long enough to swing the faltering Timothy up on his. Ephraim and Joshua picked up their small children, and their wives already carried the babes.

Louise, still grimly carrying her flintlock and ammunition pouches, lengthened her stride until she reached Cornelia's side, where she put a strong arm under the other woman's. With George on one side of her and Louise on the other, Cornelia straightened up and lengthened her own step. The servants hurried along behind us under Henry Pepper's urging.

I turned once to look back down the long, winding road. I could glimpse the tall chimneys of Cloudmont rearing up above the thick trees. Far beyond it, smoke was still climbing darkly in the August sky from the burning homes to the west.

George stopped abruptly, standing dead still in the road. He held up his hand. Faintly to our ears came the sound of drumming hooves. Horses were on the road and galloping hard. There were many of them, too, for the sound was like faint but growing thunder. I knew a fresh touch of cold terror. Had Judith been forced to tell Railo our destination? Were they riding now to cut us all down as the enraged Ezekiel had Mary and Andrew, leaving us to lie in our own blood?

Bibsey began moaning. Pepper told her rudely to be quiet.

George's voice lifted with sudden hope. "They're coming from Williamsburg. It's Charles with the militia!"

The sound grew louder and louder and, at last, far

down the road in the ever brightening east, we saw a great crowd of men on horseback. As they drew nearer, we ran to meet them. There looked to be better than two hundred of them, all armed with muskets and pistols. It was the Williamsburg militia, with Charles Alexander at their head.

The men drew rein as the distance between us shortened, and George led us to the side of the road. As they surrounded us, their horses' sides heaving, Charles was off his horse in a flash.

"Where are Mary and Andrew?" was his first question after his eyes found Laura.

"They are victims of the insurrection," George said grimly. "Their bodies and that of Ezekiel are in the woods, just outside that old tunnel beneath Cloudmont."

Charles's face paled and his eyes went to the small Andy, who drooped sleepily now on Amanda's shoulders.

Noah approached the girl, saying, "I'll take him, Miss Amanda, do you carry my flintlock." Smiling gratefully, Amanda did so, as George spoke to Charles and the colonel of the militia.

"There are nearly four hundred slaves surrounding Cloudmont," he said, his voice carrying clearly to the horsemen who moved restlessly about us.

Colonel Gray spoke up. "Captain Madison, can you give us the details of what has transpired since Mr. Alexander left you?"

"I can," George replied grimly, and proceeded to inform him of the hours we had watched—how we had seen the Livingston plantation burn, then Lindens, and that we did not know the fate of those at Tulip Grove and Rose Hill. "Noah here has told us many were slaughtered. He got to us with word of the insurrection before the slaves reached us—giving us time to defend ourselves."

"Good man, Noah," the colonel said tersely. Noah, holding the sleeping Andy in his arms, nodded in recognition of the commendation.

After that, there was a short discourse between George and the men on horseback. While we waited, Laura and I sat down at the side of the road to rest ourselves.

Louise and Cornelia stood straight and silent, tensely awaiting the decision of the men.

Colonel Gray said at last, "We've enough guns and men here to break it up—and we shall take the ring-leaders too. Railo shall pay for his slaughter." He glanced at our tattered crew. Bibsey, Pepper, Clementine, and Abigail had seated themselves silently nearby, and poor Beady, so plump, was looking for a comfortable spot. Most of us still carried pistols and flintlocks. "You have a number to be got to safety, Captain Madison. I will give you a detachment of fifteen men, who will ride your group into the forest to hide until we can quell the rebellion."

"I shall join you in the fight we have on hand, Colonel," George said shortly. Then to us, "We'll take you back to the tunnel on horseback and you can take refuge in there. Railo's people will be scattered when the battle begins, and we shall have enough to deal with without fearing you might fall victim to their knives."

We were unceremoniously hoisted upon the horses behind the militiamen—in some instances, three to a horse—and we cantered into the woods as the balance of the men rode off to Cloudmont. In a very short time, we were back at the spot where Mary and Andrew and Ezekiel lay. The horseman I rode behind swore as we came upon them.

As we dismounted, Charles said, "God—I can't believe that Mary and Andrew are dead."

"And we have to leave them—here on the forest floor," came Cornelia's anguished voice.

"Never mind, dear Cornelia," Charles said with great tenderness. "We shall fetch them to Cloudmont for a proper burial when this is over."

Cornelia wore a dazed look. It was strange to see her, always so in command of herself and every situation, now looking uncertain and haggard. I went to her as the others dismounted and prepared to enter the dank tunnel.

"Cornelia," I said softly," I know you grieve as we all do—but we must go on. You must not let this tragedy kill you, too."

"I know, I know—but I have only one left—my George."

"No, Cornelia," Charles said gently but clearly above the champing horses about him. "You have me too."

Her eyes filled with tears and her throat worked, but no words came.

Louise stepped forward, tall and lean in her leather clothing. "And you have me, Cornelia, willy-nilly. I will never desert you. Too many years have passed. My hatred long ago turned to a kind of love." Before my astonished eyes, the two women embraced.

"You are kind," Cornelia said huskily, "too kind."

George said crisply, "Hurry now, all of you. Into the tunnel, and don't come out for any reason until we come for you. I do not want any of you where some errant slave can fall upon you with knife or scythe."

Henry Pepper balked. "I'm going with you, Mister George," he declared, and he moved back from us to join George and Charles.

I did not allow my mind to touch on the possibility of what would happen to us if the militia should fall victim to the slaves.

When we had all gone back into the damp, dark hole in the ground, George and the men pulled the brush over the opening. Exhausted, we sank down in sitting positions, our backs to the moist earthen walls. The crack of musket fire as the militia began the battle against the slaves could already be heard.

We were clustered near the opening and for a long time after the men left, we sat there wearily and silently, trying to rest.

Suddenly Andy asked clearly, "Will my daddy and Aunt Mary wake up when this is over?"

Timothy spoke, his voice shaky and tearful. "Your daddy and my mama are dead."

"Forever?" Andy asked with disbelief, gazing in the gloom at his cousin.

For a moment, no one answered, then the tall, quiet Ephraim cleared his throat and said, "Don't you worry none, Andy. We'll all be together after a while."

Timothy started to say something else, but Amanda pinched him. He burst into tears, but said nothing more. Amanda's face was white and drawn as she wiped her brother's tears away with the hem of her skirt. Then she turned her eyes to Noah.

"Noah, do you think they were all slaughtered at Tulip Grove?"

Flustered, Noah hemmed and hawed a moment and then said, "Miss Amanda, I were in such a hurry to get to all of 'em, I can't truthfully say. I 'spect they got away."

Amanda looked away from him. "They did not get away," she said numbly. "My darling Clay is dead. I feel it."

"Aw, now, Miss Amanda, you don't either know that," Ephraim said, consoling her. "Some of 'em was bound to get away."

"Not the way Railo had it planned. My beloved is dead." She fell to weeping softly. I went to put an arm around her.

"Do not borrow grief, Amanda, dear. Keep your hope. If all goes well with the militia, we shall know before the day is over if Clay got safely away."

She shook her head. "If he had gotten safely away, he would have come to Cloudmount for me."

I said nothing, for I knew she spoke the truth. I turned my mind away from the carnage I conjured up when thinking of the other planters and their burned homes.

The crack of musket fire was steady now, and I wondered if George and Pepper had found horses. Knowing George, I thought grimly, he had found one and was now in the thick of the fighting.

CHAPTER 19

We stayed nearly the whole day in the tunnel. We were all very hungry and thirsty and the children slept a good deal of the time. The only really comfortable ones among us were the two little black babies, who nursed at their mothers' breasts and needed neither food nor water.

The rest of us dozed, but fitfully and unevenly, due to the distant sounds of sporadic battle. Once there were hoarse shouts and screams of pain just beyond the tunnel mouth, causing all of us to stiffen and Louise to ready her gun. The sound of conflict moved away and we all sank back, but remained tense.

I had never been so tired in my life. Timothy and Andy were silent and wide-eyed when they wakened. Neither of them seemed to fully comprehend the tragedy that had befallen them. Domino snuggled between them, his pink tongue licking out occasionally to touch their hands.

During those dragging hours in the damp gloom, while the August sun burned outside our hiding place, I had too much time to think. My constant worry about Mélisse increased. I wondered if Mincy had been able to keep her whereabouts unknown to the slaves, or failing that, if she had been able to keep the slaves from wreaking vengeance upon my child as a symbol of the tyranny they were fighting against. Interspersed with these anxieties were thoughts about my feeling for George Madison. In my vivid imagination, I could picture him with head severed, dying in his own bright blood. The sick horror that scene engendered was equal only to my fears for Mélisse and her safety.

Laura, at my side, murmured once, "I keep thinking of Charles—and if he should be caught by the slaves and hacked to pieces——"

"Hush!" I said fiercely. "We *will* not think of such things!"

She sighed. "I wish I were as strong as you are, Lilibel."

"I'm not so strong. Inured is the word, Laura. Misfortune has been my lot on too many occasions during the last ten years for me to break now." I set my teeth and added, "We are going to come through this all right—all of us."

As the hours crept by, in my own heart I was uncertain, despite my brave words to Laura. So dim had my hopes become that I could scarce believe it when, at last, George and Charles called to us as they pulled the brush from around the mouth of the tunnel. Henry Pepper was with them, and they had several horses waiting as we straggled out wearily into the late evening sunset.

We were all so glad we could have wept. Cornelia and the two black women did so, unashamedly. Cornelia kept stammering over and over, "You're safe, George, you and Charles. Thank God!"

Louise, stoic as always, gave her son a swift kiss upon his cheek. Bibsey and Abigail clung to Pepper half crying, half laughing, while Beady blew her nose noisily on her skirt and Clementine hiccuped in her effort to choke back tears of relief.

As we drew about the men, George said, "We are taking you back to Cloudmont. We brought enough horses for all to ride comfortably." He gestured to the waiting animals.

The bodies of Mary and Andrew and Ezekiel were gone, but the leafy bloodsoaked ground beyond the tunnel mouth was grim evidence of the reality of our nightmare.

"Is the rebellion over, Mister George?" Joshua asked cautiously.

"Yes, Joshua. We've rounded up over two hundred

slaves, but some have vanished into the forest and many are dead. Railo is among those who escaped, but Judith is among those we have captured, and I think we can get her pardoned because of her aid to us. The pity of it is that so many had to die."

Ephraim asked slowly, "What will they do with them as captured?"

George sighed. "Hang the ringleaders, and sell the rest to planters further south. But you and Joshua will soon be free men. Come, mount up. 'Tis getting dark fast, and you should all be safe inside when night falls."

"Mary and Andrew——" Cornelia began huskily.

"They have been taken to the coach house to await burial, Mother," George said briefly. "And your brother's body is with his widow, Ephraim."

Amanda, holding Timothy and Andy by the hand, asked in a small voice, "Have you heard if any others of our neighbors have escaped alive?"

Noah glanced at her uneasily before swinging himself up on one of the bays.

George, lifting her up to the bare back of a gelding, said brusquely, "We'll tell you all the news when we reach the house." Hoisting the two small boys up behind her, he turned to his mother. "You'll be glad to know that Cloudmont still stands, my dear." Domino bounced around the feet of the horse carrying Amanda and the boys, giving short, joyous barks.

Pepper held my foot as I swung up on another big bay and Laura mounted behind me, putting her arms about my waist. Soon we all set off through the woods and away from the James. Looking back, I could see the sunset sky reflecting on its waters through the trees. It looked like a river of blood and I suppressed a shudder.

I wanted to ask about Mélisse for I felt sure some of the militiamen must have sought out Aunt Mincy's cabin looking for escaped slaves. They would have brought my child home to Cloudmont, surely. I was afraid to ask, but I kicked the smooth flanks of the bay and cantered past the others to reach George.

"What of Mélisse?" I asked over a great lump that had risen in my throat.

He glanced at me in the dimming light and there was

quick, warm reassurance in his smile. "She is still with Aunt Mincy. Colonel Gray and a squad of militia went there to seek out any slaves who might have found a hiding place with her. But you know Mincy! She wouldn't let him take your daughter. Informed him in no uncertain terms that she harbored no slaves and she was to keep Mélisse until you yourself came to get her."

"Was she—did Mélisse seem well?"

"Colonel Gray would have brought her back to Cloudmont despite Mincy's protest, but Mélisse herself seemed determined to stay there until you came."

My little laugh was choked with relief. "I vow, I believe that old lady could win my child from me. Nevertheless, I should like very much to go and get her." My voice was thick with fatigue.

George's black eyes went over me like heat lightning. "Liliane, you know Mincy will care well for her. The insurrection is over and you need sleep more than you need Mélisse with you at this moment. You and I will fetch her as soon as possible."

I drooped and Laura's arms tightened about me protectively. In my ear she whispered, "I know how you feel. If 'twas Andy, I should be the same as you—but you know George is right."

We reached Cloudmont and circled around to the rear, where we found a small army of militiamen had made a campground of the bowling green.

At Cornelia's cry of dismay when she saw the trampled turf of that once lovely sweep of lawn, George said quietly, "Mother, you should thank God it is they and not Railo's men who camp there. Besides, this is only half the militia. The other half are marching the captured slaves to Richmond. These remain to search out strays—and we've Railo to deal with yet."

Suddenly Joshua and Ephraim gave a great shout of joy and in the closing rays of light, I could see there were many slaves in the quarters. Candles were lit in windows and small children played in the dust of the little yards and gardens. At their cry, the doors opened and black men and women rushed out to greet us. I was dumfounded.

George said dryly, "These are our Landon people, my dears. They declare and swear that, except for Ezekiel, they were never party to Railo's rebellion. After hiding from the insurrectionists in the woods, they are more than grateful to be home and under the protection of the militia."

I murmured, "But they *were* part of his army. I *saw* them——"

"No," George drawled. "You only thought you saw them. They have sworn loyalty to the Madisons and wait only for the freedom they are promised."

By now the slaves had swarmed about us with glad cries and were assisting us to dismount. The militiamen had laid down their bedrolls for the night and stacked their weapons on the bowling green. It was with a dazed sense of disbelief that I trailed after the servants and the others to the house. I was utterly exhausted, and wanted only to rest.

But Beady lit the lamps and Pepper lighted candles as we all went into the kitchen. In a very short time, we were all seated about the dining table—a sadly depleted family—and Beady was serving cold roast with stewed fruit and cold, hard bread. There was wine, which revived us almost as much as the food.

Over the table Amanda fixed George with hard eyes. "Uncle, you said you would tell me which of our neighbors escaped, once we reached home."

George put his arm around her and said, "My dear, at Rose Hill, they all escaped, thanks to Noah. Vance and Sara and all five children. They hid in the woods while the Negroes sacked the house—we were wrong in thinking they burned it. They burned only when they had to force the issue. But at the Livingstons', Tulip Grove, Lindens—none escaped. You must be brave, Amanda. All the Reeds lost their lives."

"I knew it," Amanda said, two shining tears slipping down her cheeks. "I felt it all along. I shall never see my darling Clay again—but I've a part of him that no one can take from me."

In the flurry of sympathy that welled up around her, no one took notice of this comment.

"George—you said Mary and Andrew were in the coach house?" Cornelia asked.

"Over the stables—in the visiting coachmen's quarters."

Charles said abruptly, "Cornelia, my dear, I shall ride into Richmond and order headstones for them at the earliest possible moment. George and I have already given orders for coffins to be made for all three."

"This settles any scruples I ever had about slavery, Laura said bitterly. I shall never trust Judith again. They are all savages, and they can stay slaves and do our bidding forever."

George said quickly, "My dear Laura, we will have no such thing at Cloudmont. I intend to free them all as soon as possible, without waiting for too much schooling now. Judith will go with them. Colonel Gray is aware of her saving our lives and she is free to take up quarters with Sal, Ezekiel's widow."

Laura was cool now. "Then who's to bring in the crops this fall? All your farmers have fled."

"I shall go into Norfolk and recruit a number of workers if I must. We shall not lose our harvest." His voice grew heavy with irony. "And we've all those *loyal* Landon people out there now to help, too. Besides"—his tone lifted—"the farmers who escaped will no doubt return now the rebellion is quelled."

Cornelia said sadly, "I want to see my darlings buried tomorrow—no matter what else takes place."

But I was thinking of Mélisse and the joyful moment when I would hold that small form to my breast once more.

I awoke at dawn, stiff and bruised in body and mind, but I leaped from bed and began a hasty toilette. I had slept in the same torn muslin dress I had worn throughout the last two nights and all yesterday in the tunnel. Now I stripped it off, wishing with all my heart that I had time to call for Abigail and Clementine to bring me a hipbath of piping hot water.

But the pressure to see Mélisse was too great. I splashed like a porpoise in the basin of water I poured, scattering droplets as I bathed myself the best I could. The day was already hot and the cool water was refreshing.

Hurrying to the tall chest of drawers, I drew on a fresh chemise and petticoat, then began to comb my long, tangled hair. I did not bother with doing it up, but tied it back with a ribbon. Finally I donned my riding habit in anticipation of going to Aunt Mincy's with George.

When I reached the foot of the stairs, I saw that Louise Alexander and Cornelia were already in conference with the captain in charge of the militia.

Glancing up, Cornelia said, "Come down, my dear. We are so relieved. The slaves did not have time to strip our smokehouse and gardens. We have plenty of food. Louise and I are going to give provisions to the militia so they can prepare their meal."

Both women wore fresh summer dresses, and Louise, giving me her sardonic smile, said, "They've even rounded up some of the horses that were taken. Your Dandylion is among them."

As she spoke, John Seabury and George entered the great hall from the dining room. I said, "Oh, John, I am so glad to see you! When did you arrive from Richmond?"

"This morning—but an hour ago," he replied, his face still marked by shock and sorrow. "I am greatly relieved that so many of you survived."

"And I am going after Mélisse now. She stayed——"

George cut in firmly, "My dear Lilibel, you must wait until I can accompany you to get Mélisse. We have to consider the danger of stragglers in the woods. Railo himself is hiding out somewhere. As long as he is at liberty, there could be another uprising, for he is a strong and determined man."

"After breakfast, we are going to have services for Mary and Andrew in the church," Cornelia put in. "John will conduct them. And I had so hoped we would all be together for that." Her eyes filled with tears and she added brokenly, "Lilibel, you are very dear to me—please come to the services with us. After all, I know how grieved you must be—I have lost a son, but you have lost your betrothed."

My anxiety to be with Mélisse was nigh to choking me, but I managed to murmur tenderly, "You know I shall be there, Cornelia."

"And I will accompany you to get Mélisse this afternoon," George promised. I had to be satisfied with that.

Breakfast was served as soon as the rest of the family

gathered. Beady had done herself proud, making up for our day of fasting in the tunnel, with grits and ham, eggs and slices of homemade toasted bread, bowls of fresh fruit, and hot coffee, the aroma of which set my appetite tingling.

Amanda was very pale as she sat across from me, barely nibbling at her food. Cornelia remonstrated and she said listlessly, "I'm not hungry, Grandmother." She looked at John Seabury, her big blue eyes with dark smudges beneath them. "Will you conduct services for the Reeds and Montagues, John?"

John replied, "Of course, my dear Miss Amanda."

Cornelia said hesitantly, "But you know—you may not see them. 'Tis said they were burned beyond recognition, and we shall have to seal their coffins.

Amanda's eyes filled with tears and she brushed them away with her hand, murmuring, "At least Mama's won't be—I shall see her one more time. And Uncle Andrew. But I can't believe Clay is gone—that I shall never see him again!"

"Time will help," Cornelia said with a trace of bitterness, "but nothing really ever erases the pain of loss." Then she turned to her remaining son and said gently, "Dear George, I hope now you will let someone else handle your shipping and importing business in Norfolk, for you are so needed here."

George, setting down his coffee cup, looked at her squarely. "As a matter of fact, Mother, I have given some thought to Cloudmont and its operations since the loss of Mary and Andrew. I have come to the conclusion that Charles Alexander should be granted a share of his rightful inheritance."

Charles's black head jerked up and he stared in amazement at his half-brother. His mother, who stood in the door to the pantry, stiffened with shock.

Cornelia's face, however, did not change as she nodded her head soberly. "I think that would be wise, my son."

George went on, "Charles knows as much as I and more about operating Cloudmont, for he has been here most of his life. Of course, Andy will have his share. And Amanda and Timothy have Jackson's Landing, which is a paying plantation in its own right."

"I must say, I didn't expect this." Charles's handsome face was a study in disbelief. I saw Louise wipe her eyes vigorously on her apron. The change that crept over Charles's face was powerful. The wild recklessness that had resided there, the arrogance and wilfulness, the truculence were wiped away as if by magic. As he squared his shoulders, his resemblance to Andrew was so marked, I wondered if any beside myself could see it. He and Laura exchanged glances and there was concealed passion in both their eyes.

And I looked at George through new eyes. I saw in him now a strength and justice I had not dreamed he possessed. It made him all the more admirable to me, and I thought dismally of the days ahead when he would be gone.

Now he said, "When we have sorted things out here, Charles, you and I will go into Richmond to our lawyer, Amos Biddle, and have your inheritance legally drawn up." His little quizzical smile at his half-brother broadened. "And I shall expect in return that I may leave Cloudmont in your hands when I take to the sea, or to my business in Norfolk."

Charles nodded, inarticulate for once.

"Then you will not give up the sea and your Norfolk enterprises?" Cornelia asked sorrowfully.

"No, Mother. I cannot. I love them too well, but I shall come to Cloudmont often enough to keep my hand in." He pushed aside his coffee cup and added, "Now if you good ladies will forgive Charles and me, we shall leave. We must arrange the burial details, for the militia has recovered almost two hundred bodies that must be buried and soon. But we shall return by eleven of the clock for the services for Mary and Andrew."

As he and Charles got to their feet, he looked at me, frowning. "Lilibel, you and I will fetch Mélisse sometime this afternoon. I know how anxious you are to see her, but you cannot go riding alone in the forest." His eyes swept the table. "Indeed, none of you is to venture out of the house alone, do you understand?"

We agreed. As the men left the room, apprehensions rose afresh in my mind about Mélisse. I thought of Railo and those implacable eyes. He had suffered so terribly.

The injustices he had endured had hardened him like a rock. There would be no mercy in that bruised heart. But George had said the militia had searched Aunt Mincy's cabin and he was not there. My Mélisse was safe, I told myself firmly.

The services for Mary and Andrew were short, but moving. Yet, the macabre fact that kept inserting itself into my brain was that all the while we sat in the church and listened to John Seabury extoll the virtues of the departed, the militia was in an empty field digging graves for nearly two hundred souls who would have none but the most scanty service said over them—and no coffin to hold their bones. The practice of slavery had taken on new and terrible dimensions in my mind, and I knew it would hang like a sword over my head as long as I lived with it.

The afternoon drew on, but George and Charles did not return. I found myself pacing restlessly about the house, unable to concentrate on any chore or diversions. Cornelia was grieving now over the fire damage to Cloudmont and the breakage that had taken place in the brief time the insurrectionists had poured into the house. I made an attempt to console her, reminding her that George had promised to make all repairs and restitutions very soon, but my heart was not in it.

I had just about made up my mind to ride out alone to fetch Mélisse when George returned, looking harassed and worn.

"Are you ready to go?" I asked without preamble.

"Let me wash up and change shirts and I will be ready."

Though he seemed quite himself, I felt a touch formal with him. I tried to pinpoint this feeling and concluded that it was an effort on my part to wipe out the intimacy I had shared with him the night of the rebellion. It was only because of interruptions that we had not consummated our desires. I was sorry and glad of this alternately, but I reminded myself for the hundredth time that George would never marry me, and that thought helped to harden me against the undeniable magnetism he held for me.

He returned to me, looking exceptionally attractive

in a full white shirt with a small ruffle down the front. I looked away quickly, so that he might not glimpse the yearning I knew to be in my eyes. He had two pistols thrust in his waist, and a long, sharp knife in a scabbard hung from his belt.

I felt a flash of uneasiness, but put it firmly from my mind. We would not need those weapons. The militia had scoured the forest for miles around and found nothing and no one.

It was late afternoon when we went out the rear door of the great hall, where George untethered his big horse, and then to the stable, where Noah saddled up Dandylion for me. We would have to hurry to be back before dark, a singularly unpleasant thought.

As we trotted past the quarters and the other outbuildings, we were both quiet. Once away and into the dense forest, I felt compelled to speak. "You are very silent, George."

He looked at me squarely. "Two things are on my mind, to the exclusion of most others today."

"And they are?"

"My overwhelming desire for you—and my abomination for slavery. Both are powerful disturbances." Then with a twinkle of his customary audacity, "And what has preoccupied you, madame?"

"The desire to be reunited with my daughter as soon as possible," I replied. Though I could have told him his two disturbances were mine as well.

"Then you have thought no more of our close communion the night of the insurrection?"

I attempted a shrug. "We were under great stress—and people do and say odd things when their lives are in danger. I have given it no more thought," I lied. *No more thought!* Only George and Mélisse had been in my mind.

"Perhaps you are right," he said lightly. "But at the time, it seemed very important." His smooth, tanned face closed against me and was unreadable.

We were silent for the rest of the long ride to Aunt Mincy's cabin. When at last we reached it, the sun was low on the western horizon and sparkled through the tree trunks like shafts of molten gold. Mincy's small cabin looked lonely and empty. No smoke emanated from the rock chimney. Fear clutched me.

"It looks empty," I said, panic in my voice.

"No—she's there. The curtains are open. And look, here comes old Gypse to greet us." The dog came from around the house and at the sight of George and me, his tail began to wag and his trot quickened.

Dismounting, we tethered our horses to the hitching post. The windows of Mincy's cabin were open and the cool wind belled the curtains out toward the porch.

"Mincy!" George called as we stepped up to the porch. " 'Tis George and Lilibel—are you and Mélisse there?"

The door flew open at once and my child darted out from behind Mincy's skirts. I stopped to catch her in my arms.

"Why Maman, you are crying!" Mélisse said with wonder, pulling back from me, her long, faintly curling black hair neatly combed and tied with a blue ribbon. "Whatever for? I have had the most wonderful visit at Aunt Mincy's. Did you know I can bake cookies? I mixed them and baked them and all Aunt Mincy did was tell me a little bit. *C'est vrai*, Tante Mincy?"

"Oui, ma chérie," replied Mincy haltingly.

"She taught me to cook and I am teaching her French," Mélisse said proudly. "Do not cry, Maman!"

I wiped my eyes and laughed shakily. "I cry from joy, *ma petite*," I told her. "I have not seen you for two whole days and two whole nights."

"Come in and eat some of my cookies," Mélisse said, pulling me into the house. Mincy greeted us. It seemed to me there was a certain restraint in her bearing, but she followed us into the cabin, declaring she would make a pot of tea to go with the cookies. She left the door open and the evening air was cool through the herb-scented cabin.

I was reflecting on the fact that Mincy's cabin always was filled with the most delicious fragrances, when an odd feeling stole over me. It was the same sensation I had experienced when I first visited there. And with it, apprehension and cold fear spread through me.

As George and I seated ourselves, my eyes went automatically to the coarse sacking curtain at the side of the room. It was very still. There was no movement, but there was a prickle at the base of my neck and my hands grew cold.

Mélisse was prattling happily as she helped Mincy get down the cups and saucers and set them on a tray. I scarcely heard her, for my premonition of danger was so strong, it drove everything from my mind.

Then my child said, "Even Railo said my cookies were 'licious." And her eyes grew big and round and she put a hand over her mouth, turning to Mincy. "Oh, Aunt Mincy—I forgot—I didn't mean— *Non*, *non*, Maman! That was long ago that Railo said that!" She floundered helplessly, but George was already on his feet, his hand at the pistols in his belt.

He said, "Aunt Mincy, he's here. I know it—but the militia said they were here and searched your place. Has he come since then?"

The old woman straightened up, her back like a ramrod and her voice steely. "I done give him harbor in my root cellar." She gestured to the edge of a trap-door, half hidden by a rag rug. "Mr. George, you got to let him go."

The curtains moved then and Railo stepped out from behind them, tall as George, his wide chest and shoulders bare, a bloodsoaked rag tied about one thigh. His right hand still wore the bandage, soiled and bloody now.

George leveled his pistol at him and said, "By God, I hate to do it, Railo, but I must take you in. Too many have died. Man, why did you do it?" His voice was shaken and I knew that despite the slaughter that had taken place, he felt compassion for this big black man who had been so cruelly mistreated.

"No, Cap'n, I ain't goin' back," he said, and like a flash of lightning, his arms shot out and enveloped me, held me pressed against him, his knife at my throat.

I was frozen with shock and Mélisse began screaming, "Let my *maman* go, Railo!"

George's face whitened slowly as he put the pistol down on a little table by a chair. He said carefully, "You will be caught and if you harm Madame Sevier, I can promise you I will kill you. Release her."

I felt Railo shake his head. "I don't want to harm her,

but you got to let me go. I'm takin' her with me an' her safety depends on you not following, Cap'n."

"You will not take her with you," George said between his teeth. And in the twinkling of an eye, he flung himself forward, his hand shooting out faster than I could see, to grasp Railo's wrist where he held the knife against my throat. I heard the knife fall to the floor and I was suddenly released as Railo locked himself in combat with George.

I fled to Mélisse across the room, catching her in my arms, as the two men rolled about on the floor, Railo trying to reach his knife and George kicking it out of his reach.

They broke apart, then half crouching, circled each other like wrestlers. Aunt Mincy stood like a statue in the corner beside us, unmoving as her eyes followed the violent movements of the two men. Their breathing was rough and panting and they sounded like animals fighting. I shrank back, holding Mélisse close.

Swiftly, George drew his second pistol, but had no more than gotten it into his hand when Railo with a single fluid movement kicked out, striking George's wrist and sending the pistol flying across the room.

Once more they circled each other. Then with jarring impact they came together, each seeking to bend the other to his will. They were very evenly matched, both being big, muscular men and, for what semed an eternity to me, they grunted and struggled, exchanging heavy blows, then clenching together fiercely.

First George was on top, then Railo, and my heart was in my throat. If Railo should kill or cripple George, Mélisse and I would be at his mercy, and he would no doubt hold us as hostages until he could get away.

George's shirt ripped suddenly as he struck out and Railo winced under a terrific blow to his stomach. George followed this up by swiftly circling him and catching his neck from the rear in a hold that bent his head forward, rendering him unable to use his arms, though they flailed wildly.

George said, breathing hard, "Railo, I can snap your neck—but I don't want to. If you'll give me your word you will return with us for trial, I'll release you on your honor."

Railo's laugh was derisive. "They'll hang me! I would rather die here and now!"

Holding his head down in an iron grip, George tried to reason with him. "I'll go to court for you—explain the brutalities of Livingston, and justice can be tempered with mercy. You may get off and I'd see you got out of Virginia. We've Judith safe at Cloudmont. You two could go north together."

"That's a lie! They'll hang me—you know it!" He gave a great lunge against George's iron grip and broke free. He slid forward across the rough planking as George, off balance, fell backward. Railo, on his knees, flung himself toward his fallen knife. And George whirled to the hearth where his gun had been sent by Railo's kick. Both men seized their weapons simultaneously and turned to face each other. Railo raised his long knife and plunged at George, who had cocked the pistol.

The two men came together as the gun exploded. As Railo fell, I saw his glittering knife rip George's shirt from shoulder to wrist and the quick, bright blood began to flow.

George looked down, panting heavily, at where Railo sprawled on the floor. Blood was welling slowly from the slave's chest as the silence drew out for a timeless moment.

George groaned. "My God, what a waste!" Then in a choked voice, "God damn the practice of slavery!" He seemed unaware of the blood that covered his right arm, the pistol dangling from his hand. He dropped the gun suddenly and stooped to straighten Railo's powerful legs, so that the great, symmetrical body lay straight upon the floor, the bandaged thigh and hand, the bleeding chest mute reminders of man's inhumanity to man.

As he stood up, George said, "I didn't intend to do it. I thought I could persuade him." There was a wealth of sorrow in his voice. "But he was right. They would have hanged him. Poor Judith. God, I hate to be the one to tell her—and that I did it, too."

"You did it defending your own life," I said quickly.

"Railo knew what he was risking. I think he intended to die here and now."

"That's true, Cap'n," Aunt Mincy said slowly. "He swore to me he'd never be taken alive." Then, roughly, "Lemme see that arm."

George ripped the torn remains of the sleeve of his shirt from his bleeding right arm. " 'Tis a long scratch—not deep."

" 'Tis enough to kill you," Mincy said, with an inscrutable glance from her black eyes, "do blood poison set in." She went to her cupboard and brought forth three jars and a long roll of white cotton cloth.

Mélisse suddenly began to cry. I took her up in my arms, whispering soothingly to her, "Hush, *ma petite*, 'tis over. You are safe," but it seemed to bring no comfort, for she sobbed silently against my shoulder. I sat down in Mincy's rocking chair and began to rock her back and forth, while the old woman bathed George's arm carefully with strong lye soap. By the time Mincy had put her salves upon it and bound it tightly with the bandaging, Mélisse had grown quiet, but she kept her head against my shoulder.

When Mincy had finished, George got to his feet and looked down once more at Railo "We shall have to take him back to Cloudmont with us," he said slowly. "Jesus, I hate to tell Judith."

"I will tell her," I said. "I will make her understand that you did not do it voluntarily."

Mélisse began to cry softly once more, and George took her suddenly from my arms and held her against his broad chest. "Don't cry, little one. I will take care of you and your mama and see you get safely home to Cloudmont in only a little while now."

She lifted her tear-filled eyes to him and drew a great shuddering breath, but her arms slipped up about his neck. He kissed her cheek tenderly. He held her a moment longer as her sobbing lessened, then handed her back to me.

My heart went out to George, for his face was a study in sorrow, regret, and frustration. Mincy was watching him also, and said soothingly, "Mister George, they's been killin' on both sides—an' us in-betweens that would've prevented it all, can't break our hearts over wickedness abroad in the land. I knows you didn't want to kill Railo—an' somewheres, he knows it, too."

George looked at her from under brows still drawn in sorrow. Light was growing dim in the cabin now, for the sun had set and Aunt Mincy struck flint to a candle. Its gentle glow softened the harsh reality that lay upon the cabin floor. She bent to Railo and with a soft cloth wiped the blood from his chest.

"We must get back to Cloudmont. There may be some insurrectionists still roaming the woods, Aunt Mincy," George said somberly.

"No," the old lady said with finality, "they all gone now. With Railo gone, they gone."

"I can't take that chance," George said shortly, reloading his pistol. "I'll tie Railo on the back of my horse and take him with me to Cloudmont for burial. The colonel will want to know he is accounted for and can make no more trouble." There was bitterness in his voice.

Mélisse had ceased crying at last, but she clung to me with a desperation that reminded me sharply of our flight from Paris.

Mincy insisted on binding the big black's fatal wound. When she was done, George lifted the lifeless form of Railo onto the horse's back, and we made ready to leave.

Before we mounted our horses, Mélisse turned to Aunt Mincy, holding her arms up to her. When the old lady picked her up Mélisse said, "Tante Mincy, *je t' aime beaucoup*."

The lined black face moved in a warm and loving smile. "I loves you very much, too, *ma chérie*."

George turned to Mincy. "Aunt Mincy, have you a poultice, a potion to cure a sick heart?" His eyes were on the form of Railo, flung over the horse, and I could see the pain in his strong face.

"God and time take care of that, Mister George," she replied soberly. "You a good man an' you have a kind heart. It mend itself one day soon. My peoples should love a man like you an' work with you."

"I'm going to free every one of them I can," George said violently.

We rode back to Cloudmont in the dark, but the sure-footed animals had no trouble in picking their way along the faint trace between Mincy's cabin and Cloudmont.

Our ride back was singularly quiet, both of us preoccupied with our own thoughts. Mélisse was very quiet and a few moments after our departure, I felt her small, warm body sag against me in slumber. It was such a sweet relief to feel her near, to know she was unharmed, that my heart was lightened despite the recent tragedy—though I dreaded facing Judith.

As it turned out, I did not have to face her. All of the Cloudmont slaves were so disturbed by the militia camped right across from their quarters that they were up and alert as we came clopping up the graveled pathway past them. They had been awaiting us, for all had expressed concern for Mélisse.

The moment we were within hearing distance, they came out with lanterns to greet us, Judith among them. When her eyes fell on the body of Railo across the back of George's stallion, a low, wailing cry was torn from her. I had never heard a sound so full of pathos, of tragedy and grief. I felt my own eyes filling with hot tears as she and the slaves holding lanterns fell back at the sight of Railo's great, still form. Then Judith ran to him and cradled his head against her bosom.

Over and over, she wailed, "Railo—my love, my heart, my life! They have killed you!"

Mélisse roused as we drew near the stables and Abigail and Clementine came rushing out of the house, followed by Cornelia and Amanda, then Laura, all relieved to see we had returned safely. The militiamen came to us and Captain Duncan loosened the cords that held Railo, easing him to the ground, where Judith knelt to put her arms about him and weep silently.

Everyone was asking questions at once and we were hard put to answer them all. Cornelia took Mélisse in her capable arms, murmuring, "Thank God, we have you back safely, my darling."

The sounds about us boiled up as others from the house came running to the stables. It seemed an eternity before the confusion simmered down.

As those about us conversed in lowered voices, Judith

looked up at George and said coldly, "You killed him, didn't you, Cap'n George?" In the light of the lantern, her eyes were as hard and cold as her voice.

"It wasn't quite like that, Judith," George said slowly.

"How else could it be? You killed my Railo."

I stepped to her and said, "No, Judith, Railo brought on his death himself. George tried hard to get him to surrender, offered to speak for him at his trial, but——"

"You tryin' to tell me my Railo shot hisself in the chest?"

I drew a long breath. "No, but Railo said he would rather die than surrender. He tried to kill George with his knife, as you can see." I gestured to George's bandaged arm. "George had to shoot to save his own life."

"Cap'n George killed my Railo and I will never forgive him." Judith cradled the strong face of Railo against her breast and the eyes she turned on George were implacable.

"I'm sorry, Judith. I would have saved him if I could, believe me or not. But he would not have it. The choice was his and he made it."

Captain Duncan said, "We will make a report and bury him first thing in the morning, Captain Madison."

Judith's eyes flashed. "Make your report—but my people and I will bury Railo in a proper service ourselves. He was brave and strong and he deserves a proper burial—not in that mass grave with all them other ones."

They acceded to Judith's wishes. The following morning, a long funeral procession of slaves, stretched out behind a hastily constructed coffin, moved into the woods for a private burial. They had asked John Seabury to say a funeral service over Railo and he had reluctantly agreed, the only white man among all the blacks who mourned the passing of Railo.

It was swiftly over, but Judith and Laura were estranged. Judith remained with Ezekiel's widow, Sal, and Laura did not send for her, nor did Judith make any overtures to her former mistress. George indicated that he would send her north at the first possible moment, with her papers of freedom.

In that first week, with the help of the militia, George and Charles arranged funerals and burials for our neighbors. John Seabury, a source of strength for us all during these ordeals, conducted the services with dignity and sympathy.

The militia left and the English gardeners returned the day after. More of the farmers than we had hoped returned too, and it began to look as though George and Charles would not need extra help for the harvesting after all.

Life at Cloudmont settled down. Charles and George went to Richmond to buy headstones for Andrew and Mary. After that, they traveled to Norfolk, where George inspected his new house and found it almost ready for occupancy, but for the furnishing, which he planned to produce through his import business.

He bought new rugs for Cloudmont and had artisans in to repair the damage the torches had done to the floors. New drapes were brought in and hung. Exquisite new vases and ornaments were delievered, and by the last of September, it was impossible to tell that any damage had been done the house.

We heard that the slaves were swiftly tried in Richmond and several of them were hanged. The rest, as George predicted, were sold to planters further south. The relatives of the Reeds, Montagues, and Livingstons were traced and we heard that they would undertake to rebuild the plantations.

The Chenaults came to dinner at Cloudmont and recounted the harrowing details of their escape from the slaves. Like Laura, they were bitter and their hearts hardened toward the slaves. They showed no disposition to do away with slavery at Rose Hill, but spent some time discussing the purchase of new slaves to replace those who had been sold south. No one seemed to have learned from the slaughter that man cannot enslave man and find peace.

George and Charles were extremely busy between harvesting the crops at Cloudmont and attending to business in Norfolk, and we saw little of them. That was just as well, for each time I saw George, my heart yearned for him, even as reason told me it could never be.

However, it seemed to me that a new tenderness had

sprung up between Laura and Charles, and I was very glad for it. The tragedy appeared to have brought them closer together, and I began to hope things would work out for them.

As for myself, deep within me a decision was being made as well. Though I should never reveal it, I knew Mélisse and I had no blood claim to the Madisons. We could not stay at Cloudmont, parasites on the family. I knew I must pull strength from somewhere and make a break with them. When we were alone, I mentioned this briefly to Laura. Her reaction was one of angry protest, and she pointed out that I had as much right to stay at Cloudmont as she, since she could not openly claim Andy as her son.

But I could not face the long days ahead, waiting for George's return when he was gone, yearning over him when he was at home, perhaps even succumbing at last. I felt his eyes upon me often when he was at home, slightly mocking, the ready laughter just behind them, but I would not look at him. And in my heart I silently vowed to make my departure quietly and secretly if I must, when the moment presented itself.

Only Amanda looked as though she shared my heavy heart. She ate but little and her face was pale and troubled. The others thought it grief for Clay, but I noticed the thickening at her waist and sensed the burden she carried. I wondered how long she could maintain her silence.

She approached me one evening shortly before bedtime, coming to my room in her nightgown, her eyes haunted and sad. "Aunt Lilibel—I must talk to you. I *must* talk to some one."

I drew her into my room and we seated ourselves on the couch. Mélisse had fallen asleep and I spoke softly, so as not to waken her. "I know, Amanda," I said compassionately.

"You know?"

I nodded. "And my heart aches for you."

"Aunt Laura said you spoke to her of leaving Cloudmont. Oh, I know 'tis a secret and I swear I won't tell, but please don't leave me. *Please!* How can I face the others? How can I tell Grandmother? No one knows. Oh, it will kill Grandmother! You're the only one who understands." She flung herself into my arms, and I held her shaking shoulders through a storm of weeping.

"Please tell me you'll stay until my baby is born, Aunt Lilibel—though I don't see why you want to leave, unless it's because Uncle Andrew is gone and you grieve as I do without him."

I soothed her, whispering comforting words to her and holding her close until her tears subsided. Finally, I said, "Yes, Amanda, I will stay until your baby is born, and I will help you in every way that I can."

She wiped her eyes, relief plain on her sweet face. "You can help me when I must tell the others. Oh, Lilibel, I do wish you didn't want to leave—maybe you will change your mind after your grief lessens."

I smiled and said, "Perhaps," but in my heart I knew I would not. Still, I would stay long enough to comfort this young girl who had neither mother nor husband to stand beside her during this trying time.

So September drifted on and the harvests were laid by The great wagons, filled to the brim with cotton and covered with canvas, set out down the road for Hampton and the new and wonderful cotton gin. The tobacco was picked, and hung to age in the tobacco barns, before being packed in barrels for shipping to the lands across the sea.

Finally the day came when, as we sat in the second drawing room after breakfast, Cornelia looked at Amanda with suddenly alert eyes. "My dear, your appetite is very light, but you seem to have gained a great deal of weight."

Amanda flushed. "Yes, Grandmother, I have."

Laura looked at her critically as well, and I discerned a sharp suspicion in her blue eyes.

"Most of it is around your waist. Your little face is quite thin," Cornelia said slowly.

Amanda, looking down at her embroidery, said nothing. Laura asked, "Are you feeling well, dear?"

"As well as can be expected in the circumstances," Amanda said shortly. " 'Tis my heart that hurts—my mind and my memories that ache."

Cornelia's black eyes had narrowed. She asked slowly, "What is it, Amanda?" I felt that the truth was slowly making itself known to Cornelia at that moment, for her lips grew taut and her face slowly lost its color.

Amanda raised stricken but defiant eyes to her. "I am expecting Clay's child—I do not know when. These matters were kept secret from me by my mother. She would never discuss such with me."

The breath went out of Cornelia in a great sigh and Laura's eyes were wells of sympathy, as Amanda went on swiftly, "We would have been married long ago, but for mother and Uncle Andrew. And I loved Clay with all my heart and soul. I wanted him! Just as he wanted me—and they made me wait—until it was too late!"

Then at the silence about her, she cried, "I'm not sorry! I'm glad! Glad, do you hear? Clay will never be gone from me now. I shall always have a part of him in our baby."

Cornelia said sadly, "We must get Mincy to examine you, dear. She will be able to tell us when your baby is due."

"You mean you aren't going to turn me out of the house for the sin I have committed?" Amanda asked bitterly.

"Don't be cruel, darling," Cornelia said softly. "You know you and your baby will be welcome at Cloudmont the rest of your lives. It's just that I fear for your child—it will have no name, unless we could arrange a marriage for you with one of the young men in Williamsburg. With the dowry you will have, it should be easy to——"

"No!" Amanda cried. "I'll not marry a stranger and a fortune hunter just to give my child a name—one that doesn't even belong to him. He will be a Reed, and if I cannot claim that for him, he'll be a Jackson. And he shall be a great landowner when he grows up. Half of Jackson's Landing will belong to him." She burst into tears.

Cornelia rose and went to sit beside her granddaughter on the sofa, putting her arms about her. "Do not cry, my darling little Amanda," she said softly. "What is done is done. We will not look back, but to the future instead. Your baby will be greatly loved. It's only that I think of Charles and the stigma that has been attached to him over the years, and I dread it for your baby."

Amanda said stiffly, "Charles is one of ours, now. He was Grandfather's natural son—and he loves you well. So shall my son."

Cornelia was silent, but I knew she was thinking of the way of the world. A bastard was always a bastard in the eyes of our society, and Amanda could know little of the slights that could be handed out by the narrow-minded and obstinate. But Cornelia straightened her shoulders and her voice contained a rueful kind of joy as she said, "Ah, well, 'twill be another baby in Cloudmont—and we shall love it well."

Amanda put her arms about her grandmother and her voice was muffled. "Dear, dear Grandmother—you are so kind to stand by me." Her eyes, I saw, were filled with relief and gratitude.

I said briskly, "We shall make your baby a beautiful layette over the coming months, Amanda."

CHAPTER 20

The busy social life we had known the previous spring and summer was no more. The Chenaults were involved in replenishing their looted home and buying new slaves to replace those they had lost through the insurrection. The heirs and new owners of the Reed, Livingston, and Montague plantations, all firm believers in slavery, were using slave labor to rebuild their mansions on the ruins of the old. We had the same evil practice all about us once more.

Cloudmont seemed more beautiful than it had ever been. True to his vow, George freed all of Cloudmont's slaves. Judith and Sal he sent north with Joshua and Ephraim and their families at the end of September, giving them each a small bag of gold for the trip.

Judith and Laura did not say good-bye to each other. The rift was too deep and both were too bitter.

By the time November drew to a close, all of the former Cloudmont slaves had left Virginia except Noah. He was given his freedom, but preferred to stay and accept employment and regular wages.

Amanda was still painfully sad, but her health was excellent, and we all concentrated our energies in trying to lighten her moods.

It was John Seabury, oddly enough, who provided the solution to Amanda's problem. The first of December, when Cornelia, Laura, and I were seated about a blazing fire, each with a cup of hot tea, John approached us. He came directly to the point.

"Mistress Madison, I cannot stand by and see Amanda suffer the stigma of bearing a child out of wedlock," he said grimly.

We were all shocked at his forthright mention of so delicate a subject. For a moment, I thought he meant to propose marriage to Amanda himself. Cornelia must have felt this also, for she said cautiously, "Amanda has determined not to marry, Mr. Seabury, and is willing to face the consequences."

"I know that," John replied, "but I would prevent those consequences. I propose that we have something concrete to show the world. Here." He held out a scroll, and after some hesitation Cornelia took it.

"Why"—she spoke in shocked surprise—" 'Tis a wedding license for Clay and Amanda!"

"I have dated it the first of April and signed it as the officiating pastor. It will be simple enough to proceed on the premise that Clay and Amanda were secretly wed by me in April. Amanda's baby will be quite legitimate—the secret was kept because of her mother's refusal to consent to the marriage."

Amanda, who had been standing for some time in the doorway behind John, flew across the room and flung her arms about the young pastor, a sob in her voice. "Oh, John! How kind you are—how thoughtful! Will it really be official?"

"As official as I can make it. I will swear that I performed the ceremony in secret, while I was visiting the Reeds at Tulip Grove in April—months before I came to work at Cloudmont. Which I did—and I would have indeed performed the service had I been asked to at the time." He held Amanda's hands in his and, looking into her glowing face, added, "God will surely forgive a lie such as this, when it will give an innocent child of love an easier life."

Amanda's voice was light as thistledown. "And my baby will have his rightful name."

A great burden was lifted from all of us by John's license. He even forged Clay's signature on it after

Amanda wrote hers with a flourish. When Cornelia told George and Charles of the minister's kindly deception, both were astonished and pleased.

George gave a great roar of laughter and said admiringly, "By heaven, Seabury's a *man*. There will be some consternation at Tulip Grove, I'll wager, when they learn young Clay has a legitimate heir, but Amanda can put them at their ease quickly enough when she tells them she will make no claim on the plantation."

As December drew on, so did Amanda's time. Mincy was much in evidence at Cloudmont. She remarked one day, "T'wouldn't surprise me none at all if Amanda don't have a little Christmas present fer all of you."

It was on this day, three weeks from Christmas, that Laura urged me to ride with her along the James. I had been embroidering fine lawn handkerchiefs for Christmas gifts, but her request was so weighted that I knew she wanted to talk alone with me.

In a short while we were trotting along the banks of the cold glittering river. She was so silent that I prodded gently, "I feel you have asked me to ride for a purpose, Laura."

She gave me an oddly dreaming look, at variance with the cold, crisp air about us. "I'm going to marry Charles," she said. "I've told him *everything*—and he still wants to marry me. I wanted to tell you before anyone else."

"Then you *do* love him?" I asked somewhat dryly.

"I love him deeply," she said simply. "I thought you, of all people, would know that."

"I did, but it surprises me that you have finally discovered it." I smiled. "Ah, Laura, I am so happy for you!"

Her look was sober. "I know you are preparing to leave us at Cloudmont. I want your promise to stay and see me wed to Charles. You have become my dearest friend."

One more bond, I thought. First Amanda and her baby to come. Now Laura and her wedding to Charles. I asked reluctantly, "When is the marriage to be?" afraid it might be as far away as spring.

"Charles and I have waited too long already. We are

going to tell Cornelia tonight, and we will be married by John on New Year's Eve when all our friends"—sadly—"those that are left—are here for the Open House."

"I have promised to stay until Amanda's baby is safely born, and I will stay to see you safely wed to Charles."

Laura said hesitantly, "You still don't want me to tell the others you plan to leave?"

"No. I know what Cornelia would say and I don't think I could bear to refuse her. Nor can I endure the remonstrances from the men and the platitudes of the servants."

She said slowly, "You were Andrew's affianced—they all believe Mélisse to be Andy's cousin. You should stay, Lilibel, and you know that."

I shook my head. I could not blurt out the harsh truth to Laura, that I was fleeing my love for George Madison, that I feared to stay at Cloudmont because my passion for him grew daily and I did not know how long I could hold out against him. My frequent proximity to George and the futility of my love for him were making me more and more unhappy.

George's attitude toward me was one of alert courtesy and an unnerving watchfulness. I strongly sensed that he was only waiting for a sign from me to make another suggestion that we become lovers, and I could not be sure what my answer would be. This was the thing that drove me to the hard decision to leave and put temptation out of my way.

The days drifted by. Beady and the servants were busy preparing all sorts of festive foods, from mince pies to fruitcakes and many varieties of sweetmeats and comfits. Mélisse and the two little boys grew wild with excitement and anticipation and raced through the house with Domino panting behind them. Even Amanda smiled often now.

Charles and George brought home suspiciously happy looking boxes and packages from their journeys to and from Norfolk and Richmond. And before long, the head gardener, a new man named Tom Scranton, brought in two young pine trees, which we stripped of their boughs to decorate the house.

While others smiled indulgently, I thought sadly of my daughter and me alone in the world once more, as we would surely be when we left Cloudmont. And I remembered the long-ago coach ride from Hampton after our storm-tossed voyage on the *Maidee Love*. I had been so sure Cloudmont would be home.

I thought bitterly, *I was born a fool.*

CHAPTER 21

A week before Christmas, Amanda went into labor. At the start, we all rejoiced that the baby would be here in time for Christmas. With Aunt Mincy in attendance, veteran of hundreds of births before, all of Cloudmont was sure it would be a swift and easy delivery.

But as the day wore on, Amanda could not stifle her cries of pain and Mincy came out to tell us gravely that the baby, unusually large, was breech, and Amanda had young and narrow hips. By dark, Amanda was calling for me, and I went into the chamber, Mary's former room, to try to comfort her.

She looked at me with great ringed eyes and said starkly, "Lilibel, my baby and I are going to die. He cannot be born."

I took her hand and said reassuringly, "That is not so, *ma petite*. You are having a bad time of it, true enough, but you both shall live to be very old people."

"No. God is going to punish me for stealing my love with Clay when we were unmarried."

"What nonsense!" I said firmly. "God gave you this baby and he means for you to be happy with it.

A sudden scream was wrenched from her and she drew her legs up tensely. Mincy said urgently, "Flow with it, honey—don't tighten your legs—flow with it."

For two hours, I sat with her, and the others crept into the room and out, anxiety and apprehension thick about them. But Amanda would not let me go. She clenched my hands until I was forced to clench them to keep her from bruising me. All this while, Aunt Mincy was dosing her from bottles, moving her hands over Amanda's abdomen and urging her to bear down.

Midnight drew on. It seemed to me that the young girl was growing weaker, and real fear struck my heart. I looked at Mincy over the candle beside the bed and said, "Aunt Mincy, is there nothing we can do?"

"She so narrow, Miss Lilibel." Then she came to a harsh decision. "I'm goin' to try to turn this baby. He gonna die, if he don't be born soon."

The entire household was still up, for no one showed an inclination to sleep with tragedy possible at any moment. Cornelia and Laura kept coming to the room, but Mincy did not encourage them to stay. "This chile wants Miss Lilibel nearby an' that's enough."

Now with every cry of agony, I felt the pain in my own loins for Amanda. I said thickly, "Do you think you can turn it, Aunt Mincy?"

"I'm goin' to try—she so narrow, it's goin' to be tetch an' go." From her row of jars beside the bed, she opened one and dipped her hands into it. It was a thick, viscous liquid and once her hands were slick with it, she said, "You come help me, Miss Lilibel. You hold her legs—up, like this."

I did as she bade, conscious of the low moans of agony from Amanda. I knew that a few more hours of this and we would lose both mother and baby, and I began to pray hard that Mincy might turn the baby, no matter how narrow the birth channel.

She slipped her hands inside slightly and began manipulating the child, so near the opening, gently. Then with sudden strength, she widened the opening and pushed with great force.

As Amanda's scream rent the air, Cornelia flung the door open and she and Laura rushed into the room. "What is it?" Cornelia cried. "Is Amanda dying?"

Mincy, busy with her efforts, made no reply and I told the women that she was attempting to turn the baby. It seemed to me an eternity that Mincy's hands were busily at work inside Amanda's vagina. We were all tensely silent, for each of us knew that if this failed, we would lose both Amanda and the baby.

Suddenly Mincy cried, "It's turning! I've most nigh turned it!" Then after a fraught pause, she cried, "It's done—the head is down now!"

I looked down to see the small round head emerge, slowly followed by the shoulders, arms, and legs. It was a beautifully formed baby boy. Amanda's cries ceased and a great sigh came from her.

Mincy was swift in her ministrations then. She gave the baby to me to hold, while she dosed Amanda once more, saying, "This make her sleep, poor little chile."

Cornelia and Laura clung to each other, crying with joy that both mother and child were saved. Then Mincy put us all to work. The baby's umbilical cord was neatly tied and Cornelia was given the job of bathing him in a bowl of warm water on the washstand. Mincy went about the business of cleaning up Amanda and the bedding, and I was glad to see that the girl had fallen into a deep sleep. Only then did I realize that every muscle in my body was trembling from fatigue and fear. When we left the room, the baby was cozily and warmly wrapped, a small bundle of perfection beside his mother so that she might see him at first awakening. Mincy took up her vigil beside the bed, telling us all to get some sleep.

Amanda was weak for the next few days, but her appetite was good and her pride in her young son was enormous. But Mincy told us that she should not get up for Christmas, and the holiday was rather subdued.

Word of Amanda's secret spring wedding and the holiday birth of her child spread through the neighboring plantations, resulting in a rash of visits and gifts for the baby. The Chenaults were especially happy and expressed great joy and pleasure, remarking that it was a fine thing there would be one of the Reeds' own progeny to carry on the name.

Cloudmont was soon in a turmoil over the upcoming wedding of Charles and Laura and plans for the traditional Open House to be held afterward. It was agreed that Charles and Laura should stay until morning and leave for their wedding trip to Richmond on New Year's Day.

If Beady and the servants had cooked up a fabulous

feast for Christmas, it was nothing compared to their efforts toward the wedding and Open House. The kitchen was filled with savory fragrances each day.

The smokehouse overflowed with hanging turkeys, pheasants and ducks shot by George and Charles, geese, great haunches of beef, dove and quail, all smelling deliciously of smoke and tenderness. Laura and I peered in at the amazing store one morning before our ride along the James. The weather was crisp and clear, just brisk enough to invigorate, and we made the most of it.

Charles had brought Laura's trousseau from the sisters Chandler in Richmond, who had her measurements and made the dresses and lingerie to fit perfectly. We discussed it as we rode along looking at the twinkling waters of the James.

"I think of all those lovely things we made and had made for your wedding to Andrew, Lilibel. I grieve that you have no use for them yet—but you shall meet some wonderful man someday and find your own happiness."

"Perhaps."

Her look was sympathetic. "I know you did not love Andrew, my dear, and I am truly sorry it did not work out. And I know you are unhappy now. I can see it in those great golden eyes of yours."

"I am content," I said evasively. "And I am very happy for you and Charles, *chérie*. Too, it pleases me to see Cornelia so joyful that you plan to live at Cloudmont. She is in her element with little Clay to love, and now she has the prospect of more babies. Your wedding should be a beautiful ceremony. John Seabury has even bought himself a new suit in which to perform the service." I smiled, thinking of the tall, serious young man and his fondness for all of us. John had proved his worth to Cloudmont a dozen times over. Under his tutelage, Mélisse, Timothy, and Andy were making great strides in their lessons. Mélisse could write her name and even read simple sentences, though she was still under six. I regretted the prospect of removing her from his classes.

We rode along silently for a long time and I drank in the beauty of the land thirstily. This was magnificent country, evoking more love from me than France, now, and the thought of leaving it all to work in the tight little confines of a millinery shop—or even as a tutor for some great family in Norfolk—made my heart ache with loneliness. I would miss Cloudmont terribly.

Laura's wedding day dawned bright and clear and I went into her room and sat with her as she bathed in the scented water of the painted wooden tub, lathering herself luxuriously with French milled soap. As I sat there, for the first time Laura confided in me about her unhappy affair with Andrew.

"I thought I loved him. I *did* love him, and Yve was very possessive, Lilibel," she added apologetically. "I thought she gave him much trouble. I had married Thomas, thinking 'twas his brother I loved and, naturally, as a young widow I was very vulnerable. And Andrew could be very subtle—could be most charming. I thought I knew him well." She wore a strange, oblique smile. "But Mary knew him better. And after I became pregnant with little Andy, I began to fall out of love with him. I—He was not the man I thought him to be. He was—weak." She fell silent.

"I know," was all I said.

"As you might suspect, when love died, contempt took its place—as I expect it was with you. But he wanted Andy, and I was not so brave as Amanda," she finished sorrowfully. "But now I shall be able to watch Andy grow up—even teach him some things about life, now that Mary is no longer here to prevent me."

When I left her, she was singing cheerfully and donning her wedding dress, with Abigail, Clementine, and Bibsey all hovering about to help. And I went to my own room to get ready for the festivities.

The wedding was over and it had been beautiful. Laura wore a pale pink satin dress that set off her lovely face and figure. The guests, among them the Stuarts from Richmond and all our new neighbors, including the Livingston nephew and niece, filled the great drawing room.

George looked exceptionally handsome in a fawn coat and ruffled white shirt, with beautifully polished Hessian boots on his trim, muscled legs. His white cravat with a diamond stickpin was quite elegant. I found myself seeking him out among the guests, and often felt his eyes on me.

I was aware he still desired me. It was in the tension between us, in our guarded conversations, in the air when we were in close proximity. But become his mistress I would not. Mélisse deserved better than that from her mother. Besides, he had expressed a wish to accompany the *Tern*'s next voyage to England. He would be gone six months—and I would be gone from his life when he returned.

When the dancing began, I went from one pair of arms to another. The young Cholmondeley from Richmond sought me out now that I was no longer affianced and his ardor increased as the evening wore on. After one dance with him drew to a close, he led me to the punch bowl, where George stood, drinking a pony of bourbon. As the young man ladled our glasses of punch, he began to talk of the future. In a warm and winning voice, he informed me that he had a beautiful plantation home under construction on the York River but that the wife he wanted to grace it had not yet said Yes. George listened unabashedly as my suitor's voice grew warmer, indeed impassioned. "Miss Liliane, I have fallen desperately in love with you. Is it possible—would you consider becoming my wife?"

I murmured that I must have time to think it over, but he continued to press his suit. He held no appeal for me, and I could not marry coldly—not again. I had married Jacques, for whom I bore only affection, and very nearly married Andrew for reasons much too similar—and I had not been happy.

In the midst of Cholmondeley's persuasions, George stalked off, his face unreadable, but I was glad he had heard. I was glad, too, that I had taken great care with my appearance this evening, wanting perversely to stir George further. Kohl was faintly about my eyes, making them large and luminous, and my cheeks and lips were delicately rouged. The amber satin dress, one from the ill-fated trousseau, showed my figure to the best possible advantage. And as the evening progressed, I did not lack for partners. One of them, slightly tipsy and immoderately complimentary, informed me that I was the most beautiful woman he had ever seen. I was grateful, and hoped that George noticed my popularity.

He did. But he did not ask me to dance until the evening was drawing to an end. Then we danced without a single spoken word. As his body touched mine in passing, I was acutely conscious of it and of the turmoil it stirred within me. I told myself, *Enjoy this while you may, for it will not come again.* Warm, fluid, acquiescent and willing, my whole being opened up to him.

Still without speaking he whirled me out of the drawing room door and through the great hall, where groups of guests were conversing and sampling tidbits from trays carried by the servants.

I did not ask him where he was taking me. I merely followed as he went to the drawing room on the west. There was no one there, and in its privacy, his arms closed about me. He tilted my face upward. Still without a word, he began to kiss me. His lips were gentle at first and I responded fervently, arms tightening about his broad shoulders as I pressed myself against him. We stood fused together for long minutes and when finally common sense struggled upward, it was almost too late. His hands slipped down the curve of my back tenderly, pressing me ever closer and they melted my heart.

"No!" I cried, as I flung away from him. Frustration and rage swept like a tide through me.

"Ah, but you want me as much as I want you! I've watched you—your eyes. You'd never be happy with a milksop like Cholmondeley and you're a fool to consider his proposal. I'm the man you want."

"That may be, for you are a powerfully attractive man, and I'm no hypocrite as so many of these *good* ladies about us are. But I'm no simpering schoolgirl either—to be taken in by you and the uncertainties you offer."

There was faint puzzlement in his deep voice. "But why? Why won't you, Liliane?"

"Because," I said, my voice rough with anger, "what you are offering simply isn't good enough. One Louise Alexander in this house is enough. So keep your freedom, George—I want none of it."

I turned to go, but he reached out, caught my arms

and, with a powerful pull, jerked me against him once more.

His mouth came down on mine demandingly, fiercely, and something hot and deep rose within me to meet it. I was drowning in desire for this man. I had to get away. And I promised myself in the heat and turbulence of that brief moment of surrender to him that Mélisse and I would leave as soon as possible.

I tore loose from his arms and fled from the room.

Early the following morning, Charles and Laura left in the carriage for Richmond. It was loaded with enough baggage to make one think they planned to stay a year, but I knew there would be many balls and parties given for the newlyweds by all their friends in Richmond, and ballgowns and evening clothes took a great deal of room.

All of us stood in the cold clear morning air of the new year of 1804 to see them off. We waved gaily as long as we could see them, until they turned off the road to the west and toward Richmond. Amanda was with us, but because of the chill air outside, she had left baby Clay with Abigail.

A feeling of deflation fell over us all, as we returned to the house. It was a bright and beautiful January first, with the air crisp and cold, and our lack of wraps sent us hurrying through the door into the great hall.

"I shall miss Charles," George said impatiently, "and he says they may be gone a month. It means I will not be able to sail with the *Tern* and our cargo of tobacco to England this month."

Cornelia smiled. "Do not expect sympathy from me, my dear. I would that you never went to sea again."

"I know, Mother," he responded with a rueful grin. "You may rest easy. I shall be here under your nose until Charles and Laura return. I must ride out to the acreage beyond the tobacco fields to see to the winter wheat even now. And I have to teach our new overseer how we refertilize the tobacco acreage each year."

When George had donned his heavy riding coat and taken his departure, Cornelia said to me, "Dear, do come and help me with the first-of-the-month accounts.

I have come to depend upon you greatly, Lilibel. You are excellent with ciphering and your hand is very clear on the ledgers."

Mélisse and the two little boys, followed by their shadow, Domino, came tearing through the drawing room as we made our way to the morning room.

"Maman," my daughter cried, "Beady has baked a fresh batch of gingerbread and says we may have some, if you say so."

"You children have eaten so many sweets during the holidays——" I began.

"Gingerbread is healthy. Aunt Mincy said so," Andy cried, his blue eyes bright with mischief. "Do let us, Grandmother and Aunt Lilibel!"

Cornelia and I exchanged glances and succumbed, so the trio went scampering off to the kitchen.

Cornelia said comfortably, "My dear Lilibel, I do not know what I should do without you. You have been such a courageous and helpful girl. I have come to love you as dearly as if you were my own."

"Thank you," I replied in a muffled voice, dreading the moment when I must hurt this kind woman to whom family meant so much. "You are very dear to me as well, Cornelia."

"Am I? Truly? That affords me such happiness. I respect you deeply, my dear, for you are a gallant and brave young woman. I had so hoped to see you my daughter-in-law." We had reached the morning room, where the sunlight spilled in over the many green plants Cornelia had set about the room. Her indoor garden cheered me each time I entered it.

Together we made lists of supplies to be brought from Richmond, tallied those we had used, entered the servants' wages. I did the ciphering for Cornelia. It took us a little less than two hours to balance the sheets nicely.

All the time I sat cozily beside her—this woman who had come to love me and my child so deeply—my heart beat heavily with the sad knowledge that within the next few days, Mélisse and I would leave her.

But some deep, hard core within me rebelled against pining for and dreaming over what could never be. George was like quicksilver, and though his moments of laughter, his times of grim sobriety, his even-handed justice, and his warmth toward all those about him were dear to me, I could not live on dreams and I would not lend myself to a second-rate alliance. It went against every fiber of my being. George had told me in the beginning that he did not intend to marry, that his life was full. I had only myself to blame for the emotions that were driving me to leave Cloudmont.

By the first of the following week, I had begun my preparations to leave. I took Noah into my confidence, for he would have to saddle up Dandylion and help me strap my portmanteau and valise on the horse's back before the dawn hours. I explained to him that I really had no claim on the Madisons and I must make my own way in the world. He did not understand and was most reproachful, even condemning me for leaving without telling the others.

"But good-byes are so hard—especially to those you have come to love, Noah."

"I know, ma'am. That's why I stayed on at Cloudmont. I loves these people and they been good to me. I can't see why you don't feel the same."

"I do, Noah, but it is best that Mélisse and I leave."

"But you was Mr. Andrew's bride-to-be—an' Miss Mélisse is little Andy's own blood cousin. You family, Miss Lilibel. You family peoples. You gonna break Mistress Madison's heart."

"I have reasons for leaving, Noah, that I can't explain to you. I only ask that you have Dandylion saddled and ready for me by four o'clock tomorrow morning. And that you keep my secret. I shall write Cornelia a letter explaining my departure to her. She will understand and forgive me, I'm sure. And perhaps we shall all meet again in Norfolk for a visit. You will keep my secret, won't you?"

He said slowly, "Yes'm. But I don't like it. I'll keep it till you're gone—an' I'll have Dandylion ready and waitin' for you and Miss Mélisse."

When George returned early in the evening, I took my last meal with the family. My heart was so heavy, I could scarcely eat Beady's delicious food. Talk at the table was desultory, of the neighbors, of the crops last fall, of the departure of the *Tern* and the riches her cargo would bring in return.

George and I were polite to each other and distant, but when I looked up once to find his black eyes on me there was a small raw flame in their depths that sent the old familiar desire through my veins. Tomorrow before dawn would be none too soon for my departure, I thought.

After dinner, John Seabury left to work on his Sunday sermon. The rest of us sat in the parlor drinking coffee and relaxing. Amanda had brought the baby down and we took turns cooing over him. He was truly a beautiful child, lovely as a picture cherub. When Cornelia held him the hard etched lines of grief left her face for a time. She looked younger than her years, and traces of the girl she had once been were plain to see.

As George took him from her arms to look into the tiny pink face, I thought how much I would miss Cornelia—Amanda, Laura and Charles—all of the wonderfully warm-hearted servants. But I set my mind against the claims of love, and my decision was rock firm.

"You're looking very determined, Lilibel," George said lightly, as he handed the baby back to Cornelia. "A penny for your thoughts."

"I—I was thinking of all the things that must be done this spring—and what the future holds."

"And what does the future hold?" he asked lightly, a touch of the old mockery in his voice.

"A very busy year, I should say."

"We will go visit in Richmond next month, Lilibel, and you shall have some new clothes——" Cornelia began.

"*Alors!* No more clothes, dear Cornelia! I have that monstrous trousseau already."

"But it holds such sad memories for you—and styles are changing every month," she said placidly, tucking the handknit blanket closely about the warm bundle she held.

"*C'est vrai,*" I said absently. "That is true, dear Cornelia."

"Then it is settled. I will write the servants to get the house ready, and write Lucy Stuart and her husband that we are coming. There should be some lovely winter parties this season, and Charles and Laura will be there." She sighed, "Things are so dead in the country now. We don't even have the hunts organized yet and I so love to follow the hounds."

George tamped tobacco into his pipe, smiling. "You are a true sportsman, Mother. We have all missed the hunts this fall, but you know we have had our hands full getting the countryside back to normal."

"I know," she said regretfully. "We who live along the James will be a long time forgetting the horrors of the August insurrection."

We talked a little longer and then I made my excuses. I planned to get Mélisse from the nursery upstairs and we would retire early, against our predawn rising. I had already packed my portmanteau and valise with a few clothes and the personal things we would take with us.

I dreaded making explanations to my daughter. She would be six next summer, and was quite old enough now to realize the enormity of the step I was taking. I knew that she would weep when she found that we would no longer live at Cloudmont. Mélisse had found happiness here, complete and unalloyed, and it would be hard for her to adjust to the catch-as-catch-can life that awaited us in Norfolk. But I felt sure I would find good employment in that busy port city.

When Mélisse was sleeping peacefully in the big bed, I went to the table that held quill and ink and penned my note to Cornelia. I told her how much she and the others had come to mean to me and that it hurt me deeply to leave Cloudmont, but I explained that I could not be any longer a charity, as indeed I was, and must therefore find employment elsewhere. I did not mention George, the true reason for my departure. I closed with the optimistic remark that we would see each other occasionally, since Norfolk was not too far from Cloudmont.

I put the finishing touches to my packing, taking as little as I could get by on. I laid out my dove-gray riding habit and the worn fur-lined cloak I had been wearing the long-ago night of my arrival at Cloudmont. I blew out the candle and crept up the steps and into the high feather bed, where I sank into its warm, enveloping folds beside my sleeping daughter for the last time.

I lay awake an hour or more, then dozed fitfully, watching the sky beyond the window and wondering if the hour to leave would never come. The sky was heavily overcast and there were no stars, and a cold wind whistled about the house, reminding me that we were deep in winter's grip. I dreaded the long ride to Norfolk, but I would be there by evening, with such an early start. I thought comfortingly of the leather bag filled with gold and silver coins, generous gifts from Cornelia, who often remarked she loved the feel of her own little gold reserve and was never without it. She meant, of course, for me to spend it on clothes for Mélisse and myself when we finally visited Richmond. Instead, I would use it to live on until I could find employment. We would be very hungry before we reached Norfolk; I had not dared to risk asking Beady for a knapsack of food.

At last I slipped from bed, trembling slightly from nerves and the chill of the room. I struck flint to the candle and looked at the little gold watch on a chain, a gift to me from George at Christmas. It was four-fifteen in the morning.

Swiftly I bathed in the icy water I poured in the bowl from the pitcher, and even more swiftly donned the dove-gray riding habit. As the warm garment covered me, my shivering ceased and I moved to waken Mélisse.

She protested, "Maman—'tis still night!"

"But we are going for an early morning ride, my darling," I said with false gaiety. "We are going to Norfolk, and we will have such fun there!"

She rubbed dimpled fists against her eyes. "A visit? Who else is going? Andy and Timmy?"

"They will come later," I improvised. "This is a surprise for you—you shall see!"

"And Tante Cornelia?"

"*Aunt* Cornelia, *chérie*. Hurry! We must be dressed and get on Dandylion and be gone, if we wish to make Norfolk before dark."

I hurried her, keeping up a running whispered chatter to divert her. When she was ready, I blew out the candle. Soon we were tiptoeing down the long hall to the stairs, with the portmanteau in one hand and my reticule in the other, Mélisse carrying the small valise. I made a *shhhing* sound, adjuring her to silence. "We do not want to wake the others."

We moved quickly and quietly down the long stairs, through the blackness that was the great hall, unerringly to the rear door. I had decided against risking a candle. Mélisse was even more surefooted than I, so familiar had she become with the house.

I closed the door silently behind us and, in the pale light of the winter sky, we followed the long path to the stables, where a candle glimmered faintly in the tack-room.

Noah's black face appeared at the tackroom door as we entered. I put the portmanteau down breathlessly.

"I reckoned you an' Miss Mélisse wouldn't ask fer no food, your leavin' bein' a secret an' such. So I done begged a bit off Beady, claimin' hunger. Here 'tis." He held out a coarse cloth sack to me. " 'Tis ham and bread an' two apples an' cookies."

"Noah, you are truly a *bon ami*," I said fervently, taking the sack.

"What's that, ma'am?"

"A dear and good friend," I replied. "Where is Dandy-lion?"

"Jes' inside the stable—all saddled fer you. An' I'll strap on your portmanteau an' valise, do you give 'em to me now."

He picked up the candle and gave it to me. "Hol' it fer me, Miss Lilibel, whilst I sees how to do it."

In the dim, pungent confines of the stable, Mélisse and I stood silently as Noah strapped the two small pieces of luggage across the mare's rump firmly. Then he held his hand for my foot and I swung up into the saddle, taking Mélisse when he handed her to me.

"Thank you for everything you've done for us, Noah," I said, my voice thick with unshed tears.

"Maman," Mélisse said with sharp awareness, "why are you crying?"

"Oh, I'm not," I replied with a choked laugh. " 'Tis but the cold makes me sound so."

Noah stood watching, holding the candle, as I trotted

out of the stable and down the road away from the big house. I would swing around through the woods to the front, to make sure no one heard the sound of Dandy's hooves striking against the graveled road that encircled Cloudmont.

I could not look at the house looming up through the trees, chimneys tall against the starless sky. Instead, I kept my eyes on the woods path that led us around to the road that ran between the great plantations and Norfolk. I put Dandylion into an easy gallop, wanting to put as many miles as possible between us and those we had come to love so dearly.

"Maman," Mélisse said suspiciously, "I do not see why we had to leave without saying good-bye—as if we were running away—the way we did when we went to Marseilles. What is the surprise you promised?"

"Oh, 'tis not at all like that other time," I said quickly. "No one is chasing after us. We do not have to hide." But I was thinking how much like that time it was, and I wondered bitterly if my life would always be made up of flights to escape.

"I think if we do not hide, at least 'tis a secret you keep—our leaving Cloudmont," she said shrewdly. Then she whimpered, "I'm cold!"

I slowed the horse and drew the fur-lined cloak up about her snugly. "There, *chérie*. You must not worry about these things. Maman will take good care of you. We shall have a gay time in Norfolk. And if I told you the surprise, it would be one no longer. Now try to sleep a while."

Mélisse made no reply, but I could feel resistance in her little body against mine. She was suspicious now, and with good reason.

We rode for what seemed a very long time, no longer at a gallop, for the wind against us had too great a bite in the predawn darkness. When at last the east began to pinken, I drew a long breath of relief. Slowly the sky brightened and the towering black trees beside the road became merely tall green pines and arborvitae.

As the sun rose higher, it warmed us, and Mélisse stirred restively. I shifted her about so she sat astride before me. Her little legs would be warmed by the silken sides of Dandylion. I slowed the horse still further to rest her.

We had been three hours on our way when I first heard the pound of hooves in the distance. I looked ahead, thinking it came from Williamsburg, through which we would pass on our way to Norfolk. Then I realized it came from behind us.

I turned and looked behind me, but the road curved among the trees and lost itself after a stretch of a hundred yards. I debated whether to seek a hiding place beyond the ditch at the road's side. The trees were thick and forbidding in appearance, and I decided to wait and see who approached.

"I hear someone coming, Maman."

"I know, my darling. No doubt 'tis another traveler on his way to Williamsburg or Norfolk." The sound drew nearer and the road made another sharp turn. Unconsciously I stepped up the mare's pace, instinct driving me ahead. Then suddenly, with a quickened thunder, the horseman was beside us, hauling back upon the reins sharply, causing his big stallion to snort heavily and stamp about. Dandylion shied, but steadied as the stallion nuzzled her shoulder, and I looked into the unsmiling face of George Madison.

Mélisse cried in joy, "Oncle! *Je suis heureuse*—I am so happy to see you!" Her glad laughter sounded loud in the cold morning sunlight.

"And I to see you both," he replied, but his eyes held mine.

"I left a note of explanation for Cornelia——" I began lamely.

"Noah came to me long before breakfast. I found your note."

"Noah should not— My note was not meant for you——"

"And I took the liberty of exchanging it for one of mine. See?" He held up my note. I could see the slanting black script clearly.

"George, you had no right to do that!"

"I had every right to do it, madame. The note I left

my mother will make her much happier than this cold little missive of yours."

"It's not cold! I love her dearly and I told her so——" I broke off, then asked very coldly indeed, "And what brings you here on the road to Norfolk so early of a morn?"

"The same thing that brought you to it, Liliane."

Was there a note of pleading in that arrogant voice? "I do not understand you," I replied, looking straight ahead.

"I think you do." There was the old teasing mockery in his words now. "Are you not curious to know what I wrote to my mother?"

I made no reply, but my daughter asked pertly, "What did you write Tante Cornelia, Oncle?"

"I wrote her that your mother and I were leaving for Norfolk together, where we would be married and all three of us live happily ever after."

"Oh," crowed my daughter, "So *that* is Maman's surprise!"

"I'll wager it is no surprise to your mother."

"But it is! You said you would never marry——"

"My dear," he interrupted, "that was before I knew you well. Before you set your cap for me with such delightful thoroughness."

"*I* set my cap—for *you!* How——"

"Come now, Lilibel. I have run off from my responsibilities at Cloudmont and in all likelihood my poor honeymooning brother will have to return and take them up, while I chase after you like a lovesick calf!" His merry laughter rang out. "Do you think lust is all I am capable of, Lilibel? Surely you will not deny me the chance to show you my other sterling qualities—such as love and tenderness and respectability? What an oaf you must think me, indeed." His laughter was as infectious and warming as the sunlight.

I laughed with him suddenly, gaily and without restraint. "No, George—oaf does not at all describe what I think you are."

"And I shall have my very own papa," Mélisse said with great pride and contentment.

So near was joy to the surface now that her words set us off in laughter once more, as together we three followed the winding road toward Norfolk.